Shadow Princess

INDU SUNDARESAN was born and raised in India and went to the United States for graduate studies. She is the author of *The Twentieth Wife, The Feast of Roses, The Splendor of Silence,* and *In the Convent of Little Flowers.* She lives in Seattle, Washington. Visit her website at www.indusundaresan.com.

ALSO BY INDU SUNDARESAN

The Twentieth Wife
The Feast of Roses
The Splendor of Silence
In the Convent of Little Flowers

Shadow Princess

Indu Sundaresan

HarperCollins *Publishers* India

First published in India in 2010 by
HarperCollins *Publishers* India

P-ISBN: 978-81-7223-997-8
E-ISBN: 978-93-5029-443-7

10 9

HarperCollins *Publishers*
A-75, Sector 57, Noida, Uttar Pradesh 201301, India
1 London Bridge Street, London, SE1 9GF, United Kingdom
Hazelton Lanes, 55 Avenue Road, Suite 2900, Toronto, Ontario M5R 3L2
and 1995 Markham Road, Scarborough, Ontario M1B 5M8, Canada
25 Ryde Road, Pymble, Sydney, NSW 2073, Australia
195 Broadway, New York, NY 10007, USA

Typeset in 10.5/12.5 Adobe Caslon
InoSoft Systems

Printed and bound at
Thomson Press (India) Ltd.

For my mother Madhuram

and

my daughter Sitara

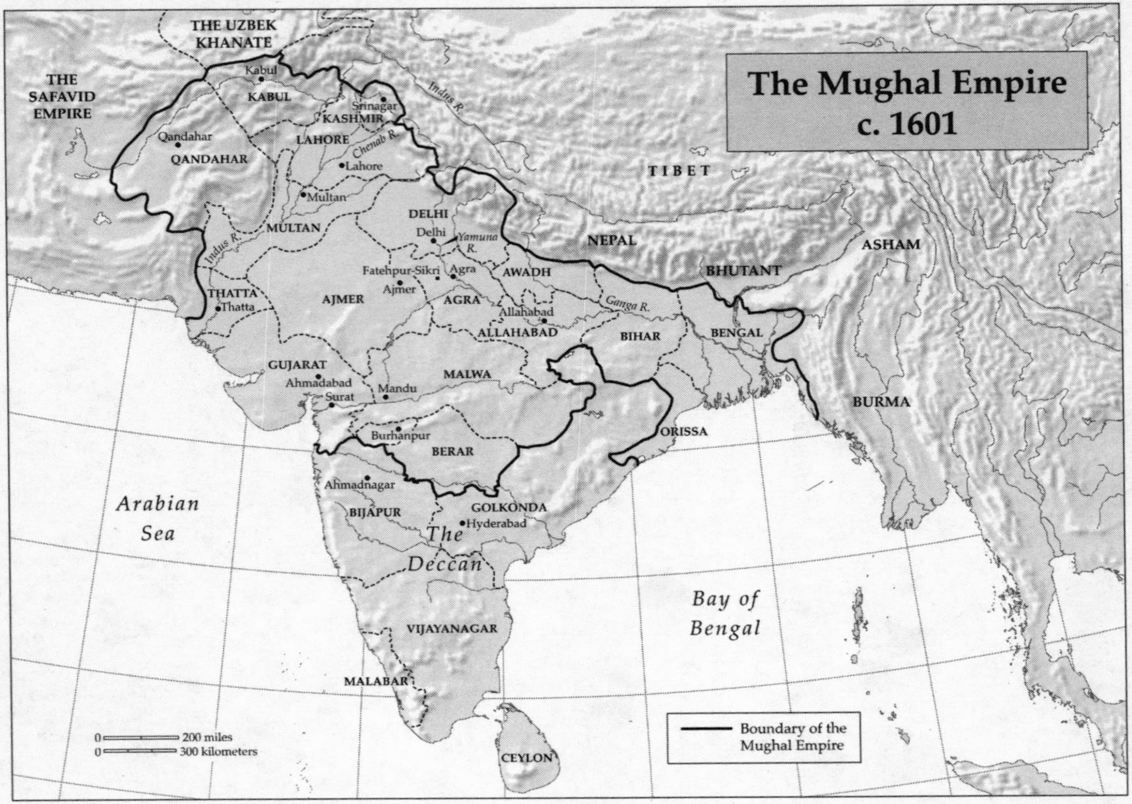

The Mughal Empire
c. 1601
THE UZBEK KHANATE
THE SAFAVID EMPIRE
Kabul
KABUL
Srinagar
KASHMIR
Qandahar
QANDAHAR
LAHORE
Chenab R.
Lahore
Multan
MULTAN
Indus R.
TIBET
DELHI
Delhi
Yamuna R.
NEPAL
ASHAM
BHUTANT
Fatehpur-Sikri
Agra
AWADH
Ajmer
AJMER
AGRA
THATTA
Thatta
Allahabad
Ganga R.
ALLAHABAD
BIHAR
BENGAL
GUJARAT
Ahmadabad
MALWA
Surat
Mandu
BURMA
ORISSA
Burhanpur
BERAR
Ahmadnagar
Arabian Sea
BIJAPUR
GOLKONDA
Hyderabad
The Deccan
Bay of Bengal
VIJAYANAGAR
MALABAR
CEYLON
0 200 miles
0 300 kilometers
Boundary of the Mughal Empire

Selected Members of Princess Jahanara's Maternal Family *Selected Members of the Mughal Imperial Family*

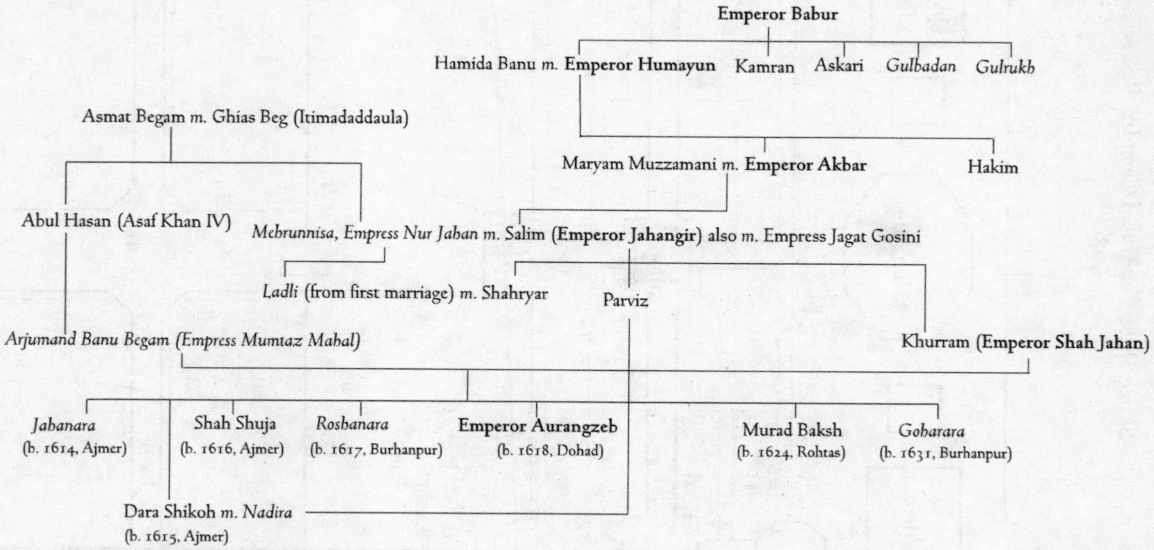

Key: Sons, *Daughters*

Sketch of the Taj Mahal Complex
c. 1648

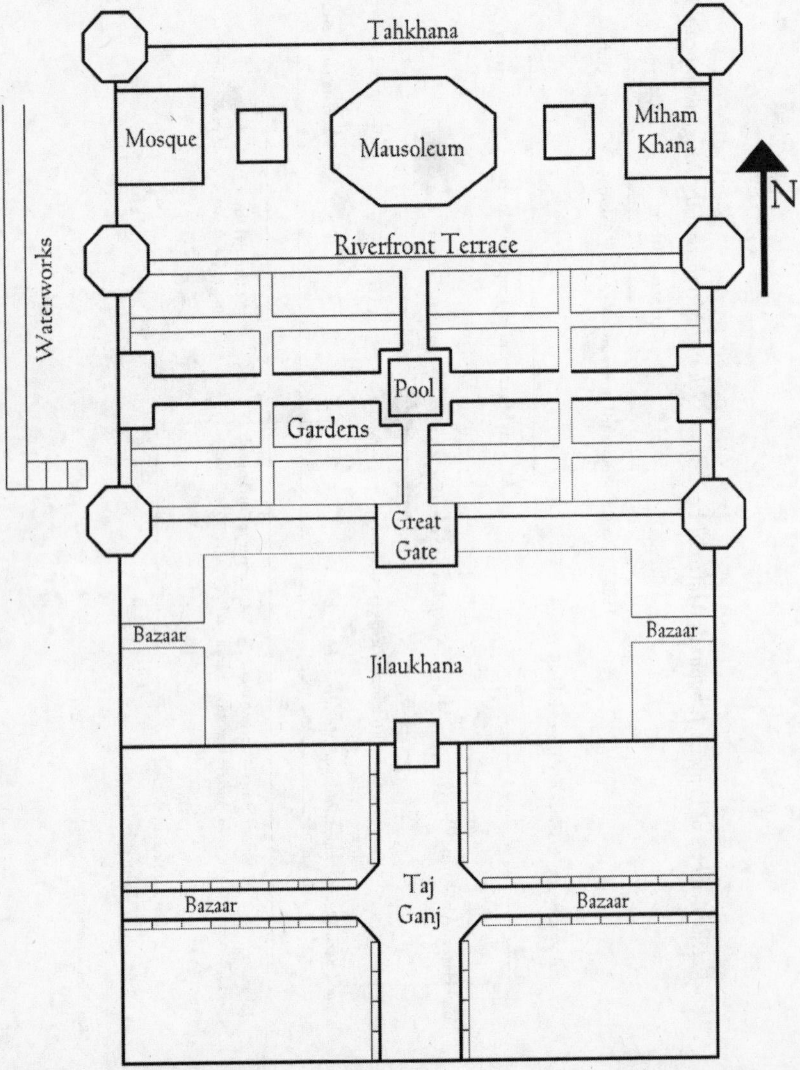

Principal Characters
(In alphabetical order)

Abul Hasan	Jahanara's maternal grandfather
Ahmad Lahori	architect of the Luminous Tomb
Akbar	third Emperor of Mughal India (r. 1556–1605)
Amanat Khan	calligrapher employed at the Luminous Tomb
Antarah	Jahanara's son
Arjumand Banu	titled Empress Mumtaz Mahal; Jahanara's mother
Aurangzeb	Jahanara's third brother; later, the sixth Emperor of Mughal India (r. 1658–1707)
Babur	first Emperor of Mughal India (r. 1526–30)
Dara Shikoh	Jahanara's first brother; the expected heir to the Empire
Ghias Beg	titled Itimadaddaula; Jahanara's maternal greatgrandfather
Humayun	second Emperor of Mughal India (r. 1530–40; 1555–56)
Ishaq Beg	Jahanara's eunuch
Jahanara	Shah Jahan and Mumtaz Mahal's first daughter and oldest surviving child
Jahangir	fourth Emperor of Mughal India (r. 1605–27); Jahanara's paternal grandfather
Khurram	titled Emperor Shah Jahan; Jahanara's father
Mahabat Khan	the Khan-i-khanan; Commander-in-Chief of the imperial armies
Mehrunnisa	Empress Nur Jahan; Jahanara's maternal grandaunt; Emperor Jahangir's twentieth wife
Mumtaz Mahal	Jahanara's mother, for whom the Taj Mahal was built
Murad	Jahanara's fourth brother
Najabat Khan	noble at court; Jahanara's lover

Raja Jai Singh	Raja of Amber; noble in the Mughal court; original owner of the land on which the Taj Mahal was built
Roshanara	Jahanara's sister
Shah Jahan	fifth Emperor of Mughal India; Jahanara's father
Shah Shuja	Jahanara's second brother

Shadow Princess

one

After the passing of midnight . . . a daughter was born to that tree of the orchard of good fortune; whereupon her feverish temperature (mizaj-i-wahhaj) transgressed the bounds of moderation . . . This unexpected incident and soul-rending disaster filled the world with bewilderment.

—From the *Padshah Nama* of Abdal-Hamid Lahauri, in
W.E. BEGLEY AND Z.A. DESAI,
Taj Mahal: The Illumined Tomb

Burhanpur
Wednesday, 17 June 1631
17 Zi'l-Qa'da A.H. 1040

The empress's howl, splintered and exhausted, stretched thinly into the night air and then fractured into little pebbles of sound. One a.m. The coming dawn, still hours away, smudged the horizon in ghostly grey. Oil diyas and candles rippled in an impulsive draught of air, spilling light from the apartments fronting the Tapti River.

Mumtaz Mahal screamed again without a sound, lips drawn back over even, white teeth, eyes shut.

'Mama,' Jahanara desperately said, grasping her mother's hand in her young, strong ones. 'Can I give you some more opium?'

Mumtaz shook her head and leaned back on the pillows, shivers racking her body. Now, once the contraction passed—

despite the long day and night of suffering—her features settled into an immeasurable beauty. It was there in the perfect cut of her nose, the seamless curve of her chin, the glowing skin and liquid eyes, irises ringed in darkening shades of grey. She had retained the newness of youth, though she was thirty-eight years old this year.

Empress Mumtaz Mahal, the Exalted One of the Palace—a title Emperor Shah Jahan had bestowed upon her a few years after they wed—let her hand lie in her elder daughter's comforting hold. In another minute, the pains would begin again. As she struggled to give birth to her fourteenth child in nineteen years of marriage, she was grateful even for the fact of it, for she was married to a man more beloved to her than anyone else, Khurram. He had been Shah Jahan for many years now, but she still thought of him as Khurram—the name his grandfather, Emperor Akbar, had bestowed upon him at birth.

A roar filled her ears. Opium. She briefly considered it in the filigree silver bowl, sweet to the taste, mixed with dates, the juice of the tamarind, a sprinkling of crushed cashews and almonds, studded with raisins. She had already eaten five round balls, each the size of a jamun fruit, since her waters broke . . . when was that? But the opium, always effective before, had only just razed the edges of the pain this time; she was hesitant to take more. The midwives, with their constant chatter and advice, had said that it would not harm the child already formed inside her. Mumtaz did not believe them. Her belly began to throb again, and she screamed, frantic with worry that Khurram would hear; he was sure to be nearby, though he was not allowed to enter the birthing chamber. There were some rules even the emperor of the Mughal Empire could not circumvent.

A gaggle of midwives flitted around the room, keeping their distance from the bed where their Empress lay. She could not bear their touch upon her so soon.

Jahanara's fingers constricted, and Mumtaz, through her screaming, gasped, 'Let me go, beta.'

The girl did in fright, covering her own face instead. When Mumtaz could rouse herself, she reached out blindly.

On her left side, a voice said, 'I am here too, Mama. I will comfort you. If you do not want your hands held too tight, I will hold them lightly.'

The empress sighed. She turned to her second daughter, Roshanara, and then back to Jahanara. How similar they were to each other, though, and she smiled within; they would hate that comparison. Jahan was seventeen years old, willowy and upright. She had a thin, sharply structured face, all planes and angles, brows that had been plucked to arch thickly above the bones surrounding her eyes, hair drawn back in this heat and plaited down her back. Roshan was a smoother version of her older sister, her skin more fair, her eyes coloured with flecks of green, her face round. And yet, despite this outward physical sophistication, she was only fourteen years old, three years younger than Jahan in age, a lifetime in understanding. She should not have been here, but she had insisted and Mumtaz had given in, unable to argue once the labour began. After all, the girls would one day be mothers themselves; let them see and learn and know what a woman was to do in her life. Between the two of them, there was already a slender rivalry, so inconsequential now as almost not to exist. But, Mumtaz thought, she was here to control them, for they needed a mother's hand; Khurram was of little help, he had too much love for one child and a bland indifference to the other.

When her belly strained with the next contraction, Mumtaz wondered why her thoughts were so clear. During the thirteen previous births, she had no memory of actually thinking anything. Those experiences had been simple, practically easy, an ache in her lower back, a sucking of opium, the child brought out splitting the room's seams with its cries, each successive yell painting smiles on all their faces. Laughter from outside as Khurram heard the news, his ear pressed against the wood of the door. Then there had been those early years when Khurram and she, and the children, had been sent in official exile to stumble around the empire, pursued by his father Emperor Jahangir's troops. Some of the births had taken place in tents, on the roadside. Even now, in these comparatively restful times, with the whole empire in the palms of their hands, Mumtaz could hear the distant rumble of pursuing horse hooves and felt an overwhelming fear for their lives if they were caught.

Not all the children had lived. There had been a girl before Jahanara who had died when she was three years old, and Mumtaz had to struggle to remember her name . . . and her face. They were still in Emperor Jahangir's good graces at that time, and so he had sent his condolences to his son and his daughter-in-law upon that child's death. Some of the other children had been stillborn, mercifully so, not giving her the time to create an attachment with them. Some had died within a few days; some, like that oldest girl, had died of smallpox or of a mysterious and stubborn fever just as they were beginning to crawl, or walk, or babble or talk. But she still had six children. Jahan and Roshan—the only two girls—here with her and four fine boys in the outer room with their father. And if this child lived . . . She touched her belly gently, and for the first time came this thought—*if this child lived and she herself did not die,* there would be seven. And she still had some childbearing years left in her, and though Khurram and she had been married so many years, despite the burdens of the empire, despite the women in his harem, he would visit her bed. And so there would be other children. In the end, this, and everything else, was in Allah's hands.

'Jahan, you are of an age to marry soon,' she said faintly when the contraction had passed.

'I am?' And then, softly, 'I am.' Those two words were fraught with longing, and Mumtaz watched her child. So she had felt too at her age, well before her age, with none of the patience Jahan had. 'We will speak of it when you are feeling better, Mama.'

'Your Bapa and I have been talking,' Mumtaz said, the words rushing from her mouth, determined to use this precious, snatched moment of calm. She had realized the truth of what was to happen to her, suddenly and with clarity. Her only anxiety was that she would not be able to see Khurram before . . . and she wanted to see his face, touch him, hear his voice. But she had her duties to her children too. She beckoned with a tired hand. 'Come closer.'

She had meant this for Jahan, but Roshanara also crowded over her. 'There is an amir at court, of a good family who have been servants of the empire for generations. They hail from Persia, descended from the Shah, though their ancestral lands are in Badakhshan. Your Bapa and I will not force you into a marriage you do not want, Jahan, but—'

'You know that I will want what you do, Mama,' Jahanara said. 'Why all this now? We will have plenty of time later, save your energy for the child.'

Empress Mumtaz Mahal closed her eyes, exhausted, and lay unmoving on the bed for so long that the two girls gazed at each other in trepidation. Roshanara bent to her mother's ear and whispered, 'What is his name, Mama?'

'Najabat Khan.'

Neither of the girls knew anything about Mirza Najabat Khan. They had been at court only a few times in the zenana balcony behind their father's throne, not paying attention to the names of the nobles presented to the emperor, mesmerized instead by the glittering gold and silver standards, the absolute quiet in a room thronging with men, the rows of turbaned heads bent in deference to their Bapa.

Mumtaz took a deep breath as pain bit into her lower back again. 'Jahan, call for your father.'

Jahanara rose; orders from her mother were obeyed almost before they left her lips. When she realized what was being asked, she dithered. 'Bapa cannot come here, Mama.'

'He has not until now,' Mumtaz said. 'But I want him.'

The midwives grabbed veils and drew them over their heads, falling into submissive attitudes even before the emperor had stepped into the room. Someone clucked, in disapproval, and Mumtaz, though she heard the sound, paid little heed to it.

'Tell him to come.'

Jahanara bowed to her mother. 'He will be here, Mama, as soon as I can open the door.'

'Go, Roshan,' Mumtaz said to her younger daughter. 'I want to be alone with your Bapa now.'

Roshanara went from her mother's bedside, her mouth pursed with discontent, and sat down with the slave girls, who had made a space along the wall for her. When Jahanara put her hand on the latch, the metal chill against her skin, she heard the midwife mutter, 'The head is showing, Your Majesty. It will not be long.'

~

Princess Jahanara Begam rested against the door and rubbed the back of her aching neck. Her mother had laboured for thirty hours, and now finally the child's head was crowning. At first, this confinement had been like so many others at which Jahanara had been present. The slave girls had laughed and called out for the birth of a son. The sage primary midwife sat in one corner (holding her own court among the lesser midwives), nodding at the jokes, her fingers busy with her knitting so that they would remain supple when she was needed. Aside from the opium, Mumtaz had wanted to eat only apples. Jahanara had patiently sliced and fed them to her mother. These were early apples from the valleys of Kashmir, exquisitely tiny and well formed, the size of cherries. Their aroma filled the room in this fiery month of June—in the middle of the flat plains and miles from the cool mountains of Kashmir—and all of their senses slavered. Jahanara had seen saliva drip from the primary midwife's mouth. But the fruits were for the empress, and no one, not even her children, princesses of royal blood and birth, had a right to them. And then, in the past few hours, something had changed. Not the fact that Mumtaz had laboured too long but that she had struggled too hard, her eyes vacant during the contractions, her conversation impeccably lucid in between. As though she would never find the time to speak again.

At that thought, Jahanara picked up the ends of her ghagara and fled down the dim corridor in search of her father, and when she reached the end, someone put a hand across, halting her progress. She stopped, breathing hard from the running.

'What is it, Aurangzeb? Why are you awake? You should be in bed, this is women's work.'

Her brother's figure detached itself from the shadows. At thirteen he was already almost at her height. Aurangzeb was as thin as she was, but whereas her gait and her carriage were assured, he was at that awkward, dangling age, with his torso not grown into his long arms and legs.

'Is Mama all right, Jahan? Can I go and see her?'

Jahanara drew back from him, outraged. 'Mama has asked for Bapa—I'm on my way to get him, and even he should not be in her apartments now. How can you think *you* would be allowed?'

He shook his head absent-mindedly, as though he had not heard her. 'Why would I not be allowed? You are. What is wrong? Is the child born? Why is it taking so long?'

He still had his hand on her arm, and Jahanara shook him off with an impatient gesture. In the semi-darkness of this outer corridor of the palaces at Burhanpur, Prince Aurangzeb's mouth twisted for a brief moment with pain. It was not as though they all did not like him, Jahanara thought. Aurangzeb was one of them; they shared the same father and mother—and this in itself was so unusual in these times, when Bapa could have had numerous wives and concubines—nothing demeaned their ancestry. But a minor sliver of irritation lay between them and Aurangzeb. It was . . . his intensity, his supreme confidence (so misplaced in her mind; he was a child, had done nothing yet, and would probably do nothing in the future), his insistence on what he thought was right and what wrong.

She said, as forcefully as she could, 'Don't be foolish enough to enter the birthing chamber, Aurangzeb. Remember that you are a royal prince and must follow convention.'

Her brother had turned to the doors at the far end of the corridor, but at Jahanara's words he paused. She left him and ran to her father, knowing that nothing but the casual mention of propriety (which to Aurangzeb was akin to something holy and held in reverence) would have stopped him. She ran swiftly, her heart surging in her chest, not seeing the eunuchs on guard along the way who bowed to her. Where was Bapa? Where was he? She burst into her father's apartments and shook him awake.

'Mama wants you,' she said, sobbing now. 'Go to her. She is dying.'

~

By the time Emperor Shah Jahan entered the apartments, Mumtaz had given birth to their fourteenth child and was asleep. Jahanara and he had stood outside for twenty minutes, their hands linked, listening to the empress's cries, and then the wail of the child. The Matron of the Harem, Satti Khanum, had put her head out when they knocked and said, 'Her Majesty is fine, Your Majesty. Silly child'—this to Princess Jahanara—'to rouse your father from sleep with fears such as these.'

'I want to see her, Satti,' Shah Jahan had said.

'Soon, not now. You cannot watch the birth itself. Stay outside, Your Majesty, I will call for you.'

And so they had been left at the door, leaning with their ears flattened against the wood. They had heard the child bawl, a sigh from Mumtaz, a quietness as she slept. And then Satti had opened the door for her emperor.

The baby, a girl, was in a gold and silver cradle in one corner of the room. The women around—midwives and slaves—melted away to make themselves inconspicuous as Shah Jahan bent perfunctorily over the child. She was awake, and her vivid blue eyes looked out at him from the folds of silk swathed around her little body.

'Did Her Majesty give the child a name before she slept?' Shah Jahan asked.

'She suggested—' Roshanara came flying to her father's side and clasped his arm around the wrist. 'She suggested Goharara, Bapa. Do you like the name?'

'Whatever your mother wants is what will be, my dear. Go.' He nudged her away. 'I must be alone with her.'

He went to the bed and sat down on a low stool someone had set there for him, his knees raised level with his chest, his hands on his thighs. For a long time, as the dark of night wore out and the light of day came to claim its share of time, he gazed at his wife, noted the rise of her chest as she breathed, marvelled at the sheer beauty of her features. He would never tire of this simple act. He placed a broad hand on her brow, but she did not stir. Her skin was too warm, he thought, and snapped his fingers once, without turning around. A slave brought a bowl of water scented with the attar of roses and a soft towel, which he dipped into the water and laid on her forehead.

'You must get well soon, my love,' he said gently. 'We have to enjoy the throne of Hindustan, now, when we finally have what I have laboured for.'

Four years ago, Shah Jahan had fought a bloody and terrible battle for this empire. He had killed his brothers, his cousins, his nephews without a thought for mercy, for he had known that if they in turn had the throne within their grasp, none would have been shown to him. Minor rebellions still abounded, to be sure, and one such had brought them to the southern boundaries of the empire, all the way here to Burhanpur, where they had once spent years in a sort of near exile, where some of their other children had been born, where the throne—set so far away at Agra, hundreds of miles to the north, with its immense treasury of jewels—had seemed unreachable. But Mumtaz and he reigned now over this mighty, stupendously prosperous land, and their names would forever be etched in history, and when posterity spoke of the Mughal Empire, it would be in hushed tones of awe and reverence. And *his* name, and his beloved's name, would come to signify everything Mughal. There was very little of the self-effacing in Emperor Shah Jahan—in any case, it was not humility which had put the crown upon his head when his own father had designated another son as heir and chased him out of India.

On the bed, Mumtaz Mahal stirred. It was a little, restless movement, caught by everyone in the room watching their emperor at the bedside of the woman who was his world, who had been similarly taught to consider their empress as constituting the entirety of *their* world. It was not a difficult task for these retainers, for in following their emperor's wishes came some wealth, some influence in the imperial zenana, and the simple ability to preserve their heads on their shoulders so that they might see another day.

When her breathing evened again, Shah Jahan captured his wife's wrist and laid his lips upon the skin on the inside of her elbow. The child in the cradle raised a tiny voice, and a wet nurse with engorged breasts rose to feed her. Earlier in the day, this woman had been chosen from the many others who had presented themselves at the palaces, their persons neat, their hair combed, their teeth brushed rigorously with twigs from the neem tree. For, to nurse a royal offspring meant riches, unimaginable affluence, perhaps even devotion from the child. Who, if a boy, could one day wear the crown of Hindustan, and who would remember even in adulthood the woman who had nursed him in infancy. Satti had picked this fortunate woman, with her thick peasant face, her lush and rounded body, her clean mouth, and her honeyed milk, which Satti had tasted herself.

'Is she all right, Khurram?'

Shah Jahan stumbled in his haste to rise from the stool and kneel by his wife's bed. He laid his arms over her waist and thighs. 'Yes, Arju. Are you, my love?' So he also called her, Arju, short for Arjumand, the name she had been born with.

She seemed to wait a long while before answering. 'I'm tired. It was . . . harder this time. I'm glad for this moment when I can see you.'

'What sort of talk is this?' he asked lightly, even as his heart began a mad thumping within his chest. So something was wrong. Arjumand had never before been so distressed. The birth of a child was an occasion of joy, and no matter how much she had suffered, she had been smiling and happy when he came to her. The fears evoked by his daughter's distraught words, laid to rest by Satti Khanum at the door, came flooding back in him. When his wife's lips moved, he bent over her and laid his cheek by hers, not allowing her to speak. She would be fine, surely.

'Let me call for the hakims,' he said.

'Wazir Khan?' Her voice was barely audible. 'He knows nothing about women's matters, and he has never been allowed into the imperial zenana before. What would he do?'

'But you—'

'I am all right, Khurram. Tired, that's all. All right now that I have seen you. Will you stay here?'

'Yes,' he said simply, and then he felt the brush of her eyelashes upon his skin as she closed her eyes and slept.

When day broke over Burhanpur and the muezzins' voices floated over the air to call the faithful to prayer, Shah Jahan left Mumtaz, still asleep, and went to his chambers to pray. He moved slowly through the zenana, worn from his vigil by his wife's side. In the last hour, Jahanara had come to sit by him and had put her head on his shoulder as they watched Mumtaz Mahal. When he departed, he left his daughter by her mother's side. She was sleeping also, still sitting on the floor, leaning against the mattress, her face against Mumtaz's hand.

Two hours after Emperor Shah Jahan left his wife in her apartments, Princess Jahanara woke with a feeling of dread. Her mother's hand was cold. Jahanara scrambled up and saw that her chest was stilled of breath, her face calm, as though she was still asleep.

'Bapa,' she howled. Her voice brought the women of the zenana flocking into the apartments. She pushed them aside and ran out again, tears streaking her face. Down the corridors, into her father's room, where he was resting. She did not know what to tell him, how to tell him of this. Even as she ran, she knew that something had changed in their lives from this moment. Who would look after them now? Who would look after Bapa? He was the supreme ruler of the Mughal Empire, but he would not think his life worthwhile without the woman he loved.

two

And that treasury of modesty and coffer of chastity was buried according to the custom of temporary burial (amanat) in the building ('imarat) inside the garden of Zainabad at Burhanpur, which is situated on the other side of the river Tapti; and the said building is constructed in the midst of a tank.

—From the *Padshah Nama* of Abdal-Hamid Lahauri, in
W.E. BEGLEY AND Z.A. DESAI,
Taj Mahal: The Illumined Tomb

Burhanpur
Wednesday, 17 June, 1631
17 Zi'l-Qa'da A.H. 1040

The child who had entered the world and sent her mother from it had been taken away, her whimpers fading with the wet nurse's footsteps. Rain came soon after the second *pahr* of the day was struck, after the noon hour. The day had begun clear as a diamond of the first water, the sun brilliant, the heat suffocating in its intensity. Then the skies had gathered a fistful of clouds over Burhanpur, ominously dark, laden with rain. The first streak of lightning outlined the somber black stones of the fort at the banks of the Tapti, the first boom of thunder rattled the windowpanes of the chamber where Mumtaz Mahal had lain on the birthing bed.

Then, the skies opened up, and the rains, mild at first, raged into a fury. A few short hours after the empress had drawn her last breath, she was laid in the ground and covered with the wet earth—Muslim strictures and the heat did not allow for delays in burial.

They stood in a line behind the imam, linking hands: Jahanara, Dara, Shah Shuja, Roshanara, Aurangzeb . . . and even Murad, who was only seven years old. Murad moved closer to Jahanara. His greatest worry was that the egret feather Bapa had given him two days ago—to plume in the pearl aigrette on his turban—would be in a sad state of drooping. He touched his head surreptitiously. His turban felt tight on his forehead. He wiped his nose, and the imam droned on. His sister's hand clutched his a little too tightly. As he wriggled his fingers, Jahanara said, 'Quiet, Murad. Pay attention to the imam.'

She shivered, and by her side, Aurangzeb said, 'Yes, listen to the prayer for our Mama.'

Jahanara had chosen this spot where their mother was to lie in Zainabad Bagh, on the eastern bank of the Tapti and across the river from the fort. If she turned her head, she could see the windows of the apartments where Mama had died, and, as that thought came, she did turn to look and saw the lone glimmer of white in the massive courtyard of the fort, built twenty feet up from the water level. Bapa. Also standing in the rain, watching them all from afar. He had refused to come for the burial, refused as Murad had initially, choked with grief, with disbelief, with the conviction that if he did not attend this hurried funeral, he would find his wife alive again.

There had been no such luxury for Jahanara, for even as her mother died, she had become Padshah Begam, the chief lady of the harem, in her place. The shift of status was almost unnoticed, from that first moment when she had run down the corridor, leaving the door to her mother's apartments open behind her. 'The empress is dead,' attendants had wailed. In a gossamer deference, eunuchs had bowed more deeply to her. Her father had been rising from the bed when she flew into the room. She had not been able to speak, only mouth this, *Mama is dead, Bapa.* He had fainted, falling with such abandon that his right elbow would ache for the next week. An hour later, questions had begun quietly in her ear.

Where should Her Majesty be buried, Your Highness? Jahanara had lifted her gaze to the vista beyond the windows, to Zainabad Bagh, to the pond in the middle of the gardens with its flat-roofed baradari where Mama had ordered entertainments for them all—music, dance, wine, and food—on moonlit nights.

She had washed her mother's body herself with Satti Khanum. The tears had come, again, as she wiped Mama's face with the pure Ganga water they used for drinking. Once. Twice. A third and final time with little cubes of camphor powdered in the water to perfume the body. Three silk shrouds, scattered with a hundred tiny diamonds, were wrapped around Mumtaz Mahal. The strictures demanded that the cloth be plain, but Jahanara had set twenty seamstresses to embed diamonds into the silk. Mumtaz's hair had been smoothed down and coiled behind her head. Jahanara had left on her mother a pair of diamond studs, the diamond ring that pierced her nose, twelve bangles with diamonds on each of her wrists, refusing to listen to any reason about divesting her of her jewellery.

'She is an empress,' she had said. 'She cannot go to her grave like a pauper.'

No one had argued with her beyond that, not even Satti Khanum, whose voice rose in the zenana on all occasions, who had had Mumtaz Mahal's ear in every matter, who was almost as powerful in the imperial harem as the empress herself.

Jahanara then had gone in search of her brothers and found them huddled outside their father's apartments. Dara sitting on the floor, watching his hands. Shuja weeping in one corner. Murad rolling a wooden toy horse and cart on the carpet. And Aurangzeb pacing so furiously that his bare feet slapped on the stone floors of the outer chamber.

'The funeral will be after the second watch,' Jahanara had said.

'I will not go.' This from Dara, his face pale, his eyes a dull red, his whole frame shaking.

'Nor will I,' Murad had cried. 'Mama will come back if I do not go for her funeral.'

'We will all be there,' Jahanara had said, almost shouting. Her eyes had smarted with a flash of tears, but she had brushed them away impatiently. She did not have the time for this sort of weakness; who would look after them if she began to cry again? 'Bathe first, you must be clean, and eat a little, and when we go to Zainabad Bagh to lay our mother in the ground, we will conduct ourselves with the dignity befitting our rank and our status. Dress simply, in white.'

At the sound of her sharp tone, all their heads had snapped around, and they had stared at her in disbelief. 'Bapa will not even come out,' Dara had said.

Jahanara had felt a slight chill. The skin on her palms was still wrinkled from having been immersed in the water used to bathe her mother's body, and an arrow of pain seared a previous cut on one index finger, which still throbbed even after she had washed the camphor out of the wound. But her tears were stanched, because she seemed to be the only one who had some control over what was happening. With their mother's unexpected, so unwanted death, the rest had all disintegrated.

'I will go talk with him,' she had said. But the conversation had led to nothing other than an overwhelming sense of fear. Jahanara had never seen such utter hopelessness in her father before—the thickness of his voice, the debilitated movements of his arms and legs, which could not be quieted, the strange laughter at inopportune moments—it had left her afraid for all of them. To the boys waiting outside, she had simply said that their father would not be there when their mother was laid in the earth. He had not even questioned this simple burial for Mumtaz.

She turned back towards the baradari on the pond. It was a small building, perhaps thirty feet long on each side, with a flat roof and sets of three cusped arches per side. The island itself, in the middle of the pond at Zainabad, was barely bigger than this baradari that perched on most of the land, leaving a thin skirt of grass and mud around it. And it was on this slender patch that they all stood. The centre of the pavilion had been dug up, the flat black stones that paved its floor removed, mud loosened and heaped to one corner. The imam who was leading the funeral prayer for their mother stood on the first step leading up.

When he had finished, Aurangzeb went up to the man and tapped him on his shoulder. The imam bowed to his prince and walked backward until he was behind the five of them. He did not lift his head once, acutely uncomfortable and disapproving in the silence that swelled around them.

Jahanara peeled the wet chiffon veil from her face and wiped the rain off her forehead and her eyes. Dara had protested against coming to the funeral because he had been repelled by anything to do with death and dying, even though this was their mother. Murad had insisted against being here because he was a child. And Aurangzeb . . . he had protested against *their*—Jahanara's and Roshanara's—being at the funeral because they were women and not allowed to take part in so public a ritual. So also the imam felt now, his distaste evident, his eyes fixed upon the ground just a few inches around his feet so he would see where he stepped but no more. This man—like Aurangzeb, Jahanara thought with a sense of mirth—was as rigid and obstinate as an ass. He had been so cautious that he hadn't even dared to look at Mumtaz's covered body by the graveside, because she was a woman.

Murad cried gruffly, great sobs ripping out of his little frame. Shivers shook him even in this heat, for all the rain had done was increase the cloying humidity. Murad put his arms around Jahanara's waist and clung to her, burying his face in the damp folds of her ghagara. She kissed the top of his head and said, 'Hush. Hush, little brother.'

'He wouldn't make such an indecent display if you were not here to comfort him,' Aurangzeb said.

'Will you keep quiet, Aurangzeb?' Dara spoke for the first time since they had come across the pond in a convoy of boats to lay their mother to rest. He had stood on Aurangzeb's other side all this while, his head bowed, his face sombre. 'You've said enough. You always speak more than you should. Words such as these are more of an indecent display than a child mourning for his mother . . . or his sister comforting him.'

Standing at the first step to the top of the baradari, Aurangzeb flushed, in rage and in embarrassment, because all their retainers were ranged around them, and, even through the pounding of the rain—lessened now somewhat—Dara's incisive words had been clearly audible. On various other boats bobbing gently in the pond were the ministers of state, seated and watching. Had they heard also?

Dara moved to occupy the place left by Aurangzeb and patted the sobbing Murad on his shoulder.

The prayers said, the empress's body was lowered into the rectangular grave, with her head pointing west, towards Mecca. The six of them climbed the steps and stood around the grave, looking down upon their mother's shrouded figure—no coffin had been built for her, in keeping with the strictures. Then, one by one, they scooped up handfuls of the moist earth and flung it in. The mud splattered over the unsullied white of the cloth that sparkled with its hundreds of diamonds, and slowly, as they threw in more, the sparkle dimmed and then was extinguished.

From the palaces in the fort across the Tapti, the man on the raised courtyard could not see this action—his children covering his wife's grave with mud—because the rain had begun anew its strengthened pounding, all but blotting out the severe outer lines of the baradari. The man held a white umbrella over his head. Beyond the confines of the fort at Burhanpur, Shah Jahan's authority flung out wide over the lands of Hindustan, and an entire empire would have been willing to fall on its knees in gratitude had it been given a chance to perform this minor duty of shielding his august head from the rain.

Emperor Shah Jahan was cold inside and out; his skin felt clammy, his heart fragmented into so many pieces that even breathing seemed torturous. He wondered if he would himself last many days more without Arjumand; it was unimaginable, a life without her. Would his children be performing the same duty for him in a few days? His tears fell. His ears were filled with the crashing of the rain on the white canvas of his umbrella; the folds of his white churidar, scrunched up around his ankles, were soggy; the lower edges of his white coat, the *nadiri,* clung to the fabric of his churidar. He would wear only white for the next few years. His shoulders stooped under the slender weight of the umbrella's gold-encased stem, and he felt himself age. Something had died inside him also.

Behind him, some thirty paces away, were two women who stood erect, their veils pulled over their faces, their backs firm. They were the empresses who remained. One, the first woman Shah Jahan had married, was descended from kings herself; her lineage was impeccable—she was linked in blood to the Shah of Persia. The second woman, whom Shah Jahan had married after his marriage to Arjumand (making her his third wife), was the granddaughter of the man who had been Emperor Jahangir's Khan-i-khanan, the Commander-in-Chief of the imperial forces, a powerful, well-respected man.

The first wife glanced thoughtfully at her husband. She was thirty-eight years old herself, but her last child, her first and only one, had been born some twenty years ago—in 1612, the year Shah Jahan had married Mumtaz. Having performed this perfunctory duty in giving her a child, albeit a girl child, he had not come to her bed again. What had been Mumtaz's charms? A pretty face? She herself had had one. Grace and elegance? Here also she could not be faulted. Noble blood? Mumtaz was the granddaughter of a Persian immigrant, a nobleman, true, but one who had been hounded out of his country. She could claim no ties to the Shah, no hint of royalty, and yet . . . she had been so ridiculously adored that the first wife was ignored, and the third wife—who also had been given the opportunity to produce a royal offspring after the marriage—was treated no better. The first empress inclined her head to the third wife. She had borne him a son, but the child died when he was two years old, so she literally had nothing any more.

But now—and here the first wife smiled to herself—now Mumtaz Mahal was dead. And their husband would return to them, for where else could he go? He would grieve for the dead empress, to be sure, but would find his happiness and content among the living. The first wife began to sketch out plans in her mind—which apartments to occupy here in Burhanpur and later in the capital city of Agra; which servants to retain and which to let go; which eunuch to create as Chief of the Harem; how to pension off Mumtaz's seven children; when to begin negotiations for the marriage of her twenty-year-old daughter. And then she remembered that she had not been consulted on the funeral arrangements, as a Padshah Begam of the harem ought to be. That her messages of condolence sent to the empress's apartments had been ignored. That Satti Khanum, who officially bore the title Matron of the Harem but in reality had been Mumtaz's chief lady-in-waiting, had not come to pay her respects to the newly powerful woman in the zenana. That, instead, that child Jahanara had taken over all the duties she, the first empress, should have performed for her lord in his time of need. How could a daughter take the place of a wife?

The first wife shifted on her feet, moved involuntarily out from the sheltering protection of the umbrella, and was drenched. She cursed under her breath, not daring to raise her voice. Even in death, Mumtaz Mahal cast a long shadow over the women who had been such pitiful rivals for her husband's heart.

But at least, the first wife thought, grasping at something, *anything*, Mumtaz was being buried here in Burhanpur, and here she would remain. In a small and indistinct baradari on the outer rim of the empire, in a city that could well be captured by the Deccani kingdoms which raged south of them. Then, no one would remember her, no one would take her name in their mouths, nothing would be said by posterity of this fierce and unreasonable love that her husband (and *her* husband, the first wife thought viciously) had had for her.

When Emperor Shah Jahan turned and stumbled back into the fort, she slipped her arm through his. He let her, left now with no strength even to protest.

She did not know how wrong she was. Mumtaz Mahal had died in Burhanpur, but she would live for posterity in the brilliant tomb that Emperor Shah Jahan would build for her in Agra, four hundred and thirty miles away—the Taj Mahal.

rauza-i-munavvara
The Luminous Tomb

As there was a tract of land (zamini) of great eminence and pleasantness towards the south of that large city, on which there was before this the mansion (manzil) of . . . Raja Jai Singh, it was selected for the burial place (madfan) of that tenant of Paradise . . . a lofty mansion from the crown estates (khalisa-sharifa) was granted to him in exchange ('iwad).

—From the *Padshah Nama* of Abdal-Hamid Lahauri, in
W.E. BEGLEY AND Z.A. DESAI,
Taj Mahal: The Illumined Tomb

Agra
Wednesday, 17 June 1631
17 Zi'l-Qa'da A.H. 1040

A thicket of sparrows launched itself from the branches of the tamarind on the banks of the Yamuna. The birds flew in a rush, first in one direction and then neatly in another, as though scrambling to make sense of what had disturbed them just as dawn laid open the horizon in Agra.

The man below lifted his head and followed the path of the birds until they disappeared and their confused twittering faded. Mirza Raja Jai Singh bent to sit in the lotus position on the mat his servants had laid out.

It was still night, but the darkness had begun to fade away. Through the mat, Jai Singh could feel the coolness of the damp earth. He was clad in little this early in the day—his chest was bare, he had dropped his chappals on the sandstone terrace of his mansion before descending the steps and the slope to the water; all he wore was a white silk dhoti tied around his waist, its edges decorated with a thin lining of silver *zari*.

'Huzoor.'

Mirza Raja Jai Singh inclined his head.

'The mistress—'

'Which one?'

'I beg pardon, sire, the first lady requests your presence when you have the time.' The eunuch hesitated. 'As *soon* as you have the time. In fact, forgive me, Mirza Sahib, without fail and the sooner the better.'

The eunuch stopped and waited. Raja Jai Singh could hear big intakes of air, a slow leaking out with a tuneless whistle. So his first wife had commanded him to her presence, as she usually did, demanding and not always diplomatic. And this eunuch who was her servant, he did not know how to knead her orders into more palatable words; the stupid fool trembled and shook, and even drooled in his fear. Raja Jai Singh turned back to the water and took a deep breath of the freshly moist air. Here was the hint of the monsoon rains; they would come soon, and every morning when he rose to walk to the tamarind tree, the grass would lie soft and spongy under his bare feet, the thirsty earth would sing, trees would flourish a joyful green.

He put up a hand. 'I heard you; go now. And do not return. This is the last time, you understand?'

The eunuch bowed, intelligent enough not to speak another word. Caught as he was between his master and his mistress—one sent him away, the other filled his ears with tales of neglect—he had no choice but to obey both of them. His master was obsessed with his mistress, who was a houri, an enchantress, and she in turn would rise every morning to spoil his master's time before sunrise . . . only because she could and because she wanted to. It was a game they played.

As the man backed up the slope, Raja Jai Singh heard him bump into someone, another servant perhaps, and say in a low voice, 'The Mirza does not wish to be disturbed.'

Mirza, Jai Singh thought wryly; he had been born a mere noble and would die a mere noble, despite his title of 'Raja' and his 'kingdom' of Amber.

Jai Singh had inherited his family fortunes and his title from his grandfather Raja Man Singh upon the latter's death in 1615. Man Singh, also a vassal to the Mughal Empire, had nonetheless managed to live with the extravagance of a king, with sixteen hundred wives populating his zenana, a veritable swarm of children, so many sons he could not remember all of their names. In the end, all of them had preceded Man Singh in death, except for the man who was Jai Singh's father. And so, despite that many wives, that many children—that many ways to split Man Singh's extensive properties in Amber and here in Agra into thin and equal shards to be absolutely fair to the numerous male offspring—all the property, the lands, the palaces, the immense bounty of gold and silver jewels, and this lovely mansion at Agra had fallen into the hands of Jai Singh.

He was a fortunate man, he thought. Even the fact that he had been allowed to retain his grandfather's property almost entirely unmolested was due to—among other things—the mercy of his being Hindu and of the emperors being Muslim. In the Mughal Empire, the emperor was the sole and only custodian of wealth, which he distributed to the nobles of his court at his discretion—this wealth was a gift, a privilege, a reward for faithful service. When a noble died, according to the law of escheat, so also died his right to his estates—his heirs could not inherit *anything*; it all reverted to the state, to their emperor. This was so in theory; in fact, the emperor usually passed a cursory glance over the property and a more than cursory glance over the heirs and their loyalty to his crown, and handed the estates back to the next generation almost intact. For some unspoken reason—a reason Jai Singh did not question—Hindu Rajas were exempt from this rule of escheat, and deaths in their families were not automatically accompanied by the arrival of the emperor's bailiffs.

A pale pink brushed the skies in front of Raja Jai Singh. From where he sat, without stretching his neck too far, he could see the red sandstone walls of the Agra fort pick up the blush of dawn. He mused over his fortunes again, over his luck at having this magnificent haveli on the banks of the Yamuna at Agra—a piece of land coveted by many of the nobles at court—which he had inherited from his grandfather. Amirs newer to court, or even those with lineages as extensive as thoroughbred horses, turned jealous eyes upon the lush copse of trees that surrounded the mansion, the sweet air that floated up from the river, the glimpse of the fort, why even the proximity to the fort, which allowed Jai Singh to present himself to his emperor in response to a summons before most amirs even had the time to call for their cummerbunds. But all of this—the land, the title, the wealth—had been well earned. For Raja Jai Singh came from a family that could trace its service to the Mughal emperors and to the empire from the time of Emperor Akbar. But his family had not just been servants—they had some much-cherished imperial ties also. Jai Singh's great-grandaunt, an Amber princess, had been Akbar's wife and Emperor Jahangir's mother. His grandaunt had been Jahangir's wife. The son born of this latter union, Prince Khusrau, had been unfortunately killed by his brother Emperor Shah Jahan on his way to the throne. If Khusrau had lived . . . if he had become emperor, perhaps Jai Singh would have been more powerful at court, inheriting this power instead of having to work for it.

He waited for the wink of the sun's rays before he turned east and touched his palms together in the first movement of the *surya namaskar*—the salutation to the sun. Even as he performed the motions of his exercise, some four hundred miles away, Empress Mumtaz Mahal went to meet her death. Raja Jai Singh dreamed desultorily of a small chhattri to cover his ashes when he died, here by the banks of the river, the jalis of the chhattri filtering the cool breezes from the Yamuna. But it was not to be, for his emperor wanted his land and his mansion for a loftier purpose—to house the remains of his beloved wife at Agra.

Jai Singh did not know then that his haveli would be demolished before the year was out, and in its place would rise a Luminous Tomb.

three

Even though the Incomparable Giver had conferred on us such great bounty, more than which cannot be imagined, through His grace and generosity, yet the person with whom we wanted to enjoy it has gone.

—From the *Padshah Nama* of Amina Qazwini, in
W.E. BEGLEY AND Z.A. DESAI,
Taj Mahal: The Illumined Tomb

Burhanpur
Tuesday, 23 June 1631
24 Zi'l-Qa'da A.H. 1040

The days wasted themselves in Burhanpur, in a daze, slowly moving into night and returning again. The town heard the gurgle of the ghariyalis' vessels filling with water to measure time, heard the men strike the brass disk hanging above their heads to announce the ends of the watches, saw light turn into darkness, but it was for all of them with a sense of unreality.

The shops in the main bazaar street were open, awnings held up on vertical poles to shelter from the sun, but business was not as usual. If money changed hands at all—for flour and rice, vegetables, copper pots, gold and silver—it was with a reluctance, as one hand hesitated in handing over the coins, the other grabbed a little too greedily at the first income of the past week. Even after their purchases, customers tarried outside the shops, trying to make conversation that did not sound stilted. They talked of the weather (it was hot, fiercely so), about the lack of dependable rain (and again about the weather), about the emperor's presence here at Burhanpur (such a blessing to them all). But of the death of Mumtaz Mahal they could not speak. The men in the streets, the few veiled women of a higher class who strayed for goods, the more common women who wandered with their heads bare to the gazes of all; they had none of them seen their empress, but news from the fort palace that loomed over the bazaar seeped into every corner. And what they heard most of was their emperor's grief at this lady's death. A day after she had died, after she had been buried on that small island in Zainabad Bagh, in the centre of the Bagh's pond, they heard that their emperor had died also.

At that news, the shopkeepers pulled wooden shutters over their storefronts, locked them securely, and crept into their houses behind the shops as a mob of young men racketed through the street, shouting profanities and wrecking anything they could find. Three hours later, the dust settled only when the Ahadis, the emperor's personal bodyguards, thundered through the street on their horses, swords drawn to slice down a head here, an arm there. The rebellion—if it could be called that—of the miscreants ended then, as abruptly as it had begun. Burhanpur settled into a state of long-drawn-out waiting accompanied by a hush, a silence, a burgeoning fear.

Outside the fort at Burhanpur, the highest amirs of the empire waited also, day and night. It was customary for the nobles to take turns of a week or more in guarding their sovereign—they would arrange themselves and their retinues in the courtyard just beyond the guard of the Ahadis, set up their sleeping and cooking tents, array their men in semicircular bands around the palaces and on the banks of the Tapti. But since Mumtaz had died, all the nobles in Burhanpur, most of them normally present at court, found themselves crowded in the courtyard. When night fell, small fires sprang to life, over which meats were roasted, water boiled, wine warmed. Their voices were subdued. A stillness hung around them. When one of them moved, on the sixth day after the empress's death, they all turned to him with some hope. He could do something. He was the Khan-i-khanan.

Mahabat Khan was the Commander-in-Chief of Shah Jahan's armies, in some senses the most powerful man in the empire after the emperor himself. He was a soldier, and the empire, through all the years of its existence, had been forged by the sword, dyed by the blood of fallen princes and commoners, wrought into existence by wars and not diplomacy, and so Mahabat had more authority than the Grand Vizier himself, who was merely the Prime Minister of the empire.

He had tarried under the shade of the canvas awning of his square tent for six days, eating and drinking in the courtyard with the other nobles, as he awaited the summons from his emperor. Now it finally came in the form of Ishaq Beg, Mir Saman, or Master of the Household, to Empress Mumtaz Mahal.

'His Majesty commands your presence, Mirza Mahabat Khan,' Ishaq Beg said, standing behind Mahabat, to his right. From the corner of his eye, Mahabat saw that Ishaq Beg's back was a little too stiff, the tilt of his chin too arrogant. He had not the demeanour of a man who had just lost his employer—and so his employ—and his very means of existence. The Khan-i-khanan set his wine goblet down on the table by his side and nodded. He rose, and the entire assembly of nobles around him rose also, their gazes firmly upon him as though he could tell them already what he would find when he entered their emperor's presence.

Mahabat Khan rinsed his mouth with some water and waited while his servants combed back his hair, ran their hands over his shoulders and his *peshwaz,* straightening out creases and ironing wrinkles between their broad fingers.

Ishaq Beg stood back, and when Mahabat passed him, he raised his eyes in a sly, almost condescending glance. Mahabat worried about that look all the way into the fort, beyond the Ahadis who parted to let him through, the eunuchs slinking in the outer reaches of the zenana, the stolid Kashmiri women who guarded the emperor's most private moments. These women were told to shield their tongues as jealously as they did their emperor; one slip, one misplaced word, one frivolity and their tongues would be cut out. They were rewarded richly for their services and punished without a thought if they failed even a little in rendering those services. As Mahabat Khan approached Shah Jahan's apartments within the fort on the banks of the Tapti, he could feel the coolness wafting from the river's fragrant waters through an open window. He paused when a Kashmiri guard barred his way with her spear.

Despite his standing in the empire, Mahabat Khan did not make a murmur as the guards searched him. They shook the turban from his head and, deftly holding the aigrette in place, fingered the folds of cloth. They ruffled his hair—a sliver of a blade could bring harm; his clothes were agitated, his cummerbund examined, the soles of his bare feet (he had removed his footwear outside the main entrance) rubbed. Then they stood aside, and Mahabat wondered if they had not been too meticulous in their search, if the other nobles commanded to His Majesty's presence were subjected to a similar indignity each time. But then he also remembered his long and chequered past with his emperor and thought briefly that if their positions had been reversed, he would not have trusted himself either.

When he entered Shah Jahan's chambers, Mahabat lingered, blinded by the gloom around. The windows were all sealed with tightly woven khus mats, and silken drapes covered the edges to shut out all light. A breeze whirled around the room, caught and tossed about by the punkahs held by the fifteen slave girls standing in the corners and against the walls. There was a little light from a candle on a low table in the centre, which flung shadows around. Mahabat took in all of this when his eyes had adjusted somewhat painfully from the glare outside. He heard the rustle of a woman's skirts and saw the back length of a ghagara slip around the door to his right and a hand with glowing diamond rings pull the door shut, but not before she had hesitated for a while. The oldest princess, he thought, Jahanara Begam. Now they would all depend upon her, lean upon her slender shoulders for counsel, advice, strength. Who else was there? Satti Khanum, perhaps. But Satti, for all her intimacy with the members of the emperor's zenana, was in the end a retainer, and she would remain in that capacity. The emperor's own mother was dead; and he had not been close to his father's other wives—especially Mehrunnisa, the last one—so which woman could help him carry his burdens other than this child of his?

Mahabat then became aware that he had been lost in musing and had not yet been noticed by his emperor. He peered around the room, his eyes going from the slaves at the walls (to whom he paid little attention; they were akin to the furniture) to the bed in the centre of the room, which was empty, the two steps leading to a raised indoor verandah with arches that looked out over the Tapti. And here, leaning against a pillar, he found Shah Jahan clad in the white of mourning. Mahabat padded over the length of the room, and, as he approached his emperor, he stopped and performed the *chahar taslim,* bending with some difficulty from his waist, laying his right hand on the ground and raising it to his forehead four times. When he had completed the salutation, he straightened his back with a groan, which he hoped was inaudible. Then he waited again, his gaze to the ground. He could not speak until Shah Jahan chose to begin the conversation.

When his emperor's voice came to his ears, Mahabat felt a deep sense of shock.

'You are here, Mahabat,' Shah Jahan said, so hoarse as to be almost inarticulate.

'Yes, Your Majesty. At your command, always.' And now Mahabat looked up at the man seated on the stone steps and felt his heart stop. Even in the room's dimness, he could see the ravages of six days of constant weeping and no eating. Shah Jahan's frame had wasted away, the skin was carved tightly over the bones of his face, his eyelids were swollen and puffy, and his back was stooped. But what astounded Mahabat the most was the white on his head and his face—almost overnight, or so it seemed to him, the emperor's hair had greyed. Mahabat would not have thought it possible if he had not seen this for himself. He almost reached out a hand to Shah Jahan's clasped ones, then stayed that comforting action. What was he thinking? He could not dare to touch his sovereign.

He could not speak any words of solace either. What could he say? That the empress would be missed by all of them, that she had indeed been the brightest light in Shah Jahan's palace, that her loss was so great as to cause them all grief? Mumtaz Mahal had been the most precious jewel in Shah Jahan's zenana, and it was not Mahabat's place to comment, even in such an innocuous manner, about a member of the imperial harem. This much he had learned well. Many years ago—frustrated, without paying heed to any advice—Mahabat had cautioned Emperor Jahangir about the immense power he was granting his twentieth wife, Mehrunnisa. For his pains, he was trounced in a chess game by that empress (and that still rankled) and sent to Kabul, a frozen fringe of the empire, to serve as 'governor'. Mahabat Khan was a tired old man, now in his seventh decade, and no longer stupid. He kept quiet, his head bowed, his heart knocking against his rib cage.

Finally, Shah Jahan spoke again. 'I am going to give up the throne, Mahabat.'

Caution was forgotten, etiquette damned.

'You cannot, Your Majesty,' Mahabat cried. 'You are a young man yet, only thirty-nine years old. Your life stretches in front of you. This is the empire you have battled for and won; it is rightfully yours. Your grandfather Emperor Akbar considered you his heir. You . . .' Mahabat stopped speaking, but it was only to sob instead, an action that astounded him. He thought, through tears that he could not stop, that he was indeed growing old and feeble, but only because he should have anticipated talk such as this when he was summoned to Shah Jahan's presence. He wiped his eyes and waited again, for a smile or some mockery from Shah Jahan. But his emperor behaved as though he had not even noticed Mahabat's reactions. Instead he was examining his thin fingers and considering Mahabat's words carefully.

'I have no wish to live, Mahabat, let alone reign any more. What use is it to possess these lands and this wealth? When . . . *she* was alive, there was something to fight for, a reason to be Emperor. It was so that she could forget all those years we were persecuted and chased over the lands, so we could rest our aching bodies on ground that did not move, so that we could get the respect due to us.' Emperor Shah Jahan raised his head, and for a moment, even among the ravages that grief had produced, Mahabat saw the arrogance and confidence that had made him a monarch. 'Allah Himself ordained that I would be king,' Shah Jahan said. 'My grandfather wanted me to rule after my father. My father . . . he was besotted and led astray by a devious woman who wanted to put another on the throne—you know this history well, Mahabat Khan, you were a part of it.'

'I know, Your Majesty, and apologize for my role,' Mahabat said. After his near exile to Kabul as a so-called governor, he had come back to court, begging for an audience, and then Mahabat had surprised himself and almost everyone else he had known by effecting a coup and imprisoning Emperor Jahangir and the empress. But he had been a weak leader—and that woman indeed had had crafty ways, for even under guard she had managed their escape. Then Mahabat went into hiding from the royal couple. He later agreed to hound out of the empire the son who was giving them so much trouble. Long before he had become emperor, Shah Jahan had forgiven Mahabat, but he was not above remembering or reminding him of it. Even in the typical, much convoluted, loyal-one-day-blithely-unfaithful-the-next history of Mughal nobles, Mahabat's fortunes had swung so wildly, he himself could not believe he was still alive.

'I was destined to be emperor,' Shah Jahan continued, his voice much smoother now, and Mahabat realized this was the first time in days that his emperor had talked to anyone. 'I was fated to be a great ruler. But there are times, Mahabat, when there is a reason to step down and give up ambition. Without'—and he hesitated again, as he had before, not willing to call out his wife's name in front of another man, a mere minister—'her.' Shah Jahan passed a hand over his eyes.

Someone sneezed in the next chamber, and Mahabat's head whipped to the door through which Jahanara (or so he thought) had left when he entered. She had shut the door, he had seen her do it, though now it was ajar by a few inches. But she had not made that sound—it was a man's sneeze. One of the princes? Either them or one of the eunuchs, but no one other than the royal offspring would dare be caught listening at the entrance to the emperor's chambers. Which one? Mahabat thought. And then Shah Jahan said, 'Which one of my sons do you think should rule in my stead, Mahabat Khan?' And he knew why he had been summoned to his emperor.

Dara was sixteen years old; Shuja fifteen; Aurangzeb thirteen; and Murad a laughable seven. Mahabat Khan had opinions about the emperor's sons that he kept to himself. Dara was a disrespectful puppy, too inclined to think only of himself; Shuja was merely a puppy—he followed and he could not lead; Aurangzeb was a leader, but he was inflexible and resistant to advice, dangerous qualities for a leader to have; and Murad was . . . well, Murad was nothing yet, unformed and little.

Mahabat Khan did not think the emperor had, yet, one son who could rule the empire. What was Shah Jahan's purpose in calling him here? To offer him a regency? How could a son rule when his father was still alive? It went against all Mughal law; to whom would the people bow their heads—the boy king or the emperor who had willingly ousted himself?

Mahabat Khan chose his words with care. 'It is a difficult situation, Your Majesty. I say, with all respect for your wishes, that your time to leave the throne has not come yet. You are our sovereign; in your happiness and well-being is ours. The empire, as you well know, Your Majesty, is a great responsibility also. There are millions of people who depend on you, who cannot live without the sight of your face in the mornings—as they wake to greet the sun so also they revere their emperor. In these past few days, your absence from the jharoka appearances has caused unrest and distress among your subjects—'

'If you were to choose, Mahabat'—Shah Jahan cut into his minister's speech and forced a decision from him—'which of my sons should rule after me?'

And so Mahabat Khan, Khan-i-khanan, aware of the partly open door to the next chamber and not knowing which of the four princes was behind it, responded the only way he could. 'Your choice is mine, Your Majesty.'

It was an unsatisfactory answer. But after so many years of intrigue and rebellion, the Khan-i-khanan of the Mughal Empire knew that the grasp on the world's richest throne was tenuous at best, and any one of Shah Jahan's sons could feel the weight of the crown on his head, and so he was not going to part his sixty-five-year-old head from his equally old body with words from his own mouth.

~

Prince Aurangzeb waited until he had heard Mahabat Khan leave and then grasped at the door's handle.

His father's voice, tired and barely audible, stayed his action. 'Close the door and leave, Aurangzeb. You should be ashamed of yourself, listening at doors like a common spy. You are a royal prince.'

Aurangzeb flushed, and his hand trembled. Bapa did not like him; he had never liked him, not since his birth. It was Dara who was his favourite, Dara who could do no wrong, who was the crown prince, who would rule the empire. How had Bapa known that he was there? He glanced around and realized that light poured into this room from an open window, and in leaving the door connecting to his father's chamber ajar, he had let some little light seep into the murk in there. But how had Bapa known *he* was there? Aurangzeb thought for a brief while, pushed the door open a little more, and his father said, 'Go. I do not want to see you now.'

At that, Aurangzeb stepped back into the room and shut the door gently. Blood rushed under his skin, and a fighting madness rose in him at the injustice of those words. His father could not possibly have known it was him. Emperor Shah Jahan had merely guessed which of the boys was at the door. But guessing was not definite knowledge. Let him think what he wanted; Aurangzeb could act better than anyone else he knew, and Shah Jahan would soon doubt his own thoughts, and . . . begin to cast suspicion upon the other sons. Perhaps even the much indulged Dara.

He slipped out of the room and ran fleetly through the zenana in search of Jahanara. He went to the series of rooms she now occupied, which had once belonged to their mother. Among so much else, Jahanara had now gained possession even of these rooms in the fort at Burhanpur, and this Aurangzeb did not mind, for he thought it her right. But one person minded, very much, and when he burst into the innermost chamber, fronting the river Tapti, Aurangzeb saw Roshanara seated on the divan in the outer verandah, her hand shading her face from the harsh sunlight.

He stopped, panting. Her mouth drooped at the edges.

'What is it now?' he asked. It was always something with Roshan, some disgruntlement, some anger, some spite at quite anything. In that they were alike, this much he recognized, but Aurangzeb was a man (well, a boy yet who would grow into manhood), and he would fight in battles, own lands, rule lands, perhaps even this empire of theirs. 'Where is Jahan?'

'Why do you want her?' Roshan asked. 'Am I not enough? What have you heard now?' For she also recognized a kinship between them. Dara and Jahanara were allied; she thought

Aurangzeb and she should similarly be allied. To Shuja, older than Aurangzeb, she gave little importance; he was a nonentity.

Aurangzeb walked across the room toward his second sister, mulling over in his head what he had heard of the conversation between Shah Jahan and Mahabat Khan. If Bapa were to leave the empire to one of them now, it would be to Dara. Dara, who was sixteen, old enough to be king, though not old enough to rule the empire—that would mean a regency. Would Mahabat Khan be made regent? But Mirza Mahabat Khan was more *his* friend. He sat down beside Roshanara and told her what he had just overheard.

Her eyes gleamed with excitement. 'One of us will be emperor.'

'Dara,' Aurangzeb said shortly. He made an exclamation of disgust. 'It will always be Dara.'

'And Jahan will rule beside him. She will be his Padshah Begam; she will rule over his harem, she will tell him what decisions to take at court.'

'There will be a regency; Dara is too young.'

'If only you could be emperor, Aurangzeb,' Roshan said.

'Then you can be the head of my zenana?' he asked. 'I am thirteen years old, Roshan. Why would Bapa even think of handing the empire to me when Dara is there to take on those responsibilities? Where is Jahan?'

Roshanara shrugged. 'Somewhere, doing something, being Padshah Begam already. She does not need Dara to be head of the imperial harem; Bapa has as much as given her that title already, just six days after Mama's death. If only you paid attention to what was actually happening around you, Aurangzeb, you would know.'

'What has happened?'

As Roshanara began to speak, the door to the apartments opened and a young girl drifted in. The slave girls in the room, out of earshot of Aurangzeb and Roshanara, bowed to her, and she acknowledged the salutations with a wave of a hand. Nadira Begam was fifteen years old, her skin as fresh as a flower at the break of dawn, her figure softly rounded in the hips and the breasts. She moved with an innate grace, her eyes clear and untroubled when she came to sit beside them. Nadira was their cousin, daughter of Shah Jahan's brother Prince Parviz. She had been born at Burhanpur and had lived all of her life here, since her father had been governor here during their grandfather's reign.

They both looked at her with affection. If Nadira had been a male child, that affection would have been somewhat wanting, for in being a boy she would have been a threat to the throne and would have, perhaps, died in the battle for succession in 1627. But a girl child, left to be brought up by servants at the southern edge of the empire, was not to be thought of as a hazard. Her father had been a wastrel during his life, succumbing to the lure of drink, as so many Mughal princes had. At one time, Emperor Jahangir had hauled up this sluggish son and sent him, under Mahabat Khan's care, careening around the empire in pursuit of Shah Jahan and Mumtaz Mahal. But Shah Jahan could hardly hold a grudge against his brother's daughter for her father's faults—and if Parviz had lived until 1627, he might very well have died by Shah Jahan's sword, but he had drunk himself to death, conveniently, and left behind this languid girl.

Roshanara continued to speak, ignoring Nadira seated at their feet, her face resting against her cousin's thigh. 'Bapa has increased Jahan's income to one million rupees.'

'Mama's income,' Aurangzeb said reflectively. 'What will she do with so much money?'

'And he has given her most of Mama's estates. Five million rupees are to go to her—all of Mama's parganas, her lands, her jewels—and the other half of five million is to be divided among the rest of us, a million each.'

Aurangzeb grinned. 'If Bapa could make Jahanara emperor, he would. Dara would be nothing compared to her.'

'This is not funny,' Roshan said sharply.

'But so much money.' Nadira spoke for the first time, her little voice in a half sigh. 'You are all so rich. My father was never anything compared to yours.'

'And now Dara will be emperor,' Roshanara said.

'He will?' Nadira sat up and looked at the two of them. Then she collapsed back into her pose at Roshan's side. 'How nice for him.'

'I want to be emperor,' Aurangzeb muttered, and when Nadira opened her mouth, he said, 'Nice for me too, Nadira, but only one of us can be Emperor. If your father had had much more of a spine and less of a liking for wine, he could have been king himself.'

They continued talking thus for the next half hour, until Jahanara came back to her apartments. When she returned, Aurangzeb began to bring up the topic of his father's conversation and found himself hesitating more than once. Closer in age than any of them, Jahan and Dara had a special friendship that he had not been able to break into. Jahanara was always kind to him, but it was not pity he wanted from her; he wanted her to respect him as she did Dara, he wanted her love and her affection, and he wanted all of that to be firm and unwavering.

So he did not talk to Jahan in front of Roshan and Nadira, waiting for a time when they would be alone, when the only voice she heard would be his. He was well aware that he was still considered a child, although he had moved out of the zenana apartments into the *mardana* quarters—the male half of the household. He had a better seat on a horse than Dara, he knew almost all of the Quran by heart, and he cultivated the nobles at court with an assiduousness Dara should have employed but did not. He was cut from the cloth of kings, Aurangzeb thought.

'You must go now,' Jahanara said, sinking slowly onto a divan in one corner. 'Draw the curtains.' This last was to the slave, who moved noiselessly around the room in response to her command.

'Are you tired, Jahan?' Roshanara asked, her voice tinged with more malice than sympathy.

'Yes. Go.'

'I want to see Bapa.'

Princess Jahanara raised her head from the velvet bolster and gazed steadily at the three of them. Roshanara, watchful, chewing her lower lip. Aurangzeb, all aglow with excitement, betrayed by the restless movement of his hands. Nadira, sweet and . . . well, stupid Nadira, looking away into the light beyond the thin muslin drapes.

'Bapa does not want to see anyone yet, Roshan.'

'He sees you,' Roshanara said bitterly.

'Because she comforts him, Roshan. Don't be stubborn about this.' Aurangzeb put his arms around his sister's and his cousin's shoulders and shepherded them out. 'Let's go now. Rest, Jahan.' When Roshanara resisted his touch, he whispered in her ear, 'Later, Roshan. This is not the time to fight. Later.'

And so they left Jahanara on the divan, alone in her room, wretchedly unhappy. She was exhausted and bewildered by the duties rapidly forced upon her. The harem scribes who came to her apartments every night to read from their journals—intimate and intricate details of all that had happened within the zenana's walls. The begging for daily orders from the Mir Bakawal, the Master of the Imperial Kitchens—what delicacies should be prepared for the emperor's table, Your Highness? The excessive obsequiousness from the slaves, eunuchs, and servants. The constant struggle to keep Bapa's two wives appeased and Satti Khanum in her place.

She closed her eyes and tried to calm the riot of thoughts that raged through her brain. There had not been a moment to think of Mama in these past few days, and she was crushed by the change in Bapa. He refused to eat; she had managed to coax a few mouthfuls of chicken biryani into his mouth, feeding him herself, and a couple of sips of wine. But he had had no interest in more. Of anything, it would seem.

A benevolent sleep came to claim her then, and as she slept, she cried softly, tears escaping down her face to dry in rivers of salt.

Outside her rooms, Aurangzeb, Roshanara, and Nadira parted and went on to their own quarters. Prince Aurangzeb skipped as he ran. Jahan must have noticed this little service he had done for her, and soon he would speak with her in private about what he had overheard. No one else knew of this, he was sure; Mahabat Khan would not speak until it was made a fact.

But Roshanara and he had talked enough in front of Nadira, after a while not really noticing that she was even there, so light was her presence. And that princess let her slave girls run ahead of her, waited until they had disappeared, and then sent a message to the mardana through a eunuch she found passing by. The next day, Nadira took the boat to Zainabad Bagh, to pay her respects to her departed aunt, she said, and when she was alone at the baradari, another boat docked on the other side, and she turned eagerly to meet the man who had come in response to her summons.

rauza-i-munavvara
The Luminous Tomb

> *Across the river Jumna . . . is the tomb of I'timad-ud-Daulah . . . This exquisite mausoleum, the first example of inlaid marble work in a style directly evolved from the Persian tile-mosaics, was raised by the Empress Nur-Jahan to the memory of her father, Mirza Ghias Beg.*
>
> —C.M. VILLIERS STUART, *Gardens of the Great Mughals*

Agra
Tuesday, 23 June 1631
24 Zi'l-Qa'da A.H. 1040

Once upon a time, not so long ago—fifty-four years to be exact—a young Persian nobleman packed his belongings in the middle of the night and fled his homeland, heading east in the year 1577. The family took with them only as much as they could easily transport, having left in shame and in stealth. Ghias Beg had three children, two boys and a girl, and his wife carried a fourth in her rounded belly. When they stopped at a nomadic encampment in Qandahar, on the outer verge of the mighty Mughal Empire, the wife gave birth to a baby girl in the midst of a winter storm. This child they named Mehrunnisa—the Sun of Women. A desolate Ghias sat outside the tent in the battering baying of the wind and pondered his fate—a new baby to feed, a family to keep safe, nothing but three gold mohurs in his cummerbund. The bejewelled court of Emperor Akbar beckoned from the capital at Agra, and if fortune was kind to Ghias, he could, perhaps, join the ranks of the lower nobility, earn a living, and die an inconspicuous death.

He did not know then that this last was not to be. For that child named Mehrunnisa, born in the tattered black tent in the desert near Qandahar, would become, thirty-four years later, Empress Nur Jahan of the Mughal Empire when she married Akbar's son Jahangir and came into his harem as his twentieth wife. Ten years after the marriage, when Ghias Beg died with the title Itimadaddaula, or Pillar of the Government, Nur Jahan would raise a wondrous white marble tomb over her father's remains on the eastern bank of the Yamuna. She would herself never see it completed, for by the time the last stone was laid, Mehrunnisa had been sent into exile by the current emperor.

As powerful as Ghias's daughter would become—in fact, the most powerful woman in the Mughal dynasty—it would be his granddaughter's name that would adorn the thoughts of posterity. And that granddaughter—Mumtaz Mahal—who was Nur Jahan's niece, had just died herself. The plot of land where her glowing tomb would come to be built was on the western bank of the Yamuna—southwest of her grandfather's spectacular tomb.

The penniless and not-always-honest Persian nobleman who had had to flee his homeland would find a permanent home in Hindustan. The women of his family would light up the harems of the Mughal kings. His own tomb, exquisitely wrought with his daughter's vast wealth, in marble inlaid with semi-precious stones, would be a veritable jewel. His granddaughter's tomb would eventually be built along the same lines—in white marble, with brilliant red and purple inlays of gems, a crimson sandstone platform, a massive gateway of red sandstone speckled with white marble.

None of these details, in their specifics or even in their totality, had taken shape in Emperor Shah Jahan's mind as he mourned the death of the wife he had loved above everything else in the world . . . perhaps even more than the empire he had fought so hard to rule. But now he was emperor; the treasury vaults under the fort at Agra shimmered with jewels and stones of astounding value; his lands stretched hugely across the map of Hindustan; every plate he ate from, every goblet he sipped his wine from was studded with diamonds and rubies—this immense wealth, in a sense, was what he had fought for. With this wealth came his power.

As the skies settled into a deep cobalt over the fort at Burhanpur on the night Emperor Shah Jahan had decided to give up his throne, he knew that his wife's final resting place would not be humble. She had been precious to him when alive, the mother of fourteen of his children. She would rest for all eternity at Agra, he thought, not here at Burhanpur. And where in Agra? There were the vast grounds that Raja Jai Singh had inherited from his grandfather, which Shah Jahan had let him take upon Man Singh's death, unquestioned. And now . . . he wanted that land.

In the undulating light of the diyas, that very night, Emperor Shah Jahan wrote out a farman—a royal edict—to Raja Jai Singh, ostensibly requesting the land and his mansion at Agra, in reality ordering him to hand them over. In return, because he was going to build something so sacred upon that land, the tomb that would house Mumtaz's remains, he gave Jai Singh four other mansions in Agra as a gift. He signed the farman, affixed the royal seal at the head of the orders, and sent the paper to his daughter Jahanara to read it over.

Then he set the goose-feather quill down with a shaking hand and covered his eyes.

He had no idea yet what to do with the land or how to construct the tomb upon it. Only a few months later would he begin to think of Itimadaddaula's tomb of white marble on the eastern bank of the Yamuna, to think in terms of something similar for his wife, pure and chaste in marble so untarnished that the colour would bleed white in the harshness of the sun and emit coolness on the night of a full moon. Nowhere as tiny as Itimadaddaula's tomb, but mammoth in its lines, yet graceful and elegant, as only his vision could make it. But for now, he knew that, no matter what the tomb looked like, he would call it the *rauza-i-munavvara*—the Luminous Tomb.

four

In our quarter of the globe, the succession to the crown is settled in favour of the eldest by wise and fixed laws; but in Hindoustan the right of governing is usually disputed by all the sons of the deceased monarch, each of whom is reduced to the cruel alternative of sacrificing his brothers, that he himself might reign.

—ARCHIBALD CONSTABLE (ed.) AND IRVING BROCK (trans.),
Travels in the Mogul Empire, A.D. 1656–1668
by François Bernier

Burhanpur
Wednesday, 24 June 1631
25 Zi'l-Qa'da A.H. 1040

When Emperor Shah Jahan woke that morning, he felt the chill of the metal disk under his cheek where he had laid it the night before, and when he rose to look at his grief-ravaged face in the mirror, he saw the imprint of the Persian script upon the disk on his skin. He stared at his image for a long time, his fingers brushing over the writing on his face, then glanced at the royal seal in his hand. Impressed on the heavy gold were the names of his ancestors—Timur the Lame, Babur, Humayun, Akbar, Jahangir, and in the very centre his own, Shah Jahan, the King of the World.

Eunuchs and slaves moved around in his apartments soundlessly as he went to the balcony attached to his rooms and stood in the morning sunlight. From here he could see the dusty plains around Burhanpur stretching out for miles, a few splashes of green where trees grew with dogged determination, low hills on the horizon. He owned all of this land, as far as he could see, and so much more of India—Kabul and Lahore in the northwest, Kashmir in the north, Bengal in the east, and here in the south pushing against the edge of the Deccan kingdoms. The emperor laid the seal on its side upon the balustrade of the balcony and watched the chunk of gold glow, faint smears of ink darkening the grooves and furrows of the writing upon it. It had been hard won, this empire of his, with a bloody history he had engraved upon his heart, along with which came the knowledge that nothing worthwhile was achieved easily.

Some hundred years before, in April of 1526, an upstart Timurid prince had brought his twenty-five-thousand-strong army in battle to the plains of Panipat near Delhi. His name was Babur. In that battle, Babur, with his pathetically small army, met the one-hundred-thousand-strong forces of Sultan Ibrahim Lodi, who was the ruler of the Delhi Sultanate—and routed them by firing with muskets from behind a barricade of carts on the battlefield. With that stunning victory over the Lodi king, Babur became the first emperor of Mughal India. With the conquest came the vast wealth of Hindustan—gold coins, jewels of magnificent lustre and value, trim and well-fed horses to populate an immense cavalry, war elephants, and an astounding and new collection of subjects, who looked strange and spoke in stranger tongues—all prostrated at the feet of the new emperor.

But Emperor Babur hated Hindustan—he loathed the heat, found the topography too flat, too uninteresting, and yearned all the while for his gardens in Kabul until he died four years later.

Babur's eldest son, Humayun, became emperor after him and found that his father had bequeathed upon him an unsteady empire and also three half brothers, who thought themselves as much sovereign as the eldest son. Ten years later, beset by family troubles, he was driven out of India by Sher Shah Sur, who set up court in Delhi instead. It would take Humayun fourteen more years to set foot in Hindustan again with the help of the Shah of Persia, and when he did, in 1554, it was only to rule for two short years before he died. His son Akbar was only thirteen years old when Humayun died and already on campaign far from his father's side.

Emperor Akbar ruled for forty-nine years, expanding the boundaries of the empire his grandfather had laid the foundations for well beyond Emperor Babur's imagining. He conquered kingdoms and married daughters, nieces, and sisters of the vassal kings to demand thus their everlasting fealty to his Mughal crown. He built monuments, tombs, and forts, palaces and entire cities so lavish that they would survive for hundreds of years. He was a great king, a good king, a just king, known for his liberality, his generosity, even his patronage of arts and culture.

When Emperor Akbar died, in 1605, only his oldest son, Jahangir, was alive, and he ascended the throne when he was thirty-eight years old after a long and bitter struggle with his father (and indeed with one of his own sons) to feel the heft of the Mughal crown on his head. When Jahangir became emperor, his father bestowed upon him—the first of the Mughal emperors to be given this bounty—a more or less peaceful empire, a firm throne, and an unshakable legacy free from any threat from the outside. Most of Jahangir's troubles came from the inside.

When he was forty-three, Emperor Jahangir married for the twentieth time and brought into his harem a Persian woman, Mehrunnisa, whom he made influential within his harem and without, at court. Mehrunnisa would, eventually, become the bane of one of Emperor Jahangir's sons—Shah Jahan. When Jahangir died, Mehrunnisa attempted to put on the throne another son, a weakling prince named Shahryar, nicknamed most unflatteringly *nashudani*, good-for-nothing. In the end, it was Shah Jahan who ascended the throne at Agra as the fifth emperor of the Mughal dynasty, and he sent to their deaths his brother Shahryar and, for good measure, a couple of his cousins, thereby ensuring even in 1627 that, if anyone would lay claim to the throne of the mighty Mughal Empire, it would be only someone who was directly descended from him and his wife Mumtaz Mahal.

And now, in June of 1631, a week after his wife's death, Emperor Shah Jahan leaned his arms on the railing of the balcony and closed his eyes wearily against the glare of the royal seal when the sun lit upon its golden face. He was contemplating erasing his name from the centre of the seal, divesting himself of the imperial turban, having the *khutba*—the official proclamation of sovereignty—read out in the name of one of his sons instead. The question was . . . which one?

~

When the heir apparent to the Mughal throne, Prince Muhammad Dara Shikoh, was born, in March of 1615, his father and mother were still firmly in the good graces of their emperor, Jahangir. Dara's grandfather was overjoyed to hear news of his birth, for he was the first son of a then-favourite son, and Jahangir gave the infant boy his name, which was to mean 'the glory of Darius'. Five years after Dara's birth, his family fell into disgrace. He remembered some of that mad flight around the empire with his parents and his brothers and sisters—his grandfather's imperial troops filling in their footsteps in the thickly packed mud of the countryside almost as soon as they had made them. Or so it seemed to Dara. They roamed the empire for five years, sleeping in one palace one night, another the next, and a strange succession of princes and nobles came to lay their arms down before his father, who was then only a prince, a disgraced and defamed prince whom Emperor Jahangir and his twentieth wife, Mehrunnisa, were determined to crush. Even in circumstances such as these, the then five-, six-, seven-, and nine-year-old Dara watched fealty being sworn to his handsome father, leanly muscled and dark-hued from days spent in the saddle, and he learned what it was to have royal blood imbuing his veins.

Only later, in fact, on that mid-afternoon in June 1631, a few days after his mother had died, did Dara understand more of the situation in his childhood as he stood at the keel of the boat that rowed him over the clear waters of the Tapti to the other bank and to Zainabad Bagh, where his mother lay buried. It was the time of day, all over Hindustan, when not a creature stirred outside shelter. In Dara's eyes, there was the hot, still dazzle of the sun hovering overhead. It had rained earlier, but the glisten of the water on the walls of the fort behind him and the roofs of the buildings in Zainabad Bagh in front of him had long since burned off in a quiet sizzle when the sun showed its face again. The heat picked up, the land dried under its fierce intensity, and people and animals fled to the safety of coolness and dark wherever they could find it—under trees, below rooftops, beneath cloth and canvas awnings, even in the cover of shadows cast by lounging cattle and camels.

Dara stood bareheaded in the boat and turned impatiently to the man rowing him across. 'Can you not go any faster?'

'Yes, Your Highness,' the man said, his muscles straining against the oars as they dipped cleanly into the water and then out again.

Their pace did not pick up even in the slightest. Dara had known that the boatman was rowing as strongly as his age and body would allow him to. The boatman would never use a negative with Dara or any other member of the royal family; his answer had been steeped in etiquette and in generations and centuries of servitude, and so he had said yes when, in fact, he *could* not physically have rowed any better or brought them to the other bank any quicker.

Dara tutted, thinking that he should not have wasted his breath in futile conversation with a menial. But he was anxious all of a sudden since his mother had died. Bapa would not see any of them, except for Jahanara, and each night she had returned to her own chambers from their father's with a droop to her shoulders, with few words left in her mouth, and slept the nights away as though she would never again wake. Dara had waited by her side for two nights, watching the rise and fall of her chest as she breathed, waiting desperately to know what was happening with Bapa. Was he all right? he had asked, and in reply Jahan had waved her hand and brushed him away. He had stayed on in her rooms, unmindful of the clucking maids and even the shooing gestures of Satti Khanum, as Jahanara dressed and departed again to be with Shah Jahan. He had paced the hallways outside the royal apartments his father occupied, waiting for a summons or a sound from within. At times, he thought he had heard a fine keening wail, brokenhearted and reedy, which had sent a cold hand to clutch at him. Could that be his Bapa? Even here, on the outside, his legs trembled at that sound; how could Jahanara hear it up close, how could she bear it, what did she do to comfort their father? After that day, Dara spent the rest of his time in his own apartment, growing more and more restive. Now, the day after Mahabat Khan had been granted an audience with his emperor, Prince Dara Shikoh was on his way to the other bank of the Tapti to meet a woman who had sent him a summons for another audience. And he went, Dara thought, rubbing sweat from his forehead, because she would fill these silences that had surrounded him since his Mama had died. Nadira knew something, else she would not have sent a furtive message to him through a eunuch in the harem or insisted upon their meeting so far from the palaces at a time of day when few ventured outside.

The boat docked, and Dara swung over the side and onto the wooden boards of the jetty before the boatman had had time to fasten the rope over a post and bring the boat's rocking to a halt. He flew through the entrance to the garden. Guards raised their spears in threatening gestures and lowered them in one move when they recognized the slight, muscled figure of the man who swept past them. Their heads bowed to the ground, but Dara did not notice their salutations, just as he had not expected to be stopped.

In the Bagh, it was finally a little cool, and huge mango trees spread their many-armed branches over the paths, creating a permanent shade from the assault of the sun. As Dara ran, he could smell the sweet-sour aroma of the warm sap that ran down the sides of the fruit hanging from the trees, the branches so low that he had to duck his head in places. The Bagh was full of guards, lining the pathways, at the crossroads where one pathway met another, all clad in mourning white for his mother. A lone boat, bleached into paleness by the sun, drifted along its mooring rope on the pond, and Dara hauled it in towards him, shading his eyes as he did so in search of Nadira's figure in the baradari on the island. He could not see her, but he knew that she was there. He climbed into the boat, waving off offers of help from the guards around, and rowed himself to the island. When he docked at the other end, hands came to help him, and Dara tripped as he swung his leg out over the side of the boat. Upright, he stayed standing where he was, on the rocks that lay strewn over the thin lip of the island. Now that he was finally here, his haste cooled and his breathing slowed. For a few steps away, under the stone awning of the baradari, lay his mother, a woman who in life had enchanted him, as she had so many others, a woman who in death he had not yet had the time to mourn.

The island in the middle of the pond in Zainabad Bagh was little more than a gathered mound of mud carted over in boats and flung on a bedrock of boulders and gravel that the emperor's engineers had carefully designed. The foundation for this island was so solid that a tiny pavilion had been built upon it—just as Mumtaz Mahal had envisioned—as a place of repose where she could lie down on a blistering afternoon with the breeze swinging through the open arches. As time passed, she opened her baradari to her husband, and they had a quiet dinner here on some evenings, with the slaves stacked against the baradari's pillars, or to her children when she brought them here to listen to music on moonlit nights or to the sounds of the dark—a partridge startled from its rest; a jackal's brusque and childlike howl, intended to entice other animals to it for slaughter. And so, Dara, her favourite son, the one upon whose shoulder she had rested a light hand so often, had come here enough times to have accumulated memories only of Mumtaz Mahal.

He remained where he was, his head bowed in prayer. When he looked up, over the steps of the pavilion and into it, he saw Nadira kneeling in front of the smooth, flat slab of marble that was his mother's gravestone. Whereas the rest of Zainabad Bagh was quiet, here, on the island, there was the melodic beat of the imam's voice as he chanted verses from the Quran. Day and night, this sound rippled out over Mumtaz Mahal's remains by the emperor's orders. Every man chosen for this task sat facing west, towards Mecca, his eyes lowered only to the Quran by his side, not daring to look at the sheet of icy white marble, even though there was nothing to be seen of the woman herself and she was long dead.

Dara recognized the sura the imam was chanting and joined in, and he saw Nadira's lips move in a like fashion. When the imam continued, Dara slipped off his thin sandals and climbed into the baradari to kneel alongside his cousin.

Nadira was nothing if not practical, and even in the sight and presence of the newly dead, as soon as Dara had settled himself and bowed to touch his head to the stone under which his mother rested, she said, 'The emperor wishes to give up his throne.'

He paused in the act of straightening his back and then continued until he was vertical. Nadira had spoken in a low voice, hovering somewhere over a whisper, and he knew that no one could hear them. Dara knew also that, although they had both come to Zainabad Bagh and met at Mumtaz Mahal's grave as though by chance, even if they were seen, like this, close to each other, their knees and thighs touching, there was nothing in the least inappropriate. Nadira was his cousin, his uncle Parviz's daughter, and Parviz had been their father's half brother. A brother, Dara conceded realistically, who had done little good in his life and had conveniently drunk himself to his death before the Mughal throne became vacant again. Even this little fact was in Nadira's favour, and in the past year and a half, during the time they had been at Burhanpur, Dara had discovered anew this cousin of theirs who had been born here and brought up here, a woman, a girl, who knew nothing of politics and whom he would not have thought possessed of much intelligence. Until now.

He did not question her statement. Here, finally, was a reason for the thick solitude and quiet that had surrounded them all in the past few days since his mother had died. Bapa was considering dispossessing himself of the crown of Hindustan, which he had fought so bitterly, and for so many years, to gain. Dara reached out and rubbed his palm over the stone in front of him. Had she meant so much to their Bapa then? He was old enough (and in a zenana full of women with little to do other than gossip he would not have needed to be very old) to understand the import of the child who mewled away in the wet nurse's apartments in the palace—she had been the fourteenth child of his parents' union, which meant that over the past nineteen years no other woman had captured his Bapa's fancy and imprisoned his heart like his mother had. She *had* meant so much to him in life that, at her death, Emperor Shah Jahan was willing to throw away everything else he had and to live the rest of his days, aged beyond his time, in obscurity, with a son on the throne instead of him.

'Where did you hear this?' he said at last, thoughts humming in his head. What did this mean? Who would be his regent? For Prince Muhammad Dara Shikoh knew that he was the heir to the Mughal throne and that, if this news were indeed true, in a few days he could find himself emperor at sixteen years of age.

'Aurangzeb,' Nadira said.

'How does he . . .' Dara shook his head. 'He probably listened at the door when the Khan-i-khanan was granted an audience in the fort. Bapa would not have called Mirza Mahabat Khan for counsel—he rarely does such a thing—he would have informed him of this decision . . . which means,' Dara said more to himself than to Nadira, 'that he has made up his mind.'

'No one but you can be emperor,' Nadira said softly. She was not looking at him, though her head was turned towards him and slanted to one side, her eyes cast down upon his hands.

Of the four princes, Dara was the one who had been granted his mother's beauty, her spectacular physical attractiveness, her height and erect carriage. He was also a poet at heart, and his interests lay more in thinking and philosophy than in the saddle or on the battlefield. But, as with most things, Dara was equally accomplished in either. He could ride a horse with such grace that it seemed as though the animal, finely tuned to every twitch of the reins in his hands, was but an extension of him. His childhood masters, great generals themselves, had been awed by the fluidity with which he wielded his sword, his mace, his spear, surpassing their expectations of him. At study, the mullahs found him steady and with an unshakable concentration. He asked questions of them about Islam and Hinduism and Buddhism that they could not answer, or did not dare to think about; his grasp of languages was stellar—he seemed to do anything he set his mind to effortlessly. And in that lay Prince Dara Shikoh's only fault. He was well aware of his talents, and so he was lazy, indolent, uncaring, and unnecessarily disrespectful to others, even his teachers.

Dara glanced down at Nadira when she spoke. She had uncovered her face, and her veil lay on the floor beside them. It was woven of a thin white muslin, and the cloth had a sheen to it. Dara picked up the veil and wrapped it around Nadira's shoulders. At his touch, she seemed to tremble, and he looked at her more fully.

'How old are you?'

If Nadira realized this to be a strange question—they were cousins and had been in close contact with each other for the past few months in the imperial zenana—she did not show it.

'Fifteen,' she said. 'A year younger than you, Dara.'

It was the first time also that she had used his name; thus far, when they had talked or played board games together, she had always begun and continued conversations without any form of address. The sun had lurched lower into the sky, and its rays now slanted into the baradari, and in this illuminating light, Dara saw Nadira as though for the first time. He had watched her take off her veil with a sense of shock, although he had seen her face many times before. Here, in public, with the imam at the other end of the baradari and the guards outside, the gesture had seemed indecent and exciting, as though he was being offered a glimpse of something sacred and forbidden. He saw the long lashes resting against cheeks that were glowing with red, a blush, because of him and his presence. He saw her hair curl against tiny ears in which were two small diamonds—her inheritance did not allow for the immense riches they all took so carelessly for granted. He even noticed her hands resting on her knees, the fingers long, the nails oval, the entire tips—nails and skin—coloured a faint orange. Like the others, Nadira was in mourning and had not coloured her hands with henna since the empress's death. What would Mama have thought of Nadira as a bride for him? He had to marry, all emperors were obliged to beget heirs for the empire, and here was a woman whom they all knew, whom they would not be wrenching away from another kingdom and another home—whose loyalty could never be questioned. Who had no living and powerful relatives to invoke rebellions. And yet, Nadira had little to offer. She would bring no magnificent dowry to the marriage, no alliances with powerful kings, no fealty sworn to the Mughal throne. Dara knew, as he stood at the cusp of becoming the sixth emperor of Hindustan, that Nadira Begam, daughter of the poor, dead Prince Parviz, could never be an emperor's wife. Rulers could not choose where they married or marry for anything akin to love.

He smiled wryly. His grandfather *had* married for love, a twentieth wife who was both Dara's step-grandmother and his grandaunt. But these two intimate relationships had been only trouble for Bapa and Mama—and a lesson to all of them in consanguinity. Much better to stay with the dictum that politics and love did not mix well.

Dara took Nadira's hand in his and kissed the fingers. Her skin gave off the aroma of sandalwood, and the hand lay soft in his large ones. She was trembling.

'Did I do well in telling you, Dara?'

'Brilliantly, Nadira.'

He rose abruptly and backed out of the baradari without a word of farewell, leaving Nadira to find her way back to the palaces across the river. This time, Dara allowed himself to be rowed across the pond and pondered as he went to the boat that would take him across the Tapti. Once on the other side, he went to Jahanara's apartments and, when he did not find her there, sent word to her in their father's apartments for her to come and meet him immediately. She did, and they talked together for three hours, until the emperor roused himself and asked for his daughter again.

She went back to her father with an ache in her heart. The empire would be Dara's, this they all knew well already—but how could Bapa even think of giving it up now? When Jahanara neared the door, Aurangzeb came up to her. 'Have you heard, Jahan?'

At her nod, he said, 'I wanted to be the first to tell you.'

She frowned. 'This is not a race, Aurangzeb. Bapa is in there, dying slowly and—' She looked hard at him. 'What do you care if Bapa . . . Why is it important to *you*?'

He took a step back and flushed, his neck and cheeks stained crimson, his face mutinous. 'Yes, why to me? Dara is the one who would care, who should care. Isn't that what you think?'

Jahanara turned away, disgusted. Surely her other brothers could not be salivating over the throne already. Was this an indication of things to come? Had Mama's death changed so much in their lives? She stayed at the door, pointedly ignoring Aurangzeb until he stumbled, spun around, and then ran to his apartments. When his footsteps had faded away, Jahanara opened the door and went inside, suddenly terrified that if her father took this decision he could plunge them into a civil war.

And the empire would disintegrate.

rauza-i-munavvara
The Luminous Tomb

Nur Jahan's great monument to her father is important . . . because it reflected architectural transitions . . . that were to achieve full flower in the tomb of Arjumand Bano . . . against the extraordinary visual success of Itimaduddaula's tomb, the . . . use of white marble was . . . already a foregone conclusion by the time Shah Jahan began to plan for the Taj Mahal.

—ELLISON BANKS FINDLY,
Nur Jahan, Empress of Mughal India

Agra
Thursday, 25 June 1631
26 Zi'l-Qa'da A.H. 1040

Ghias Beg died in 1622, forty-five years after he had fled his homeland of Persia in shame, dogged by debts unpaid. He had arrived in India with four children, a wealth of nothing, and a reputation that could not bear close scrutiny. For all his faults—and these were mostly related to his appetite for money—he was a man who made friends with ease and kept them firmly by his side.

Prince Dara's paternal grandfather, Emperor Jahangir, exercised his right of escheat when Ghias Beg died and took all of his immense property—his lands on the banks of the Yamuna at Agra, his mansions, the jewels in his safe house—and bestowed it upon the woman who had come to mean more to him than anything else in the world, his wife Mehrunnisa. It was an expected move on his part, but not a very politically correct one. Mehrunnisa was already empress, supreme in the harem, formidable in court dealings, and possessed of a vast income of her own . . . but she was, in the end, a mere woman. When Ghias Beg died, his oldest surviving son was Abul Hasan, Dara's maternal grandfather, and it was to Abul that all of the father's property ought to have gone, not to the daughter, not to a woman, even if she were an empress. Besides, Abul's daughter was married to Prince Khurram, and both Khurram and Arjumand had been sent into exile by Mehrunnisa while Abul himself was at court, at his father's deathbed, and mocked subsequently for the loss of his father's property to his sister.

Jealousy flamed through Abul at the thought of this injustice, and then he heard that Mehrunnisa intended to convert the gardens that their father had owned on the Yamuna's eastern bank into a tomb for him and for their mother.

The tomb took a mere six years to build, and politically for Abul and Mehrunnisa those were turbulent years—Mehrunnisa was still the empress and her word held sway, but Abul clung to her side, determined that, when Jahangir died, it would be Khurram, the third son, who would become the next emperor, not a puppet of Mehrunnisa's manipulations. And so it came to be in 1628, the year Ghias Beg's tomb was completed. Abul imprisoned his sister and any other man who would dare to claim the throne, sent word to his exiled son-in-law and daughter, held a fierce and tight grip over the empire until Khurram could be crowned Emperor Shah Jahan and he could finally become hugely powerful himself—as the father-in-law of the fifth emperor of the Mughal dynasty.

But Abul did not know then that the sister whom he had once adored, whom he had grown to loathe in later years, would leave a legacy in the shape of the tomb for their father, which she commissioned, which she designed, and for which only she could pay with her wealth. When it was completed, Abul knew that his hand could neither have shaped this graceful building nor reached into his purse for the money required—only Mehrunnisa had the incalculable elegance, the determination to succeed, and the imagination to raise a building over their parents' remains that was an oddity for its time.

The tomb, Itimadaddaula's tomb (for this was the title by which Ghias would always be known), was built in the traditional *charbagh* style that the Mughal kings had brought into India from Persian gardens. The main garden was walled on four sides to keep out heat and dust and prying eyes. When she first looked over Ghias's gardens after his death, Mehrunnisa decided to keep the charbagh that her father had built—the garden crossed over with two raised stone pathways that bisected at right angles in the centre, where was housed a baradari, a small pavilion. The bisecting pathways created the charbagh—or the four compartmentalized gardens. Mehrunnisa had the centre pavilion demolished, for there the tomb would rise. And at the centre of each wall, where the pathways began, she constructed four ornate gateways of red sandstone inlaid with marble, each identical to the others, and had three of them bricked up, so that the only entrance to the tomb was from the eastern gateway, and the western gateway would overlook the riverfront.

For six years, a fine powder of marble and sandstone clotted the air around Ghias Beg's gardens, and the chink and click of chisels and hammers on stone plagued many a child's dreams in the stonemasons' huts that sprang up around. When the dust subsided, the tomb radiated charm and allure, but Mehrunnisa was never to see the finished product of her creation—by 1628, she was already deposed as empress, her brother had imprisoned her, and when Khurram became emperor, he sent her into a semi-official exile to Lahore, three hundred and seventy-five miles from Agra.

The elevated stone pathways that created the charbagh met in the centre of the garden, and here was another raised red sandstone platform, on which the tomb stood. The platform itself was unornamented, simple slabs of stone mortared to one another, but the sides were inlaid with hexagonal patterns in white marble. The tomb was wholly built in the white marble that came from Raja Jai Singh's quarries in Markana. At one point during the construction, Mehrunnisa had thought of covering the walls of her father's tomb with beaten silver sheets that would glow in the sun and smoulder under an overcast sky, but her architects persuaded her otherwise, citing the weather, the wear on silver, the fact that stone would be more enduring. And what stone? Until 1622, none of the emperors' tombs—those of Babur, Humayun, or Akbar—had been built in anything other than the red sandstone that came from the quarries near Fatehpur-Sikri. Marble was used as an inlay, but in small quantities, sparingly; it was expensive, it had to travel many miles from Markana and arrive intact at Agra.

Mehrunnisa, Empress Nur Jahan, was disdainful of the price; by the time she came to build her father's tomb, it meant more to her than just a memorial for her parents, it symbolized her power, her authority over the empire, her immense wealth (which was why she wanted to adorn the walls with silver sheets)—it also meant that she, and not Abul, had the opportunity of leaving something for posterity to wonder at. Thus far, only the Mughal emperors had had the privilege of raising a marble dome over their remains, but Mehrunnisa decided to build one for her father, who, not so many years ago, when appointed treasurer of the empire because of his merit and reputation, had almost wiped himself and his family's name from Mughal documents by embezzling fifty thousand rupees from the imperial treasury. But then his daughter married Emperor Jahangir, his granddaughter married Prince Khurram—for all his greed, his teetering on the edge of honesty, Ghias Beg was an extremely fortunate man.

The tomb was designed after a jewel box that Mehrunnisa

owned. It was square, sixty-nine feet long on each side. Each corner had an engaged minaret, which was octagonal until the flat roofline and circular beyond, topped with a rounded cupola. On the centre of the flat roof was a square baradari, its walls punctured by marble jalis, and inside were two cenotaphs in white marble signifying the resting place of Ghias and his wife Asmat. Their actual remains were in the central room on the ground floor. Here also were two cenotaphs in the centre of the room, this time covered with a polished chunam, a lime plaster that had been dyed yellow with limestone. The floor here was marble inlaid with semi-precious stones; the jalis on the ground floor were again delicately fashioned out of lightweight pieces of marble.

But it was the outside surface of the tomb that was designed to awe a visitor. Every surface, *every surface,* was covered in a profusion of precisely rendered patterns of stars, hexagons, squares, flowers, curves, and arches, all this display inlaid into the base of white marble so that it seemed more inlay than base.

When she had thought about the colour scheme for this *pietra dura* inlay, Mehrunnisa had spread out chips of semi-precious stones on the carpet in front of her and pondered for a long time. In the end she had opted for muted colours—sard for brown, yellow limestone (the brightest of her choices), a dull green jasper, and the sharp black-olive of bloodstone. The reds, the blues, the pinks were left on her carpet. Abul had participated even in this choice and had laughed at her, but she had been resolute. 'You will marvel at it, Abul,' she had said.

And a marvel it was. A passer-by strolling on the western bank of the river and looking east towards Itimadaddaula's tomb would see the sheer red sandstone walls of the gardens rising from the bank and in the centre of the wall the western gateway, embedded into the stone, its detail picked out in white marble. And behind the arches of the gateway, there would be a little glimpse of a hushed white marble tomb, with its four minarets, its flat roof, its square, domed pavilion on the rooftop. But when the passer-by crossed the river and entered the tomb from the eastern gateway, he would be confronted with a spectacle his eyes would not at first be able to believe and his mind would never forget. A serene tomb in translucent white, daubed in ochres, blacks, and greens, perfectly framed by the gateways of its gardens, a glimpse of the river beyond the tomb, the dark of the cypress trees on the lawns, the grey of the monkeys romping along the stone pathways. Mehrunnisa had thought of everything in planning the tomb for her father, and in the end nature and artifice collided to bring her imagination to life.

And so, Emperor Shah Jahan would see this tomb that the woman who had sent him into exile had built and use it as a model for the one he was thinking of building for his wife at Agra.

On the other bank of the river, and south of Itimadaddaula's tomb, Raja Jai Singh had received the imperial farman from his emperor with the royal seal at the top and, by its side, the imprint of Shah Jahan's thumb dipped in a saffron dye. It was mid-afternoon, the air blighted of moisture; heat hazes wavered over the placid waters of the Yamuna, and Jai Singh sat under the shade of the tamarind at the very edge of his property, the farman on his lap. Behind him, he could hear the muffled breathing of the runner who had brought the emperor's orders as the man wiped his forehead and splattered sweat on the dry ground.

Jai Singh put a hand up in dismissal.

'An answer, Mirza Raja?' the man asked in a low voice, his head bowed in deference. 'I am to bring back a letter to his Majesty.'

He would not himself, of course, but his orders were to take a missive from Raja Jai Singh and run with it to the next stopping post—nine miles away—where another fleet-footed messenger waited night and day, hand held out for the bamboo tube that enclosed the letter, his legs moving into a run even before this man would have come to a halt. In two and a half days, perhaps just a little more, Jai Singh's response would be in his emperor's hands in Burhanpur—some four hundred and thirty miles away. This system of communication, wrought in Emperor Akbar's fertile mind, had reached an efficient peak in his grandson's rule. In the emperor's service, distances evaporated under the runners' feet; they had smooth roads carved out for them that spun through the entire length and breadth of the empire, so that an event had only to occur in one corner of Shah Jahan's lands and it would be breathed into his ear before a week had passed.

'Yes, there will be an answer to His Majesty.'

Raja Jai Singh called for his writing materials and penned the only reply he could—he was overwhelmed with joy and gratitude on receiving His Majesty's farman; he was blessed indeed that he could be of such service to His Majesty; the grant of the four other mansions in return for this worthless piece of land of his on the Yamuna was too generous, not necessary, but as His Majesty had seen fit to give these to him, he would accept with a deep thankfulness. Raja Jai Singh signed the letter to Emperor Shah Jahan and then added a small postscript—one he knew would be of great interest to his ruler: he would be packed and would leave his haveli by nightfall. Under all the writing, Jai Singh placed his own seal—at the very bottom, as befitted his status inferior to his emperor.

And so Raja Jai Singh, willing or not, gave up his land. The four mansions in Agra that he received in return were but a poor trade, that much he did think privately, although the buildings themselves were superior to the one he had just relinquished, the lands more extensive, his total assets greatly augmented.

The land was now Emperor Shah Jahan's (and it had always been his; he was emperor and Jai Singh a vassal king who had enjoyed his tenancy on the land for so long), and the idea for the tomb was already present, in Mumtaz Mahal's grandfather's tomb across the river.

As much as he abhorred her, Emperor Shah Jahan very briefly acknowledged Mehrunnisa's contribution to Mughal architecture in deciding that Mumtaz's tomb would be constructed in white marble. But there the similarities would end, for the Taj Mahal would be of a purer white, flawless, such as the world had never before seen—a Luminous Tomb.

five

The elder daughter of Chah-Jehan, was very handsome, of lively parts, and passionately beloved by her father. Rumour has it that his attachment reached a point which it is difficult to believe . . . it would have been unjust to deny the King the privilege of gathering fruit from the tree he had himself planted.

—ARCHIBALD CONSTABLE (ed.) AND IRVING BROCK (trans.), *Travels in the Mogul Empire, A.D. 1656–1668* by François Bernier

Burhanpur
Thursday, 25 June 1631
26 Zi'l-Qa'da A.H. 1040

'Bapa.'

Princess Jahanara sat down beside her father, wrapped her hands around his arm, and rested her head on his shoulder. From this close, with his spent breath fanning her hair, she could hear the sounds of his chest. He had caught a cold the evening he spent outside on the ramparts of the fort, watching as they buried their mother. The servants were supposed to have wrapped him warmly, held an umbrella over his head, brought him inside after a half hour, but none of her instructions had been followed. So Emperor Shah Jahan had tarried in the rain too long, until he had come inside shivering, his *qaba* drenched, his hair clinging to his head, the skin on the palms of his hands shrivelled as though he had immersed them for a while in water. Jahanara, drained as she had been after her mother's burial, had undressed him herself, wiped him down, put him to bed, and slept on the floor on a mattress so that he could hold her hand through the night.

'What madness is this?' she said, her voice muffled in the cloth of her father's white cotton kurta.

When he responded, she heard the smile in his voice and her heart eased. After so many days he had found mirth in something, a little, inconsequential statement that had a wealth of meaning in it. 'So you have heard?' Emperor Shah Jahan said. 'And from which one? No.' He put her away from him. 'I do not want to know. Aurangzeb was at the door to the next room when Mahabat Khan was granted an audience. That boy needs a horsehide whip against his back for listening in. Dara or you would never have done something like this.'

Jahanara kissed her father's hand and tried to keep her voice even. 'You cannot give up the empire, Bapa. Whom will you grant it to? We are all so young, so untried . . . and you have fought too long for this crown.'

'Yes,' Shah Jahan said deliberately, 'you of all people would remember the trials I have faced. You were with us all the time.' He looked down at her young, earnest face and thought for a moment he was looking into Arjumand's face in those early days when they were just married. But it was a fleeting thought—although Jahan was uncannily similar to her mother in personality, physically, they were very dissimilar women. When he used that word, *woman,* in his mind, the emperor felt a sense of upset. His wife's death had created a woman out of their daughter, who had always seemed like a child before.

'If Dara, Shuja and Aurangzeb take your past troubles lightly, Bapa—' Jahanara began, and Shah Jahan hushed her, holding his fingers over her mouth.

'I do not say they are irreverent,' he replied, 'not in my presence. But they were not here, with us, during those last few years before the throne of Hindustan became mine. Empress Nur Jahan'—here his forehead furrowed with a frown of loathing for his father's twentieth wife—'demanded them as surety in 1626, and so your Mama and I had to send them to the imperial court. She thought that if she retained the sons, I would not rebel again. She was right, but my sons were her husband's grandsons; my father would not have allowed them to be harmed.' His voice faltered at the end, for he still doubted what he said. His father had been swayed by that evil woman and had disinherited Shah Jahan after declaring him heir. The boys would not have been safe if his father-in-law Abul had not kept them out of Mehrunnisa's reach. He had never asked them about their life in the imperial court during those last two years of his father's life, if they had been happy, discontented, homesick for their parents . . .

'Dara talks sometimes, Bapa,' Jahanara said, thinking back to those days herself. 'The empress was kind to them; they were treated as royal princes, provided mullahs for study and entertainments to amuse them, but kept under guard. Aurangzeb once said that it was only right—Emperor Jahangir and his wife were victorious, and they, the boys who would one day inherit the empire, were the spoils of the battle between you and your father.'

'Aurangzeb talks a little too much.' The emperor rose and walked into the verandah, fretting the raised embroidery around the neck of his kurta with his fingers. In his father's place, with a quiverful of male heirs given as a guarantee, he too would have posted a rigid guard around the boys, and perhaps not given them as much liberty, but he disliked being reminded of any thoughtfulness on Mehrunnisa's part. He stood still as the thin silk curtains pushed inward, carving out his figure, their skirts whispering on the speckled marble floors. Every piece of fabric in the emperor's apartments—the covers on the bed, the cushions and the pillows, the drapes on the windows, the overhead punkah's rectangular cloth, even the light Persian rugs on the floors—had been changed to a shade of white for mourning. The absence of dark colours in the rooms created a cool and clean space. Shah

Jahan stretched his arms over his head and swayed lightly on his feet. His body ached, his eyes hurt from the weeping, his chest seemed blocked by tears and grief, and in all these days that he had cried for his wife, and cried himself to sleep, Jahan had been by his side. He turned to see her watching him, her grey eyes sombre. She was worried, he knew that, even though she had said little, only called his conversation with Mahabat a madness. These past few days *had* been an insanity to him, unbelievable, astounding, implausible. Yet here they were, the two of them, bereft of a wife and a mother whose every word had been a blessing to them, whose every deed a revelation. Allah had seen fit to call Mumtaz to His side and had taken her from them.

He drew in a deep breath and let it out in a fit of coughing. At once, Jahanara was by his side, leaning into him, allowing him to rest upon her sturdy shoulders. Emperor Shah Jahan put his arms around his daughter and held her, as much as she held on to him, her arms around his waist, her head on his chest. Girl children, he thought, were blessings from Allah; sons only caused worry. Almost from the beginning, Jahanara had been steady, calm, and had passed through her childhood without actually touching it. She was old beyond her years, and now, when he most needed the will to live, he remembered that he had her. Shah Jahan knew her every mood, her every wish (often subordinated to his), her sense of sacrifice, her pride—this last of immense importance to a princess.

'When did you think of this?' she asked.

'When your mother died,' he answered, knowing she was talking of his madness. 'There did not seem any necessity to rule any more.'

She clutched at the sleeve of his kurta until the fabric tightened around his arm. 'And who do you think must follow you?'

'Do you need to ask that? Dara.'

'Is he ready to be emperor in your stead?' A tremor in her voice. 'Think, Bapa, the boys are so young and likely to be easily led by the amirs at court. Where will you be? Who will pay attention to an emperor who has deposed himself?'

'Does it matter so much, Jahan?'

'Only as much as the empire does. If the nobles array themselves into cliques, the land will be fragmented.'

A long silence followed as they stood there together by the railing of the balcony. The sun had dipped into the western sky by now, and its angled rays bathed the fort at Burhanpur with muted light. The day's heat had diminished with the coming of the night, and, in the river below them, fishermen cast their nets out into the waters from their little dinghies with audible thumps. The river swallowed the wide nets as soon as they touched its surface, leaving only small blue and red floats visible. They watched as the nets were gathered in and hauled up to the boats, tiny fish writhing in masses of silver and white.

'I had thought of a regency. But only briefly.'

'Who? Mirza Mahabat Khan?'

Shah Jahan nodded. 'Or your mother's brother Shaista Khan, or your mother's father, Abul Hasan. Of the two, perhaps Abul.'

Jahanara stepped back and glanced at him. 'A regency would also be unwise. There is no precedent for this, Bapa. Would you be willing to allow another man to counsel your son in matters of state?'

Shah Jahan rubbed the side of his neck thoughtfully. 'Tell me, how much has this lunacy of mine affected your brothers?'

'Dara . . . he thinks he will be your choice, as I think also. Shuja does not know yet. Aurangzeb wants to be emperor, but Bapa, he is only thirteen.'

Even as she said this, they both remembered that Shah Jahan's grandfather and Jahanara's great-grandfather Emperor Akbar had also been a mere thirteen when his father died and he had been hastily crowned on a makeshift brick platform. But a regency had followed, for the next six years, and it was difficult to think now that the man who had left them this solid, glorious empire had struggled to rid himself of his regent, and even of his controlling wet nurse, to both of whom he had given his affection, his love, and far too much power.

'Go now.' Shah Jahan pushed his daughter gently towards the steps and the outer door to his apartments. 'And tell your brothers, and all who will listen, that I will be at the jharoka balcony at dawn tomorrow. In the afternoon, I will visit your mother's grave.'

Jahanara reached up and kissed her father's cheek. His beard, unkempt since he had not allowed a barber near him all these days, scratched at her lips. When she had crossed the length of the room, she looked back and almost ran to her father again. He stood framed in the light of the setting sun, his back bent with grief, his right hand over his eyes.

'How will we go on, Jahan?'

'By stepping firmly through life, Bapa.' She tried to keep the quaver out of her voice.

She knew of this Luminous Tomb her father meant to build for her mother. No other emperor before, and none after, would ever think of honouring a mere woman with such radiance in marble. As her mother lay dead, Jahanara would take her place in almost everything, but she did not think her own life, or Roshan's, or even that of poor little Goharara, whose coming had killed their mother, would amount to much in the centuries to come. They would remain Mumtaz Mahal's daughters—always in the dark when held up to her light. They would be the princesses in the perpetual shadow of the queen who had died.

When she stepped into the darkened and cool antechamber, Jahanara tarried awhile. Her heart slowed with an effort and she realized that a crisis had been averted. And it was of her doing. On the other side of the door, her father moved around his room with a faltering step. Beyond, in the corridor, she heard the scrabbling of the flock of retainers who awaited her commands on matters trivial and important. Jahanara took a deep breath and went out to meet the servants. Young as she was, in the coming years, she would be asked to arrange marriages for her brothers or consulted on court affairs or act as a crutch upon which her sorrowing father leaned. This she would not mind. But she did not know that performing these varied duties would eventually cast a lingering shadow upon *her* life most of all. That posterity would only know her as a beloved daughter and an adored sister. Nothing more. Perhaps.

Emperor Shah Jahan had said, entirely in jest, that Princess Jahanara should tell anyone who would be willing to listen that he would, finally, a week after his wife's death, give an audience at the jharoka early the next morning. It was a little joke. *Everyone* in and around Burhanpur paid heed—which meant any man of even the smallest standing in the empire, for the emperor had moved his court to Burhanpur and with him came the imperial army and the entire administration. The Mughal Emperor was the court, the country, the empire, and in his august person, in his crown—even if won by some very mortal and immoral means—lay the fate of the one hundred and thirty million people in Mughal India.

Word flew as if on wings of fireflies, flickering first here and then there, until the whole of Burhanpur knew that they would get a glimpse of their Emperor's face at sunrise. The jharoka appearance itself was one of the many Hindu customs the Mughal Emperors had adopted as their own, even as they had been gathered into the lap of the country that made them immeasurably rich and made them and their heirs into one of the most powerful dynasties on Indian soil. It was properly called a *jharoka-i-darshan*—a privileged viewing of, a glimpse of the hallowed monarch. Emperor Akbar, Shah Jahan's grandfather, gave the jharoka its sunrise timing, thinking that the first face his subjects should catch sight of upon waking and commencing their day's work should be his own—who else's?

Emperor Jahangir had tripled the jharoka appearances during his rule, emerging three times into special and ornate balconies built into the bulwarks of his forts and palaces: at sunrise on the eastern side, at noon on the southern side, and at sunset on the western side. The citizens never tired of these jharokas, for each day they satisfied themselves that their emperor was alive, interested, and engaged in his responsibilities. The jharoka came to signify the well-being of the emperor and the empire. Emperor Shah Jahan's presence at the jharoka was *that* important to his position as emperor—and not since Emperor Humayun began the tradition of the jharoka a century ago, had a Mughal emperor missed seeing his subjects for more than a week of days. In Emperor Shah Jahan's case, it was a full eight days, for he had decided to return to his duties on the second Friday after his wife's death, and he would also visit her grave for the first time on this holiest of days in the week.

But his absence had had its effect. Rumuors sprouted on the dry, dusty mud around Burhanpur and grew into great fears, fanciful tales, and some complete untruths. The emperor had died, killing himself by his own hand. The emperor had been deposed, killed by his sons. Which son's hands were bathed with his father's blood? One prince or another was considered by the rumormongers and dismissed . . . and reassessed as the murderer of his father. The Afghan kings, having heard of the empress's death and the emperor's demise, were planning another rebellion from the north and the east—soon, very soon, there would be another dynasty upon the throne of Hindustan. And so forth.

One accusation, vile and torrid, fluttered even this soon after Mumtaz Mahal's death, based eventually on the premise that the emperor was indeed alive. He was said to have used his daughter in the place of his wife, because she had so much the look of her mother and the personality of her mother—and so, Emperor Shah Jahan bore the same love for Princess Jahanara Begam that he had for Mumtaz. These were early days yet, filled with fear and uncertainty, so this rumour did not take wing as it could have. But it would later on.

After Jahanara fell in love with an amir from the court.

SIX

Before sunrise musicians played to wake the court and at the moment of sunrise the emperor presented himself in his jharoka-i-darshan . . . The custom . . . to reassure them that he was alive and well and all calm in the kingdom was an old one . . . this . . . was an occasion for common people to make personal requests direct to their ruler.

—BAMBER GASCOIGNE, *The Great Moguls*

Burhanpur
Friday, 26 June 1631
27 Zi'l-Qa'da A.H. 1040

By the time the sun rose in the maidan that had been hammered out in the dust and scrub outside the fort at Burhanpur, men had been gathering in front of the marble jharoka balcony for hours. As dawn broke, lanterns and torches were extinguished and people turned to one another in the first light of the day with questions and sleep-deprived faces. But the questions could wait. They combed their hair, rubbed clean hands around their necks and behind their ears, wiped their faces, and straightened their clothing. This was no usual jharoka, on this Friday morning, and in their haste most had hurried with their toilettes, a huge breach of etiquette in appearing before the emperor. The men stood in three loose tiers leading up to the jharoka. Under the balcony itself were the Khan-i-khanan Mahabat Khan, solemn and upright; Mirza Abul Hasan, the emperor's father-in-law and a grandee of the empire; and the Grand Vizier. Behind them were the other nobles at court—Hindu rajas, Muslim amirs, holders of high rank, much wealth, quite a bit of magnificence. In Emperor Jahangir's or Emperor Akbar's court, some of these men could have called themselves fathers-in-law to the emperor and been proud of having their blood mingle with the emperor's, but Shah Jahan had been contrary to his father and his grandfather, limiting his wives to a mere three.

Behind the amirs of the empire were the tradesmen, the businessmen of affluence but not equal rank, and travelling merchants. In court, the demarcations between these classes of men were marked by railings of gold, silver and wood, and by the texture and value of the carpets each class of men stood on. But the jharoka, by its very definition, was not a court, not even an audience, merely a looking upon the emperor to be assured of his well-being. It was as casual a royal ritual . . . as royal rituals could afford to be casual.

And yet, the war elephants from Emperor Shah Jahan's stables were mustered behind the standing men. The imperial horses were brought in; two cages with newly captured leopards were wheeled by the keepers of the royal menagerie. The first announcement of Shah Jahan's presence at the jharoka was preceded by the beating of the huge kettledrums in one corner. The heart of every man in the maidan thudded to the accompaniment of the drums, as the beaters' muscles strained and stretched and sweat began to pour from their foreheads. The trumpets joined in, a twirl of breeze swung the yak's-tail standard, held high above the assembly, and finally, the conch bearer raised his shell to his lips and let out a huge blast.

The crowd bowed in unison as Emperor Shah Jahan filled the empty doorway of the jharoka and then stepped outside, dressed in splendid, pure white. His qaba and the wrapping of his turban were silk; there were diamonds in his aigrette, pearls around his neck and on his hands, diamonds glittering on the broad cummerbund around his waist, just visible to the men standing below through the stone railing of the balcony ledge. But what astounded them most was that the man they beheld, their emperor, was not the man they had seen under these very circumstances just over a week ago. Where was the clear gaze fixed upon them in benevolence and firmness? This man was crouched over his own stomach, his hands seemed to shake as he put them out to balance his weight on the balustrade, his face was aged, the hair on his head more white than they had imagined.

'Padshah Salamat!' they shouted, their voices petering into nothing.

This was not Emperor Shah Jahan. Whether in court, or at a private audience, or at the jharoka, no one was allowed to move even the slightest bit in the emperor's presence or speak before being spoken to or asked for a response to a direct question. Every event where the Mughal emperor was present was silent—thronging with men and animals but quiet as a stillborn wind. Coughs were to be stifled, itches scratched later; even breaths had to be hushed. For the first time, when the men below the jharoka balcony raised their heads and doubted the evidence of their eyes, a slow quiver of movement passed through them. They glanced at one another. They bumped shoulders. They gazed at the man on the balcony, their master, with a steadiness unbecoming to servants of the empire.

Her heart thumping, Jahanara leaned against the opening of the jharoka, just out of sight of the men below. The balcony itself was of a slender width and length, two feet by five, and from where she stood, she could reach out and touch her father. When the sun lifted itself from the arms of the night and bathed the upper ramparts of the fort at Burhanpur, it would light up Shah Jahan's face with its newly minted glory and create awe, just as the jharoka appearances were always meant to do. Bapa would speak very little during the jharoka—he rarely did, even when small petitions were brought to him—this much he, and previous emperors, had decided would be the practice at these appearances. So how then to convince them that the man who stood before them was their king?

Even as she thought this, Jahanara felt a warm flush cover her face, for she had in her own mind created a doubt, or rather picked up on it from the outside.

'What is happening?' said Dara in a low voice.

'I don't know.'

'They think . . .' But he did not finish his sentence; he could not either.

Jahanara glanced at her four brothers and at Roshan, hovering behind them. She had ordered them all to be awake and present at this jharoka appearance without really knowing why. Complaints had poured into her bedchamber all night, in the form of letters from Dara and Shuja and a visit from both Roshan and Aurangzeb. They had not wanted to rise so early, they did not think it necessary to be present at the jharoka—this was their father's duty, not theirs. She had responded to all of them with a simple injunction to be ready by daybreak, and they had all listened, but this did not surprise her; she was used to being obeyed. The youngest, Murad, she had kept by her side all night, had roused him and overseen his dressing herself. For the past five minutes, ever since their father had stepped outside, the four boys had grumbled in their throats, yawned widely, and rubbed their eyes in a pantomime of sleep, but now they were alert. They all sensed the change in the atmosphere, from adulation into something more threatening.

Then the whispers began, and Jahanara felt her heart plummet. Little noises at first, arising from one part of the crowd, then another, then yet another, until they all seemed to rise in the air and meld together in one melody, like a thunderstorm's wind.

Jahanara saw her father stagger. Emperor Shah Jahan's hands shook, and he wrenched them from the balustrade to clasp them behind his back. He cleared his throat, half turned towards his children.

'Jahan,' Shah Jahan said, pleading, his eyes fixed upon the crowd below.

She pulled Dara up to her and said, 'Go.' And then she propelled him out onto the balcony, edging him around her father and to his right. He went without a word. One by one, she sent the other three sons out also. Shuja to stand at Dara's right. Aurangzeb to stand at Shah Jahan's left; Murad to his left, until the four heirs of the empire bounded the emperor on either side. Murad, too short under the balcony ledge, stuck his toes in between the railings to hoist himself up and hung from there, his arms dangling over the side.

When Roshanara made a movement towards the balcony, Jahanara pulled her back. 'Are you crazy? You cannot show yourself to the men of the empire.'

'I will cover my face,' Roshanara said. 'Empress Nur Jahan held audiences at the jharoka, and our grandfather allowed her to.'

'No,' Jahanara said, clutching her sister's sleeves. 'No woman will step out onto the balcony in such a brazen manner while Bapa is emperor. Do you think the amirs respected Nur Jahan for her actions? They laughed at her. A woman's place—our place, Roshan—is behind the veil, behind the zenana's walls, and if you want to do anything at all, do it here, in this space. But,' she added, unable to be kind to a sister she did not like, 'you can do little, Roshan, you are but a second daughter. Stay away from the jharoka.'

Anger flashed through Roshanara, and she had opened her mouth to speak again when a wave of sound blasted from below, thrilling them all as the men clapped their hands and the trumpets played.

'Padshah Salamat!' the crowd shouted.

The Mir Tozak, the Master of Ceremonies, who was situated below the balcony, took up the chant and then recited the emperor's name and title as if affirming that he indeed stood above them, that there was no trickery, that the four glowing and brilliant boys who ensconced their father had shown to the crowd that this man was their king. They stood together, linking hands under the balcony's ledge, where their hands could but barely be seen, but their shoulders touched at each side, their backs were straight, and these princes looked out into the crowd with open and courageous gazes.

As though introducing Shah Jahan for the first time, the Mir Tozak said, his voice swinging over the now-silent courtyard, 'Bow to the mighty emperor who bears the names of his ancestor Amir Timur and the titles of Abul Muzaffar Shahabuddin Muhammad Sahib-i-qiran-i-sani Shah Jahan Padshah Ghazi.'

Jahanara heard her father's name being called out and bowed her head, as did her brothers on the balcony. Then, with a soft touch, she nudged Dara and Aurangzeb on their elbows.

'Come back,' she said.

The four princes shifted from their father's side, and one by one, as they had entered the balcony, they stepped away from it and from the sight of the crowd.

But their purpose had been achieved. Jahanara quivered with excitement as the jharoka progressed, knowing she had been instrumental in this immediate acceptance of Bapa (who had still not said a word to the people below) and knowing somehow that she had gained some power here in the zenana, on the other side of the balcony. The jharoka went on for forty more minutes, and the boys went back to their chambers to sleep; only the two princesses stayed on, sitting now on either side of the balcony's opening, glowering at each other, both cast in the morning shadow of their father's figure on the balcony.

~

That evening, after the sun had set, Shah Jahan ascended the three short steps into the baradari in Zainabad Bagh and knelt by the side of his wife's grave. In his hands was a folded silk sheet, six feet by four, into which were sewn seed pearls, an inch apart. The emperor laid the silk over the marble and unrolled it carefully, smoothing as he went, until it covered the whole grave.

In the centre of the sheet was a single pink pearl, the size of a *rudraksha* seed.

Shah Jahan sat back on his knees and wiped his face. It was dark outside, and here, a single sesame oil diya cast its light over the pearl-embedded sheet, which glowed like the fresh snows of Srinagar at sunrise.

He rubbed his fingers over its glimmering surface. Facing west towards Mecca, he raised his hands and whispered the Fatiha.

In the name of God, the Lord of Mercy, the Giver of Mercy!
Praise belongs to God, Lord of the Worlds,
the Lord of Mercy, the Giver of Mercy,
Master of the Day of Judgment.
It is You we worship; it is You we ask for help.
Guide us to the straight path:
the path of those You have blessed, those who incur no anger and who have not gone astray.

An unhurried breeze dissolved his shadow, cast large upon the walls of the baradari, and cooled the heat on his face. He had almost given up his empire, floundering in his sorrow, and the thought that he could spend the rest of his days by his wife's side had come upon him in a brief moment of lunacy. How could any of his sons rule yet? He bent down to kiss the hem of the sheet of pearls and remained thus for a few minutes, his head touching the ground. He could hear a rustle of clothing and small murmurs around him as the amirs bobbed in their boats in the pond—they had accompanied him to the edge of the island. Shah Jahan put their presence out of his mind and prayed for his wife again, this time in silence. He was emperor, lord of those men, their king—while they could not have seen him in conversation with his most loved wife when she was alive, it was only fitting that they witnessed his first meeting with her after she had died. Kings had no privacy and no right to expect any.

Emperor Shah Jahan returned from his wife's graveside to the palace at the fort at Burhanpur, all the while immersed in thought. His fingers brushed over the long rope of blush pink pearls that adorned his neck, weighted by a ruby pendant encircled with diamonds. He could still feel the warm clasp of his sons' hands, on either side of him on the jharoka balcony, and feel their presence around him, which had lent him credibility in the eyes of the empire. Arjumand and he had had these children because they were the result of their love for each other, but over the years, each child had adopted his or her own personality, brought it to the fore, become something and someone other than his or her early self. Today, this morning, subduing their distinct natures, they had supported their father together in a time when he had most needed them.

His tears had dried as he pondered all this, and he felt, with a slight pang, that one of the hands holding his ought to have been his beloved Jahanara's, for it was she to whom he had called out when he was so overwhelmed, she alone who had known how to react in an instant.

He took his pearl necklace off and weighed it in an open palm—by the end of this evening it would adorn Jahanara's neck. A small gift from a grateful father who would never forget this act of kindness.

And so, Emperor Shah Jahan and Princess Jahanara thought thus of the jharoka incident, as they began calling it over the years—that it had been beneficial. This too was true, useful it was, and to all of them. For the first time, Dara, Shuja, Aurangzeb and Murad (young as he was) had tasted the heady power of arranging themselves in state above the crowds on the jharoka balcony. And from that time onward, each of them nurtured that thrill, even as the crown reposed on their father's head. In attending to her Bapa's immediate want, Princess Jahanara had inadvertently allowed her four brothers to see what it was to be emperor . . . before their time. And they all wanted this. Yet, though each had a right to the throne of the empire, only one of them could eventually be emperor.

And when he did so, *to* do so, he would take the lives of his father and his three brothers.

rauza-i-munavvara
The Luminous Tomb

When a period of six months had expired after this grief-gathering event, prince Muhammad Shah Shuja' was appointed to convey the holy dead body of that Queen of angelic temperament to . . . [Agra] . . . and all along the way, they provided food and largesse to the poor.

—From the *Amal-i-Salih* of Muhammad Salih Kambo, in
W.E. BEGLEY AND Z.A. DESAI,
Taj Mahal: The Illumined Tomb

Burhanpur and Agra
Monday, 15 December 1631
21 Jumada al-awal A.H. 1041

In Burhanpur, it rained on the day they unearthed Empress Mumtaz Mahal's body from her grave, as it had when they had buried her. It was an unseasonable rain, falling in thin, sharp and evenly spaced needles like a silver curtain with a single weave. And unlike that day in June, every member of the royal family, including Emperor Shah Jahan, was assembled in the baradari.

He had visited the grave every Friday since her death. Life had come back in slow increments as the days passed. When his distress had abated somewhat, he remembered her voice, the sound of her footsteps as she approached his chambers, the comforting hum of her breathing as she lay in bed beside him.

Shah Jahan watched the diggers slice mud and carefully deposit it in piles around the grave. Jahanara stood at his right, her hand in his. They still wore white, for they had not begun to end their mourning for Mumtaz. Dara was at his left, Aurangzeb next to him, and by his side were Shuja and Murad. Roshanara stood a little behind Shah Jahan and Jahanara, trying, every now and then, to part them.

The workers had uncovered the grave by now, and with gentle movements they lifted the empress from the ground and carried her body to a waiting coffin built of sandalwood. The wood was hinged with clasps of beaten silver; the lid was decorated with the same silver inlaid into the material. The imams in the baradari intoned verses from the Quran, their musical voices soothing. The coffin was then lifted to a waiting boat, which rowed its lone way across the pond to the other side.

Emperor Shah Jahan and his children followed in another boat. He leaned upon Shah Shuja on the way over the waters of the Tapti, intent upon the boat ahead. Go in peace, my love, he thought, soon I will follow you to Agra.

'Guard your mother carefully, Shuja,' he said.

'I will, Bapa,' Prince Shah Shuja said. He patted his father's arm awkwardly. 'I am proud to be the son chosen for this task. Thank you.'

The next morning, at sunrise, Shah Shuja, Satti Khanum and Wazir Khan, the head of the royal physicians, set out with an entourage to Agra, where the land for the yet-to-be-built Taj Mahal awaited them all. Jahanara watched them leave, Dara by her side. She said, just once, 'You should have gone, Dara.'

'My place is here, with my father,' he said.

She shook her head. 'I cannot go, and so Satti Khanum goes in my place. But . . . now Bapa will have a special fondness for the son who has performed this duty for him. You should have offered your services.'

Dara made a small, impatient gesture, which Jahanara knew meant that no one could take his place in his father's affections, and she knew also that this was true. Aurangzeb had wanted this task, Shuja had wanted it, and in the end Emperor Shah Jahan had chosen Shuja. For this insult, as he deemed it, Aurangzeb had sulked for the past few days. But Shuja was older than Aurangzeb, and so it fell to him. Jahanara felt a sense of unease as they stood together on one of the upper balconies of the fort at Burhanpur and watched the dust from the caravan diminish into the horizon. Dara was selfish—no, perhaps not exactly selfish but self-centred, his vision stunted at any point beyond his own immediate needs. The empire was his to have, and she prayed that her brother would realize that, while the future seemed assured for him, in the end, the crown still rested upon their father's head. And their father was himself only the third son of Emperor Jahangir.

She chewed on her lip, still thinking, now of the journey that they also were to make, northward to the capital city.

Some six months ago, Raja Jai Singh had departed for the final time from his haveli on the banks of the Yamuna during the fleeting twilight that cast its coral hues over Agra. His effects were bundled, his household dismantled, his horses led out of the stables, his cows and goats and chickens hustled onto the road in the few short hours after he had received his emperor's orders to donate his land. In those hours, his servants had packed swiftly, stripping the rooms of curtains, piling rugs upon bullock carts, extinguishing kitchen fires that had burned for years (kept at a low ebb during the night and fed again in the morning), toting larger pieces of furniture on their backs and down the road to the first of the residences that Emperor Shah Jahan had given him. His wives had sobbed with frustration at the move but kept their tears hidden behind veils so that even the servants would not notice or think them anything less than joyous at obeying the emperor's commands. His children had swept through the empty, echoing rooms in glee, tripping upon the workers, injuring a shin here, an ankle there.

As night came, Shah Jahan's bailiffs thundered into the empty and silent courtyard of the mansion, leapt from their frothing horses, called for the torches to be carried in. They scoured the haveli, peering into every dark corner, throwing water on the cooling ashes of the kitchen's chulhas, digging up the flat marble stones that had paved the floors under beds, all in search of some treasure the Raja might have forgotten. But Jai Singh's servants had been conscientious and thorough. Every piece of jewellery had been unearthed from its decades-old hiding place, every silk drape and bedspread had been folded and stowed away. There was nothing left but an empty house, a broad red sandstone terrace facing the river, the mud path down to the waters, and, at the very edge, the ancient tamarind tree, which seemed to droop at the loss of its owner.

The next morning, work began at the site, even though Jai Singh's letter of yielding was still running its way through the vast plains of Hindustan to his emperor's hands, for there had never been a doubt in anyone's mind that Jai Singh would give up his land gracefully, and so there was no need to wait for Shah Jahan's further orders.

The tomb was still a myth, nebulous in shape, unknown in size, wraithlike in its presence. But here it would be built, and here would be laid to rest forever the woman whom their Emperor had loved . . . and perhaps still loved, more than anyone else.

The morning brought legions of peasants into Raja Jai Singh's courtyard standing close to one another, their callused hands holding the tools of their trade—a hammer, a block of stone, a chisel to pick out mortar between brick. The foreman, appointed only for the task of demolition, spoke his few poetic words.

'Everything must be destroyed,' he said. 'In three days, this haveli must seem to be a dream, and nothing else.'

The destruction began. The men wrapped the poor, thick fabric of their turbans around their noses and their mouths, squinted their eyes against the dust, and strained their muscles. The rooms of Raja Jai Singh's haveli, which had been designed and built by his grandfather fifty years before, crumbled into powder. The walls came down, the bricks were chopped up and carried away, the floors were carved out of the earth and thrown into a refuse heap. The red sandstone terrace, mighty and grand above the river, was cut into pieces and later, as the tomb began to take shape, slabs of stone from this terrace would be used to fashion walls and floors for the workers' huts. At the end of three days, as promised, there was nothing left of the mansion, just a deep gouge in the warm earth and the tamarind at the waterfront, its diminutive leaves smothered by a fine red dust.

As the months passed, the earth itself was moved from one place to another as Shah Jahan's engineers took meticulous measurements and pondered on the acclivity and declivity of the site. Early word from the emperor's court at Burhanpur called for the land to be perfectly flat and for the waters of the Yamuna to run close by the site of the tomb. So the peasants lined up in unending rows—hundreds of them, men, women, and children as young as five years—with rolls of cheap cloth on their heads, atop which they balanced battered and curved vessels. These were filled with mud, and the workers swayed towards another part of the site and dumped the contents there as ordered, and the mud was raked down as soon as it fell upon the ground. Shah Jahan had mentioned, briefly, to one of his nobles that he wished for the Yamuna never to dry into its summer sandiness in front of the tomb. So the course of the river was changed, to curve closer along the work site, and again the workers carried their burden of earth across the river and piled it on the northern side, to nudge its waters closer towards the other bank.

In flattening the land, trees were cut down. Raja Jai Singh's grandfather had planted a guava orchard in the front of the haveli, and of those trees, forty-three had survived the torrid heat and aridity of Agra and flourished and grown to provide shade and colour. When the trees were felled, despite their age, their trunks were as slender as a woman's waist, but their branches were laden with the second, rain-brought fruiting—guavas the size of oranges, a mild green on the outside, pink and honeyed on the inside. The two enormous mango trees of an inner courtyard came down also, and their roots were harder to dislodge from the reluctant ground.

By December 1631, there were no more signs of inhabitation left on the land that Raja Jai Singh had 'gifted' to his emperor—the earth finally lay quiet and deserted, awaiting a new history.

Along the way to Agra, everywhere the funeral cortege stopped for the night, a guard was set up around the coffin, torches kept burning, the Ahadis posted in a solemn circle, standing through the hours in full armour. Word had fled along their path of this coming procession, and in the towns and villages of Hindustan, people turned out in vast numbers to wait for their empress and pay their last respects to her. In return, Prince Shuja dipped his hand again and again into bags of gold mohurs and silver rupees and threw them into the crowd to give thanks to the empire that had come to honour his mother.

They reached Agra on the eighth of January 1632, about three weeks after they had set out from Burhanpur. They had travelled fleetly these past weeks, stopping only briefly for the night, unhindered by the entire contingent of the imperial zenana, and made the journey to Agra in a relatively short time. At the site of the Taj, Shuja presided over a small tract of land as his mother's body was buried with haste and a small, domed building of red sandstone, some twelve feet high, was raised over her remains. He looked at the tiny furrows that marked out the lines of the mausoleum his father was going to build. The temporary resting place was in front of the future platform on which the tomb would stand according to the architect's plans. Here—once they moved Mumtaz yet again—would be the top left quadrant of the charbagh gardens in front of the Taj Mahal.

Before he left Agra some twenty days later, Prince Shah Shuja knelt at his mother's grave and prayed that she would come to his father in his dreams and speak of Shuja as a favoured son. This he had not been when Mumtaz was alive. But there was some hope surely, he thought, in the fact that his father had entrusted this sacred duty to him. He put his lips to the cold stone slab, then rose. Through the morning fog that rolled landward from the Yamuna, he saw another tomb take shape, resplendent in white marble, its very platform towering over the small structure in front, its frosted white minarets floating apart from the main building. The fog shifted in a streak of breeze and dissolved the outlines of the Luminous Tomb.

seven

Whenever the King travels in . . . pomp he has always two private camps; that is to say, two separate bodies of tents. One of these camps being constantly a day in advance of the other, the King is sure to find at the end of every journey a camp fully prepared for his reception.

—ARCHIBALD CONSTABLE (ed.) AND IRVING BROCK (trans.), *Travels in the Mogul Empire, A.D. 1656–1668* by François Bernier

Burhanpur
Wednesday, 17 March 1632
25 Sha'baan A.H. 1041

'Will we return here, Jahan?'

'Bapa will not want to.' Princess Jahanara straightened from the edge of the balcony and stretched her arms above her head, easing the heaviness in her neck. It was early morning, and the air was still scented by the night and lay lightly upon the shoulders of the two women who stood atop the ramparts of the fort. Tea, fragrant with cinnamon, cloves and nutmeg, steamed gently in white and blue Chinese porcelain cups that had been laid on the flat edge of the balustrade.

'Too many memories,' Roshanara said softly, more to herself than her sister. 'Of the unwanted kind. And yet, there are others also; I was born here, Jahan.'

'This is the first time Bapa and Mama have been apart.' Jahanara leaned over to search through the lightening gloom below. She could not see very well yet; the eastern skies were a melody of russets and reds, but the sun had not broken through, so the courtyard, lit only intermittently by torches, was more shadow than light. But they could hear sounds—the snickers of horses, a low trumpet from an impatient elephant, the clank of armour, swords against shields, buckles against mail, a water vessel falling to the ground with a thud. 'Think about it,' she said, 'in all the years that they were married, they were always together, and even in death . . . Mama lay but a mile away, but now, with her in Agra, Bapa did not want to delay our journey there. No'—her voice grew stronger—'we will not come back to Burhanpur.'

Roshanara reached out a hand to the delicate china cup and sipped her chai; it had cooled in all of their talking, though not even enough to form a skin of cream. It was still hot, not the blasting heat that would come later in the day, but enough for a bead of sweat to break from her forehead and run down the side of her nose. 'Will we'—she hesitated—'you and I, have what they had, Jahan? Will you find this sort of happiness with the amir Mama mentioned—what was his name, Najabat Khan?'

'I would hardly speak to you of it, Roshan,' Jahanara said with asperity. 'You should not take his name. He is my intended.'

'Oh?' Roshanara raised her eyebrows. 'So it is settled, then?'

A horn blasted in the courtyard, low and sweet, its sound floating up to them, and they both pulled their veils over their heads to just below their chins. In the six months since their mother had died, the colour at court and in the imperial zenana had been predominantly white—a blinding, snowy white that allowed for no relief. Emperor Shah Jahan still refused to wear any other colour, steadfastly showing the world that he had not stopped grieving. But a month ago, Jahanara had sent orders to the cloth *karkhanas*—the imperial ateliers—to brush her whites with a tinge of crimson. She wore rubies in her hair, their colours so washed out that they were more pink than red, and her tight *choli,* which left her slender waist bare, was trimmed on the sleeves with tassels of red. A few days later, Princess Roshanara had sent a similar order—her clothing was of the palest green, emeralds glowing upon her person. The emperor had seen but said nothing to his daughters when they altered the prevailing fashion. They were young, he had thought.

~

When the sound of the horn melted away, the sun broke free from the horizon and cast its low rays over them all, bathing them in a golden, liquid light.

'Not settled,' Jahanara said in a flat voice. 'Nothing is decided yet about Mirza Najabat Khan. We have had no time for festivities, Roshan.'

'I know. Shall I talk to Bapa?'

'You?' Jahanara swung around quickly, smiling below her veil. 'What would you say to him? Why would he listen?'

'Who then?' Roshanara asked. 'Would *you* dare yourself? Ah'—she paused—'you think Dara will. Why do you like him so much, Jahan?'

'This is a stupid question,' Jahanara said slowly. 'It is not any of your business whom I marry or how the alliance comes to life. And Dara'—she searched her sister's face under the sheer covering of chiffon—'he is our brother. He's the heir to the empire and we love him. Or we should. What kind of a question is that?'

Now they both saw the crowd in the courtyard below clearly. Splendid Arabian horses from the imperial stables, all black with white fetlocks, their bridles and saddles picked out in silver and velvet, stood right in the front. The men mounted on them, the Ahadis, who were the most elite of the imperial bodyguards, held aloft their spears and also the emperor's standards and banners. Behind them, and for a mile or so that Jahanara and Roshanara could see, were ordered rows of camels, elephants, and men on foot—all carrying burdens, wrapped in cloth, strapped on their backs in howdahs or baskets. This was the *paish-khana,* the advance camp, which was leaving Burhanpur three days before the royal party departed, with a complete set of tents, cooking vessels, chairs and tables, bed linen and bedding, vegetables and spices. When they reached their first halt in the journey, this city of tents, glittering with silk and damask, the floors smothered by the finest Persian carpets, would be waiting for them.

'Do you remember when Bapa almost gave up the throne, Jahan?' Roshanara said as the elephants, a hundred in all, lumbered by. They transported the heaviest equipment of the emperor's camp—the tents, the tent poles, and the furniture. 'Aurangzeb thought that he ought to be considered . . . for the position. It was not wrong of him to think so; he has as much right to the crown as Dara, doesn't he?'

Jahanara held her hand over her nose and mouth as the elephants' passing raised a fine mist of dust. When it had settled, they saw the white cows and gray bullocks swing through; they provided the milk, cream, yogurt, buttermilk and ghee for the imperial kitchens. The most well-fed of them went into curries and biryanis. 'He does, by law, such as it is. But it was Bapa's dearest wish that if he gave the throne to anyone, it would be to Dara. I think he was right.'

Roshanara's mouth twisted. 'Why do you like him so much?'

Jahanara shrugged. 'He is my brother; that should be enough. For you too, Roshan.'

Just then, the thud of hooves quieted and four horsemen drew under the balcony where they stood. One of the two in the centre was mounted on a magnificent white horse, its head plumed with a heron feather. The rider was similarly clad in white; Prince Aurangzeb had not dared to follow his sisters' example and show in open court that he disregarded his father's mourning for his mother. The man next to him, an amir of the court who had been asked to accompany him, rode a few paces behind, and flanking them were the two other horsemen—canopy bearers—who held long poles over their heads linked by the thick white cotton of an awning fringed with white silk tassels. As they passed under the princesses, the canopy bearers reined in their horses, and for a moment, Aurangzeb and his companion were visible. The prince looked up, smiled, and raised his hand. Jahanara and Roshanara answered his salute and saw the amir glance up in surprise, then quickly drop his gaze to the ground when he realized who they were.

They went on, followed by five hundred camels and the four hundred bullock- and ox-drawn carts. A hundred men had been employed for the special purpose of carrying the fine china that they ate from, the gold and silver vessels they served themselves from, the earthenware matkas that bore water from the holy Ganga—the only water they drank.

When they left on their journey back to Agra in a few days, they would travel in an enormous entourage with at least as many animals of burden as the paish-khana. So long was their procession—for it could hardly be called by any less lofty name—that it would take twelve hours for the horses, the camels, the elephants and the foot soldiers to pass by one single point, even given that they would travel with a considerable breadth about their forces, not just this mammoth length. When they encamped, the traders accompanying them would set up bazaars in an orderly manner wherever the Mir Manzil, the Quartermaster of the Empire, had determined the shops to be, and in these bazaars—which would each serve the nobility, the soldiers and the more common people who accompanied the camp—there would be found every necessity: milk, ghee, eggs, meat, spices, cloth, needles and thread, grains, flour, jaggery, toys for the children, jugglers for entertainment, indigo for dyes, carpet weavers and coppersmiths.

The encampment would stay at a place for a few days, perhaps a week, and then move on to the second paish-khana—which had left Burhanpur a few days before—so that all they had to do was descend from their horses, camels and palanquins and find their accommodations exactly similar to those they had left behind in the day's journey. At any given time, the emperor's campsite would accommodate about four hundred thousand people.

The first major city they would reach would be Mandu, then Ajmer, and then Agra. But along the way there would be other, frequent stops wherever they found water in the form of a lake, a river, a pond, and where the land could be flattened out to pitch their camps.

'How long will we be on the road?' Roshanara asked.

'Two months, perhaps more; if Bapa wishes to take us to a hunting ground for some new game, we will be longer. It all depends on him.'

'And you?' Roshanara said.

'And me, Roshan,' Jahanara said firmly. In the past few months, despite frequent skirmishes, they had settled into an amicability that had been surprising. But one day, without any warning, Roshan had stopped arguing with her, and Jahanara, preoccupied with her mother's duties, had not initially noticed. Of all her siblings, she loved Dara the best; why was hard for even her to articulate—especially under such persistent questioning from Roshanara. Perhaps because they were closest in age, or perhaps even because they were alike in temperament. But now, with Mama dead, it had suddenly become important for Jahanara to have an ally in the zenana, and who better than her own sister? So Roshan's unexpected calm had been a blessing. Jahanara sighed. She was very tired, exhausted almost, burdened with too many tasks.

'I heard Satti calling you Begam Sahib,' Roshan said. 'Are you the Padshah Begam now, Jahan? What of Bapa's other wives?'

Jahanara smiled with a little, wry upturn of the edges of her lips. Satti Khanum had stayed back at Agra after accompanying their mother's body to the work site of the tomb, and Shuja had returned in early February—this Jahanara had wanted, and she had petitioned their father to order it. Satti had been, still was, the first lady-in-waiting in the imperial zenana, perhaps almost as authoritative as Mama had been. And when Mama had died, Satti had transferred herself to Jahanara with the same role, supposedly that of a friend and an adviser. But the relationship was not the same. Jahanara, used to having her way in most matters, found Satti Khanum's presence too cloying, too domineering, almost too condescending because Satti was older. Satti had thought that this difference in her behaviour would not be noticed, and though she would never have dared to take liberties with the empress, she did with the princess. So Jahanara had waited with a patience she had taught herself, to find the appropriate time to send her caretaker away and to teach her a lesson in humility. For as valuable as Satti's role had been in going to Agra to accompany Mumtaz's body, her staying was a definite statement.

'Do you know why Satti called me Begam Sahib?' she asked. 'It was in jest, a comment on my supposed arrogance in giving the order for her to go to Agra and wait for us there.'

'Was it good to anger her, Jahan?' Roshanara's face was suddenly very young, anxious.

'Roshan . . .' Jahanara paused to choose words carefully. 'We are . . . supreme now. Bapa's other wives had little consequence when Mama was alive, and while they might have risen somewhat in eminence now, the plain truth is that he does not love them. Not as much as he loves us. Would you want them to order us around?'

'Of course not. But only one of them has a living child, and a daughter; where is the value in that?'

Jahanara smiled. *They* were girls also, but what Roshan meant was that they had living brothers who would inherit the throne, so their positions in the imperial zenana were assured—they were women with power, and Bapa's other wives, loved but with affection and not passion, could not create trouble for them with that lone daughter, who would be married and have children and die one day, without ambitions.

'Satti needed some time away from here,' Jahanara said, 'so that she can learn to really call me Begam Sahib when we return. She must know never to cross me again.'

'No one must?' Roshanara said faintly.

'Not even you.'

They were silent for a while after this. Jahanara had decided to travel by palanquin for the first few days, so Roshanara had decided likewise. It would be a leisurely journey—the distance from Burhanpur to Agra had been accomplished by Emperor Shah Jahan's runners in a little more than two and a half days; by Prince Shah Shuja, travelling back on his horse and stopping merely for the night, in about fifteen days; and by them, moving in a huge mass of men, livestock, artillery, and the imperial zenana, in something more than two months.

'That amir,' Roshanara said as she turned to leave her sister still at the ramparts. 'The one by Aurangzeb's side—that was Mirza Najabat Khan.'

Jahanara caught her arm and pulled her back. 'How do you know?'

'As I know most things, Jahan. You are not the only one in the imperial zenana with resources.' She wrenched her arm from her older sister's grasp and ran over the brick terrace towards the staircase. Perhaps that noble had been Najabat Khan, or perhaps not. The little lie would keep Jahan thinking for a while—thinking about opportunities missed, a glance at a lover lost—and she would perhaps, just perhaps, not be so strident and demanding in the harem.

A little before noon, the palanquin entered a stand of dying laurel trees, too small to be called a forest, too large to circumvent. The laurels were leafless now, bare branches extended overhead in a cobweb, linking one into the other, but the unremitting sun seared through every gap. No escape from the heat here, Jahanara thought, wiping her forehead and neck, her hand coming away wet with sweat. She picked up the gleaming peacock-feather fan and waved it ineffectually, moving the burning air around the confines of her palanquin. The curtains, of a glowing silk weave in chartreuse, were closed. Inside was a fine netting of English lace that some traveller had brought from England as a gift for Emperor Jahangir—ten bolts of it, distributed casually among the wives and sons. He, and Jahanara strained to remember his name, Sir Thomas Roe perhaps, had come as an official ambassador from the court of a King James, striving for a trade treaty for the peppercorns, the indigo, the fragrant sandalwoods and the calicos of Hindustan. But he had not lasted for long—much like Emperor Babur, she thought with a smile; he had hated the heat in India (because he still insisted upon donning his English gear: stockings, doublet, fitted coat, a frilled and close collar), and they, the Mughals, were much more refined at diplomacy than the English. Roe did not get his treaty, though he got many assurances of affection from Jahangir. So he went home. Since, the English had not sent any more ambassadors, but they were still here in Hindustan, setting up 'factories', which were merely warehouses to collect and store goods until they could be laden on ships to England.

In the early days after Shah Jahan had become emperor, he had considered briefly the value of the English on Indian soil. Why not drive them away? Jahanara had asked. And he had said that the foreigners—the Portuguese Jesuits, the Dutch, the English—all served a purpose to the empire. They wanted Indian goods, poured millions of rupees' worth of gold and silver into the treasuries in return, and keeping them all in Hindustan was a surety against any one of them becoming too powerful or too demanding. Look at the trouble Emperor Jahangir had with the Portuguese, he had said. And that too was well-known history. Jahanara drew her knees up and tucked her chin over them. At first, the Jesuits had controlled the trade routes in the Arabian Sea, to the extent that even pilgrims from India travelling on the Haj to Mecca had their passports stamped with pictures of Jesus and Mary. The emperor had deemed it a small price to pay for security from piracy. But then, in retaliation for the privileges being given to the English at court, the Portuguese viceroy had captured and burned a hundred and twenty Mughal ships—not ships of the navy, for the empire had no navy and so had to rely on foreign help, but trade ships—in Goa's harbour. That was when Emperor Jahangir and Mehrunnisa had crushed them, taking away treaties, restricting their movements within the land. And now this.

She pulled the lace curtains apart, their aroma sweet in the fiery heat, since they had been washed, as the merchant had suggested, in goat's milk and hung to dry in the sun until they gleamed like snow. Then she reached out and parted the silk and realized that she was alone for the first time in so many days. The laurels had been planted, or had taken root, close to one another. Once in full leaf, they would have provided shade and shelter to animals. Now there was little left other than their branches and their trunks—the bark patterned in scales like a crocodile's back. And so the eunuchs, ladies-in-waiting, and aged amirs on horseback who were her companions and her guard were spread out among the trees. As the four bearers of her palanquin jogged in an unsteady rhythm, bending here to duck a low-lying branch, cracking branches like twigs there, the others moved alongside but blessedly away, unable physically to come any closer.

Somewhere up ahead was the imperial elephant that Bapa rode upon, seated in a silver-and-gold howdah, surrounded by the nobles at court, all jostling for a position close to him, hoping for a benevolent glance, a dropped word that would change their fortunes forever. Dara, Shuja and Murad had also decided to ride their horses; Roshanara was somewhere behind, and the baby, Goharara, had been sent ahead with her wet nurses a few days ago.

Princess Jahanara gazed out into the patchwork of light and shadow cast by the trees, and she heard the soft pants of the palanquin bearers, smelled the metallic odour of the sweat that poured off their bodies. Strewn around her were books from the imperial library, but she did not want to read now, she desired only to exult in this freedom—the ability to put her face through the curtains, to watch the light, feel the heat, and know herself alone and yet protected.

'Jahan,' someone said. She sighed.

'Did Bapa send you with a message?'

'No,' he said, and as he leaned in towards her, his horse stumbled on a stone.

Jahanara screamed, 'Dara!' and lunged out to grasp his collar as Dara slid from her view. Just then, another strong hand clasped Prince Dara's arm and held him upright. Half in and half out of the palanquin, and aware that she was unveiled, Jahanara pulled herself back to the safety of the curtains. Who was that man? Then, when Dara spoke again, she knew.

'Jahan,' Dara said, panting, 'Mirza Najabat Khan says that there will be trouble in Bengal. The Portuguese are creating terror among the people; they've raided their houses, kidnapped their children and their women for slaves, and captured their lands.'

'How does he know this?' Jahanara asked, clasping her shaking hands tightly in her lap. So Roshan had lied about his having left with Aurangzeb and the paish-khana. It didn't surprise her. Her heart hammering, she peered out carefully and saw a tall, sunburned man who had an easy seat on his horse. He had an angular face, a jutting chin adorned with a short, clipped beard, a beaked nose in profile, a thin neck. His forearms were muscled and scattered with hair, and he wore a red string around his right wrist—for what? Jahanara wondered. The hands that held the reins were large, with a single gold ring on his right index finger. He had fallen back again, and Jahanara had to turn her head and lean forward to see him better. But he kept his head bowed and his gaze stolidly away from her.

'Tell her of your news, Mirza Najabat,' Dara said.

Jahanara heard him say, 'I dare not, Your Highness. It is better coming from you, in any case. You are too kind in allowing me to speak with Her Highness, but it is not my place.'

'News was brought to Bapa, Jahan,' Dara said, 'and he has to decide what to do about it. The Portuguese grow too conceited.

Bengal does not belong to them; they forget this and assume that they can bully the empire's subjects and we will do nothing about it.'

'It is not merely that,' Jahanara said thoughtfully, and she sensed that both the men outside had come closer to listen. 'They are being disrespectful to Bapa. Do you remember that they had kidnapped Mama's slave girls and refused to return them when Bapa asked?'

'During his flight from Emperor Jahangir, Your Highness,' Najabat Khan said to Dara.

'Mama was furious; I don't remember her being as angry before. She did not care very much for the slave girls—it was the insult. Since Bapa was in hiding from his father, they thought they would be safe from retribution. But Bapa,' Jahanara said, 'has a long memory.'

'And so do you,' Dara said.

'Some things you must always remember, Dara. What does Bapa say?'

'He waits to talk with you, Your Highness,' Najabat Khan said, and she noticed that he did not falter this time. He had the voice of a poet, she thought, with music threaded into it. It was an unreal conversation to Jahanara, for she could now see Mirza Najabat Khan more clearly. His face was open, and when he smiled, his teeth flashed white against his skin. He could not see her, did not know what she looked like or how she carried herself, but he had heard her voice, which was more than most of her father's courtiers had done until now. She let him see her hand by reaching out to arrange the curtains, unable to resist this small vanity. Then she yanked her hand back inside, flushing, furious with herself. Now that Mama was dead, who would remember that a marriage had been considered between Mirza Najabat Khan and Jahanara? Would Dara know? Would Bapa even allow it? How could she speak of it herself? All of a sudden, Jahanara wanted to marry Najabat Khan. The small conversation they had had was enough. She had looked at him, seen the strength in his face, felt herself glow when he smiled. And this was more than most other women were allowed.

She put her hand over her chest, feeling her heart still thumping wildly within. Speak again, she could not. Dara and Najabat Khan kicked their heels into their horses' flanks and rode on ahead.

As they passed, Najabat said, 'Your first instinct was right, Your Highness. Whether this report has any truth to it or not, the Portuguese must be taught a lesson in Bengal. There is only one sovereign in Hindustan, and he is Emperor Shah Jahan.' He glanced at the palanquin as he said this, speaking to Jahanara now, rather than Dara, but it was Dara who nodded, who took the words to be addressed to him. Jahanara simply sat mute and watched until they were out of sight.

They broke out of the laurels soon after this, and somewhere in the front of the procession, Jahanara heard a call to halt for lunch stringing down the line as one soldier sang the command to another and another. Musing, thronging with excitement, she did not notice that Roshanara's palanquin had drawn apace and she too was looking out through the mesh of her curtains. Princess Roshanara asked a passing eunuch for the name of the man with her brother, and he told her. 'Find out all you can about Mirza Najabat Khan,' she said to the man, and he bowed and left on his information-gathering mission.

Later that night, as she listened to the eunuch, Roshanara brought out a map of the encampment and spread it on the carpeted floor of her tent. The royal family's tents were clustered around the middle, stained red on the map, a colour only they were privileged to use. Their tent poles stood the highest, and the tents themselves were elaborate two- and three-storey structures with numerous rooms partitioned by thin wooden boards clad in gold and silver cloth, second-floor galleries screened with netting behind which sat the musicians, and thick Persian carpets flowing from one wall to another. Around the royal tents were the structures of the Diwan-i-am and the Diwan-i-khas—the halls of Public and Private Audience—for the business of the empire could not stop merely because the emperor was on a two-month journey. There were even special tented balconies erected for the jharoka appearances and a Naubat Khana—a drum room—which housed the imperial orchestra that announced Shah Jahan's arrival at and departure from each ceremonial function.

The amirs at court arranged themselves around the royal enclosure, depending upon their ranks and their importance to the emperor.

'Which one?' Princess Roshanara Begam asked quietly.

In response, the eunuch knelt and laid a stubby finger on one tent, a quarter of a mile from the zenana tents.

'Always?'

'Of course, Your Highness,' he replied in a wooden voice. 'The Mir Manzil does not change this plan during the trip, unless some topographical deformity forces him to do so. And,' he said, when she raised an eyebrow at him, 'he does not foresee any such problems.'

Roshanara drew in a deep breath, a plan taking shape in her mind. She shook her head once. Such folly even to think thus. But then, what was the harm in it?

She dipped her goose-feather quill into a jade inkpot, drained the red ink along the side, and unhurriedly marked a circle around the black tent the eunuch had pointed out to her.

eight

We can only imagine Raushanara's . . . spleen at having to play second fiddle to Jahanara. Raushanara exerts less influence, rates less privilege—not merely because she is younger, but because she is also less beautiful and less intelligent. By the time Raushanara emerges dramatically from Mogul history as more than a mere name, it is too late to find out how she evolved; in the climactic autumn of 1657 she will be forty years old, rigidly hardened into a scheming and ruthless virago determined to rule the Mogul harem.

—WALDEMAR HANSEN,
The Peacock Throne: The Drama of Mogul India

Mandu
Saturday, 10 April 1632
20 Ramadan A.H. 1041

Some three weeks after the departure from Burhanpur, a girl walked alone through the vast encampment of the paish-khana. She was heavily veiled, clad in black, and nothing was visible of her, neither her feet nor her hands, which—if rough or silken—would indicate whether she was a noblewoman or a creature of the night. And yet, no one dared to accost her, for she was followed closely by two sturdy eunuchs, grim-faced and unsmiling, their grasps on daggers tucked into their cummerbunds, their eyes examining every face with suspicion. The woman, the girl by her confident, swaying stride, ignored the men guarding her. She held her back rigid and her gaze ahead, weaving through the tents purposefully. The amirs had just returned from their nightly audience with Emperor Shah Jahan, and this girl had come almost at their heels, so behind her a straight line of torches still blazed into the sky delineating the route to the Diwan-i-am. The air was beginning to thicken with thousands of cooking fires from every nobleman's chulha. In an hour, the smoke would smother the camp, and on a night such as this, with little or no breeze, the fug would wrap tightly over the encampment, dense as fog rolling off a cold ocean. Men and women routinely lost their way from their tents to their privies and back and spent the rest of the hours either roaming around blindly or huddling in a corner to await dawn. And so few ventured out unless it was necessary.

But the girl was bold, her steps assured, her head held high on a slender neck. As she passed the torches along the street, their heated flames seemed to touch her cheek, and she lifted her hand to cool her brow. In twenty minutes, the street was deserted, except for the oil boys toting long-spouted oilcans, with which they kept the rag heads of the torches burning through the night. The oil boys did not dare bother her either—when one tried, pursing his lips in a whistle, a eunuch smacked the sound from his mouth and he tumbled to the ground. After that, she went on unmolested.

When she slowed her steps, one of her guards came close to her and said, 'The tent on the right, Your Highness, is the one belonging to Mirza Najabat Khan.'

She nodded, turned smoothly to the tent's entrance, lifted the flap, and entered.

Najabat Khan was seated in the middle of his tent eating his dinner. Like the emperor, most of the amirs at court had their own miniature paish-khanas, so that they too could arrive at the next halt and find everything in readiness for them—their sleeping quarters set up, their kitchen tents erected, the chulhas burning, the privies dug behind the tents. While they were forced to accompany Emperor Shah Jahan on foot or on horseback during the actual travel and spend many hours in an uncomfortable saddle as if they were on a hunt or at war, they were given the privilege of preparing for their night's rest in advance. A few simple rules had to be followed. None of the amirs' tents could be red—that colour was reserved for Shah Jahan and those ladies of his harem whom he chose to honour. None of their tents could be pitched on higher ground than the emperor's—and this was the Mir Manzil's duty in assigning places in the encampment. None of their tents could be bigger or decorated more lavishly than the emperor's—and this last rule was relatively easy to follow, for no single person in the empire was possessed of as much wealth as his emperor.

Earlier in the day, Najabat Khan's servants had put up his tent and then sprinkled the ground with water to settle the dust. Upon the earth, they had laid out jute mats, their edges overlapping, and atop the mats, three thick cotton mattresses, one upon another. The very top layer was covered with Persian rugs.

When the girl came into the tent, she found to her surprise that, as richly as it was appointed, it was but one big room with a few windows woven into the corners, now with their flaps down for privacy. Why, she thought, her own tent had three rooms—an entrance hall; a sitting room, where she received her guests; and a sleeping room beyond. She entered, her feet sinking pleasurably into the thick Persian rugs, and stood there awhile watching Najabat Khan eat. She thought that a man's nobility, his grace, could be demonstrated only when he was at his meal, and Najabat Khan ate exceptionally well. He chewed his food carefully, his head bowed over his plate; he did not lick his fingers; and when he was done he made a small movement with his head. A male servant appeared to bear away the plate and bring him a finger bowl of warm water with a wedge of lime.

She started when Najabat Khan spoke harshly. 'Who are you? What are you doing here, wench?'

He had not seen her properly, she thought, as she stood in the gloom of the doorway, and so she came forward and began to lift her veil. Then, realizing what she had been about to do, she dropped the fabric over her hands again.

Najabat had risen, grabbing his sword in the same instant. He hesitated; his breath caught in his throat when he saw her more clearly. He sheathed the sword again and killed the silver light that had darted around the room from the blade's reflection.

'Your Highness,' he said, and performed the *chahar taslim* as he did for his emperor, stooping, placing his right hand on the floor and raising it to his forehead four times. 'I beg your pardon, I had no idea it was you. I thought you were some errant woman who had strayed into my tent . . . like the others who have—' He caught himself in time, felt a flush warm his face, and said again, 'Pardon me.'

'Did you not expect to see me?' the girl said, and Najabat glanced at her with a mild surprise. Her voice was different from the one he had heard in the laurel forest, a little higher, the tone a little more unsure, but even then he had caught only snatches of her conversation; the rest had been muffled by the sounds of their horses' hooves and the palanquin bearers' concerted panting as they trotted along.

'No,' he said honestly. For who could have anticipated something like this? He had been diffident in speaking with her, in public, her brother by his side, and to see her appear in his tent at night . . . and alone . . . His face began to perspire, and his neck felt very tense on his shoulders. If someone were to see them together, to catch them in conversation like this, his life would be worth less than an ant's, squashed under the heel of the emperor's wrath without a thought.

'You must leave, Your Highness,' he said. 'It is . . . this is a great honour for me, but you must now depart. Allow me to escort you back into the royal enclave. It is the least I can do.'

'Will you not ask me to sit, Mirza Najabat Khan?'

'Please.' He gestured towards a divan and remained standing as she settled upon it.

'Tell me about your family, Mirza Najabat.'

'Your Highness wants to know about my background?'

'Tell me.'

Deeply uncomfortable, he complied, though he did not know then that the princess in his tent knew all about him already. Najabat Khan's family also descended from Timur the Lame, much as the Mughal kings were, and could trace their lineage back to Tamerlane for eight generations of sons and sons of sons. Closer in that timeline to Najabat, his grandfather Ibrahim had married Emperor Babur's widowed daughter-in-law, and that union had resulted in the birth of Najabat's father, Shahrukh. So there was this tenuous imperial link also to the Mughal royal family; they were related not by blood but because Najabat's grandmother had once been a royal princess.

Najabat's great-grandfather had been the ruler of Badakhshan—one of the many Timurid princes like Emperor Babur to be given small kingdoms in far-flung places—and some relation of his from that connection still ruled Badakhshan. So he was royalty also, of a minor sort, nowhere near as grand or wealthy as the Mughal kings. His grandfather had been in service to Emperor Akbar, and so also his father, both in fairly elevated ranks at court—holding *mansabs* of five thousand horses each. Najabat Khan, twenty-five years old at the time he narrated this family history to the veiled princess seated on his divan, was merely a noble in the emperor's court. He could not inherit either his title or estates from his grandfather or his father—such was the rule in Hindustan—but had to work to prove his loyalty to his new sovereign, create his own alliances, forge his own way at court. However, the ancestral connections to the Mughal courts were not *all* for naught—both the men before him had built up enough goodwill to have Najabat accepted readily in Shah Jahan's regime and, more important, to bring the imperial couple's glance upon him as a prospective suitor for their daughter.

They had found out about his connection to Emperor Babur and the light strain of royalty that ran through his veins, but what had impressed them most was that the family had always been dedicated subjects to the Mughal kings. He was a handsome man, with a physique muscled and strengthened from his hours in the saddle, a clean-cut and honest face, capable hands, and light blue eyes that bespoke his Timurid ancestry. Jahanara, Mumtaz Mahal had thought, would fall in love with him, and because he had strength of character, he would match her feisty daughter well.

When Najabat finished speaking, he stood dry mouthed and shaking. He had been enchanted by the glimpse of Jahanara's slender hand through the curtains of the palanquin, had appreciated her fine mind and her decisiveness when confronted with the Bengal problem, but this—coming to his tent to scrutinize him in person—was absurd. She had put him in jeopardy by such foolhardiness; she had most probably caused a raging jealousy among the nobles who had seen her come here. She was veiled, true, and in black, in contrast to the imperial mourning white, but *he* had known who she was after a moment—there was something in her carriage, the way she held her head, her haughty walk. Najabat Khan, who had never seen a woman from the imperial zenana before, let alone a royal princess, had even so immediately recognized one when he glanced at her. There were many other men who would have also. Najabat knew nothing of his dead empress's interest in him as a husband for Princess Jahanara—such talk had not reached his ears, and, in the normal course of events, he would only have received from the emperor an order for marriage, one he would have obeyed unquestioningly. Taken as he had been by Princess Jahanara a month ago, he felt a small sense of repulsion towards the girl on the divan.

He had stopped talking and stood in the centre of the tent, looking down upon her. She rose and said, 'Thank you, Mirza Najabat Khan. That was all I wanted to know. Perhaps we will meet another day, who knows?'

With that she left, even before Najabat had a chance to bow to her. He wiped his forehead on the sleeve of his qaba, and it left a damp spot of sweat upon the silk. He had heard of Princess Jahanara's strong will, more so since her mother had died. There were whispers of her being supreme in the zenana now, in possession of the royal seal, and growing more powerful each day. But no one had mentioned to him that she was also a stupid girl.

Princess Jahanara Begam, however, was not dim-witted, not given to act on impulse, did not lack a keen sense of self-preservation. Whatever she did, she deliberated carefully upon, and in the coming years this purposefulness would be the cause of strife between Najabat and her—because she knew what was right, what wrong, and what her role was in the empire. But it would be a while before Najabat would realize that while he had been correct in thinking that one of his emperor's daughters had come to visit him, he had not been right about which one.

The girl stole away through the congealing smoke of the kitchen fires, finding her way to the royal tents by the *Akash-diya*—the light in the sky—an enormous lantern set on a forty-foot-high pole in front of Emperor Shah Jahan's Diwan-i-am which burned night and day, formed the centre of the emperor's camp, and could be seen from miles away on a dark night to guide lost contingents back to their sleeping quarters.

When Princess Roshanara had reached her tent, she slipped inside quietly and lay down on her bed. She would be fifteen years old this year, the same age Mama had been when she had been betrothed to Bapa. They could have been married soon after. So why not Roshanara? She had first been curious about Mirza Najabat Khan because she had seen him talking with Jahanara—that in itself was an unusual occurrence; neither Dara nor any of the other brothers had brought a strange man into their sisters' company before. That made her sit up. Was it deliberate then on Dara's part? Under normal circumstances, mention of Najabat Khan in the imperial zenana would have come from

Bapa, though the brothers could well have brought up the topic, as could their uncles—any men connected with and invested in the imperial family. But so soon after Mama's death, Bapa would not have been interested in marriage alliances for either his sons or his daughters.

Had Jahan spoken to Dara earlier and asked him to bring Mirza Najabat Khan to her? No, this was not likely. So openly, so much in public—Jahan would never give anyone an opportunity to gossip about her; she was too aware of what propriety demanded. Outside, the sounds of activity diminished until there was only the crackle of campfires and the subdued step of the watchman as he patrolled the lane. The torches, left burning all night, gave off a muted glow, their light seeping in through the material of Roshanara's tent's walls, a pale blue. The acrid tang of the enveloping smoke came to her nostrils, and she flipped over and buried her nose in the pillow. Jahan could not want him, and there was no marriage contracted yet between them. And she had so much else; she could not possibly care about a man who had ridden a few yards by the side of her palanquin. If she did care . . . Mirza Najabat Khan would be the best judge of which sister he found most appealing. And there was only one way to give him that opportunity, by letting him see her. But at the tent, her courage had faltered and she had not been able to lift the cloth that covered her. She thought, though, that she had made an impression upon him, that he knew who she was—it did not strike Princess Roshanara Begam that Najabat Khan could have mistaken her for anyone else, for she was a royal princess, proud and certain that everyone who crossed her path would not only know her but remember her for the rest of their lives.

Lying on her bed, she made her plans methodically. She would have to wait until Jahanara married, as Jahanara was the older sister, but when she did, Roshanara was determined that, somehow, she would become the wife of Mirza Najabat Khan.

rauza-i-munavvara
The Luminous Tomb

A period of one year had elapsed since . . . the sudden death of the Lady Mumtaz al-Zamani, and the time had arrived for observing the customary ceremony, known in this country as 'Urs.

—From the *Padshah Nama* of Jalala Tabataba'i, in
W.E. BEGLEY AND Z.A. DESAI,
Taj Mahal: The Illumined Tomb

Agra
Tuesday, 22 June 1632
4 Zi'l-Hijja A.H. 1041

Prince Aurangzeb knelt, and beside him Abul Hasan and Muhammad Ali Beg also went down on their knees, much more slowly. The three of them closed their eyes, raised their hands, and recited the Fatiha. When they had finished, they sat back on their heels, reflective, and in a while, as the imams began to chant suras from the Quran, they settled more comfortably against the silk-upholstered bolsters which lay strewn on the divan.

The long night passed thus, voices raised in prayer and praise of Mumtaz Mahal on the first anniversary of her death, Aurangzeb upright in the main tent, flanked by his grandfather and the Persian ambassador. The tent was filled to thronging—all the important amirs at court, the mullahs and Hindu priests, Buddhist and Jain monks, the Jesuit cleric Father Busée, who presided over the church in Agra that Emperor Jahangir had allowed the Portuguese to build. Aurangzeb stiffened and glanced at his hands, clasped rigidly in his lap. Bapa had been too tolerant in allowing these other men into the Jilaukhana of the tomb, where the 'urs, the anniversary, was being held. At other times, especially during Emperor Akbar's rule, they had actually been invited to take part in religious discussions—to express the merits of their own religions and perhaps discount those of others. A philosophic conversation, Aurangzeb's great-grandfather had called it. The prince reddened and covered his face. How could that even be? Islam was the one true religion, Allah the only true God—why even invite other talk?

There were arguments in favour, of course, that even Aurangzeb, only fourteen years old, understood. The acceptance of other faiths was necessary in an empire that was largely populated by infidels—Hindus, Buddhists, Jains, the Christians whom the foreigners had converted—and it created the basis for political solidarity. He turned and scowled at the Jesuit priest again—he had forgotten his name, but Dara would know, because he was friendly with this man. The news from Bengal about Portuguese aggression on the empire's subjects had led Emperor Shah Jahan to retaliate—swiftly and powerfully—and yet this priest came with a put-on solemn face and listened to the holy words from the Quran. He came, Aurangzeb thought, not as a man of God but as a representative of the crushed Portuguese in Bengal begging for the emperor's mercy, insinuating himself into this sacred assembly.

'Are you tired, beta?' Abul Hasan asked, touching his shoulder.

'I think you must be, Nana,' Aurangzeb replied, turning to his grandfather and clasping his hand. Much to both their surprise, he kissed Abul's hand, then let go, his face crimson. 'You loved Mama very much.'

'I did,' Abul said, wiping his eyes though he had not shed a tear. All of his crying had dried up in Burhanpur when he saw how his son-in-law and his emperor had been devastated by Mumtaz's death and how the children had begun to loosen their ties to the family and spiral out into minor acts of rebellion that their father had not noticed or tried to control. 'It is terrible to lose a child before her time, worse yet to be sitting at her first 'urs knowing that she will never return to me . . . to us. If things had taken their proper course, I would have gone first and she would have done something like this in remembrance instead, as it should have been, Aurangzeb.'

They sat quietly awhile, Aurangzeb thinking that his grandfather was not so old yet, only in his sixties, but Mama's death had aged too many people because she had been deeply loved.

'What are these 'urs, Nana?'

Abul turned to him in astonishment. 'You don't know? You should have asked the mullah at the mosque. It is a custom here in Hindustan, among the Chistis—the Sufi order in Ajmer—to celebrate death. Not a strange ritual if you think about it. The word 'urs come from Arabic, meaning marriage, a meeting between Allah and the soul of the departed.'

Prince Aurangzeb had been born in India, and he was Indian in every aspect—his knowledge of the countryside, the customs of the subjects of the empire, the passing of time and seasons, the varieties of foods. He had not lived anywhere else or even visited anyplace where he could not claim to be master and of the royalty. And yet, when his father had chosen to mark the first anniversary of the death of his mother with a ceremony called the 'urs, he had not known what it was. His upbringing had been Persian and Turkish, much like those of his ancestors, and this was the first time that one of the Mughal emperors of India—some one hundred years after becoming sovereigns here—was adopting one of the local death customs for his own. It was unusual enough that a royal prince had to ask for an explanation.

Upriver from where they sat, in the fort at Agra, Emperor Shah Jahan prayed alone, for the same amount of time as they did in public—as the 'urs ceremony recommended—one whole day and one whole night. At the end of which, they would distribute food to those who were assembled and alms to the poor who had been gathering outside the Jilaukhana.

Dara, the favoured one, and Shuja, only a little less in favour, were with Bapa, and he, Aurangzeb, had been dispatched here. But he did not mind very much, for it gave him an opportunity to present himself to these grand and powerful men of the empire, for them to see him and to know him in circumstances such as these. Aurangzeb knew, even this young, that if he was to become emperor after his father and displace the much-lauded, much-blessed Dara, it would be with the help of these amirs.

'Look how magnificent all this is, Aurangzeb, and remember to be grateful,' Abul said. He gestured around them at the silken tent, thirty feet by thirty feet, the first of three in the courtyard. There were twelve smaller ones around, all coloured a pale blue—butterflies perched on the open earth left after the demolition of Raja Jai Singh's haveli.

'Grateful, Nana?' Aurangzeb said with a quick flash of a smile, which disappeared almost as soon as it had appeared. That little movement softened the fire in his normally intense gaze, made him look more youthful, more of the child he really was, his face smooth with its darkening of hair on the upper lip and the few hairs on his chin that he resolutely refused to shave. 'Why?'

His grandfather took hold of his hand and drew him closer. 'I can remember when my father, your great-grandfather, made us leave Persia in the middle of the night. And on the way, in the great desert, we were beset by dacoits. Somehow, we survived, but they took everything we had. And then Qandahar . . .' His voice trailed away, and Aurangzeb, who had heard this story in some form or another many times from this man, knew that he was thinking of his sister's birth at Qandahar, of her marriage to Emperor Jahangir, of her perfidy towards Shah Jahan and towards her brother. 'And then,' Abul continued, 'we came to Agra. My father was nothing very much at court for a very long while, even though Emperor Akbar had noticed him, been benevolent enough to grant him a mansab, but he worked hard, beta. Well before my sister married Emperor Jahangir'—and this time he talked of her without flinching—'my father was made Treasurer of the Empire.'

'I know, Nana.' Both of them conveniently forgot other misdemeanours on the part of the family—Abul's older brother Muhammad had tried to assassinate Emperor Jahangir, and his father had embezzled fifty thousand rupees from the treasury—all of which were magically forgiven when Mehrunnisa became the twentieth wife. They forgot that, responding to Abul's pleas, she had made the marriage between Mumtaz and Shah Jahan happen. That she had built her father's tomb north of where they sat, on the other bank of the river. But they did remember that it was this tomb—Abul's father's and Aurangzeb's maternal great-grandfather's—that had provided the plan, the sketch, the very idea for Mumtaz Mahal's tomb.

'So this,' Aurangzeb said, looking around, though seeing nothing more than the walls of the tent, 'is going to be the part of the complex where the Jilaukhana will be.'

And they both thought of the vast plans that the architect had drawn up for Emperor Shah Jahan and the exquisite miniature model he had made of the Taj Mahal's complex, intricate in every detail, attention paid to every facet.

The complex was to be in three parts—the tomb itself on its red sandstone platform at the edge of the river, flanked by a mosque on one side and an assembly hall on the other. Its gardens, with a red sandstone reflecting pool along the centre, would be in front of the tomb—landward, naturally. At the southernmost end of the gardens was to be a massive gateway in red sandstone—the main entrance to the tomb. This gateway was part of a forecourt called the Jilaukhana, and this was the second of the three parts—on the land for which the first 'urs for Mumtaz took place.

The third part, beyond the southern gateway to the Jilaukhana, was to be the Taj Ganj—a mammoth square complex that housed bazaars and four caravanserais, the incomes from which would fund the care and upkeep of the tomb and the forecourt.

The tents for the first 'urs were pitched on a flattened piece of land, ready and awaiting the building of the Jilaukhana. The forecourt would be a rectangular courtyard, built especially for the purpose of allowing visiting nobles to dismount, tether their horses, and refresh themselves before entering the tomb's gardens. It had four gateways—east and west, from which, down a long corridor of verandahs, there were two bazaar streets; and the southern gateway, up a short flight of stairs because of the slope of the land, which eventually gave out into the Taj Ganj. But the courtyard, the other three ancillary gateways, the bazaar streets trimmed with red stone *chajjas* or eaves that sluiced rainwater down into the yard—everything paled in comparison to the northern gateway, the *darwaza-i-rauza.* Quite simply, the entrance to the tomb, but really called the Great Gate.

This darwaza was to be a magnificent structure, seated on its own sandstone platform, the floor of which was inlaid with white marble. It would have a high central arch flanked by four smaller arches, two on each side, and every arch would actually be a rectangular portal culminating in a peak on top. There would be four engaged minarets on the four corners, octagonal in shape, topped by white marble cupolas, and the front and back portals were to be capped by eleven freestanding marble cupolas. The building would house a central hall, decorated with marble inlay, with tiny transom windows along the roofline to let in natural light, and when it was completed, a shimmering Aleppo glass chandelier, lowered for lighting by thick chains, hung in the centre of the ceiling.

The front of the darwaza would also be built of the red sandstone so prolific in the quarries around Agra but inlaid with white marble, into which would be carved, in calligraphic script, the eighty-ninth sura from the Quran, which invited believers to step into Paradise.

'There's hardly anything here now,' Aurangzeb said. 'But the architect's model was meticulous. Mama would have liked it, but then, she liked anything Bapa did.'

Abul Hasan nodded, his heart brimming. Even in times of such plenty, he could not forget those early days of the flight from Persia or his envy when his sister became an empress. Now his child would lie for eternity in splendour; one day her husband would join her here, or he would perhaps construct a tomb for himself elsewhere; such were the privileges of royalty. Something his grandson took so much for granted, mocking him when he spoke of being grateful. He studied the boy next to him and felt an abrupt tug of fear. These children his Arjumand had borne, each was an independent, fiery spirit. At times he wished she had had only one son; then there would be no question of succession, no fighting, no fragmenting of the family. But he was nonetheless thankful that she had been so fertile—four sons, three daughters, these were all good, wanted, blessings from Allah. Though he was still uneasy, somewhere inside, knowing Aurangzeb well. The boy was affectionate and could be kind if he wanted, all hidden, alas, under a mask of strictness and rigidity, so unappealing in someone this young.

Unaware of his grandfather's ruminations, Aurangzeb listened to the chanting, joining in, falling silent. He desperately wanted to be king after his father, and he wanted them *all* to agree to this, even Dara, who thought himself secure and the position rightfully his. And he wanted his beloved Jahan to laud him, to put her hands on his face and smile as she did upon Dara and Shuja. But as he sat through that night, he was afraid, because he knew that none of this would be easy and that, like his father, he might have to wash—forever—the blood of his brothers from his hands.

As day dawned, fifty thousand rupees were distributed to the destitute who clamoured outside the chintz screens which had kept the ceremony from the view of the common people. The men left an hour later, and the grounds were cleared of every living person before the ladies of the zenana came into the enclosure to perform their own 'urs. This too went on, for a day and a night, and in the end, Princess Jahanara and Princess Roshanara gave out an equal fifty thousand rupees, with their own hands, and from their own incomes, to the poor women assembled.

And so ended the first 'urs in the Jilaukhana, the brilliant entrance to the tomb.

Emperor Shah Jahan viewed the final resting place for his wife thus, a little slice of Paradise, set in lush gardens. He had thought of everything in designing the tomb, consulted for hours with his architects on the buildings that would decorate the waterfront and house the grave of his wife, so the entrance to the gardens could not be any less grand for this Luminous Tomb.

nine

His Majesty also plays at chaugan in dark nights, which caused much astonishment even among clever players . . . It is impossible to describe the excellency of this game. Ignorant as I am, I can but say little about it.

—S.L. GOOMER (ed.) AND H. BLOCHMANN (trans.),
The Ain-i-Akbari,
by Abul Fazl Allami

Agra
Monday, 22 December 1632
10 Jumada al-thani A.H. 1042

By the time the male players had left, the *ghariyali* was ringing in the end of the second watch of the night. It was so quiet that the sound of the brass gong being struck by the leather-headed mallet rolled cleanly over the walls of the fort and into the *chaugan* field. The ghariyali paused for five seconds when he had concluded measuring out the *gharis,* seven in all, and then lifted his mallet to follow up with two more strikes in quick succession to indicate the end of the second watch. Midnight. And the moon was centred in the sky, its pearl-like face streaked by wisps of thin clouds.

Jahanara stood alone in the middle of the polo grounds, a silver brilliance of moonlight around her. Dara, Shuja and Aurangzeb had played here earlier in the evening, and Roshan and she had watched from a zenana enclosure on one side of the field. Aurangzeb's team had won—Dara and Shuja had played on the opposite side, but they were no match for their brother. When they had been younger, he had run faster than all of them, pumping his arms and legs, his face red with effort; he could ride better, straddling a horse as though he had been born on one; his mouth, even, was quicker to retort. So Aurangzeb had won, because he had *wanted* to win, and because he had not been expected to do so. Dara was slothful, assured of his position and so uncaring about 'little' wins and losses, as he termed them.

Then they had all left. The torches lining the length of the chaugan field had been extinguished, the slaves and servants had carried away the refreshments, the noblemen watching had gone to their homes and their beds, and the moon had climbed higher, breaking through the low clouds that thronged the horizon. When Roshanara had ascended into her palanquin, Jahanara had made as if to follow her, then slipped back quietly.

Around her, a few men pounded divots of tufted grass back into the steaming earth, which still seemed to throb from the reverberation of the horses' hooves. Their heads were bent doggedly to the ground, and they kept their distance, for behind her Ishaq Beg, her Mir Saman, Master of the Household, ranged along the perimeter of the field. Jahanara turned to him finally and beckoned. When he had run up to her, she said, 'Is he here?'

'No, Your Highness.'

The moon was directly overhead now, flooding them with light—but it was a strange blue-black light that cast heavy shadows where it did not touch and set the diamonds in Jahanara's hair to such a glittering sparkle that it was as though her head was aflame with an icy fire. She could see little of Ishaq's expression, but she knew he was fretting, even angry. She knew him well, almost as well as Dara and Shuja, for Ishaq had been brought into Shah Jahan's zenana when he was still very young, a boy of less than ten perhaps (for his parents were too poor or too indifferent to keep measure of time or dates), to be brought up there as a servant, and since he could not have stayed on in the women's quarters once he hit puberty, he was made a eunuch.

'I have to see him, Ishaq,' she said.

'This is not right, Your Highness,' he mumbled, gazing around him into the murk of the kinshuk trees in the distance and the looming bulk of the Agra fort, from where an upturned bowl of light from the streetlamps embraced the skies. 'There are other ways to meet a man. He could come into the zenana perhaps . . . but no'—he checked himself—'that would not be correct either. Marry him, Your Highness, if your need is so great, then you can visit with him for as long as you like.'

'I intend to,' Jahanara said. 'And I will, one day, but not for some time to come yet; I am wanted in the imperial harem.'

Ishaq Beg glanced at her in surprise; despite what he had said, this was the first he had heard of her wanting to marry. He had spoken to her as no other man would have dared—not her father or her brothers—chastised the propriety of what she was going to do, suggested a marriage instead, but Jahanara did not mind. There was little Ishaq and she had not talked about when they were growing up together. He had sat by her when the mullah came in for lessons, adjusting her veil, helping her with pronunciations; he had lain by her feet when she was unwell, grasping the heated skin of her shins and calves; he, not her mother, had held and pacified her at the sight of that first monthly blood, though he had not known what it was or why it had happened. A few years ago, curious, Jahanara had asked him what it was like to have no . . . feeling, no tug of the sensual, the sexual being within. He shrugged and gazed into her eyes directly, with no sense of embarrassment. 'It happened before I knew very much about it. I know no other life but this one. I've seen other men maddened by their lust for women, blinded by it, so perhaps I am better off.'

'Do you regret it, Ishaq?'

It had taken him a long while to respond to that question, months, in fact, but Jahanara had not forgotten that she had asked it of him. And when he said, 'No, Your Highness, for I would not then have had the privilege of serving you,' she knew it was nothing other than the truth. Even with astounding candour such as this, neither of them had forgotten their place in the world—she was a royal princess and Ishaq Beg her eunuch, her slave, and her servant.

They were, Jahanara thought now, as close as two human beings could be, with an undefined friendship. He was not her brother, her father, her mother, or her sister, and yet he was all of these, in some ways more devoted because his life was hers. And yet, she had not said anything to him of meeting Mirza Najabat Khan in March, nor that she had thought of him every day, watched for him as Bapa sat in the imperial court, and finally sent him this summons because she could not bear not being near him any longer. Ishaq, who had been her mother's favourite eunuch, and still *her* closest friend in the imperial zenana, had not known until this moment that his princess had fallen in love with a courtier.

'He is here, Your Highness,' Ishaq said, turning towards the right end of the chaugan field, where a man waited, his horse's reins held secure in his hands, the animal quiescent and obedient. 'And I will be within call.'

'I do not fear him, Ishaq,' Jahanara said softly. She raised her right hand and snapped her fingers. Two grooms, their eyes to the ground, brought a gleaming white Badakhshan horse up to her and fled as soon as her hand had touched its bridle, not even daring to stay on to help her into the saddle, though it had been many years since she had needed such assistance. But they ran because she had shed the long length of her white chiffon veil on the earth before she walked to the middle of the field, was clad now only in a white silk choli, which hugged her figure, the sleeves caressing her wrists, and a pair of pantaloons gathered at her waist in folds which narrowed down to her ankles. Her hair, rolled and pinned neatly at her nape, was studded with diamonds, and the stones glittered on the silk of her outfit also. Jahanara laughed, the sound breaking out of her as she put her foot into the stirrup and swung up into the saddle. She had ordered specifically for this horse to be brought from the imperial stables for her tonight because it was from Badakhshan, where Mirza Najabat Khan also found his lineage, and because of the spray of black, like an ink spot, on its pristine white forehead—the only colour it had anywhere on its body.

The horse rode well, a little inclined to spiritedness, but it wanted only to fly, not trot, across the empty chaugan grounds. Jahanara had covered part of the way to the end of the field when the man met her halfway and reined in his horse beside hers. Perhaps he had not seen her fully in riding towards her, but when his horse had stilled to a mere moving of its hooves, he glanced at her naked face and then away.

'Your Highness, I beg your pardon,' he said.

'Look at me, Mirza Najabat Khan.'

He did, turning back not with reluctance but with an eagerness and a boldness that sent a thrill through her. In the sparkle of the silver light that surrounded them, his eyes were almost black, and the moonlight touched the planes of his face, painted his broad forehead, the slant of his cheekbones, and dipped into darkness in the hollows of his eyes and under his nose.

'I would not have thought . . .' He went no further with that statement.

'That I would be so daring?'

He nodded uncertainly. She had been brave here, in letting a man who was not her husband see her face, audacious in inviting him to the polo grounds in the middle of the night for a meeting, perhaps unwise also. But in that first moment when they talked, Jahanara forgot everything else. Their mounts snickered, and Najabat Khan's gaze fell upon the mark on her Badakhshan horse's forehead.

He reached out to stroke it, his hand moving involuntarily. 'I had only heard of this horse in His Majesty's stables; it traces its bloodlines to the Macedonian Alexander's horse, Bucephalus. That horse was a brute in legend, known for its speed and strength, and it is said that all its descendants have this splatter of black on their forehead and one blue eye.' There was awe in his voice, and when Jahanara's horse whinnied and shook its head, Najabat yanked his hand away. Jahanara watched him with a small smile, amused at his admiration for a mere horse, irritated as well that he had not glanced upon its rider again.

'He has a blue eye,' she said.

'How did His Majesty acquire him?' Najabat asked, still engrossed by the animal. 'There is a story that one of the aunts of Badakhshan's king, whose husband had owned the only stables with the descendants of Bucephalus, killed all of them, rendering the line extinct. I cannot believe that one such still exists.'

'He was bred in the imperial stables, Mirza Najabat Khan.' Jahanara was suddenly weary of this talk and of Najabat's obsession with a horse. She had asked for it to be brought to the chaugan fields as a mount for her this evening precisely because of its history and its lineage. There were thirty-nine others like this one in the stables reserved for the horses of Badakhshan, each said to be bred from Alexander's horse, and they *were* magnificent animals. But so was she.

The man opposite her lifted his head in acknowledgement and gazed directly into her eyes for the first time. His expression gave nothing away, but he did not leave either. Jahanara was certain that there were people in the field watching them—her grooms and syces and Ishaq Beg were there, of course, but others whose business it was to spy, to whisper into ears, to spread calumny. But she had not cared when she asked for Najabat Khan to come here, in part because she was the Begam Sahib of the imperial harem, the most powerful woman within, and in part because she had wanted to be with him. Now, a shiver racked her body when she felt his eyes upon her, this close, a few feet away at most, and if he lifted a hand to reach out to her as he had to her horse, he could touch her.

'You do not have to be here, Mirza Najabat,' Jahanara said quietly. 'I thank you for coming, but it is dangerous, as you well know, and I am better protected than you are.'

He did not reply for a while, and Jahanara felt a flush warm her face under his fixed scrutiny. Here, in the cobalt darkness of the night, she was shy in his presence. What would it be like, she wondered, in a bedchamber with candles glowing on the walls, his every expression open and lit for her?

'Are we to have a race, Your Highness?'

'Do you play chaugan, Mirza Najabat Khan?' Jahanara had to steady her voice when she spoke.

He drew in a breath. 'Ah, that is it then. I play.'

Laughter radiated from her face, and her expression softened; the cool blues of the moon's overhead light set the diamonds in her hair to dazzling. 'What else, on a chaugan field?'

'What else indeed, Your Highness? I was stupid to think that you might not be able to—' he said, and in his voice there was a trace of admiration.

'I hear you are a stellar player.'

'No, Your Highness. Merely good; and I don't think it immodest to say so, since there are many others better than I. His Highness Prince Aurangzeb is superb.'

'A game?' Jahanara asked. Her right hand lifted casually into the air, and two grooms materialized by their sides and offered them polo sticks. Najabat Khan's was fashioned with silver casings on the wood, and even in this light, verses in Persian that lauded the game were visible in the silver. Jahanara's stick was similar to his, a little shorter and encased in gold. The metals gleamed dully in their hands.

'It is a dangerous game, Your Highness,' Najabat said.

'Only if your seat is not good, Mirza Najabat,' Princess Jahanara replied before digging her heels into her horse's flanks and riding away. Her voice came floating back to him through the cool night. 'They tell me I'm one of the best. If *I* may be immodest enough to say so.'

As they reached the centre of the field, Ishaq Beg shouted, 'Hup!' and they saw him set fire to a puck and fling it into the sky. The fire burned sparsely as the puck flew in the air and landed on the ground between them. At the same time, tiny torches flashed around the field, marking out the boundary. Earlier in the evening, these grounds had been lit by bigger torches, held aloft to throw their light into every corner, and the puck that had been used was embedded with glass and semi-precious stones so that it sparkled in the firelight.

Jahanara and Najabat used a plain wood puck, fashioned out of palash or kinshuk wood, a dense and thick hardwood that burned slowly. The kinshuk tree, which grew everywhere in the Indo-Gangetic plains, thrived in the beating sun, arid conditions, and poor soil. Even as Jahanara bent to knock the flaming puck into the air again and towards Najabat's goal at the far end, the grove of kinshuks growing at the foot of the Agra fort's battlements were in full and early bloom. By this time of the year, the leaves had fallen from the trees' black and gnarled branches, and they were thickly laden instead with clusters of orange and vermilion-coloured flowers. The flowers had no discernible perfume, merely an unmatched beauty—on a bright day when the sky was a cerulean blue, the trees stood out starkly against this background with their burning flowers, and so they were locally called flame-of-the-forest.

They played for a third of a ghari—approximately an hour—and did not talk for the whole time, even at the ends of the *chukkars,* each of which lasted seven minutes. Seven minutes of play, and five minutes of resting in between. And for each chukkar, Jahanara changed her mount—a groom came to lead away her steaming animal and replace it with another, cooler, fresher horse. Every horse had the mark of Bucephalus on its forehead, and Najabat Khan slowly became used to the luxury of being around these precious animals, used so casually in a chaugan game. There was a string of horses for him also from the imperial stables, lesser mounts than those Jahanara was riding, but Najabat did not mind. In the beginning, Najabat Khan had reined in his horse, allowed his princess to knock the puck from his control and even take it towards the goal. But a short while into the game he realized that she was no amateur either at riding or at chaugan, and he stanched his impulse to be generous or kind. And so, they thundered up and down the polo grounds, riding hard, breathing even harder, their arms and thighs aching by the end. As they played, a robust fog rolled off the Yamuna and crept around the streets inside the Agra fort, then broke free to march over the grounds. Soon, the only sounds they could hear were of their panting and their horses' breathing in the silence, and they could only thinly discern the flaming, flying puck, glittering gold in the white of the fog.

'We should stop now, Your Highness,' Najabat Khan said, bringing his horse close to Jahanara. They were ensconced in a cocoon of white, and the temperature had dropped as time had passed, but they were both too heated to feel the change.

'Yes,' Jahanara replied. 'I can no longer see where I am going.'

He reached out to hold her hand, and Jahanara felt dizzy with joy. Her heart thundered and crashed in her chest, and she felt the warmth of his skin as his fingers enclosed hers. She let her gaze drop, too overcome even to look at him any more. 'Our path is perfectly clear to me, Your Highness,' he said. 'I know where we are headed.' He bowed from his saddle. 'I will not disagree with you on one point—you are indeed entitled to call yourself a good rider. And . . . I commend you on the Hugli problem, your Highness.'

She blushed again. 'Your help was invaluable.'

'I wrote you a few words of advice, Your Highness. You advised His Majesty well. He is fortunate to have you. Indeed, any man would be fortunate.'

When he hesitated, as though afraid that he had said too much, Jahanara said, 'A safe ride back home, Mirza Najabat Khan.' She pulled her hand out of his grasp with a half laugh. 'This is unwise.'

'As on the other occasion?' he asked. When her brows knit in confusion, he said, 'But never mind that; now I know and will wait for your call again. Until the next time, Your Highness. Thank you.'

When Jahanara Begam entered her chambers an hour later, she was tired, her entire body ached, but she was humming with exhilaration. The chaugan game had been enough for her to justify considering Najabat Khan as a husband. If Mama had been alive, none of this would have been necessary—Mama would have told her that she was to marry this man, any man, and she would have submitted. Although perhaps she would have used Ishaq Beg to find out something about him and protested the choice if necessary. But now, it was she who had to do this duty to herself. This was woman's work, and neither Bapa nor her brothers would care or be adept at this, thinking only of political connections or dowries in relation to marriages. A woman always wanted more than that. For Jahanara, Najabat would be an only husband. He was married, of course, he already had two other wives, but once he married her, Jahanara decided, there would be no others, and the previous two would cease to exist.

She slept then, a dreamless and contented sleep. In another part of the zenana, Roshanara Begam was awake and leaning over the balustrade of the balcony that fronted the Yamuna. She stood there until the sun came to claim the skies again. When she turned to go into her rooms again and prepare for her father's morning jharoka, it was evident that she had been crying. But she dressed carefully and washed her eyes with cool water to soothe the redness in them. As she left her chambers, she put a palm-size velvet sack of silver coins into the hands of one of the eunuchs outside, who had come back from the polo grounds in the middle of the night and bent to whisper in her ear as she slept.

Earlier in the year, just before Mumtaz Mahal's first 'urs was celebrated in the Jilaukhana of the Luminous Tomb, Emperor Shah Jahan had given orders for the siege on the Portuguese settlement in Hugli in Bengal, on the eastern edge of the Empire.

Since Najabat Khan had first brought Dara and her news of

the Portuguese rebellion—if it could be termed thus—on their travel back to Agra, Jahanara had sent him two missives about the situation. They had been simple communications in writing—for Najabat Khan could not come into the imperial harem, or meet her anywhere else in public, without setting tongues astir with gossip. But letters, on paper, opened and read in front of the zenana's eunuchs and slaves and any other royal woman who passed by, were disregarded. The politics of the situation did not bother most of the women, and they thought it mere dabbling on Jahanara's part.

She had had to drag Dara away from his studies of Hinduism with the Brahmin priests who came for his instruction, or from his pleasures, such as they were, with dancers from the harem, or jugglers or men with pet monkeys that performed tricks.

'Come, Dara, be serious. What should we do, really do, about the Hugli problem?' Jahanara had said in exasperation as Dara's attention wandered yet again to the book he was currently reading.

'Does it really matter, Jahan?' Dara had asked. 'We are to celebrate the anniversary of Mama's death in a week, and here you worry about the firangis who have set up a fort at Gholghat and call themselves kings of a tiny sliver of land somewhere in the steamy, heated, mosquito-ridden waters of the Bay of Bengal. What does it matter?'

'Mirza Najabat Khan thinks we should do something.'

Dara had lifted a languid eyebrow. 'He does? Why the interest in Mirza Najabat Khan?'

'He has helped me. Dara, you know Bapa is in no fit state to tackle this, and you insist upon your entertainments; Hugli cannot be ignored. The Portuguese grow more and more conceited every day, and they must be stopped.'

Prince Dara Shikoh had shaken his head, and Jahanara had sat back on her knees beside him. He would not listen to what was patently common sense because he had begun a friendship with the Jesuit priests at Agra, especially Father Henry Busée, and invited them into his apartments for religious discussions with the Hindu, Buddhist and Jain priests. As a mode of study, this was all very well, but grumblings had reached her ears from court, carried in Aurangzeb's voice, that Dara was too lax in following the precepts of Islam, that he paid too much attention to other religious beliefs and not enough to his own. As of now, the talk was so little as to be insignificant, and it was untrue, this much Jahanara knew. Dara's curiosity, his open-mindedness, were purely intellectual, but even such little talk was dangerous. They were Muslim, Islam was their one and only faith, and it was unimaginable that the Mughal Emperor of Hindustan could profess or be devoted to any other religion. Dara had to take care. But how did one tell him this? He was as obstinate about his beliefs as he had been indolent about politics.

When she sighed, he had said, 'I know as much as you do about Hugli, Jahan, and troops will be sent there. I've asked Bapa to send a farman to Qasim Khan, the governor of Bengal, to lay siege to the Portuguese settlement at Hugli and demolish it. Not a single able-bodied man will survive, and if the women and children live, they will be our slaves for the rest of their lives.'

And so it had come about. The assault on the Portuguese should have been brief, thunderous, ravaging, but to everyone's surprise, they had held out long beyond any time frame considered reasonable—a whole three months. It had taught them all a lesson, Jahanara thought now in December of 1632, about the value of allowing foreigners to entrench themselves so deeply in Mughal land that they began to consider it their own.

The Portuguese had first come to the Indian coast in the late 1400s, when Vasco da Gama landed a ship in a south-eastern kingdom, and had departed, cannily, with a vague treaty for trade from the local king, leaving behind a battalion of men to form a settlement. The first Mughal Emperor found his way to Hindustan only in 1526, over a quarter of a century later. Then there had been an English embassy at the Mughal court headed by Sir Thomas Roe and a slew of representatives from the Dutch

East India Company. All of these other firangis the Portuguese Jesuits had fought hotly in skirmishes around the empire, slowly acquiring the lands on the western coast—Bombay, Daman, Diu and Goa, at the last of which was the seat of the Portuguese Viceroy to India. They had made forays into the eastern coastline also, in and around the Bay of Bengal, settling first at Satgaon and moving to Hugli, on the river by the same name, when the river's waters near Satgaon began to silt up, leaving the port unusable for large ships.

In Hugli, the Portuguese had begun to build in earnest—a fort at Gholghat, a Jesuit church, a seminary, splendid mansions for people. And in the transferring of the crown from Emperor Jahangir to Emperor Shah Jahan, their confidence had grown, resulting in this wrecking. But they should not have underestimated either the wrath or the power of Emperor Shah Jahan and his favourite daughter, the Begam Sahib Jahanara.

At the end of the imperial siege, Hugli lay devastated. Five thousand men from the settlement died violent and terrible deaths. Their women and children were fashioned into a walking caravan and made to cover the distance between Hugli and Agra, some seven hundred and fifty miles, on foot like cattle. When they reached Agra, they were given two choices: convert to Islam or die. In the end, most of them converted, and they were given away to the amirs at court for use in their harems, or for use as slaves, or as anything they wanted.

When the news of the conquest arrived, Jahanara had come upon Dara, staring morosely out into the deep afternoon shadows under a tamarind tree in his gardens.

'What is it?' she had asked.

'The Jesuit fathers will not come to my religious sessions,' he had said.

'Dara.' She had put a hand on his shoulder. 'Don't feel compassion for them or rely so entirely upon someone else who is but a servant in your lands. A good and just emperor will not. So you must learn too.'

He'd stripped a stalk of the green tamarind of its leaves, scattering them on the ground before him. 'I want to marry, Jahan,' he had said. 'It is time this good emperor had sons for the empire.'

'Who?' she had asked, amused by his change in mood. 'You are thinking of someone, or shall I find her for you?'

Dara had said almost shyly, 'Nadira.'

Their cousin, Jahanara had thought, their uncle Parviz's daughter, who had come back to Agra with them when they left Burhanpur. There was no reason to consider this anything other than a good match—she was a royal and had no brothers who would cause trouble in the future for Dara in coveting the throne, and they had all known Nadira as children.

'I will talk to Bapa,' she had said, rising and thinking of how easy it had been to furnish Dara with a wife, and one of his wanting. If only she could herself arrange . . . And so, a few months later, she had sent a summons to Mirza Najabat Khan to meet her in the chaugan grounds, setting unwittingly into motion an open, though unacknowledged, war between her sister and her.

ten

The first-born son of King Shahjahan was the prince Dara, a man of dignified manners, of a comely countenance, joyous and polite in conversation, ready and gracious of speech . . . kindly and compassionate, but over-confident in his opinion of himself . . . He assumed that fortune would invariably favour him.

—WILLIAM IRVINE (trans.)
Storia do Mogor, or Mogul India, 1653–1708
by Niccolao Manucci

Agra
Monday, 25 January 1633
14 Rajab A.H. 1042

'The rubies, your Highness?'

'The tray sits in its own stand, on your right,' Jahanara called out. The servant looked about indecisively, shoulders hunched over by the weight he was carrying, not daring to lift his gaze in the direction of her voice. When he did not move, she sighed and said sharply, 'Near the silks, no, not the reds, the blues. Move it closer.'

She watched his fumbling movements with exasperation, her fingers entwined between the carved floral gaps in the two-inch-thick marble screen behind the throne. It was the middle of the third watch of the day, around two o'clock in the afternoon, and the winter sun had finally seared through the morning's mist to fling a sheer golden veil of light around the courtyard. But Jahanara's vision was limited by the screen, and press as she would her face to the cool stone, she could still not see what the servant was doing and whether he had followed her orders.

When she leaned back, the pattern of the marble was stamped on her cheek, the side of her mouth, and a part of her forehead. She was in the zenana enclosure behind the throne in the Diwan-i-am at the fort at Agra. The hall itself was a mammoth open courtyard, circumscribed by one-storey-high corridor arches in red sandstone. At one end of the yard was this rectangular verandah jutting out into the grass—with nine arches on the front and three on each of its two sides. The fourth side of the verandah was built into the fort itself and contained a throne room—a little corral—built entirely in gleaming white marble, whittled with niches for candles around Emperor Shah Jahan's gaddi. The marble was inlaid on every possible surface, flat and recessed, with gleaming blue and reds and greens—turquoise, corals and jasper—wrought in the shapes of blooming flowers and vines. The throne room was the jewel set within the verandah of the Diwan-i-am and had been, solely, Emperor Shah Jahan's vision. The verandah had a flat roof and sat on a three-foot-high sandstone platform. Its pillars were white but actually built in sandstone and polished with a high-gloss lime chunam.

Princess Jahanara Begam was standing behind the throne's recess, within the walls of the fort, and trying to direct from there the thirty servants who were scurrying around in the verandah. She had ordered the floor of the verandah to be meticulously cleaned and laid over with cotton mattresses, and she had had brought thick Persian rugs in deep reds and carpeted the whole from one end to the other. When that was done, the men had disappeared one by one into the zenana behind her, to a special anteroom where they were given their precious burdens, which they brought out in a procession. These were all presents that Jahanara was giving to Dara and Nadira for their wedding, and today she was going to display them for the court to see, as was traditional before a marriage took place.

Jahanara put her hand on the latch of the door which led into the throne area, and another hand was laid on her wrist at the same time.

'What are you doing?' Satti Khanum said. 'You cannot go out until the servants have left.'

The princess took her hand away from the door. 'I know, Satti, but they are dolts, with no sense about how to arrange the gifts. Look, that man has spilled the rubies.'

And so he had; as he turned, the lower edge of his qaba had brushed against the tray and sent it thumping onto the carpets. The rubies had scattered over the red Persian rugs, glowing with a fire's heart. The man glanced behind him towards Jahanara and Satti Khanum, whom he could not see, and crouched to gather the faceted stones in the skirt of his long tunic. When the rubies were collected, he stood there staring at the burden on his lap. His mouth was loose, his face filled with longing and awe. His monthly salary was three rupees, and in the folds of his clothing he held a khazana worth at least forty thousand rupees. His hands quivered with want.

'I must go,' Jahanara said, and, pulling her veil over her head, she opened the door and stepped out onto the balcony. As the servants watched in mute astonishment, she drew her long ghagara around her knees and vaulted down into the verandah.

Ishaq Beg said harshly, 'Get out!' and the men fled down the long halls of the verandah and into the tepid sunshine. The fifteen eunuchs guarding them brushed and patted them down as they exited the courtyard, tripping over each other in their haste to leave.

Satti Khanum followed Jahanara into the verandah in a much more leisurely fashion, out into the zenana at the back of the throne and down the steps.

'You are always in a hurry, Jahan,' she said. 'Some caution would have been advisable.'

Jahanara nodded, only half listening. Satti was the older sister of Emperor Jahangir's poet laureate, Talib-i-Amuli, and had lived in Persia until he called for her to come to Hindustan. Here, Talib had the emperor's ear, and he had his sister assigned to Jahangir's son's harem when she was forty years old, aged already by Mughal standards. To the young Mumtaz Mahal, she had provided counsel and companionship and stayed by her side through her numerous confinements, looking after the children as they grew older, taking over the education of the princesses.

And yet, Jahanara thought, as Satti and Ishaq fetched and carried the trays on her orders and laid them out where they would be viewed at their best, she was stifled by Satti's sternness, her constant cautions, her very chatter. Satti was an old woman now, as old as Jahanara's grandmothers would have been, her face lined deeply in the forehead and around the mouth. Her back was stooped, and some of her teeth were missing. For Satti Khanum, entry into the imperial zenana, being attached to the quarters of the woman who became empress, had been beneficial. She had an adopted daughter, a girl she had taken for her own upon coming to Hindustan, who was married to Amanat Khan, who had been recently hired as a calligrapher for the Luminous Tomb. She had continued on in the imperial harem, had amassed riches in gifts and bonuses from her mistress, and thought of herself as supreme . . . after the princesses. Satti had taught Jahanara Persian and verses from the Quran, and, in the change of power from Mumtaz Mahal to her daughter, had forgotten that Princess Jahanara Begam was no longer her student.

When all had been arranged, Satti and Jahanara stood in the centre of the verandah.

'Such treasures for the prince and his wife,' Satti said in a whisper.

For treasures they were. A month before, Jahanara had sent a hundred thousand rupees' worth of jewels and clothing to her uncle Prince Parviz's widow, who had taken a house along the banks of the Yamuna a short distance from the fort, for the first part of the wedding proceedings. That had been merely a promise. Laid out in front of her was the rest of what she was going to give Dara and Nadira.

Massive gold trays piled with lustrous raw silks from Thailand in colours of rose and pearl, ten diamond necklaces worth between fifty and a hundred thousand rupees set in heavy gold, bangles studded with rubies and pearls, muslins as fine as summer mist fashioned into pantaloons and bodices and veils—and each of these had gold and silver zari embroidered into the fabric, strewn with diamonds, emeralds, pearls, and rubies. A merchant had brought a bag full of rubies from Badakhshan, and Jahanara had bought his entire inventory for Dara, unable to resist the glow of red, like luscious pomegranate seeds, overcome by emotion because the Balas rubies were mined in the land where Mirza Najabat Khan claimed his ancestry. He would see these rubies also, later in the evening, when the Begam Sahib's gifts to her brother would be presented to the nobles at court by the light of torches and candles, the colours of the silk muted, the diamonds sparkling. And a few hours from now, Emperor Shah Jahan would visit the Diwan-i-am himself, along with the ladies of the imperial harem, to view the gifts.

Jahanara recognized the wonderment in Satti Khanum's voice, mingled with a little jealousy and some frustration, and she smiled to herself.

She had a huge income from her father, and *this* was the value of all that money. The envy was directed towards her, not Dara or Nadira, who would receive all this magnificence, because it meant she could so easily give away so much and not miss it.

There were perfume bottles at another corner filled with musk oil from Bhutan, and the bottles themselves were created out of turquoise enamel, studded with crystals and corals, their stoppers made from blue Aleppo glass.

'How much did this all cost?' Satti asked.

Jahanara laughed, her voice echoing off the walls of the Diwan-i-am, and she said, as carelessly as she could, 'About two million rupees, I think. I do not know for sure, Satti.'

'You are a generous sister, Jahan.'

'Yes, I am. But this is not everything.'

'Is all this for us?'

They both turned to see Nadira standing at one end of the verandah. She was clad in thin white muslin, six layers of *peshwaz*, flimsy pants underneath, her head uncovered. A breeze stirred through the cusped arches that linked the pillars, and her clothes swirled around her. Nadira had the capacity for immense grace, Jahanara thought, and then wondered if that was why Dara had fallen in love with her. There were others he could have chosen to marry—and he would eventually marry others—but Nadira had captured his heart. It was difficult for Jahanara to see what the attraction was for this creature who glided everywhere, whose presence was so light, whose laughter was like the tinkling of bells heard at a distance. She was a wraith, with little substance. Nadira was slight, in her physical appearance and in the force of her character.

'For Dara and you,' she said.

'How lovely all of it is. The wines'—Nadira touched a light finger over the green glass bottles embellished with gold stoppers—'are they from Kashmir? The ones you like so much?'

'Yes, Dara enjoys this wine also. Nadira'—Jahanara tried to be gentle—'do you wish to be married to Dara?'

Nadira looked up at her—she was a couple of inches shorter than Jahanara—with a steady gaze that turned her hazel eyes dark. 'What a ridiculous question, Jahan. And so close to the wedding.'

Satti Khanum cleared her throat, and Jahanara stepped back. It *was* preposterous to ask a bride this just before she was to be married, especially since the couple were all but married—the wedding presents had been sent to Nadira's mother's house in December as a guarantee, Jahanara herself had spent lavishly and worked tirelessly on the preparations, and there were only six days until the official ceremony.

'A husband,' Nadira said slowly, 'is a blessing from Allah. I could not ask for another man to be my husband, one so accomplished, so beloved, so erudite; but then there is no one such as Dara. You should know all this, Jahan.'

'I do, my dear,' Princess Jahanara said. 'I wanted to make sure you did also.'

'Enough,' Satti said, bristling. 'Enough talk. Nadira, you must go back home now; it is unseemly for you to be here in the imperial palaces looking over your presents.'

Nadira nodded. She said, with a half smile, 'Jahan, once Dara and I are . . . in a few months, I mean, we will look for husbands for both Roshan and you. As your sister, as your brother's wife, I will take it to be my duty.' She waved to them and left the verandah by the steps leading into the zenana.

Jahanara felt laughter spill out of her. 'She is not as inanimate as she makes us think. *She* is going to find me a husband?'

Satti Khanum's expression was sombre, her mouth tight, her eyebrows rigid. 'It is good you find mirth in this situation, Jahan. But remember, a married woman has more influence, more standing than an unmarried one. We are born to but one purpose—to be wives and mothers; there is no other self to us than that. You must marry too, someday, and go to grace your husband's home.'

There followed a long pause as Jahanara thought about this. She roamed the verandah of the Diwan-i-am, smoothing out the drape of a silk here, tapping the dazzling stones of a pair of earrings there. She did not believe Satti Khanum entirely—there was some truth to what she had said, but it applied only to women who had no wealth, no status, no eminence in society. Princess Jahanara Begam was the head of Emperor Shah Jahan's imperial zenana, the Begam Sahib. The title itself was constructed to place her in the harem; if she had been the ruling wife of the emperor, she would have been called the Padshah Begam. But both of her Bapa's remaining wives were shadow women, as insubstantial when her mother was dead as when she had been alive. They lived in the luxury they expected, with sizable incomes, servants at their call any time of day or night, silks and jewellery in piled masses, but without any actual authority. In the Mughal harem, the most powerful woman was the one most dear to the emperor, and in this case, for the first time in the history of the Mughals, it was the daughter and not the wife. Satti Khanum knew this, of course she knew this, Jahanara thought, as she listened to the skirts of Satti's ghagara sweeping the thick pile of the carpets behind her. This was why, after Mumtaz Mahal's death, she had attached herself to Jahanara, not Roshan, not the two other wives of the emperor.

'They could not have celebrated Dara's wedding so splendidly,' Jahanara said, more to herself than to her companion.

'No,' Satti answered, as though she had followed her ward's train of thought all the way through, 'but they are here to stay and will not leave when you do. And the gap formed from your absence, one of them is sure to fill.'

She stopped abruptly, and Princess Jahanara watched her think this time and saw a realization map her face. When Jahanara left to marry, one of her father's wives would again be supreme in the imperial zenana, and in the tussle for domination, Satti might well be left without a role to play. Perhaps she should not advertise either her attachment to or her exhilaration in being the Begam Sahib's servant so openly. Perhaps a little diplomacy, a division of affections, was advisable. Jahanara felt sudden pity for the woman, because she was herself privileged as no one else in the imperial zenana was, beloved of her father, possessed of a wealth unimaginable to any other woman, perhaps anywhere else in the world. As she stood in the midst of the shimmering stack of presents she was giving her brother on the occasion of his wedding, Jahanara knew that she was etching her name in history. One day, four or five hundred years from now, posterity would talk with amazement of her generosity, her open hand, her dominance over the glittering zenana. She had more money than Dara, the crown prince, the much-touted heir; all of this had cost her only about a tenth of her annual income.

'You have something else on your mind, Satti? Or do you wish to go?' Jahanara asked, wearied by the talk and her emotions. To think that the two of them—Nadira and Satti—so inconsequential themselves, would consider *her* so . . . just because she did not have the protection of a husband. Even more insulting was that they thought she would lose the protection of her father.

'I heard,' Satti said and then hesitated, 'about Mirza Najabat Khan. The chaugan at midnight. It was inappropriate, Jahan, so unlike you to act on impulse. If you are . . . indeed . . . wanting a man, I would advise a marriage. I will talk with your Bapa if you wish; you know I am here in the place of your mother. Give me the opportunity to do this for you.'

'It was no impulse, Satti,' Jahanara replied, fighting to keep her voice firm, even reasonable. That there would be gossip, she had known, but for Satti Khanum to talk thus, in terms of her wanting just any man, and then assume Mama's place in her heart; this was unthinkable and far beyond a servant's duties. 'And I will speak with Bapa when I consider it necessary.'

'You are young, my dear—'

'My Mama was married at nineteen, Satti, and she was betrothed to Bapa five years before that.'

'Jahan, if your Bapa should come to know of—'

'Is that a threat, Satti?'

'Of course not,' the older woman said hurriedly. 'It is impossible that you would even think so. Am I nothing to you, Jahan? Remember that I have taught you since you were a child, been by your mother's side, am still here now for you poor, motherless children.'

'I do know all of this, Satti,' Jahanara said quietly. 'And now I must be alone.'

She would not apologize. If her Mama had still been alive, there would have been at least one woman who had some authority over her; Satti, for all her sagacity and obvious interest in them, was not her mother. Jahanara thought that all of her immense power and wealth, both in the zenana and at court, had given her the merest smidgen of arrogance—but it was well deserved. And the Mughal kings and queens had learned the value of having this confidence in themselves, of heeding the advice of retainers and courtiers but paying attention to their own opinions both within and without the harem. Years ago, Emperor Akbar had had to battle his regent, Bairam Khan, for ascendancy when he attained his majority, for the regent had come to think of the empire left in his safekeeping as his own and, in the zenana, Akbar's wet nurse, Maham Anagha, had assumed a place of eminence that had been more difficult for him to shake. Jahanara knew well all these stories from the past, had studied them carefully, and just as cautiously had chosen the women and the eunuchs who surrounded her, but she never let them think of themselves as being more than what they were—servants, retainers and slaves.

Satti left, her step faltering, now eager to pay a visit to Emperor Shah Jahan's wives; perhaps she could say she had come to invite them personally for their stepson's marriage.

But the two women in the verandah had left something unsaid and hanging in the air between them. Without the persuasive influence of Empress Mumtaz Mahal, was it possible that Emperor Shah Jahan—having just lost one beloved woman in his life—would allow the other, his daughter, to marry and carry her affections away from the imperial zenana to the harem of another man?

~

A week later, on 1 February 1633, Jahanara sent henna to Nadira's mother's house on the banks of the Yamuna, and along with it the *sachaq,* the official wedding gift to the bride. Two hundred servants went on foot in a procession, bearing upon their heads, hands and shoulders round silver and gold platters heaped with brocades from Gujarat and Banaras and jewels from Satagaon and Surat. In front of the men, Ishaq Beg carried a plate with fifteen solid-gold cups, in the depths of which lay pungent-smelling henna paste, made from the crushed central veins, the petioles, of the henna leaves. To fill the cups to their brims, thousands of henna leaves had been harvested when they had just unfurled at the break of dawn, dewdrops still glittering like crystals on the young green. The leaves themselves would work well enough for dyeing hands and legs and hair with brilliant orange—but for Dara's *hinabandi* ceremony, Jahanara had ordered each tiny leaf to be stripped of its petiole, where the concentration of the dye was at its highest, and these slender veins were then powdered in marble mortars, mixed with water from the Ganges, and set to rest in their gold cups.

At Nadira's house, the women waited eagerly for the gifts and the henna, and the whole day was spent in singing, dancing, and decorating all the women's hands and legs in lush designs. Jahanara and Roshanara did not attend the ceremony, and they were not to attend the wedding itself—their role, as Dara's sisters, was to wait in the imperial palaces to welcome Dara home with his bride the next day. Dara went to Nadira's house late in the afternoon and was ushered into the women's quarters so that one of Nadira's sisters could adorn the skin of his hands and his feet with little dots of henna.

The next day, Emperor Shah Jahan went to his oldest son's apartments in the Agra fort just as he had finished dressing and fastened the wedding *sehra* across his forehead. It was a crown that tied at the back; for the common man, the sehra was made of fresh flowers woven into strings—Dara's sehra, a gift from his father, was a thick band of gold embedded with diamonds, which ended in velvet ropes at the back of his head, and in the front there were twenty strings of pearls, each eight inches long and each corded with perfectly matched pink pearls the size of cherrystones. The strings ended in a ruby apiece, lavishly faceted and glowing with fire.

Shah Jahan then took a farman from a pocket of his brocade qaba and handed it to Dara.

'What is it, Bapa?' Dara asked, weighing the rolled sheet of paper in his hands.

'A gift. Your sister has given you so much; your father can do no less.'

Prince Dara Shikoh unrolled the scroll and read its contents. As a wedding present, he had been given the city of Lahore, all the buildings contained within, the taxes from its bazaars, the people who lived there, the duties from its customhouses. He felt a rush of tears behind his eyelids and blinked them away. Lahore was one of the seats of the Mughal emperor, as much a capital city as Agra and Delhi—when his father came to stay, he would from now on come as his son's guest. In the handing over of the farman, Emperor Shah Jahan had made his oldest son very wealthy, almost on par with his oldest daughter. The revenues would be Dara's to do with as he pleased, to reinvest, to spend in constructing gardens or *sarais* or mansions anywhere in the empire.

He bent to perform the *konish* to his father, and Shah Jahan stopped his hand as it rose to his head in the salutation.

'You are my son, Dara, from you I do not expect servitude,' he said, smiling.

'Bapa, thank you. I do not know how to express my gratitude; you have given to me one of the jewels of your empire, and I will guard it jealously.'

'As you will, eventually, the empire itself, Dara,' Shah Jahan said almost inaudibly, speaking to himself, but Dara heard him, and this first concrete indication of his father's wishes sent a thrill through him. He was superstitious, so he attributed this good fortune to the woman he was about to marry—Nadira had brought all this to him. He stepped back and let the pearl strings of the sehra fall about his face again. Dara, the bridegroom, was also to be veiled during the ceremony; only later, in their bedchamber, according to custom, would the bride and groom lift the coverings on their faces and see each other for the first time.

The wedding was held in the Shah Burj at Agra fort—and here, they deviated from established custom that it take place in the bride's house. The house that Nadira's mother had rented was small, inconsequential, and unsuitable for the wedding of the heir to the Mughal Empire.

Upon his accession, Emperor Shah Jahan had begun to build in earnest, laying foundations in stone, marble and semi-precious inlay, for he knew that he would die eventually, his bones would crumble to dust, his imperial farmans shrivel in the mouths of white ants, but stone would survive and stand to proclaim to the people of Hindustan how powerful and wealthy their emperor had been. The first place he had turned his architect's gaze upon was the fort at Agra, built originally by his grandfather Emperor Akbar and added on to by his father, Jahangir. He had demolished, without a scruple, the buildings fronting the Yamuna within the walls of the fort and made plans for them to be replaced by faultless white marble in a series of halls, both public and private, and zenana apartments. One of these was the Shah Burj. It was situated where the walls of the fort curved sharply inward, an octagonal tower topped with a beaten copper dome that had already taken on a gold-green sheen. The tower had a flat roof below the dome with thick and jutting chajjas, eaves that rinsed rainwater away from the building and provided an impenetrable shade even when the sun was aslant. Five of its eight sides faced the Yamuna, each held up by elaborately carved marble pillars. The walls were slabs of marble inlaid with jewels in reds, golds, greens and blues. The entrance to the Shah Burj, on the western side, away from the river, was an open chamber with a lotus pond carved entirely in marble placed in the centre of the floor. The 'pond' was shallow, not even six inches deep, set with a single flute of water to form a fountain fed from an underground pipe, and when the water ran, it bubbled out of its source and rippled down the sides of the basin, barely breathing over the carved stone.

There were seven people at the wedding ceremony—officially, that is—a qazi to officiate, the emperor, his sons, and the bride. The qazi said a short prayer and then asked, as was expected, about the mehr, the settlement from the groom's father. Emperor Shah Jahan replied that he gave his daughter-in-law five hundred thousand rupees, which was hers to keep and use, no matter whether the marriage survived or not. The qazi gestured to ask for one of Dara's hands and one of Nadira's. He did not touch either his prince or the bride but brought them together anyhow—and in the joining of their hands, the marriage contract had been accepted and signed by both of them, and they were married.

Jahanara and Roshanara stood hidden behind the pillars leading into the Shah Burj, their heads covered, listening but not leaning out to see. Jahanara heard the tinkle of the gold bangles on Nadira's arms—twenty-five on each—as she clasped Dara's, heard also the rustle of the thickly embroidered chiffon veil as Nadira moved closer to her brother. The qazi melted away, passing the two women outside noiselessly, and Roshanara moved into the room to add her congratulations. Only Princess Jahanara Begam stayed where she was, feeling the cool of the marble seep through her clothing as she leaned against the pillar. One part of her mind was on the arrangements for the festivities—the alms to be distributed, the feast prepared for the night, the entertainment—and another part of her was beset by an unexpected yearning.

She glanced at her Bapa, who stood with a smile on his face, a contentment rarely seen since Mama's death. Would he look at her thus one day, when he gave her away in marriage to Najabat Khan? Or would he flinch at having to part from his daughter?

In the far distance, along a bend in the river, a fog of dust from the Luminous Tomb's worksite clogged the horizon. Jahanara went into the Shah Burj to kiss and hug her brother and his new wife, to hold her father's hand, to watch her other brothers glowing with joy.

She did not know that one day this octagonal room would become intensely familiar to her with its unchanging view of the Taj Mahal. Because her father would die here, bedridden for nine long years after one of his sons would snatch his crown and rule in his stead. And those nine years in the future would be the final shadow cast upon her, upon a life that held such promise today.

eleven

The first daughter whom he had was Begom Saeb (Begam Sahib), the eldest of all, whom her father loved to an extraordinary degree . . . and this has given occasion to Monsieur Bernier to write many things about this princess, founded entirely on the talk of low people. Therefore it is incumbent on me . . . to say that what he writes is untrue.

—WILLIAM IRVINE *(trans.)*
Storiado Mogor, or Mogul India, 1653–1708
by Niccolao Manucci

Agra
Wednesday, 2 February 1633
22 Rajab A.H. 1042

Later that night, after the eunuchs had left, Princess Roshanara Begam rested against the door on the inside of the bedchamber prepared for Dara. The aroma of roses in heated bloom filled the room, mixed with the scent of frankincense from the censers. Pink rose petals shimmered on the deep carpets. The bed, made of soft cotton stuffing, was in the centre, and four teak bedposts were festooned with garlands of roses, which hung in plush swathes, closely knitted to form a curtain of fragrance around the bed. The sheets were of fine cotton muslin, embroidered in delicate patterns of flowers in gold zari, so carefully done as to merely caress Dara and Nadira as they lay on the bed. Perfumed oil lamps glowed in the corners, casting domes of light upon the marble-embellished ceiling and shadows everywhere else.

Roshanara took a breath and exhaled gently. She was afraid to move from the door, for fear of crushing the rose petals underfoot—that privilege was to be Dara's and Nadira's when they came in. But she had a sudden craving to feel the smoothness of the sheets, to lay her head upon the feathered pillows, to look up into a lover's gaze. A breeze came in from the waters of the Yamuna below the apartment, billowed the chiffon curtains, and sent light skittering around Roshanara. And so, Dara was married to the woman he loved, she thought. What would they do here tonight? Her mouth twisted in a wry smile. She knew what they would do, as they all did, living in the imperial zenana, where every woman's thoughts went to love, to the caress of silks, to the pearling of sweat on skin. There was no mystery in that, but this, the first night of love, held a special magic, a togetherness; it was a private moment never to be captured again.

She picked up the heavy skirts of her silk ghagara and nudged a rose petal with her toe. It felt cool, and she shivered. Once she had thought it possible for her to have a night such as this . . . with Mirza Najabat Khan. But since last December, when the eunuch had bent to her ear with his tale of Jahanara's nocturnal meeting with Najabat Khan in the chaugan fields, she had become afraid and bitter. What Jahanara wanted, she usually got, because she was Bapa's favourite daughter, the one who had his affections, the one who had hosted Dara's wedding. So it had been before Mama died, so it was now. Roshanara settled herself against the door more comfortably and listened to the sounds of celebrations around the fort. The Naubat Khana, the imperial orchestra, was still playing this late into the night. The kettledrums boomed, the shehnai let loose its wail, men's voices clamoured in song in the darkness. It was the first time in almost two years that Bapa had allowed music in the capital, and Dara's wedding had become for all of them a time to celebrate not just his joining with Nadira but the official end of mourning for Mama.

And one day she would have all of this too—the music, the lights, the rich presents, a man in whose home she would be supreme, as she was not here in the zenana. But which man?

Roshanara raised her ghagara again and went to the bed, uncaring now that the rose petals lay scattered in her wake. She sat on the mattress and leaned back on her hands, looking up at the ceiling. She had not been allowed, no, invited to perform even this little duty for Dara and Nadira, preparing their chamber for the night. Jahan had been here, shouting orders, snapping her fingers in disgust when she found one wilted rose in a long garland and sent the eunuchs scurrying in search of fresh roses and a seamstress to stitch another one together to hang in its place. She had been harried, restless, perhaps thinking herself of a room in which to spend a night such as this . . . with Najabat Khan. Roshanara knew with a certainty that came from long association with her sister that Jahanara was in love with the courtier, or she would not have risked scandal in meeting him under the cover of darkness, she would not write to him as often as she did. And yet, when she, Roshanara, had sneaked into his tent to take his measure, he had seemed almost welcoming. She sat up. Were his affections still not fixed then? Was that possible?

She stepped away from the bed and slipped out of the room, thinking all the while. As women, even as imperial women, Jahanara and Roshanara had only one precious possession—reputation. In that lay a woman's entire worth. One report, well placed, could demolish it.

When she returned to her apartments, Roshanara sent her eunuchs out into the city of Agra. They followed her orders faithfully, letting fall a word in conversations around fires, speaking casually to travellers and merchants who had come in for the wedding celebrations, dropping hints at the shopkeepers' open windows as they passed by with a wink and a nod. And the next day, and in the days that followed, the rumours were reborn, blossomed, burgeoned that Emperor Shah Jahan had indeed ceased mourning his dead wife because he had found another, in the person of the Begam Sahib of the empire.

After attending to the decoration of Dara's bridal chamber, Jahanara went to her Bapa's apartments to see him to bed, as she had done every night since her mother died. Emperor Shah Jahan was waiting for her by the windows of the balcony. On the streets below, men shouted, women sang, drums were beaten in drunkenness.

'They still enjoy themselves,' he said when Jahanara came to rest her head against her father's shoulder and twine her arm in his. 'It is so late.'

'You are good to them, Bapa,' she said. 'They have missed the raucousness of mindless celebration, and they enjoy it now with Dara's wedding. Will you sleep?' She tugged at his arm and led him to the bed. The nights were still cool this early in the year, and coal braziers wrought in gold and silver filigree were dispersed around the bed, their warmth enough for Shah Jahan to require only a sheet to cover him. When Jahanara gestured towards the open doors and windows of the balcony, he shook his head.

'I've ordered for them to be left open. Read to me, beta.'

'From the *Baburnama,* Bapa?' She reached for a book beside him, covered in red leather embossed with gold leaf, ran her finger along the slit created by the jade bookmark, found the page, and opened it.

When she had read for ten minutes, Emperor Shah Jahan leaned out from his bed and put a hand over the pages. 'What a pity it is that I never learned Turki, in which Emperor Babur wrote this memoir, or that I never taught you. You and I, we have to read his words translated into Persian; I think he must be grieving at our ignorance. You see how learned he was, a warrior first, but a keen, observant one who detailed every bit of his life in these pages, studied the characters of his generals and his men, thundered in to take Hindustan for us.'

'But he hated India, Bapa,' Jahanara said softly. 'He loathed the heat, he did not understand the people—if there were empires to be conquered in cooler climes, he would have done so.'

'And you, Jahan?'

She shrugged, a graceful upward movement of her shoulders. 'I am at peace where you are, Bapa.'

The silk curtains covering the windows were a slip of a cloud, and the skies lit up as the late-night fireworks began. Now a cerulean blue, now a pale lime green, now a coral pink. The lights came on and disappeared without a sound, for these last festivities, unlike the evening fireworks, had been ordered to be noiseless. Itimad Khan moved around the room, extinguishing the lamps and torches one by one, and father and daughter were silhouetted against the glittering sky. They looked at each other in delight, seeing the shades of colours brighten each of their faces and dwindle into darkness.

'It was a good wedding, Jahan. Dara is happy, and so am I in his choice of a bride. But weddings seem to beget weddings. I am thinking of another one now.'

'Are you?' Jahanara asked, her heart pounding. She would be nineteen years old in April, and if Mama had been alive, perhaps she would have been married to Mirza Najabat Khan long ago. She searched her father's face, but he was looking at the windows.

'Sons must be married,' he said. 'They have to beget heirs for the empire, as many male children as they can.' He laughed, and it was a sound unheard for so long that Jahanara laughed along with him, just for the pleasure of being able to do so. 'But even sons that lived have had an unfortunate predilection to alcohol and opium, leaving an emperor originally possessed of a handful of heirs with one or two at the most in the end. As with my father, Emperor Jahangir. In his case, his being the only surviving son was a blessing; in mine . . .' His voice faded away, and they both thought of the trail of blood that had washed the path to his throne.

Jahanara kissed her father's hand and noticed that it was trembling. Bapa had never regretted sending his brothers to their deaths when he became emperor; it was a necessity. If he had forgiven their lives, he could have well forfeited his own—this was the unwritten law of the empire. Did he worry about his own four sons? Think that Dara's place as emperor after him was not so assured after all? But who else was there? Who else *could* there be?

'I grow old, Jahan,' he said quietly, 'in thinking thoughts such as these. And now that Dara is married, another one of you must be also.'

'Who, Bapa?' she asked. 'Which man have you chosen?'

His look of astonishment stunned her, and then his words did too. 'Not you, surely, my dear. They have a saying here in Hindustan that parents are but temporary guardians of their daughters, until they marry. But you are my very life, you cannot want . . . surely?'

'No, of course not. I meant'—she groped for words—'I meant Roshan. I thought that perhaps you were thinking of her.'

Emperor Shah Jahan lay back on his bed and crossed his arms over his stomach. 'I hear Roshan has lost her heart to an amir at court. If she wishes to marry him, she may.'

'She has? How do you know, Bapa? She could not have been so bold as to talk with you.'

'Beta, I may have been in mourning for your Mama, but my ears still work, and my spies do also. His name is Mirza Najabat Khan.'

Jahanara did not respond, but a weight descended upon her, her shoulders bowed. If Bapa knew this, then it must be true. He must know then also of her meeting with Najabat Khan in the polo fields. Was that why he had said this to her? That Roshan, whom he loved less, would be welcome to marry Najabat Khan, but she, so much dearer to him, must keep her place by his side?

'I am not of a mind, however,' Emperor Shah Jahan said, 'to let either of my daughters marry.'

He slept then, and she sat by his side, crushed. The fireworks ended, and the sharp smoke of spent gunpowder came coiling into the apartments. The skies darkened again, and Jahanara saw that a thin, cold moon had risen, hidden until now by the brilliance of the fireworks. Mist ascended from the river to shroud the trees and blot the moon, and she rose, finally, to return to her rooms. When she left, the Kashmiri women guards outside Emperor Shah Jahan's apartments saluted her and murmured to each other about the lateness of the hour. It was these whispers that Princess Roshanara relied upon when she sent her eunuchs out into the night to spread a vile rumour about her father and her sister, and Jahanara did not stop to think that, for such talk to have travelled abroad, it must have originated within the walls of the imperial zenana.

When Princess Jahanara Begam heard the gossip, brought to her by Satti Khanum, she paid little heed to it, not caring how it had started or how it had spread. In doing so, she made her first mistake. For Najabat Khan was a fastidious man, and, as enchanted as he was by his princess, something in him balked at such talk. He remembered how she had come to his tent in the encampment, boldly and without fear, and he remembered that magical moonlit night in the chaugan fields when he had to stop often to look at her, to see in her that woman from the previous meeting. He barely knew her—as indeed he had known little about his first two wives, but they were now established in his zenana and did not have omnipotent fathers or powerful brothers who could call for his head to be parted from his neck by sundown and would be obeyed without question. An alliance with the imperial family was advantageous, but fraught with danger all the same—for even a hundred years after Emperor Babur had established the Mughal Empire, the imperial family's quicksand fortunes made their legacy shakable, and they held on to the crown only by might and cunning, the former directly linked to money, and more specifically to possession of the vast treasury at Agra.

For the second woman, seen in the blue light of the moon, Najabat Khan would have risked the peril, though not for the first. But he thought they were the same.

Prince Shah Shuja, the second of Emperor Shah Jahan's sons, was married twenty days later, on 23 February 1633, and this was what preoccupied Jahanara soon after Dara's wedding, why she gave such little consideration to the rumours. Sons must be married, Emperor Shah Jahan had said, and so he said again to Jahanara; Shuja was of age—he would be seventeen that year, to Dara's eighteen, and would his beloved Jahan see to it?

She did, without as much preparation as she had for Dara. Shuja married the daughter of Mirza Rustum Safavid, a grandson of Shah Ismail of Persia, who had come to Hindustan some forty years ago to become a courtier to Emperor Akbar. Rustum was an old man, sixty-odd years old, but the girl Shuja married was born of one of his younger wives. Quite apart from their royal antecedents and their link in blood to the Shah of Persia, Rustum's family had a history of connections with the Mughal imperial family. Emperor Shah Jahan's first wife, languishing behind the walls of the imperial zenana, was Rustum's niece. And so, when Shuja married Rustum's daughter, he married his stepmother's cousin.

When the wedding had been celebrated, the bustle in the streets of Agra waned into its everyday regularity. In the lull, exhausted and filled with a hunger, Princess Jahanara Begam sent another restrained summons to Najabat Khan; this time it was to meet her in the zenana gardens, midafternoon, when most of the women would be indoors at siesta.

She waited for him. But he did not come.

rauza-i-munavvara
The Luminous Tomb

> *The Kinge is now building a Sepulchre for his late deceased Queen Taje Moholl . . . whome hee dearely affected . . . He intends it shall excel all other . . . There is already about her Tombe a raile of gold. The building is begun.*
>
> —R.C. TEMPLE (ed.), *The Travels of Peter Mundy in Europe and Asia, 1608–1667* by Peter Mundy

Agra
Thursday, 26 May 1633
17 Zi'l-Qa'da A.H. 1042

The heated, parched air was woven with the tuneful murmur of thousands of voices in prayer, reciting verses from the Quran. The first 'urs for Empress Mumtaz Mahal had been held in the Jilaukhana, the forecourt to the tomb, but this, the second 'urs, was held within, because by this time, a scant year later, the massive sandstone terrace fronting the Yamuna was already complete.

On this terrace would stand the Luminous Tomb, in the very centre, flanked on the left by a mosque and on the right by the Miham Khana, an assembly hall. The terrace was designed to occupy the entire breadth of the gardens for the tomb and was some nine hundred and eighty-five feet long. Its two ends, east and west (its northern end faced the river), were curved around octagonal towers that would mark the northeastern and northwestern edges of the tomb's complex. From the Great Gate, the terrace would eventually be barely discernible—not only because of the magnificent structures it bore, but also because it was only four feet high in front, higher at the back, some thirty feet, built thus because the land sloped downward to the river.

Emperor Shah Jahan's engineers had studied the sandy and silt-filled ground at the verge of the river, which had been routed earlier to curve alongside the building site. The foundations of this riverfront terrace, the very basis for the Luminous Tomb, would have to be solid and substantial. They spent hours in consultation, poring over the architect's plans, taking measurements on-site, excavating and filling mud in cavities, which they then submerged for days to simulate the Yamuna in flood in a year of munificent rains. Every test crumbled under the onslaught of the water, and this was their biggest problem. If His Majesty had decided instead to house the tomb in the centre of the gardens, and so landward, with merely a compound wall at the riverfront, all their calculations would have been accurate. But in his infinite wisdom, Emperor Shah Jahan had determined that the main buildings were to be at the north end of the gardens, at the water's edge, and the engineers then scrambled to make their sovereign's wishes into fact.

Finally, one day in December 1632, one experiment withstood every simulated natural disaster. And so, they marked out numerous circles five feet in diameter, sank wooden shafts, and dug out all the soil until they hit the bedrock below. Into this opening they packed rocks and chunks of iron—eventually the wood would rot and disintegrate, but this pillar of rock and iron would claw firmly into the ground and hold up above the weight of the terrace at the river, the platform for the tomb, the tomb itself, the mosque, and the assembly hall.

The tomb would be raised on a platform of brick and sandstone, its sides faced with white marble slabs, simply carved in blank arches that curved to a point on top. When the second 'urs was celebrated, the terrace was finished, and so also was the tomb's white platform. During the first 'urs there had been nothing much to see—the tents were pitched on dirt—but now the graceful and mammoth lines of the terrace and the platform gave some shape to the tomb itself. The empress's body had been unearthed from its temporary rest and brought into the underground chamber below the terrace; her cenotaph had been marked in stone on the platform; a gold screen, real and heavy gold, surrounded this marking. Eventually, the tomb would rise over the cenotaph. On this day, though, the tents for the ceremony were pitched on the terrace and the platform, around the screen.

As the ghariyalis struck the noon hour, an imperial barge docked on the river side of the terrace and a cry went out, 'Avert your eyes!' passed on from guard to guard. This second 'urs was to be a private celebration for the emperor and the ladies of his zenana, and panels of Masulipatnam chintz shielded the royal party not just at the pier but above on the terrace. Shah Jahan walked down the length of the pier, holding Jahanara's and Roshanara's hands. A wedge of steps had been cut into this side of the terrace, leading to cool verandahs. On the landward side, the terrace was a scant four feet in height, but here it was almost three stories high, an uninterrupted stretch of amber sandstone inlaid with graceful lines in white marble. In its walls were set a series of rooms facing the water, with red sandstone pillars fluting into arches to hold up the ceilings. This was the Tahkhana.

'You are quiet, Bapa,' Jahanara said when they were seated. The Yamuna flowed in sluggish tranquillity, and a warm breeze stirred through the room, the ceiling of which was lofty and airy, the stone screens punctured by light. Here they would wait until the afternoon sun had spent its viciousness, then go up to the marble platform to take part in the ceremonies and the chanting.

Shah Jahan clasped his hands in front of him, thinking of the woman for whom he was building all of this. When he looked up at his daughters, he found them watchful, noting his every movement, their heads slanted to one side. Jahan had grown into a beautiful woman, slender, her face planed in angles—a sharp jut to her chin, thin cheeks, strong bones around her eyes. Her mouth curved upward when his glance fell upon her, as though she knew what his scrutiny was about. Roshan had blossomed also in these past two years into womanhood, but she was softer than her sister—her eyes had a glow to them, her actions were more unhurried, and recently he had noticed fine lines of discontent on her smooth forehead. They were two sides of his wife, each imbued with different characteristics, and he found in them Mumtaz Mahal's varied moods. At times she had been strong, at times arrogant and demanding, at times welcoming. Himself he saw only in Jahanara, and perhaps only because he loved her so much, because she, more than any of her siblings, had found the time to be by his side when he wanted her, listened with an interest he found lacking in the others, counselled him with a sagacity beyond her age.

'I find,' he said finally, 'that I miss your Mama less now . . . than before.' And when he had spoken, his words surprised even him. Was it true? But it was. The ache of Arjumand's loss had dulled and retreated into a corner of his heart, and he could summon it only by will. It did not swamp him as it had in the early days, render him unable to function. His every day was filled with routine, and there was so little time left to think of her now. He woke at four o'clock in the morning to dress for the early jharoka, slept for an hour afterward, sat at the public audience in the Diwan-i-am, presented himself at the afternoon jharoka before retiring to the zenana for his lunch and his duties to the ladies. Here, as his father and grandfather had done, he discussed their problems, found ways to solve them, gave orders on budgets and allowances. In the late afternoon, there was yet another public audience, and a sunset jharoka, and then a meeting with selected amirs at the Diwan-i-khas. News of every incident in his empire came to him through these varied sessions, brought by spies and runners from the outer reaches—even things as inconsequential as what governors had misused the funds from their territorial treasuries by heaping gifts on a serving maid or a dancing girl. Everything was written down, secreted in the archive vaults under Agra fort.

At night, he returned to his chambers in the harem for his meal, but his door, figuratively, was always open for reports of an immediate nature, and he was stirred from his dinner or his conversations with Jahanara or Dara to the antechamber outside the zenana, where he received the men not allowed in. He went to sleep at midnight, and, in those few minutes before he closed his eyes, he thought of Arjumand.

And now even the memory of her face had faded. He could remember it in the absolute in certain situations, but his everyday recall had grown fainter. The part of his heart where love for her had resided had come to rest upon Jahanara.

Because they had been silent he said, 'Did I shock you?'

'We know what you mean, Bapa,' Jahanara said.

'But she lives on, Bapa,' Roshanara said, 'in this Luminous Tomb you are building for her.'

Shah Jahan grunted softly. 'I think that it is the thought of her that will live; if this tomb survives through the ages, as I intend it will, it will be my name that will flourish.'

'And wasn't that your intention in constructing this monument to Mama?' Roshanara asked. 'I mean,' she hurried on, realizing what she had said, 'that it is your tribute to Mama, so you . . .'

Jahanara clicked her tongue and put a restraining hand on her sister's arm, and Shah Jahan felt a sliver of disgust at his child's candour, if it could be called that. She spoke quickly, without thought, as she acted sometimes. He wearied too often of her talk, because she talked only thus, and he found himself not wishing to reply to this blatant statement. Why could she not be more like her sister?

'Should we go up, Jahan?'

'It is too early,' Jahanara said, rising to go to the verandah arches, 'but it does not matter. Let's go.'

They ascended the inner stairs of the terrace from the Tahkhana to the top, and then onward still up a flight of marble stairs to the platform which would hold the tomb. In the liquid heat under cover of the white tents, the golden screen surrounding the empress's cenotaph glowed. They stood there, gazing at it in awe. Bibadal Khan, the superintendent of the imperial workshops, had been responsible for its construction. It was four feet high, built in linked panels to form an octagon. The screen was made of solid gold, finely wrought with flowers and enamel work, and weighed a little over a thousand pounds. As part of the interior decoration for this central chamber, Shah Jahan had also ordered gold latticework oil lamps in the shape of a crescent moon, the sun, and stars. The screen had been bolted to the marble floor two months ago, and for this 'urs, workers had set up poles to hang the lamps over the grave. The imperial party knelt on the cotton mattresses and said their prayers until the sun set in the west, painting the vast canvas of the skies above Agra in daubs of gold and bronze. In the gardens below, Emperor Shah Jahan had arranged for alms and enormous platters of sweets and savouries to be given to the gathered men. When they left, some six hours had passed since their arrival—the sum of two *pahrs,* two watches of the day.

Emperor Shah Jahan returned later that night and prayed at the site of his wife's grave for another pahr, alone on his knees, facing west, towards Mecca. He had grieved for Arjumand for two long years. No one would, or could, take her place in his heart and his affections, but he was lonely, craving a woman's gentle touch, the scent of a woman's body, her arms around his waist, an oblivion that had nothing special to do with love.

He left, dragging his feet, only forty-one years old this year, but sorrow had greyed the hair on his head and in his beard and weakened his eyesight. When he stumbled while descending the steps from the Tahkhana to the pier, his eunuch, Itimad Khan, steadied him and said, 'You have forgotten to wear your glasses, Your Majesty.'

And so he had. Shah Jahan fumbled in an inner pocket of his qaba and put on his glasses to see better where he was going. As the vessel departed for the ride up the river to the fort, he looked back at the place where the tomb for Arjumand would stand to remind him, and future generations, that here was a woman so beloved that her husband had built for her—soon to be silhouetted forever against the night sky—a Luminous Tomb.

twelve

Aureng-Zebe, the third brother, was devoid of that urbanity and engaging presence, so much admired in Dara. . . He was reserved, subtle, and a complete master of the art of dissimulation.

—ARCHIBALD CONSTABLE (ed.) AND IRVING BROCK (trans.), *Travels in the Mogul Empire, A.D. 1656–1668* by François Bernier

Agra
Saturday, 28 May 1633
19 Zi'l-Qa'da A.H. 1042

Two days after the second 'urs, Emperor Shah Jahan ordered an elephant fight. It was to take place in the main maidan, a field of beaten mud, smooth and freed from weeds by the hundreds of men who trod upon it daily during the evening jharoka, at the base of the battlements of Agra fort, some thirty feet below the balcony of the jutting Shah Burj.

When news had spread through Agra of the elephant fight, bookmakers had swarmed in, laying odds on which elephant would win, how soon after the fight began, whether the mahout of the winning elephant or the losing elephant would die; even whether the reserve mahout was likely to die. It was as though a pall had lifted from the empire. The Mughal emperors were all keen warriors and avid sportsmen, at home in the saddle, in a tent, on a battlefield, at a blood sport—and of the last, the elephant fight was the ultimate sport. But Empress Mumtaz Mahal's death had ended all amusements; the imperial orchestra had not played until Prince Dara's wedding, the maidans had lain empty of entertainment, nautch girls had been dismissed from the doors to the imperial zenana—life had been dismal.

An elephant fight was the supreme diversion in Mughal India, because it was the exclusive prerogative of the emperor—not even his sons could order one. Of all the animals Emperor Shah Jahan owned in quantities large enough to stable—the horses, the camels, the oxen, the mules—the elephants were the most revered. They were initially captured from the forests around India, and, from Emperor Jahangir's time, their keepers had begun to breed them in the imperial stables, leading to strain after strain of fine animals used in war, in peace, as beasts of burden, as mounts for the imperial ladies of the zenana, on construction sites, and, last, for the pleasure of the emperor in the fighting field. Each royal elephant had appointed for its care nine men and a boy, noted in the imperial registers as 'nine and a half men'—five to tend to its education, to teach it to bow and obey orders; a mahout, who was its caretaker and the man who rode the elephant; three men to feed, bathe and dress the elephant in its finery when presented at court; and finally a boy, who would sit at the back of the elephant with the mahout and assist him in managing the beast and take his place if needed.

The two elephants chosen for the fight in Agra were the imperial stables' best *mast* elephants, categorized as full-blooded. They were both young males, feisty and fiery, given to trumpeting at all hours and eager to pick a fight whenever they could, and their names were Sukhdar and Surat Sundar.

By the time the sun was centred in the sky over Agra, the maidan was teeming with people who had been waiting for a place at the proceedings since dawn. A thrum of excitement swept over them as the imperial orchestra, housed in its own balcony in the ramparts of the fort above, played its music, rousing the frenzy of the crowd. Money moved from hand to hand surreptitiously, as bets were made under the keen gaze of the imperial guards, who pretended not to notice. Everyone knew that the emperor did not approve of gambling for too-high stakes during elephant fights. Coloured flags strung on ropes swung down from the fort into the crowd, tethered to poles around the field. At the periphery of the ground, vendors did a brisk business in chicken kababs rolled in flat and fragrant naan; vegetables dipped in a chickpea-flour batter and deep-fried, served with a tangy tamarind chutney; jaggery-sweetened drinks of lime, khus and orange. There was a women's enclosure on the side of the Yamuna, towards the very end of the field, and here the wives, daughters, cousins and sisters of the more common men sat in a medley of colour—splashes of bright yellows, greens, blues, pinks, magenta.

The princes came first to the maidan, and their appearance was heralded by the imperial orchestra, which played a song of welcome. The crowd parted to let them through, and in many an eye there was awe and an admiration that Emperor Shah Jahan, their lord and their master, was possessed of such magnificent sons. And they *were* splendid, mounted on perfectly matched white steeds from the imperial stables, the bridles of silver and gold, velvet woven around the reins in their hands, diamonds embedded into the leather of their saddles. Dara rode first, solemn and upright, raising his hand to acknowledge the love directed towards him, the press of fervent gazes taking in the sight of their future emperor. He was newly married, this young man, and his responsibilities sat well upon his shoulders. Shuja received his share of adulation also, but it was more muted, although he smiled and nodded to the men. A ripple of laughter went through the people when they saw the youngest, Prince Murad, who was only nine this year, a child next to his brothers but with a stern expression that slipped when he smiled with delight at a juggler's monkey that sprang up from its master's arms and waved at the prince. After this his face lightened and he did not stop grinning.

Behind them was Prince Aurangzeb. In the two years since their mother's death, he had retreated into himself and his studies, and this was the character he adopted most of the time. The reading of the Quran gave him something to do as he waited to grow older, and he knew most of the verses by heart. He glanced at Dara's back, listened to the murmur of adulation from the people, and looked away again, his eyes smarting with tears. What was the matter with him? He had always known Dara to be so beloved among the masses; it was only at court, among the amirs, that this reverence was tempered with disapproval of his easy manners. And Dara was a fool, spending too much time with the Jesuit priest Father Busée, giving him far too much money for his churches and his missions, interested in every religion in a dabbling, casual way, and neglecting his own true faith of Islam.

Aurangzeb shifted in his saddle as they reined in their horses by the side of the maidan. The sun blighted the sky, turning its blue so pale that it was almost white, and the colours of the clothing, the glint of jewels from the turbans of the amirs gathered around the field, the sheen of metal in the horses' bridles, all gave him a headache. In this heat, without even the relief of a cool draft of air from the Yamuna—for it was a still, airless day—the smells were intensified, and Aurangzeb held his breath from time to time, trying not to inhale the odour of the perspiration that flowed freely on brows and dampened underarms and backs, the hot smell of frying, rancid oil, the stench of old perfume. His hands shook as he held the reins of his horse and relaxed only when a series of parasols, held aloft by servants on horses, came to shade him and his brothers. The imperial orchestra announced the coming of the emperor, and they all turned towards the Shah Burj, waiting for that first sight of his person. And when he appeared, the crowd roared, 'Padshah Salamat!' Once. Twice. Three times.

They all bent their heads and performed the taslim, raising their hands to their foreheads thrice and letting them fall. Even Aurangzeb drew in a breath when he saw his father and felt his heart tug in a way it had not since Mama's death with an overflowing gratitude that this man, so glorious, so patently a king, was his father.

Emperor Shah Jahan had finally divested himself of his mourning white, two years after his wife's death and two days after the celebration of the second anniversary. He wore a qaba of raw silk in the colour Emperor Jahangir had so favoured as appropriate for royalty, and it was the deep red of a brilliant sunset captured faithfully by the dyers in the imperial karkhanas. On his head was a turban of white silk, an aigrette pinned to the centre which was a three-hundred-carat diamond, an immaculate heron's feather springing from it. There were pearl necklaces, fifteen in all, strung in different sizes and varieties around his neck. His hands were jewelled with rubies, emeralds, pearls and diamonds. His qaba was studded with a thousand tiny diamonds so that, as he moved, his entire person seemed to be on fire. With all this magnificence, the crowds below did not notice the greying of his hair or the dimmed brilliance of his eyes. Here, finally, was the emperor they adored. In his splendour was their security. And so many a heart soared with pride and affection.

Aurangzeb felt the same, and it was an emotion that surprised him. If he had been asked whether he loved his father, he would have replied, and correctly, that there was no other option available to a dutiful son, but he had never thought of love as being anything but an obligation, and, for the first time in his fifteen years, he was proved wrong. Though only momentarily. Then the heat came to plague him again, his headache returned, the scene before him whitened to a haze. He rubbed the constricting collar of his qaba and wished for the coolness of the courtyard outside his apartments, where he could read for a while or listen to the petitions for charity that found their way to him. And then the trumpets from the Naubat Khana announced the arrival of Sukhdar and Surat Sundar, the two imperial elephants, the stars of the afternoon's show. Their mahouts sat balanced and proud upon their irritable charges, goaded them with their ankhs to kneel before the emperor, to raise their trunks to their foreheads in an imitation of the taslim.

The cool tang of fresh buffalo milk came to Aurangzeb's nose—the elephants had recently been bathed in this in preparation for their fight. Their hides were a thick, rubbery grey and cleaned meticulously. Their feet were already dusty, though; even the short trip from the stables to the maidan had muddied them to their knees. They both wore a minimum of finery, thick chains of gold with large rings crisscrossed over their backs and around their stomachs and necks; the chains had large, hoop-like rings to make it easier to string in a tether if one was needed during the fight. The ankhs that the mahouts held were also of solid gold, gleaming in the sunlight. The men themselves wore a sombre white, clad only in dhotis that covered their waists and were tucked between their legs; their chests were bare. A flutter of white at the edge of the field caught Prince Aurangzeb's eye, and he saw there the mahouts' wives, in a place reserved specially for them among all of these men. The sport was so deadly that the women had shed their colours, broken the bangles on their wrists, and wiped the partings in their hair of the vermilion powder that signified marriage. If the mahouts survived, a feast would be waiting to celebrate their resurrection from the dead. If they died, Bapa would pay their families a hundred times their monthly salaries and continue to pay the widows pensions for the rest of their lives. This was why the mahouts did what they did—for the love of money, for the love of the animals themselves, and for the excitement.

Aurangzeb's headache disappeared as quickly as it had come, and he felt his heart pound madly. He noticed Dara pulling his horse back as Sukhdar roared. A low mud wall had been built along the diameter of the maidan, and the fight would begin when the elephants were given the signal and crashed through the mud wall to confront each other. Shuja, Aurangzeb could not see, for by now his gaze was focused on the two mammoth beasts, snorting and pawing at the ground. How superb they were, though so ungainly, so without line or structure. He edged closer into the field, and one of the imperial guards put his spear across his path. 'Please stand back, Your Highness.'

Aurangzeb heard Murad's childish voice shout, in an abrupt and deep lull in the racket, 'Let the fight begin!' for it was the youngest prince's privilege to do so. The elephants seemed to have heard the signal also; they shook their massive heads, and, without the provocation of the ankhs, Sukhdar and Surat Sundar rumbled through the mud wall as though it had been a mere chiffon curtain and smashed their heads into each other. The wall disintegrated in a fine mist of dirt, which billowed outward and then dissipated, and Aurangzeb saw the elephants tilt their heads this way and that and charge at each other again, their mahouts clinging on. They were well matched, he thought, raising his voice to join the clamour of the crowd, as the elephants returned to each other again and again. Surat Sundar's mahout fell off the elephant and disappeared in the dust with an awkward flailing of limbs. From the white-clad women, a thin, keening wail rose and swept across to Aurangzeb's ear.

Frightened, shaken, and without a guide now, Surat Sundar turned to flee, plowing his way through the tightly packed hordes, but paths widened to admit him and closed behind him as the men watched what Sukhdar would do. He looked around, howled his anger, and charged towards the four glittering princes on horseback.

As the infantrymen of the imperial army, clad in full armour, their shields held aloft, struggled to maintain their places, the crowd of men pushed them away. Everyone flew out of the elephant's way, and all of a sudden, one lone man found himself confronting Sukhdar.

Prince Aurangzeb felt his heart stop and his hands grow cold around his reins. Dara had fled along with the crowd. Sadullah Khan, the Grand Vizier of the empire, had yanked at Prince Murad's reins and pulled him to the side, and where Shuja was, Aurangzeb did not know. He was alone in all that din, voices wailing and crying, and he clearly heard Jahanara and his father shout out his name, telling him to flee. He looked up and saw them both leaning over the balcony of the Shah Burj. Aurangzeb bent down to snatch a spear from a passing soldier and flung it with all his strength at Sukhdar. It hit the elephant between the eyes, and three inches of the spear's pointed tip pierced the animal's tough hide. Sukhdar bawled in pain, and with his mighty trunk he whacked at Aurangzeb, thudded into his horse instead, and sent the animal flying a few feet. Aurangzeb was flung off the horse. He rose shakily to his feet and stood in the field, his fingers scrambling for the dagger in his cummerbund, but he knew even then that it was little defence against the mammoth animal.

Sukhdar rushed in again, and Aurangzeb saw Shuja ride towards the animal, yelling all the while until it stopped in distraction. That brief moment was enough. The elephant keepers, who had come armed with their *chakris* for just such a possibility, lit the two ends of their bamboo canes, which were filled with gunpowder. The canes swung around on their central axes, held up on poles, spitting fire and light, the gunpowder booming as it caught flame. Raja Jai Singh came to Shuja's aid now, peeling away from the crowd, his spear ready. He flung the spear to wound Sukhdar and jabbed at the enraged beast with his sword. The elephant tossed him to the ground and lifted a massive foot to crush him where he lay. Just then, Surat Sundar returned, butting Sukhdar from the back with a tremendous force, and his crushing foot came down a few inches from Jai Singh's head. The two elephants turned on each other, and Aurangzeb pushed his way through to haul the Raja out of the field and into the crowd.

'Thank you, Your Highness,' Jai Singh muttered, his face pale, his right arm swinging awkwardly by his side.

'I must thank you instead,' Aurangzeb said. 'I will remember that you saved my life. Now'—he touched Jai Singh on his shoulder—'Wazir Khan should look at that arm.'

'Later,' the Raja said. 'After we are done here.'

The fight went on for twenty more minutes until the unseated mahouts came to collect their charges, to part them with fireworks and torches, to calm them by leading them to the waters of the Yamuna and plunging them in until their blood cooled.

In the quiet that came afterward, Emperor Shah Jahan yelled from the balcony at Aurangzeb. 'What madness was this, beta? To stand in the path of an elephant and court death? You should have fled as the others did.'

Prince Aurangzeb turned stiffly to his father, bowed, and said in a voice that had not lost its quaver, 'Bapa, death comes even to emperors. There is no shame in that. The shame lies in what my brothers did.'

Only a few people at the base of the Shah Burj heard this statement. Dara did, and he flushed at the implication that he was a coward. Shuja bristled, because he *had* come to Aurangzeb's aid. Both Sadullah Khan and Raja Jai Singh mulled over what their prince had said, and when they raised their glances to that slight, boyish figure staring up at his father, they were thoughtful.

Long after the maidan had been cleared, during the brief twilight that swung over Agra, Jahanara stood by one of the pillars of the Shah Burj, her arms around it. Below, she heard the sweep of brooms as workers cleared the ground strewn with broken paper flags, cummerbunds wrenched off during the melee, plantain leaves that had held the kabab skewers. By morning, when her father appeared for his jharoka, it would all be pristine again. Her brow was furrowed with a frown. What *had* Aurangzeb meant by those words? She had seen the two ministers, even Raja Jai Singh, clutching his useless arm, his face wrought with pain, look at him with . . . admiration.

'Your Highness.' Ishaq Beg came up behind her and waited.

'Yes,' she said. 'I know. Is everything ready?'

He inclined his head and let her pass. Jahanara went back to her apartments slowly. Aurangzeb had said that death came even to emperors—as though he thought of himself thus. As though he already was one, even before his father had been buried.

Music drifted through Princess Jahanara's apartments, sweet and dulcet, a sitar, a pair of castanets, the low throb of a tabla, accompanying a woman's rich, throaty voice. The princess had hosted a dinner for her victorious brother Aurangzeb on the night of the elephant fight and invited all her other brothers, their wives, Roshanara, and their father. The dinner cleared, they sat now around the room on silk-upholstered divans, silent and uneasy. The orchestra was behind a screen, with only the singer's shape lightly visible, backlit by oil diyas. The walls of Jahanara's apartments had been carved plentifully with square niches, and in each a lone lamp burned, its wick vertical and steady. The floors were carpeted, wall to wall, with thin layers of jute matting overlaid with cotton mattresses and then rugs from Isfahan. Flimsy curtains, seemingly made more of air than of fabric, screened the arches that fronted the Yamuna. They hung still, their folds quiescent, not even the shadow of a breeze to incite them into movement.

They had eaten well from a menu of Jahanara's choice, cooked earlier by the imperial chefs in the kitchen attached to the harem—golden curries of lamb and goat, warm from the fires and still simmering as they were set before them; carrots and cucumbers in salads dressed with lime juice and peanut oil, sprinkled with browned cumin seeds; chicken biryani steamed in an earthenware pot with a string of kneaded dough to seal the lid and keep the rice moist until it came to rest upon their tongues; the best Kashmiri wines from the cool cellars below the fort's walls spiced with cardamom, star anise and cloves. For dessert they had a simple wheat-flour halva, cooked in ghee and sugar syrup, clad in raisins and fried cashews. The dancing girls came in when dessert was being served, and after they left, Jahanara signalled to the eunuchs to deposit the gold platters with the makings of paan—betel leaves and nuts, slivers of pure beaten silver, sugar cubes, and cloves to bind the betel leaves into a parcel.

'Ask them to leave,' Emperor Shah Jahan said.

And that was enough for all the servants. They bowed and slipped out of the apartments, and then only the emperor and his children were left. The singer lowered her voice when Jahanara raised her hand. She was part of Jahanara's personal orchestra, a woman who had been with the princess for five years now, who knew all of her mistress's various moods and just what song or verse would soothe them.

'What is it, Bapa?' Jahanara asked gently. They were all agitated and edgy, and it was not from the fright of the afternoon's elephant fight. Dara had glowered through the meal, eating with a stolid intensity, barely even acknowledging his father's presence. Nadira sat by his side, placid as ever, calling attention to herself only when she put a hand up to her nose to ward off the aromas from the food or openly sucked on a wedge of dried mango. She was pregnant, she had said, and Jahanara had heard the news with gladness and a little envy. A child would bring them all together, and a male child would be an heir to the empire. Shuja and his wife were taciturn, as was Aurangzeb, but in his silence was a pride they could not miss. His right cheek flamed from a cut; his back was bruised, and so he wore only a thin cotton kurta; and there was a bandage on his ankle where his leg had been twisted when he was thrown off his horse.

Only Murad chatted on, reliving the fight with every word, unconscious of the mood of the room. Roshanara, seated next to Aurangzeb, carried on a one-sided conversation in an undertone, answered only by grunts. But she did not seem to mind her brother's rudeness, Jahanara thought; instead, a glow of something—triumph perhaps—filled her face.

Bapa sat with his head bowed. Between dinner and dessert he had called for the zenana's scribe, an elderly woman, and given her orders that would be transmitted to the imperial court's writers the next morning. In three days, they would observe Aurangzeb's fifteenth birthday, and the celebrations were to be grand—if Jahanara could have spoken, she would have said that they would befit a king. He was to be given the same privileges Bapa had as

Emperor on the occasion of his birthday—an imperial weighing. Massive gold-beam balance scales, eight feet in height, were to be rolled into the Diwan-i-am, and Aurangzeb would step onto one scale pan, and the other would be weighted down, alternately, with bags of silver rupees, milk, flour, sugar, ghee, dried fruits, silks and clothing. He would then distribute these items himself to the poor outside, doling out alms as if he were the master of those men gathered with their arms outstretched for their king's bounty. Bapa would give him a *khilat,* a robe of honour, studded with jewels, all to be made in the space of three days, with a hundred seamstresses employed in the task of piecing together this precious coat. He would also give him a gold dagger and five thousand rupees in gold mohurs. For Shuja, for his bravery in this incident, there would be another khilat and a dagger.

Aurangzeb had risen from his seat when the scribe left and kissed his father's hand. Then, he had resumed eating, his normally sombre face splitting into smiles as though he could not help himself.

'I do not like this dissent among you,' Emperor Shah Jahan said finally. 'Dara—'

'Bapa,' Dara said heatedly, talking for the first time since he had greeted all of them, 'Aurangzeb didn't do anything special. It was reckless of him to risk his life in front of a charging elephant; why does he deserve the weighing on his birthday? You have never given me that privilege.'

Shah Jahan frowned. 'It's not your place to question my orders, Dara. If Aurangzeb was thoughtless, he was at least brave and courageous, while you turned your horse's head and escaped. You should be commending him. But I did not begin this conversation to answer you, only to say this: the four of you are blood brothers, born of the same father and mother. When you are emperor . . . *if* you are emperor after me, it will be your responsibility to take care of your brothers, to provide them with ranks at court befitting their status. And the rest of you must revere your oldest brother, support him in all of his endeavours. To the empire—and as we *are* the empire—we must represent a united family.'

'I did as much as Aurangzeb, Bapa,' Shuja muttered.

'Not quite as much,' Emperor Shah Jahan said, 'but enough for you to deserve a khilat. Aurangzeb'—the emperor turned to face him now—'what I say here applies to you also. Think more of others, beta, than of yourself. And show your smugness a little less; such an expression is improper in a royal prince.'

They all reddened. For two years Bapa had almost neglected them, and they had grown wild in their hearts, so to have him speak with such candour about thoughts they had only harboured in secret made them ashamed. But it was a short-lived shame, for they were more independent now of their father—and their dead mother—than they had been two years ago.

'Itimad,' Emperor Shah Jahan said in a weary voice. And when his eunuch bowed into the room, he said, 'Bring them in.'

Twenty-five women came into Princess Jahanara's apartments and lined up against one wall. They were clad in thin muslins, their legs bare and muscled under the sheer gowns of their peshwaz, their eyes outlined in kohl, their hair perfumed and aglitter with a freshly washed shine. In his younger days, when his wife had been pregnant, as she had been so often in their marriage, Mumtaz Mahal had allowed Emperor Shah Jahan to pick a woman from the imperial zenana for the night. Any woman he wanted or was attracted to. And in the morning, she had pensioned off the woman and banished her from the imperial zenana, so that her husband would never again see her or enjoy her charms.

With his children watching, Emperor Shah Jahan deliberated. He did not leave his seat or even change his position on the divan. The singing had stopped, and for a whole five minutes, the only sounds Jahanara could hear were Dara's and Shuja's discontented breaths, Aurangzeb grinding his teeth, Roshan with her legs stretched out in front of her, her toes tapping dully against each other. Then her father pointed. To Jahanara, the choice seemed unclear, and, yet, the others bowed and left the apartments. The emperor raised himself from the divan and went out. The woman hesitated, then followed her king to his chambers.

Jahanara put her hands over her face, her skin warm under her fingers. She could no longer recall instances when her father had spent the night, or a part of it, with a woman other than her mother, even though she must have seen this occur often enough. But in the last two years, he had been so completely . . . *hers,* she thought, a tear escaping to wet her face, that she had forgotten he was a man also. Her brothers and sister departed, mumbling their farewells, their voices subdued. But Princess Jahanara Begam stayed on her divan, sobbing quietly, her heart filled with an ache. When the pain had lessened, she realized what Bapa had done—taught them all a lesson in kingship. It was not in the choosing of a slave to pleasure him for a few hours—that in itself was inconsequential; this was her father's zenana, and the women not related to him by marriage or by blood were his to use as he pleased. And he could well have done this in his chambers, so that only the morning would bring the news to them, and they would shrug, accept it, and go on.

But Emperor Shah Jahan had paraded his women in front of his squabbling children, each itching to wear the crown, or to be able to determine who would wear the crown after him, as though he had already lost his life. So he had ordered the women, considered one carefully (although he had decided earlier; this much was clear to Jahanara from the casual pointing), and waited until they knew and realized that he was still, very much, the emperor, sovereign not just over the lands and the people of Hindustan but over them also. Mama was dead; Bapa had left off mourning for her and exercised his right as the master of his harem.

Jahanara rose, walked to the outer verandah, and looked at the blurred lights on the other bank of the Yamuna. It was a close and uncomfortable night, as hot as the day had been, without a trace of wind. Earlier, she had watched Mirza Najabat Khan in the courtyard below, but he had not even deigned to glance up or acknowledge her presence. She had not asked for him to visit her again after that afternoon spent in futile waiting in the zenana gardens. She had not asked whether her letter had gone astray; she knew Ishaq would have deposited it in Najabat Khan's hands himself.

She said without turning, 'Ishaq, are you there?'

Her eunuch came forward from the shadows to listen to his mistress, and if he was surprised, his expression betrayed nothing. And so, for the first time, Princess Jahanara Begam took a lover.

rauza-i-munavvara
The Luminous Tomb

And from all parts of the empire, there were assembled great numbers of skilled stonecutters (sangtarash), lapidaries (munabbatkar), and inlayers (parchingar), each one an expert in his art, who commenced work along with other craftsmen.

—From the *Padshah Nama* of Abdal-Hamid Lahauri, in
W.E. BEGLEY AND Z.A. DESAI,
Taj Mahal: The Illumined Tomb

Agra
Saturday, 23 July 1633
16 Muharram A.H. 1043

As the birds stirred in the trees and the indigo of the sky disintegrated into the coming dawn, two men stood on the sandstone platform of the Great Gate and looked down the gardens to the riverfront terrace.

Work for the day had not yet begun, and in this moment of peace, the men were motionless and thoughtful. The previous day's stultifying heat had died in the darkness, and it was coolest now, just before the break of dawn. The air was unsullied, scented with the imperceptible aroma of the budded ketki flowers that some worker had planted around the platform. When the sun rose, the flowers would unfurl themselves in spiky petals, each the size of a man's arm to his elbow, and send their heady aroma into the scorching air.

'Will this indeed be a paradise on earth, Mirza Amanat Khan?' the older man asked. He towered five inches above his companion. Ustad Ahmad Lahori had reached his sixty-second year on this earth, and most of those years had been spent in service to the Mughal emperors of Hindustan.

Amanat Khan laughed, the lines deepening around his mouth. He was not young himself, fifty-seven, but he was robust, stocky, and a man of means. This showed in the fine thin silk of his qaba; the gleam of diamonds on his expressive hands when he moved them in the dull light; the clean bouquet of sandalwood that curled around him, indicative of a bath; slave girls at his bidding; a palanquin to transport him so he did not have to waste energy in sweat.

'You are the architect, Ustad Ahmad,' Amanat Khan said, bowing to his companion. 'It is your hand that has fashioned this masterpiece, your name that will blaze in the minds of those men who will behold this wonder after we are dead, your—'

'I beg your pardon, Mirza Amanat,' Ahmad said, 'but you must not speak thus of our emperor's most precious possession. Our lord is the one who has planned every aspect of this tomb, it is his hand that scurried in glory across my meagre sketches, changing lines of the building here, the aspect of the mosque and the assembly hall there. He has consulted extensively with the landscapers and given us his ideas on where to plant the cypresses, the guavas, the oranges, the frangipani, so that each might bloom in one part of the garden to best showcase the empress's final resting place. I am merely his servant. And, I beg of you again, please do not call me ustad; I feel as though that title belongs to someone else. I am merely Ahmad Mim'ar—Ahmad the architect.'

Amanat Khan looked up at the man he had called a master at his craft. Ahmad Lahori had been born in Lahore, hence his name, and had attached himself at an early age to Mir Abdal Karim, who was currently Superintendent of Buildings under

Emperor Shah Jahan. This humble man was a classically trained academic, a thinker, an engineer, an architect, skilled at subjects that Amanat had never been able to fathom deeply when he was younger—astronomy, mathematics and geometry. Amanat had seen the completed plans for the Taj Mahal and had marvelled at the meticulous detail laid out by Ahmad Lahori, measurements down to an inch on every monument in the complex, thorough notes on the construction of the foundations, the consistency of the mortar that bound the slabs of sandstone and marble together, the panels for the inscriptions, and the dado panels inside and outside the marble tomb. And he denied himself the designation ustad—master—one he so richly deserved.

'You, Mirza Amanat Khan,' Ahmad Lahori said, 'will be better known. I am merely going to create the structure that will house your immense talent. An architect can be nothing in the eyes of Allah compared to the calligrapher who will inscribe phrases in praise of Him.'

And that was to be Amanat Khan's duty in the building of the Luminous Tomb. Because he was a calligrapher, because his work was to pick out the suras that would adorn the panels of the tomb, set them in writing in his beautifully formed script, supervise their printing on the marble—black agate inlaid in the white—he was revered more, granted his title of Amanat Khan and a rank of a thousand horses by His Majesty. Amanat Khan had come to India only in 1608, when he was in his early thirties and already established as a calligrapher and a scholar in Shiraz. Both he and his brother Afzal Khan had left their homeland of Persia in search of fortune and economic security in the Mughal Empire, as so many of their fellow men had done in years past. Their rise had been swift, almost astounding to the other amirs at court. Although they had both been well educated and men of letters, Afzal had always been more of a soldier and a warrior than Amanat. He had entered as such in Emperor Jahangir's service, become a favourite of the emperor, and dropped a word in Jahangir's ear about his brother's genius. As a result, the first monument of any importance

Amanat Khan had signed his name on as a calligrapher had been Emperor Akbar's tomb in Sikandra.

Afzal had subsequently—with a prescience Amanat could still not understand completely—given his allegiance to the then Prince Khurram, who was in disgrace with his father. But in the end, Khurram became Shah Jahan, and Afzal had recently been made the Diwan-i-kul, Prime Minister of the Mughal Empire, and on this new morning in 1633, Amanat Khan found himself also with a new title and the honour of adorning Empress Mumtaz Mahal's tomb with the calligraphy that would make him famous for the rest of time.

Hence Ustad Ahmad Lahori's deference to him—as brilliant an architect as he was, called upon to help with the emperor's most treasured wish to construct this Luminous Tomb, Lahori was in the end but an exalted worker, with his fingers grimed by the mud and mortar that would build this tomb.

But Amanat Khan would not allow this obsequiousness. He bowed to the older man and said, 'I hear His Majesty has charged you with another commission?'

Ahmad Lahori's mouth split into a slow and satisfied smile. 'He wishes to build an entire new city at Delhi and make it his capital. It will be called after His Majesty—Shahjahanabad. Emperor Akbar has this city'—he gestured around him to mean Agra—'he has left his mark upon it, and his grandson will leave his stamp on another. I am drawing up the plans right now, when I can get away from here to work two or three hours at night.'

'You have the vigour of three younger men put together, Ustad Ahmad Lahori,' Amanat Khan said wistfully. 'I have no doubt that Shahjahanabad is going to be a marvel for all, but this'—he gestured towards the void on the marble platform of the riverfront terrace and drew the curves and lines of the tomb's main dome—'is why we were put on this earth by Allah.'

In the end, these two men, and Mir Abdal Karim and Makramat Khan—the Diwan-i-buyutat, the Superintendent of Public Works for the empire—met every day for the next decade to pore over plans for the tomb, check for inconsistencies, make adjustments to the measurements as the work progressed, beg for audiences with their emperor so that they could discuss the changes and have them approved and execute them. By the time this lustrous mausoleum had taken root in the ground and all of its various components had been completed, the four men were to one another more akin than blood brothers. They knew one another's joys and pains, celebrated together the births of grandchildren, mourned ones lost to death, breathed as though with one breath. Of the four of them, only Amanat Khan would leave his signature embedded in marble in the tomb, but it belonged—if it could be said to belong at all to any person but its patron, Emperor Shah Jahan—to all of them. They had sweated over their creation, buried workers killed in accidents, sat in dumbfounded awe on chill moonlit nights as their vision glimmered a serene white and seemed to reach out and embrace them in a blessing. They knew, with the instinct of highly trained men, experts at their crafts—nay, virtuosos of their crafts—that nowhere else in the world would there be a monument such as this.

The tomb was built on a thin marble plinth, which sat on the marble platform on which the second 'urs had taken place. Emperor Shah Jahan had wanted it to be in white marble, each stone perfectly matched, but Ahmad Lahori had pointed out, in his gentle way, that the gradations of pale colour would provide a better contrast, frame the work, create an interest that pure white could not do. 'And from afar, Your Majesty, even from as near as the Great Gate, looking down the gardens at the *rauza,* no one will be able to distinguish differences in the stone—that will be evident only upon stepping up closer, on the marble platform itself.'

And so it was. The tomb was constructed of white marble with a marble central dome and four smaller domes on its flat roof. There were four main *pishtaqs*—portals—facing north, south, east and west, identical to one another to create a trompe l'oeil effect so that a person standing at any point around the Taj

Mahal would not be able to tell which was the true entry. The main entrance was the southern pishtaq, with its huge arched portal. Amanat Khan would exercise his calligraphy on three buildings in the main complex—the tomb itself, the mosque on the same platform, and the Great Gate. Around the portal of the main entrance to the tomb was a rectangular band of marble inlaid with inscriptions from the Quran, the thirty-sixth sura—*Ya Sin*. And it was on the inside of the tomb, on the southern arch again, that Amanat Khan had engraved in Persian, 'Written by the son of Qasim al-Shirazi . . . Abd al-Haqq, entitled Amanat Khan . . . in the year 1045 Hijri.'

The inscriptions were all in the *sulus* script in Arabic. Amanat Khan used the official court language of Persian only on the epitaph on Empress Mumtaz Mahal's cenotaph and to sign his work.

Ahmad Lahori had provided for an underground burial chamber, where the empress's body was interred and covered by an elaborate marble cenotaph with inlay. In the central and upper room of the tomb there was another, more magnificent cenotaph—a false one, meant to deceive possible tomb marauders. This room was octagonal, entirely clad in white marble, with eight arches on each of its walls in two stories, the top layer of arches mimicking the bottom layer. Only three of the archways were perforated with windows that covered the entire arch; the other four were blank, and one was the entry into the tomb. The windows were paned with sheer glass from Aleppo, in shades of jade and nephrite, the cool greens bringing the verdure of the outside inside, the colour of the light percolating into the white marble in the chamber, so that it seemed as though Empress Mumtaz Mahal rested, indeed, in the garden of Paradise. The floor was paved with marble, with a mosaic of black stone stars. A marble railing inlaid with carnelian and jade, with delicate marble screens in between cut in the shapes of flowers and circles, replaced the original gold railing upon Emperor Shah Jahan's orders, for he thought one night of the foolishness of placing so much heavy gold in full sight of every visitor—marble had a lesser value and so was less enticing to steal.

The gold latticework lamps, also commissioned at the time of the gold railing, remained, however.

The tomb had white marble dado panels both inside and outside in the pishtaqs, which were decorated with flowers in relief, their details so precise and botanical—stamens, pistils sepals and petals—that they would fool many a man into thinking they represented some actual flowers grown in Hindustan and not, as was more often true, a fancy of the artist. Ahmad Lahori had supervised even this small item in his building of the tomb and had sat over the wizened men, their fingers, faces, eyebrows and noses clogged with the fine white dust that rose as their chisels cracked away at the stone. When they had presented the first dado panel to him, he had been astonished by their handiwork—these men who let their skills out for hire wherever the empire demanded it—and let them sign the work thus with their imaginations.

The false cenotaph in the public upper chamber was in white marble, the colour of freshly drawn milk, inlaid profusely with stylized flowers in tiers—a lapis lazuli blue, a jasper red, a bloodstone black, an agate and sard brown, a carnelian orange, a chlorite and jade green, and a yellow limestone. The top tier had a band of marble inlaid with Quranic inscriptions, which Amanat Khan chose with care—as he did for every part of the tomb, the mosque, and the Great Gate.

They were still standing in the Great Gate when the sun broke into the sky and sent its rays to imbue the empty gardens of the Taj Mahal with a rosy hue as the light echoed off the sandstone walls.

'You see how splendid it is going to be, Ustad Lahori?' Amanat Khan demanded. 'All radiance, a sensation, Paradise indeed. And I am proud to be in partnership with you.'

'Thank you,' Ahmad Lahori said, and for once he did not protest the use of the title; it was as though he finally accepted his own brilliance. He spoke again, so softly that Amanat Khan had to lean inward to hear the words that dropped from Lahori's lips. 'A Luminous Tomb'.

thirteen

I . . . hope I shall not be suspected of a wish to supply subjects for romance . . . but . . . It is said, then, that Begam-Saheb, although confined in a Seraglio, and guarded like other women, received the visits of a young man of no very exalted rank, but of an agreeable person.

—ARCHIBALD CONSTABLE (ed.) AND IRVING BROCK (trans.), *Travels in the Mogul Empire, A.D. 1656–1668* by François Bernier

Agra
Wednesday, 12 October 1633
8 Rabi' al-thani A.H. 1043

Jahanara waited in the private gardens attached to her apartments, elbows on the stone baluster set in the fort's walls, her face cupped in her palms. From here, she could just discern the thin thread of the Yamuna winding its way down to the site of the Luminous Tomb. The dying end of a torrid summer, and the river's waters had receded, leaving wide banks of sand and packed silt, and somewhere in this newly acquired land there was the flicker of a cooking fire. Princess Jahanara Begam could not see the people around the fire; they sat outside its feeble rim of light to keep away from its warmth. Every now and then, a woman would step forward, stir the pot over the flames, and step back again. Each time she did that, an aroma of garlic, ginger and onions swirled upward to the princess. The cook was the singer, she thought, for each time she moved, the singing stopped. And then it began again, a lusty, guttural voice, full of promise, picking out the words in a folk song to the accompaniment of a faint dholak. It was a song about lovers—Laila and Majnu, both members of a Bedouin tribe in Arabia in the seventh century. Majnu was a shepherd in the tribe, and when he fell in love with Laila, her father did not consent to a marriage, so her hand was given elsewhere. Demented with grief, Majnu wandered out of the encampment one night and was never seen again, but desert travellers heard his voice even to this day, reciting verses in praise of his beloved.

The woman below finished her song, and a silence followed from her companions as the last notes of the dholak rumbled into the dark. Jahanara leaned out as far as she could to see if she could identify the singer. She would ask Ishaq Beg to bring her into the harem one day so she could perform for the ladies; there was a lovely, haunting quality to her voice, and though Jahanara had heard the story many times, in prose and in song, she had never heard it like this. Then, in the dark of the night, she flushed, remembering why she was here. Her hands were cold but steady, and it surprised her. For she waited for a man who would teach her what it was to love.

'Your Highness,' he said quietly behind her, and she turned.

He was the son of the lead singer in her personal orchestra and had come into the imperial zenana many times, slipping past the guards, in disguise, shedding his veil and skirts once inside. Jahanara had laughed with admiration when she first saw him, and then in a detached manner, observing a man not of the family at such close quarters. Since, he had come again and again, and his tenor lent a charm to the women's voices, his person was pleasing. She looked at him, thinking only that she had made the right choice for this night. He was tall, slender at the waist but muscled on his arms and his back. He kept his strong face shaven clean, had thick eyebrows, sparkling black eyes, loose and gleaming curls that framed his cheekbones. He wore gold studs in his ears—Jahanara had given these to him one evening—and his hands were immaculate, the nails trimmed.

There was about his mouth a small droop bespeaking weakness of character and an expression of pride at having been summoned here. That he would come, Jahanara had known, and she had not anticipated any of the humiliation she had felt when Mirza Najabat Khan left her waiting. But this man was a musician's son, and Najabat Khan was an amir at court—breeding would tell, she thought. And all she wanted from him was a night, perhaps more if he pleased her. From Najabat Khan . . . No, it was madness to think of what she so patently could not have.

'It is a lovely night, Your Highness. We have lost the moon, but the stars shed the light of a thousand sparkling diamonds.'

Jahanara tilted her head to gaze up into the night sky, and, as she did, he moved closer to her, his feet crushing the ground cover of thyme. She began to tremble then and wonder if she was doing the right thing. She was thankful that he did not touch her, merely looked out at the river.

'Are you hungry?' she asked when she was calmer.

'We do not need to do this, Your Highness,' he said, sombre, reflective. 'I will leave when you command, never return if you do not wish it, and never speak of what happened here—it will be as though it did not take place at all.'

'Thank you,' she said. 'You are kind, more than I expected. But'—and for the first time, she met his eyes—'I intend for . . . this to happen. Only . . . I do not know what to do.'

He smiled, and she shivered at the intensity of his gaze upon her. She put out her hand, and he took it in his warm one. He was the first man other than Najabat, not a father, not a brother, not an uncle, to caress her in something akin to love. They walked away from the edge of the garden into the lawn. The pathways were framed in small gold diyas, their tiny flames vertical in the still air. The verdant patch of grass was also dotted with diyas, and along one corner, framed by a sandstone arbour wound with thickly blooming jasmines, was a divan, covered in silk sheets and strewn with bolsters. There were silver trays of fruit and paan by the divan, green and purple grapes, lush slices of melons under a silver netted sheet, the tiny apples from Kashmir that Mumtaz Mahal had been fond of.

They drank a goblet of wine each, and Jahanara felt bold enough to reach out and touch his face. He kissed her palm. When he undid the front laces of her white chiffon peshwaz, she did not protest. She was wearing five layers of chiffon, each a colour from the rainbow, the weave so fine that each garment could be pulled through one of the rings on her fingers. They barely covered her, but as he loosened her clothing, for the first time he let his eyes wander over more than her face. By this time, her shyness had fled.

In the verandahs that bordered the gardens, eunuchs stood on guard, their backs turned. They were deaf to the sounds. And although questions would buzz around their ears from the next morning on, they were mute forever. The Begam Sahib had, figuratively, a gilded sword's blade against their necks—it was more than their lives were worth for them to talk.

Some time later, the man rose, arranged his clothing, and, though he very much wanted to, did not dare to bend and kiss his princess's slender foot, which nudged against him as he stood by the bed looking down upon her.

'Go now,' she said, her eyes shining. She did not thank him. For even in the short time that she had learned about love, she knew that she had given him as much pleasure as he had her.

When he had left, she rested her cheek against her hand and thought of what they had done. Her skin tingled with feeling, alive and aflame, and she felt tired, though pleasantly so. *This* was the pleasure the women of the imperial zenana sought so assiduously, risking meetings in gardens with men they did not know, imprisonment if the emperor heard, or perhaps worse, death by being pinned under a merciless sun for hours. It had been relatively easy to bring this man inside the harem, for there were—always had been—easy routes. Tunnels and back staircases, greedy palms waiting to be weighted with gold mohurs, mouths that would not flap. This Jahanara had always known, for she had grown up in an imperial zenana, and since Mama's death, when she had become supreme in the harem, she had turned away from the gossip about Bapa's numerous slaves and concubines. Though she had listened carefully and noted down each infraction, she kept that knowledge only for future use—if that need arose. She did not care that the gossip would now be about her, for what could they do? she thought. What would they *dare* to do? She was the Begam Sahib.

Her heart emptied of feeling when she thought of Najabat Khan, of how she could have been with him tonight if he had wanted, if he had only come the other day . . . for this was all they could have now. Bapa would never let her marry, in fact—and her lip curled in distaste—he had hinted, no, said outright, that Roshan was in love with Mirza Najabat Khan. What was Roshan compared to *her*? Then an ache came to settle in her, tinged with a modicum of self-pity, but she brushed it away; she had deeply enjoyed herself tonight, forgotten her cares, and not been worried about being in love . . . and being hurt, or disappointed. Perhaps it was better this way.

By the time she slept, the whole harem had heard of Jahanara Begam's visitor and that he had spent hours in her garden, on a divan, under a sky of stars that glittered like newly faceted stones. The news did not filter into Emperor Shah Jahan's apartments—yet—because the women were afraid, because his reaction was wholly unpredictable. Jahanara was not a wife or a concubine but a daughter, one so powerful that her father might well forgive her for snatching a few moments of gratification—the only thing he could not give her himself. Most of the women knew better than to credit the rumours about Shah Jahan and Jahanara. But they talked through the night, waking each other with impulsively thought-of comments, putting together with greedy avidity the few facts they had been told. What they had not heard, their imaginations supplied—for there was only one act between a man and a woman in the dark.

Later that year, Emperor Shah Jahan sent Prince Shah Shuja to the Deccan, ostensibly to oversee the campaign there and attack the fortress at Parenda. He left in great state, at the head of an infantry fifty thousand strong and a matching cavalry with horses, elephants and heavy artillery. The Deccan campaign was merely an excuse to send Shuja away, and they all—Dara, Jahanara, Shuja, Aurangzeb and Roshanara—recognized that. Although Mahabat Khan, the Khan-i-khanan, who had been left at Burhanpur to continue the Deccan wars when the imperial family had returned a year ago to Agra, had sent numerous missives to his Emperor for assistance, promising victory if it arrived.

There were amirs enough at court who would have been glad to escort the imperial army to Burhanpur, but Emperor Shah Jahan had insisted that a prince must be in the lead, and who better than Shuja, newly married and settled in his personal life—it was now time for him to take on princely responsibilities.

'Dara does not want to go, Bapa?' Shuja had been bold enough to ask his father one day. They were walking to the morning jharoka together; it was Shuja's day to accompany his father. Ever since that first jharoka after their mother had died, by tacit consent, one or another of them had always been at their father's side—if Jahanara and Roshanara went, they stayed behind the curtain screening the balcony; if one of the sons went, they stood behind their father and listened as he was approached with appeals and given news.

Shah Jahan hesitated and then continued walking as he put an arm about his son's shoulders. 'Beta, you must do something. You are a man now, married, with a child on the way. In my grief for your Mama, I have been remiss in giving all of you duties in the empire. My father sent me on campaign at a very early age, and I learned on the field what it was to be in charge of an army of men, to be accountable for their lives, to teach them to obey my every wish. This will be your first command, but with Mirza Mahabat Khan to guide you in warfare—and he is an able general—you will be victorious in sacking Parenda. If we are to make any forays into the Deccani kingdoms, Parenda must fall to us first.'

'I understand, Bapa,' Shuja said, shaking his head all the same in his ponderous way, 'and am grateful for the honour.' He stood back as the eunuchs lifted the curtain and Emperor Shah Jahan stepped through onto the jharoka balcony. Today, the horizon glowed with an early dawn, and as the Naubat Khana played its music to announce Shah Jahan's presence, the cries of 'Padshah Salamat!' escalated around them. Shuja slipped in behind his father and, under cover of the noise, said, 'Why is Dara not going?'

It seemed to him that his father had not heard what he said, for the emperor was a long time in answering. As the Mir Arz, the Master of Ceremonies at the jharoka and in the imperial durbar, read out the petitions, Shah Jahan nodded his responses or lifted his hand. He turned sideways and said, 'I thought you would prefer to be sent.'

'Oh, I do, Bapa,' Shuja replied. It was the only thing he could say, for no one dared to protest the emperor's orders—even if, and Prince Shah Shuja's mouth twisted deprecatingly—even if he was a royal prince and son of the emperor. Having grown up in the imperial court, Shuja knew that the empire's beating heart lay where the emperor was, and being sent away from court, even for glory on the battlefield, meant a loosening foothold in the empire's core. He had three brothers, and they could well steal their father's affections from him, and when he returned (if he came back at all to court for more than a brief visit), what would be his standing with the nobles? His entire circle of influence would diminish, be restricted to the generals and soldiers with whom he associated.

In his heart, as did the others, Shah Shuja wanted to be emperor, and in sending him away, and keeping Dara by his side, Emperor Shah Jahan was clearly marking his preference for heir—to Shuja and to the empire.

'Dara is needed here, beta,' his father said to him now, turning towards him and presenting his back to the assembly beyond the jharoka balcony. There was compassion in the emperor's eyes, and to Shuja it seemed as though his father was warning him against having ambitions beyond his reach. Dara was the heir to the empire—the rest of them would be given high ranks, enormous salaries, mansions and palaces around the land, jagirs and districts to administer, but before the Friday noon prayers, only one man's name would be taken in the khutba by the muezzins of the mosques—only Dara would be proclaimed as emperor for all of the empire's residents.

'I see, Bapa,' Shuja said, and kept silent through the rest of the jharoka. When he returned to his apartments, he told his wife of his plans and ordered his effects to be packed. And a month later, when the army had been readied, he departed from Agra.

As he left, Princess Roshanara touched her brother Prince Aurangzeb's arm and said, 'Shuja will never come back to court, will he, Aurangzeb?'

The young prince frowned. 'Not unless he returns as emperor. But he does not seem to care about this very much.'

'But you do,' Roshanara said quickly. 'He is the first of us to leave so that Dara and Jahan can reign supreme by Bapa's side. Your turn is next.'

He laughed. 'I will go, and willingly, Roshan. What use is an emperor who lolls around at court, who has not shed blood in wars, who has not the allegiance of the greatest warriors in the empire? I will go, and I will return.'

'You will need help here then.' It was said in an undertone, and she drifted out of the room before he could respond, but Prince Aurangzeb had heard, all too clearly, that his second sister was offering him her loyalty. She did not like Jahanara, and Jahan clearly supported Dara, so Roshanara found another brother to back. He did not mind this, Aurangzeb thought, as he had taught himself to be tolerant of almost everything—he would take Roshan's help, but his love was for Jahan.

fourteen

It is not without reason that the kingdom of which Lahor is the capital is named the Penje-ab, or the Region of the Five Waters . . . Alexander is here well known by the name of Sekander Filifous, or Alexander the son of Phillip . . . The river on which the city was built, one of the five, is as considerable as our Loire.

—ARCHIBALD CONSTABLE (ed.) AND IRVING BROCK (trans.), *Travels in the Mogul Empire, A.D. 1656–1668* by François Bernier

Agra
Monday, 23 January 1634
23 Rajab A.H. 1043

They departed from Agra for the long journey to Kashmir, which would lead them along the way to the city of Lahore—Emperor Shah Jahan's first visit to both places as sovereign.

The trip took the royal entourage through Delhi, where they halted briefly for a short pilgrimage to Emperor Humayun's tomb, and then on west and north to Lahore, some three hundred and seventy-five miles away—fifteen days of hard riding by an army unencumbered by chattel and women; a month for them as they marched steadily, day by day, in procession, their numbers a mile wide at its widest.

Princess Jahanara Begam journeyed in an open howdah set atop an imperial elephant. The howdah was a wooden structure with a gold and gilt roof, four pillars, a broad seat strewn with comfortable cushions and bolsters, thin muslin curtains enfolding the whole. The curtains were long and flitted up and down in the breeze, providing a glimpse of her face at times, or her hands, or the little child by her side, whose bright blue gaze caught every passing scene with interest. A bevy of eunuchs surrounded Jahanara's elephant, and around them were old and decrepit amirs of the imperial court, some even from the first tier in front of the emperor's throne. Though the child's delighted laughter filtered through the thick, heated air, not one man turned to look upward at the sound—they kept their horses in rein and their own heads forward, doggedly following the long road towards Lahore.

'Goharara,' Jahanara said, pulling the girl by the laces of her choli. 'You will fall out, and then Bapa will cry when he sees how his child has been hurt.'

'Will he, Jahan?' Goharara Begam asked. 'Where is he?' She leaned out farther. 'I cannot see him. The dust rises so that Bapa's howdah is masked from here. Why does he not travel with us?'

'Bapa is in conference with the amirs, beta,' Jahanara said. 'And where did you learn to speak with all those words?'

'When you were not around, Jahan,' she said with a smile that brought two deepening dimples in her rounded cheeks.

That look, and those words, caught Jahanara's heart, and she held her sister's chubby hands in her own and then bent down to lay kisses upon them. They had all overlooked Goharara, she thought, in those early days after Mama died, and so she had been brought up by her wet nurses and her maids, women of some standing at court, true, but it had resulted in the princess thinking of one of the women as her mother. When she was a year old, she had called Jahanara 'Mama', once, and a wet nurse later told Jahanara that they had been telling the child her mother was away and would come to visit her. And so Jahanara had asked for her sister to come by her apartments to play while she read over the farmans her father sent into the harem for her approval and for affixing the imperial seal, or had sent her numerous gifts of gold and silver toys, or had seen her in passing as she moved from one of her duties to another. But they had all been neglectful of her—and this was easily done; Goharara Begam was a royal princess, she had caretakers aplenty, and her older sisters and brothers had their own concerns.

'Come,' Jahanara said, drawing the child upon her knee and holding her fast against the wriggling. 'If you are quiet, I will tell you a story.'

'Laila and Majnu?' Goharara demanded.

Jahanara sighed. It was an inappropriate story for a child, that ballad sung upon the Yamuna the night she had met her own lover in her gardens, but Goharara had grown up in the imperial zenana, where gossip and tales of love never ceased from the mouths of the many women—the slaves, the concubines, the servants—where talk was free and unrestrained, where every child reached adulthood with a full and complete knowledge of the complexities of life and, consequently, little understanding of anything. Among the many rhymes and folk songs that had been sung to put the little princess to sleep, this was one. So Jahanara began her story, using the word *love* with care, so that Goharara might comprehend it as affection, as only a feeling from the heart and from the head.

'He sings for her in the desert, Jahan,' Goharara said. 'But he cannot find her again.'

Jahanara nodded. She had asked for the musician's son many a time after that one night, but for her, there was no mystique any more in this act of love. She understood now that her heart was given to Mirza Najabat Khan, and the other man was but a poor substitute, even though she knew him better. If she had been more common . . . But she was a royal princess, and he was not her equal in rank, in standing, and she had called for him for the one need that had nothing to do with her heart. Goharara grew limp in her arms and slept, a thumb in her mouth. Jahanara looked out through the netted curtains. The sun bleached the landscape to a salt white, laid calm over the stunted trees dotting the terrain where nothing moved in the afternoon. When they passed through a village on their route, children sat wide-eyed upon treetops or the roofs of the houses, watching their progress; women stopped as they drew water from wells; birds took flight from their path. She watched the rising of dust somewhere ahead in the long caravan of camels, elephants, horses and oxen, and knew that a call to halt had been made, and sure enough, in ten minutes, sentries shouted out the summons and the words came floating back to Princess Jahanara.

They had stopped in Jalandhar, almost right outside the western gateway of the Nur Mahal Sarai. Jahanara glanced out at it with curiosity, for it had been built by her grandfather Emperor Jahangir's twentieth wife, Mehrunnisa, and named after her—after one of her various titles, Nur Mahal, the Light of the Palace. Emperor Jahangir had then changed his wife's title to Nur Jahan, more lofty, of more consideration, now to mean the Light of the World. But the sarai, a rest house for weary travellers, had been built in the early days of their marriage, and it was already, some twenty years after its completion, steeped in legend—for a person in voyage, the words Nur Sarai had become a hallmark of perfection, and every other sarai in the empire was compared to this one. When the slaves from the zenana came to assemble in front of her kneeling elephant, Jahanara handed the sleeping Goharara to one of the women and descended to stand in front of the massive entrance to the sarai. Somewhere, a mile ahead in the dust and scrub, Bapa, Aurangzeb and Roshan would have halted also to pitch tents, light cooking fires, set up shamiana awnings to keep them cool. They had passed by the sarai and gone on because Empress Nur Jahan was a woman Emperor Shah Jahan detested, even though her niece had been his wife, and her brother—his father-in-law—was still one of his dearest supporters. And his children, Jahanara thought, could call the empress their grandaunt. But for her elephant to have stopped at precisely this spot, when it could well have lumbered on for the lunch meal to another, only meant that Bapa wanted her to see the sarai.

She stepped back and noted the red sandstone building's thick and blind walls that stretched on each side, ending in engaged octagonal guard towers. The gateway itself was in two storeys, the front carved in relief with exquisite depictions of court life—the chaugan, the battlefield, the peacocks in the zenana gardens, trees in full flower. Inside, the building was square, only one storey high, and had arched verandahs running all around. Set inside the cool darkness of the verandahs were thirty-two rooms on each side. There was a *hammam* in one corner, a cookhouse in another, and a group of apartments in yet another with gold padlocked doors where Emperor Jahangir had stayed to please his wife when the sarai had been built.

'She had imagination,' Dara said softly by her side. He had come upon her as she stood in the centre of the courtyard, and as he spoke, Jahanara felt Nadira's touch upon her other arm.

'She is not dead yet, Dara,' Jahanara replied mildly as an idea came to her. Mehrunnisa, Empress Nur Jahan, had been given a pension of two hundred thousand rupees a year when Emperor Jahangir died, and been sent to Lahore along with her husband's body. It was customary for the widows of dead emperors to occupy a place in the imperial zenana of the new king, albeit a minor one, and usually as revered mothers who learned to involve themselves as little as possible in the new harem's power structure. They were given a salary from the treasury, a roof over their heads, and a role to play in court occasions such as the emperor's birthday or the Nauroz festival, when they would send gifts and charity to the poor. With Mehrunnisa, such a pronouncement of a harmless retirement would have come easily to all of them, Jahanara thought, for they were related to her in two ways—she was their Mama's aunt and their father's stepmother. But then, there had been the small matter of Mehrunnisa attempting to put another son—Shahryar, who was married to her daughter Ladli—on the throne, and it had taken all of their grandfather's guile and cunning to wrest power away from her and to their Bapa; this Emperor Shah Jahan could not forget, and he did not forget.

She was forbidden to leave the city of Lahore and denied any access to the court. Jahanara did not think that her father, who would not break his journey at a rest house bearing her name, would welcome her into the palaces at the fort in Lahore when they arrived there. For the last six years, they had not spoken her name in his presence; it was as though she did not exist. This more than anything else was what Dara had meant when he spoke of her in the past tense.

They sat down in the shade of an enormous cypress growing in the centre of the courtyard on spotless white silk-covered divans. The rest of the roof, open to the sky, was criss-crossed in thin iron bars, which formed a mesh, intertwining with the branches of the cypress. The rule in most sarais was that all the travellers had to pay their fee, find themselves rooms, and settle their livestock, their mounts, and their servants before nightfall. As the sun set, the great doors of the gateway would be shut, sealing the sarai from the outer world, and guards would take their places around the structure, which had no windows on the outside walls. Come dawn, the sentry would shout, 'Wake and count yourselves and your belongings,' and he would wait for thirty minutes while the travellers did so, and if nothing had been stolen and no lives lost overnight, the great doors would be opened.

And such were the stories that Princess Jahanara Begam had only heard about the sarais in the empire. For she had never herself travelled without an escort of at least six hundred men—eunuchs and amirs—and they had paused here only for a meal; as they ate in silence, her guards took up position in the verandahs, the eunuchs facing them, the nobles turned away in two solid lines of protection. The food came speedily from the kitchens, each platter from the imperial treasury, wrapped in gold and red cloth, which the head server untied in front of them, tasted discreetly, and then ladled out. Even with stone all around, breezes dipped into the courtyard through the iron mesh, rustled the leaves on the branches of the tree, sent the patterned shade skittering in patches of light and dark. When they had finished, they washed their hands and sat back.

'Entertainment,' said Dara, clapping his hands, and two of his musicians advanced to play and sing with a harmonium and a tabla. A juggler came next, picking up gold teaspoons from the white tablecloth six at a time and flinging them into the air so rapidly that he seemed to be surrounded by blades of gold. When he was done, he laid the spoons down quickly, plucking them out of nowhere, and said, 'What next, Your Highness?'

'What do you think, Jahan? You know his skill at mimicry; shall we ask him to do that?'

'Yes,' Jahanara said, laughing, enchanted by this eunuch of Dara's who was so skilful. And she now knew why Bapa had wanted her to see the Nur Mahal Sarai—so that she could commission and build a better one herself; it would be a splendid use of her income.

'Prince Aurangzeb,' said Dara.

The man's face fell solemn immediately, his eyebrows lowered over his eyes; his forehead seemed to widen; his cheeks drooped downward; and though he wore a beard, it disappeared into his hand. He took a few fast steps, pretended to read a book, shook his head, and clicked his tongue in disapproval. Then he stood up very straight, his shoulders rigid, his ear turned towards the skies as though he were listening intently to something.

Dara roared, and Nadira joined him, but Jahanara felt a prickle of uneasiness. It was a caricature of Aurangzeb, an exaggeration of all his intensity—and it *was* real enough to be identified as Aurangzeb . . . and not humorous at all. She had expected something else, perhaps an imitation of a slave girl, or a merchant haggling, or even an animal, but this was cruel and improper. She opened her mouth to halt the excessive mirth that seemed to have bloomed all around the courtyard, when Dara's buffoon changed his expression and his manner. He bent over, let loose his beard, ran his fingers through it pensively. His mobile face aged as he created wrinkles on his forehead and around the corners of his mouth. He had not spoken, but Jahanara recognized Sadullah Khan, the Grand Vizier of the Mughal Empire, in his actions.

'Dara,' she said finally, her voice abrasive. 'Make him stop! This is ridiculous.'

'Do you know who that is?' Prince Dara Shikoh asked.

'Stop, Dara, you're courting danger.'

Dara bristled, and Jahanara saw a movement near the gateway leading into the courtyard. The guards had parted to let someone in, and for them to give way so easily, without warning to the courtyard's occupants, could only mean that the man who had entered was of some importance. The two women's hands went over their heads as they pulled on their veils to cover their faces. The man glimpsed the buffoon in the center for just a moment, but it was enough of a moment, before he turned to the side and addressed the pillars of the verandah.

'Your Highness, His Majesty requests that you start on your way again.' His voice was quiet and respectful and ended in a slight tremor. The laughter dwindled, and a stunned silence followed. Everyone looked at the princess.

'Yes, thank you, Mirza Sadullah Khan. We're ready to leave,' Jahanara said. 'Please convey this to our father.'

'I will, Your Highness.' He bowed, hesitated, and retreated.

'It was a joke,' Dara said when the Grand Vizier had left. His eunuch had melted into the verandah, transforming into his inconspicuous self. Jahanara rose and went to the waiting howdah outside filled with a sense of dread. There could be no explanation for the afternoon's events, no excuse at all given to the Grand Vizier, nothing that could be done without creating embarrassment on both sides. A royal prince could not apologize and lower himself to a noble at court, no matter how high a position he held, and she could not send word to Sadullah Khan either, so he would be offended and angered.

If it had been anyone else who had come by, they could have insisted that he had been mistaken, but not now. Perhaps, she thought, Mirza Sadullah Khan would see this as mild merriment and not an insult, but somehow she did not think so—Dara, assured of himself as the next emperor, was gaining a reputation at court for being discourteous.

A little part of her also recoiled with outrage from the brother she loved so much. Was this how Dara spent his plentiful leisure, by mocking others? The eunuch's gestures had been too practised for him to have performed this act for the first time . . . which meant that Dara had encouraged him, Nadira too, but she could only follow where her husband led. Bapa wanted Dara to be heir. Princess Jahanara Begam stayed in her howdah for the rest of the journey, refusing company even when they halted for the night or for meals. She was thoughtful, suddenly anxious. She could not talk with Bapa; he was, perhaps, more blind to Dara's faults than she, and this incident would only become small and inconsequential in the telling. If this had been narrated to her, she would have thought so also. But Jahanara had been in the sarai, had seen for herself the deep hurt in Mirza Sadullah Khan's expression, how he had struggled to keep his face stoic . . . and failed. Who could she talk to then?

In the distance, a man cried out, 'Two hours to Lahore!'

They were nearing the end of one part of the journey. Lahore, Jahanara thought, where there was one person who could advise her—one woman who knew the workings of the imperial zenana as though she had been born into it, who had conspired and schemed; who had won numerous times, who had lost in the end.

It would have to be another furtive meeting. But Jahanara was becoming quite proficient at these, with illicit lovers and now political outcasts.

fifteen

Against the prevailing tradition of keeping widowed queens at court, Nur Jahan's isolation in Lahore was virtually complete . . . Shah Jahan worked hard to sully the memory of his once-powerful stepmother, with the result that almost all of the historical works from his reign were explicitly critical of Nur Jahan.

—ELLISON BANKS FINDLY,
Nur Jahan, Empress of Mughal India

Lahore
Saturday, 25 February 1634
26 Sha'baan A.H. 1043

North and west of the walled city of Lahore—the main and massive stronghold of the empire that Emperor Akbar had built and Emperor Jahangir had added to—lay the village of Shahdara. The earth was level here, smooth and uncontoured, its soil dark, alluvial, rich in minerals. Shahdara itself was on the northern bank of the Ravi, and here, some twenty years earlier, Emperor Jahangir had given the land to his favourite wife, Mehrunnisa, who had landscaped, planted lavishly, and created terraces, pathways and fountains for a new garden so lush and pleasing that it had since been called the Dilkusha garden—that which gladdens the heart.

At Dilkusha's southern edge was a lone mansion of brick and sandstone, its lines long and elegant, with a gate through which to enter landward and a series of sandstone terraces scored down to the waterfront. It was a desolate land in many ways—as was much of the Mughal Empire itself away from the seat of the imperial court—even though Shahdara was just across the river from the greater, walled city of Lahore, and the imperial fort cut into the northwestern corner of the city.

A woman stood on the highest terrace of the mansion and looked out over the broad, sandy expanse of the Ravi. She had an erect bearing, a mass of black hair untouched by grey, the blue eyes of her Persian father, an enviably unlined face, even though she was approaching her sixth decade and had lived a sometimes turbulent and always rushed life. It was in her hands, clasped in front of her, that time showed, in fine wrinkles at the knuckles and the hardening of veins along the backs. She spent most of her time thus, in contemplation of the scenery around her—the fields heavy and green with winter wheat, the dormant waters, the walls of the fort etched against the horizon. Here she had stood a few days ago, watching the skies smudge with brown as Emperor Shah Jahan's entourage ended its long journey from Agra and arrived at the fort. The dirt had settled over one long day and one night as every segment of the eight-mile-long caravan came to a halt, as mansions were claimed again by the noblemen, as the merchants set up ramshackle shops within the city, as the women of pleasure found houses for hire and the army erected tents and encampments. The woman felt a twinge of pain in her chest and laid a hand over her ribs. Once, she would have been at the centre of it all. The welcome would have been for her, the zenana would have hummed with her orders, at night she would have laid her tired head on her husband's shoulder and slept, listening to his breathing, knowing that, when she woke, the world would still be hers to command. And now, she thought, a sardonic smile twisting the still-present beauty of her face, she had lived for six long years here outside the gardens she had constructed, where she oversaw the building of her husband's mausoleum in Dilkusha.

A movement, more a blot of dust, caught her attention in the far distance near the fort, and she raised a hand to shade her eyes, even though the sun was westerly this late in the afternoon and behind her. Yes, someone had left the walled city and was proceeding towards the river's bank, and, if that was indeed true, they could only be headed here.

Another visitor, she thought with some irony; she was not allowed at court, but in the few short days that the court had been at Lahore, she had already received one member from it.

'Hoshiyar,' she said.

Her eunuch came to stand by her side, gazing beyond her pointing finger. 'I see, Your Majesty. I wonder which one of Emperor Shah Jahan's children it will be. Not the emperor himself'—and here he chuckled lightly—'there are too few guards, but enough to make me suspect that she comes from the zenana. Which one?'

'Jahanara, I think,' Mehrunnisa said. She hesitated, and then the words came diffidently from her. 'Do you miss court life, Hoshiyar?'

He rewarded her with another laugh. Hoshiyar Khan had been the head eunuch of Emperor Jahangir's harem when Mehrunnisa entered it as a twentieth wife. He was not that much older than she, ten years at the most, though he did not know or care about his age and was not given to talking about it. But he had established himself as paramount in the women's quarters and, with an inner determination, had attached himself to one of Emperor Jahangir's wives—Empress Jagat Gosini, mother of Emperor Shah Jahan—and been her helper, her guide, her mentor in all matters in the zenana. And then, in 1611, twenty-five years after Emperor Jahangir had married Jagat Gosini, Mehrunnisa had stepped into the harem and wrested power away from her. She had known, from a long association with the zenana's affairs, that she would never be omnipotent in that world of women unless she had the support of the two principal men in it—her husband and Hoshiyar Khan. He had known this too and had disappeared one day from Jagat Gosini's chambers and presented himself to the woman whom his emperor loved beyond everything in the world, steadfastly and for the rest of his life, for Jahangir had married Mehrunnisa when he was forty-three years old and she an aged thirty-four. It was a love that was bound to endure.

'Do you, Your Majesty?' he asked now, tenderly.

'I miss the emperor,' she said. 'And perhaps if Shahryar had been a little less of a dimwit and become sovereign after his father, I might have had a place at court. But this'—and she gestured behind her, not meaning the mansion in which she lived but the mausoleum beyond it in the Dilkusha garden—'is where I am now meant to be.'

'Come,' Hoshiyar said, leading her in, 'we must prepare for our distinguished guest. She has courage, that little one, to step out of the harem and come to visit you—her father would be horrified if he were to hear of it.'

'And we both know that he probably will,' Mehrunnisa said. 'I must confess that I have longed to see this child. I know her brothers well from all the time they spent at the court as surety against their father's further rebellions, but the girls, they are an enigma, one, I think, already a little clearer as Jahanara nears.'

By the time Princess Jahanara arrived at the dwelling of her grandaunt Mehrunnisa, Empress Nur Jahan, the cool winter night had flung its cloak over the city of Lahore and the village of Shahdara. In Mehrunnisa's apartments, coal braziers wrought in silver and gold sent perfumed smoke to eddy around the room and warm the air. Mehrunnisa received the princess seated on a silk divan at the very edge of the room and forced her to enter at the far end and walk the length of the room on the thick white Persian carpets so that she could study her leisurely. Jahanara came through the door without hesitation, but as she reached Mehrunnisa, she stopped, bent down, and performed the chahar taslim with a graceful hand.

'*Al-salam alekum,* Your Majesty,' she said.

'*Walekum al-salam,*' Mehrunnisa replied, and beckoned with her finger. 'Come here, child, and kiss me.'

When Jahanara had done so, putting cool lips against her cheek, the older woman held her back and looked into her face. She had strength, Mehrunnisa thought—courage, yes, they had already established that, but also a streak of stubbornness in that firm chin and that upright neck and that balanced gaze. And something else, some sorrow that flickered in those eyes.

'You have the look of your mother,' Mehrunnisa said. 'She was always a pretty child and an exquisite woman, but I think you have your father's tenacity. How does he enjoy being emperor?'

'Very much' was Jahanara's impudent reply, and Mehrunnisa felt a smile bloom inside her, which she stifled. 'We all do, thank you.'

Now Mehrunnisa had to laugh, and she did, a rich sound that echoed off the walls and caused Jahanara's solemn face to lighten.

'Are you well, Your Majesty?' Jahanara asked.

The manner in which it was said was not patronizing, but the question itself undoubtedly was—the condescending concern of a Padshah Begam for a displaced member of the zenana—and Mehrunnisa felt herself bristle. Ten years ago, she would have reacted, but time and age had given her a wisdom she could well have used during the battle for succession, Mehrunnisa thought, and then perhaps this girl would have been just that—a child to be petted and looked after, and not the premier woman of her father's zenana. What a curious state of affairs this was. Shah Jahan's other wives were nonentities, to be sure, but the position was a burden for a daughter, which had probably led to the rumours she had heard even this far away in Lahore.

Mehrunnisa waved her hand. 'The title means little now, beta.'

Jahanara made a little sound of dissent at the back of her throat. 'We stopped at the Nur Sarai in Jalandhar on our way here. It is spectacular, Your Majesty. But perhaps more splendid is the tomb you have built at Agra for your father and my great-grandfather.'

Mehrunnisa leaned forward and pulled the girl to sit beside her—until now, she had not dared to sit without permission, and for this little courtesy, Mehrunnisa was glad. 'Tell me about it,' she said. 'I will never see it again, and when we left Agra for Kashmir that last time, it had not been completed. Tell me. Everything you saw, everything you remember.'

And so Jahanara talked for an hour about the confection of marble and semi-precious inlay that was Itimadaddaula's tomb, about the gardens, the luminosity of the inlay, the monkeys on the pathways, the sounds of a city awakening when the first rays of the sun caressed the stone. Mehrunnisa kissed her when she was done, a choking in her throat, her eyes filled with tears. Beneath all that regret was a little bit of fierce pride, for she had heard also that her niece was to be buried under another white marble tomb south of the fort, along the western bank of the Yamuna, and she knew that Shah Jahan had taken her vision for his own. Perhaps, only perhaps, he would improve upon it, though she did not think it very likely, and *she*—the daughter of a Persian refugee—would always have been the first to build a tomb of all-white marble in the Mughal Empire.

'Thank you, beta,' she said, and held Jahanara's strong hands in her own, placing both in her lap. 'Now tell me why you are here.'

Jahanara wavered, began to speak, and allowed her face to be covered with blushes.

'A man,' Mehrunnisa said slowly. 'Who?'

'Mirza Najabat Khan.'

'I know of him,' Mehrunnisa said. 'His lineage is good, his ancestors were worthy men, good servants of the empire . . . I do not understand, what is the problem?'

Jahanara would not reply for a long time, and then she said, finally, 'Bapa.'

'Ah,' Mehrunnisa said. 'I have always thought that your father's love for his wife was excessive, unusual. You are very much like your mother, my child. I can see why he wishes to keep you by his side. But what is this other ugly rumour I hear? I know there is no truth to it, but why have you allowed it to fester so around the empire?'

A note of disgust crept into Jahanara's voice. 'It is distasteful to me even to consider it with seriousness, Your Majesty. Any reasonable person would know it to be incorrect. Why'—she spread her hands—'how can I refute it?'

Mehrunnisa shook her head. 'But you must, my dear. Find the source of the rumour—it is sure to have come from within the zenana—and destroy it. Has Mirza Najabat Khan heard? But he must have,' she said, responding to her own question, 'and how has he reacted?'

Jahanara told her of that moonlit night in the chaugan grounds in Agra, and the subsequent summons, to which he had not responded. Mehrunnisa saw the princess's understanding grow as she talked. She was clever, she thought, though perhaps not with quite the amount of ruthlessness required to be supreme in the harem. She had her position because of her father's love for her, and now that love was oppressive and not enough for a girl grown into womanhood. But there were ways around every situation.

'Aurangzeb came to see me earlier,' Mehrunnisa said.

Jahanara's head snapped up. 'Why?'

'To show me what a fine young man he has become. He's a restless spirit, your brother, and if Dara and you are not careful, he has aspirations to become emperor after your father.'

'That is plain talking indeed, Your Majesty,' Jahanara said thoughtfully. 'But it will never happen; Dara is the next heir.'

Mehrunnisa gestured dismissively. 'Dara is at times a weakling, Jahanara. Remember this. Ah, I see that you already know this, but *I* know all three of them—Dara, Shuja, and Aurangzeb—well; they were with me and your grandfather for three years. Watch Aurangzeb, and make Dara watch him also.'

'I will, Your Majesty,' Jahanara said. 'I worry . . . also about Dara. His confidence is wearying. He'—she paused, but then this was why, among other things, she had come to her grandaunt—'insulted Mirza Sadullah Khan the other day. It was a little thing. A little thing only,' she repeated again.

The empress's gaze was shrewd. 'And yet it causes you anxiety? Dara can be taught manners; you must consult with your Bapa if this indeed concerns you. No,' she said, 'your Bapa will not listen; he's stubborn himself. Then you must talk with Dara, my dear.'

Jahanara shook her head.

'No? Not even that? Send an apology to Mirza Sadullah on his behalf; Dara need never know.'

'But how?'

Mehrunnisa shrugged. 'A gift for his wife—some silk, a perfume she has admired—or invite her and her daughters to stay in the zenana as your guests. Show them every courtesy when they are there. You cannot write to him directly; do so through his women. He will know and realize the reason for your interest.'

'And will it be enough?'

'Who knows? It is Dara who must make this move, but,' she said when she saw Jahanara shake her head again, furiously this time, 'you don't think he will. Watch for him carefully, my dear. Though,' Mehrunnisa said meditatively, 'I have heard of Dara's liberality also, his conversations with the priests of other faiths. He is imitating Emperor Akbar and his Ibadat Khana—the House of Worship where he invited the monks and saints of other religions—but Dara forgets that he is not yet emperor. How does this sit with the other amirs at court?'

'They dislike it, Your Majesty.'

'As they did when Emperor Akbar insisted on having his way. Him they could not dismiss, but Dara . . . it's always "but Dara". He's become a fool, Jahanara; perhaps you should support Aurangzeb instead.'

Jahanara's upper lip curled. 'The very idea is abhorrent to me, Your Majesty.'

'Oh? Well, maybe you are right. And keep an eye on Roshanara,' Mehrunnisa said slowly.

'Why?'

'Aurangzeb talked of an alliance with her. I wonder what the five of you are doing under your father's lax gaze, but she seems to dislike you. Why?'

'She wishes to marry Mirza Najabat Khan,' Jahanara said with distaste. 'But that is impossible. Bapa says so. *I* say so.'

From the far end of the room, Hoshiyar rose and came towards them. He bowed to Jahanara and said, 'Your Highness, I beg pardon, but your visit has tired Her Majesty. It is time for you to leave.'

And she *was* tired, Mehrunnisa thought with some surprise. Excited by the conversation, the intrigue, the planning, and no longer willing to be a part of it. That portion of her life was over. For this child it was just beginning. Mehrunnisa bent her head in a little prayer that Jahanara Begam, who had taken the time to call on an all-but-forgotten empress, would have the courage to see the fight through till the end and that, because she wished for it so much, Dara would be emperor after his father.

Jahanara performed the taslim again to Mehrunnisa and said, 'Thank you, Your Majesty.'

'Only one last word, my dear,' Mehrunnisa said wearily. 'If your Bapa will not allow you to have a legal alliance with Mirza Najabat Khan, you must find another way to do so. Guard your personal happiness carefully, Jahanara; no one else will be willing to do it for you.'

~

When Emperor Jahangir had died on the way back from Kashmir to Lahore, Mehrunnisa's brother Abul, who had been with the royal entourage, had performed last rites for his brother-in-law in torrid haste. Then he had sent the body to Lahore along with his sister, under guard. Later, Abul would say that these had been Emperor Shah Jahan's orders. But Shah Jahan was then still a prince in exile—it would take a full week for him to receive Abul's message about his father's death and come riding hard into Agra to lay claim to the treasury and the throne. By then, Emperor Jahangir had been interred in the Dilkusha garden. A report circulated for a few months, gaining no momentum, that Jahangir had wished to be buried in the place that he had called the garden of eternal spring—Kashmir. And Mehrunnisa, by her husband's side for all of the sixteen years that they had been married, knew the truth of that rumour, for it had been in the cool and lush valleys of Kashmir that Emperor Jahangir had been most at peace.

Five days after Jahanara's visit, another royal procession set out from the fort to the village of Shahdara and the Dilkusha garden across the Ravi. This time, messengers had come fleet-footed to Mehrunnisa's mansion with notes from the nobles at court and cautions from lesser women in the zenana—the emperor himself meant to visit his father's mausoleum and oversee the progress, and she was not to show herself to him on pain of death.

Mehrunnisa laughed, clad herself in a veil of white, still in mourning for Emperor Jahangir, and sat openly on a bench on one of the four stone pathways that bisected the garden to create the charbagh in front of the tomb. The construction was almost complete, and though the money for the building had come from the imperial treasury because Emperor Shah Jahan wanted to be the patron of his father's final resting place, it was she who had talked with the architects over the past six years, inspected every piece of the pietra dura inlay of marble in red sandstone, stood back to view the tomb rise alongside the Ravi. So she waited early one morning for Shah Jahan to arrive at Dilkusha, Hoshiyar by her side, though sitting at her feet as a servant should.

The garden was still concealed with thin ribbons of mist from the river when they heard the sounds in the forecourt, the Jilaukhana of the tomb. A colossal red sandstone gateway led in, with the four stone paths that culminated in the centre in a square and blue pool of water, which reflected the tomb itself.

Emperor Shah Jahan and his courtiers, all dressed in white, moved slowly down the centre path towards the tomb and stopped at the pool to wash their hands. As they proceeded on, Mehrunnisa leaned forward. But the group was too far away for her to see much of their expressions. They halted in front of the tomb, a low, one-storey building in red sandstone, with nine pishtaqs on each of the four sides and four engaged towers on the four corners of the structure. Inside, she had created a series of corridors, one after the other, leading to the heart of the building—a white-marble-paved room set with exquisite pietra dura inlay of agates, sard, jade and cornelian, gleaming marble walls, and a raised cenotaph in the centre. On the flat rooftop was another cenotaph, this time covered only in white marble with a marble railing surrounding it. Jahangir had said to her once that he did not wish for a roof to cover his remains, but she had not had the heart to leave her husband in the open for eternity. The two cenotaphs—one in the inner chamber, and one on the roof—were meant to satisfy them both.

Emperor Shah Jahan stayed inside the tomb for only a few minutes and came back outside with another man, who walked a few paces behind him. It was her brother Abul.

'I wonder how he likes being father-in-law to the emperor, Hoshiyar,' she said quietly.

'There is talk of his being made Khan-i-khanan, Your Majesty,' the eunuch replied.

'Abul was always a little pompous, even when we were children. It did not suit him then, and'—her voice sharpened—'it does not suit him now.'

Hoshiyar nodded. His mistress was still bitter about the way she had been treated, and rightfully so; she had been an empress and this man's sister. He spat on the ground next to him, a gesture that surprised even him—for it was such a common expression of revulsion, and Hoshiyar had always been a cultured, fastidious man. But, he thought, Abul Hasan deserved it. The small sound of him clearing his throat and spitting caused the emperor and his father-in-law to falter for a moment.

The light from the sun warmed the air and dissipated the wisps of mist in the garden. The two men turned to look down the pathway towards the lone woman seated on the bench and the eunuch by her side. A minute passed, and then two, stretching long into the silence. Then they turned and went along to the main gateway.

Mehrunnisa did not budge until the garden had emptied of the amirs from court. Then, with a hand on Hoshiyar's arm, she went inside to kneel beside her husband's cenotaph, said a prayer, and walked out again over the stretch of garden and west to the little patch of land where she was building her own tomb. She knew that no one else would do this for her. Along the way, she laughed to herself. Shah Jahan was building a new city in Delhi, he had already rearranged some of the gardens she had herself supervised in Kashmir, he had refaced all the riverfront apartments in Agra fort, he had paid for the construction of his father's tomb, he was building a Luminous Tomb for his wife. How ironic it would be if, busy scurrying around in this tremendous industriousness, he forgot to conceive or build a tomb for himself.

With four sons hankering for the throne—well, two most obviously anyway—there was no guarantee that the son who eventually became emperor would be grateful enough to raise a mausoleum over his dead father.

sixteen

The whole kingdom wears the appearance of a fertile and highly cultivated garden. Villages and hamlets are frequently seen through the luxuriant foliage . . . The whole ground is enameled with our European flowers . . . with our apple, pear, plum, apricot and walnut trees . . . full of melons, pateques or water melons, water parsnips, red beet, radishes, most of our potherbs, and others with which we are unacquainted.

—ARCHIBALD CONSTABLE (ed.) AND IRVING BROCK (trans.),
Travels in the Mogul Empire, A.D. *1656–1668*
by François Bernier

Kashmir
Wednesday, 12 April 1634
14 Shawwal A.H. 1043

Perhaps if Emperor Babur had seen Kashmir, he would have found his newly acquired empire in Hindustan a little more tolerable and would not have complained quite as much in his memoirs about this harsh, arid land.

Kashmir was the exclusive privilege of kings—a jewel in the crown of the empire, pure and untouched. Jahanara took a deep breath of the thin and clean air. They were in Srinagar, some five thousand feet above sea level, and for the first few days after their arrival, even though their journey here had been of a slow rising and leisure, they had all been prostrate with shortness of breath and headaches.

They had departed from Lahore a month ago, once news was brought to the court that the mountain passes of the Pir Panjals were cleared of snow and there was no more precipitation to be expected. Their caravan this time, unlike on the trip from Agra to Lahore, had been attenuated into a more manageable number of amirs, their families, the army, and the accompanying merchants. In the beginning, around the time of the conquest of Kashmir by Emperor Akbar in 1585, a smaller court had resided in Srinagar for the summer months with the emperor, and the reason then was that it was immensely difficult and expensive to journey north for a mere few months and every trip accumulated losses of livestock and human life. But soon, when the bounties of the vale of Kashmir in Srinagar were lauded in the blistering Indo-Gangetic plains, nobles and merchants began crowding into the city with the emperor, spilling out into the fields, mucking the waters of the lakes, augmenting the rate of crime which the overworked havaldars could not keep track of. So a bailiff was posted at the mouth of the Pir Panjal pass, and every man entering the mountains to journey up into Srinagar had to have a special permission farman granted by the court. The numbers were so tightly controlled that the bailiff would tick off the amir's name against a sheet of paper he had been given ahead of time and make sure that the person carrying the farman was indeed the person to whom it had been issued.

This was Jahanara's first visit to Kashmir, for the simple reason that, though her grandfather, Emperor Jahangir, had come here, summer and winter, six times from 1620 until his death in 1627, by the time of the first of his six visits, Jahanara's father was already in disfavour with the court and in exile in the Deccan. She gazed down at the smooth, unruffled surface of Dal Lake. If Shah Jahan had not become emperor, her brothers, sisters and she would never have tasted the enchantment of this land.

And delightful it was. Early spring, and even with the cutting chill in the air, the poplars and cypresses had begun to unfurl new, pale green leaves, the meadows overflowed with tiny white daisies, the streams were breathtakingly cold and clear with snowmelt, the very air gave allowance for repose. They had passed all the gardens her grandfather had laid out with Mehrunnisa—Anantnag, Verinag and Achabal—and at each place, Jahanara had stopped to remember and send a little message to the empress in Lahore, who now spent her days in prayer by her dead husband's tomb, whose time of power and glory was ended but who still retained the fire in her eyes and the wisdom of her experiences. Jahanara did not expect a reply from her, but she knew, even without a response, that Mehrunnisa would be grateful for the bits of news—the plastered walls of the pavilion at Verinag have a patina of warm yellow in the spring twilight, Your Majesty, or the fish at Anantnag still bear the gold rings that you had ordered put through their noses, or the mountains still rise in peace and tranquillity, their peaks brushed with the late snows. Mehrunnisa, who could not journey to Agra to see the tomb she had built over her father's remains, would have no opportunity to see Kashmir again in her lifetime because she was no longer welcome anywhere in the empire—though it was her hand that had drawn bold strokes on paper to mark out the shape and sizes of the baradaris in the gardens, her vision that had planted a row of chenar trees on the road so that they would travel in an avenue of russet golds in autumn.

And then, three days ago, they had arrived at Srinagar, crossing over the Jhelum into the broad and flat cup of the valley, with its horizontal land and its thick, linked mountains encircling every horizon. The lake spread out wide in this bowl of land, shimmering and serene, the mountains reflected on its surface. The landscape even now bore the tan hues of the departing winter—the hills were bare, the trees stretched naked limbs to the skies, the lotus and lily pads on the water were still tinged with their heavy winter greens. The tops of the mountains, floating above the mist in the mornings, were yet clad in snow, and they were immense, higher than any Jahanara had seen before. If there was indeed Paradise on earth, it was here in this tranquil land.

The Hari Parbat fort, where they had ended their journey, was perched on a small hillock west of Dal Lake, its crenellated walls mapping the hill's top. Emperor Akbar had built the fort here when he first arrived in Srinagar valley for its views—the lake below, the mountains around, the sparkling air. Mehrunnisa had constructed a garden within the fort, the Nur Afza garden, 'Light Increasing', or so Emperor Jahangir had named it when she completed refacing the pavilion with blue stone slabs, dug out a blue pool filled with cold water from the lake, created a broad and open terrace on which to sit in the early mornings and view the spectacular sunrise. Emperor Shah Jahan had given Jahanara the apartments overlooking the garden, and it was here, on a balcony looking down, that she stood that morning.

'Jahan.' She turned to see Roshanara at the door.

'Come,' she said, surprised. They were rivals now, of a sort, pecking at each other in petty matters, suspicious and wary, holding each other at bay. But ever since Jahanara had heard of Roshanara's unlikely affections for Najabat Khan—a man, she thought drily, neither of them could marry—their squabbles had become serious, every jeer filled with meaning, every snipe traced with disgust. And this over a man. Whenever she thought about this, if she thought at all that Najabat Khan was a *mere* man, Jahanara was saddened. Perhaps something more tangible lay behind their inability to truly love each other, something in the shape of the brothers they favoured. It had been easy for them to have their own lives even within the confines of the harem. Jahanara had her duties, her own apartments, her income to manage, and Roshanara—though with less to do—managed to occupy herself elsewhere. There was no need for her to be where Jahanara was, except on state occasions, when they were both required to be present. So they had not talked . . . about Najabat Khan or anything else; in any case, what was there to say about him? With all the restrictions and regulations that hemmed them into an inner, sacrosanct world, they had each still managed on a slight acquaintance to fall in love with the same man. He had no real choice between them, and they had none either, for it had been decided that they were not to marry.

But, Jahanara thought, reflecting on Mehrunnisa's last words to her, there must be some way for her to find and keep her happiness—if not publicly, then in private.

She forced herself to be polite, even welcoming. 'It is a wonder that we have not been able to come here before. Look, Roshan'—she gestured outside the balcony—'have you ever seen the sun rise in such glory?'

'My apartments are at the back of the fort,' Roshanara said shortly as she came to lean against the parapet.

'Then you will see the sun set,' Jahanara said, dreading what was to come, for she knew just from that one curt sentence.

'Why does Bapa always give you the best rooms?' Roshanara asked. 'It is unfair to treat you better than me.'

'And you ask me that? What do you expect I will say? Take my apartments?'

'Will you?' Roshanara Begam turned to her sister, her eyes alight with curiosity and eagerness.

'No.'

Roshanara grunted, her fingers moving on the fabric of her cloak. 'I did not expect you to,' she said, 'but thought I would ask anyhow. I . . . how does one say this, Jahan? You are more favoured and get the best of everything. I am Bapa's daughter also, but from the very beginning, he has shown his preference for you. You received most of Mama's income when she died; the rest was to be distributed among us. Why?'

'It's impossible for me to respond to this. Why now?' Jahanara said, feeling the weight of all that was unsaid between them come to rest upon her.

Behind them, the slave girls and eunuchs moved around on soft, padded feet, straightening the sheets, dusting the little tables, sweeping the carpets that extended from wall to wall. They heard the rattle of rocks of spent coal as the braziers were emptied, filled again, and lit. Thick smoke surged out to the balcony, and in the cool morning air, both the princesses shivered, drawing their fox fur cloaks around them closely.

'I heard about your meeting with Mirza Najabat Khan in the chaugan grounds,' Roshan said quietly.

'I know.'

'I went to see him; did you know that also?'

Jahanara felt a tightening about her chest. 'No. What . . . did he say to you?'

'Enough to make me think that he was interested.' Roshanara clicked her tongue in exasperation. 'We, princesses of the blood, are reduced to encounters with a lover in the middle of the night, under the cover of darkness, like some common woman straying from her husband's bed. It is shameful, Jahan, you must realize this.'

'When?' Jahanara asked, not paying heed to the rest of the rant, for it was self-serving. Roshanara's disgust was more for *her*, Jahanara, than for herself, though she had doubtless met Najabat Khan on a dark night also. But Jahanara had heard the word *lover* from Roshanara's mouth, and she cringed to think that her sister would consider Najabat Khan so . . . also.

'You must stop this, Jahan. Think of your position as Padshah Begam, as the Begam Sahib of Bapa's harem. He adores you, thinks that you can do no wrong, and he would be crushed to hear of your dalliances, if, that is, Bapa somehow got to know of them.'

'Is that a warning, Roshan?' Jahanara asked softly. 'Let me just say that Bapa knows of more than we think he does, his ear is always to the ground, and he is not a fool. How did he hear of your wanting to marry Mirza Najabat Khan?'

When Princess Roshanara moved to confront her sister—and this was the first time since Roshanara had stepped to her side that they had actually faced each other—her mouth was pinched, and a sparkle of tears glittered in her eyes. Jahanara almost reached out to her, but she held back, thinking that there was no place for affection between them any more, no real understanding at all. In some ways, they had all been brought up to think of themselves first, and others later, because they were royal, and invested with an immense sense of self. But over the last few years, Roshanara had schemed and shouted and whispered about her in all quarters of the zenana, mostly out of spite, and Jahanara had no feeling left for her sister.

'I am going to send him a note,' Roshanara said. 'And he will come. That, unfortunately, is all I have left now.'

'He will not,' Jahanara said without inflection, but anger raged inside her. Suddenly, it was important for her to know why Najabat had stayed away from her summons and to see whether he would indeed respond to Roshanara's. She had thought for many long hours about him and about the time they had spent together—this was all she had, all she had based her obsession upon. If he went to Roshan, he would never be hers; it was better to know that for sure than to harbour any desires that would not find their way to fulfilment.

'Call for him then, Roshan,' she said wearily. 'If he comes, you can have him.'

Princess Roshanara Begam picked up the skirts of her ghagara to step over the doorway and into the room. She did not bid her sister farewell. They both knew that something had ruptured between them; if they had stayed quiet, it would have been hidden at the back of their minds, but now . . . they had little left. They were both inmates of Bapa's zenana, both his children, both women to be cherished, treasured and controlled, and neither had to see the other again if she did not want to—once the crown found its way onto the head of either Dara or Aurangzeb.

Roshanara went to her rooms and began a letter to Najabat Khan, inviting him that night to the Shalimar gardens on the northeastern corner of the lake. As her hand trembled over the empty page, she wondered how to word this bold invitation.

Or if Najabat would even come in response to it. It was Jahan who fascinated him, Jahan who had played chaugan with him in the light of a winter moon. Of her, Roshan, he knew little and had only heard her voice. Once. But if he came, if he saw her . . . surely, he would forget her sister . . . Her mind made up, she wrote with care, unused to the handwriting she was trying to imitate. She did not sign her name at the end. When she was done, she dipped a seal in ink and deliberately pressed it on the paper so as not to smudge the edges of the imprint of the rose with its six unfurled petals—for the original seal was fashioned of silver, and this, a copy she had had made a year ago, was only of wax. It was an exquisite copy, though, and encircling the rose, these words showed up clearly: *By the order of her imperial Highness, the Begam Sahib Jahanara.*

As night descended, the muezzins' voices rose, calling the faithful to the final *salah* of the day, the last of the five ritual prayers. Their melodies, echoing around the valley of Srinagar, were accompanied by the ringing of bells in the Hindu temples and the priests' chanting of Sanskrit verses. The Muslims knelt where they were, facing Mecca, and the Hindus thronged in the incense-and-smoke-filled temples that were aglow with brilliant oil lamps.

At the end of his prayer, a man on the banks of Dal Lake covered his eyes with his hands briefly and then rose to his feet. He looked up into the cold and dry night sky, embedded with a thousand stars, whose light this high on earth seemed to be brighter and more radiant than it was in the thickly dusty plains of Hindustan. Around the lake, the many golden lamps illuminating the havelis of the amirs cast their speckled reflections on the calm water, the light flowing into darkness in the arms of the mountains and turning silver-blue in the stars of the sky. Najabat Khan stood at the very edge of his property, on the wooden pier jutting out into the waters, stamping his feet occasionally to keep the chill away from his ankles and toes. His hands were now in the fur pockets of his coat, its collar pulled up about his face so that only his nose and his eyes showed. He searched in the right-hand pocket and found the slip of paper he had been looking for. He did not need to read it again; every word was known to him as though it had come from his own hand, but his fingers curled around the paper, holding it tight. He remembered her very well from that night, the flush on her face, naked and boldly presented to his gaze, the strength in her arms as she swung the chaugan stick, that laughter. The yearning that had beset him that night had never really waned.

And then, a few months later, still in his state of happy delirium, the repugnance he had felt when he had heard the rumours of her . . . connection with her father that was so unnatural as to make him flinch. It must have been true, he had thought, for there was never talk that abhorrent that could not find its inception in a little crumb of truth. When Princess Jahanara had written again, he had crumpled the letter in his palm and set fire to it with a burning chunk of coal from his hookah, without reading it. In a few months, he had begun to doubt what he had heard, for with those rumours came the gossip of the emperor's fancy straying once more to the women of his zenana—slave girls and concubines—and also the wives of the nobles at court. Again, there was truth to all of these reports, for there was nothing secret in the empire from the emperor himself or from the amirs at court. One of Najabat's wives had visited Jafar Khan's wife and found her adorned in a splendid emerald and diamond necklace which could only have come from the treasury's coffers. So then, Najabat Khan had realized that all of his previous surmises, arising out of his fascination for the emperor's oldest child, were mistaken, since the one could not exist while the other did. He had also been misguided into believing something other than what he knew to be true of Emperor Shah Jahan's character.

Now this command from her. A eunuch unknown to him

had brought the letter in the afternoon and slipped away into the sunshine before he could open or read it.

Najabat Khan snapped his fingers in the cold, and the boatman of his shikara nudged his craft closer to the pier until it bumped against the wooden planks. He steadied the shikara as his master climbed in and then used his oar to push away into the water.

'Shalimar Bagh,' Najabat said, and settled down against the cushions, a woollen rug about his knees, as they glided through the still waters of the Dal, east and north to the slim canal that led to, and was the only entrance to, the gardens Emperor Jahangir had built for his beloved wife Mehrunnisa and on which Emperor Shah Jahan had recently constructed a series of pavilions for work and for pleasure.

By the time they reached the entrance to the Bagh, some forty minutes later, clouds had blanketed the sky and the blue light of the stars had been extinguished by a pall of greys. The air had turned more crisp, more biting, and a thin wind swept through the length of the canal, rocking the shikara from side to side. Najabat Khan shivered, wrapped his arms around himself as he stood in the glow of diyas that flickered on the first, public terrace of Shalimar Bagh.

The gardens were built in a series of three terraces, one above the other, each more than the height of a man from the ground so that, standing on one level looking up at the next, a person would see only a carved stone wall inset with niches and, in the middle of the wall, the fluid drop of water from the upper level to the one below. The first terrace was the emperor's Diwan-i-am, not so much the Hall of Public Audience as in the forts at Agra and Lahore but the only place where the amirs of the court could assemble when they came to a durbar session. It was long and flat, cut through the centre with the charbagh, and its main pathway was cleaved with a long pool of water that flowed into the canal below. Against the land end of the first terrace, Emperor Shah Jahan had commissioned a black stone throne set in a square pool, and here he had sat a day before in audience, the nobles crowded around the edges of the pool, fountains playing softly in the waters, the emperor himself, unreachable, across the expanse of blue.

The second terrace, unseen from here, was the Diwan-i-khas, again not the Hall of Private Audience as such but a garden for Shah Jahan to meet with a few privileged nobles. A eunuch came forward from the shadows of the large aspens along the pathways and motioned to Najabat Khan to climb to the second level of the Bagh. Najabat followed behind at a distance. Najabat, who had not yet been invited to the Diwan-i-khas, looked around him as he came to stand on the border of the garden after climbing the stairs. The garden was still bare, slender tree trunks, uncovered branches, the brown lawns jewelled with early crocuses in white, which glowed like pearls in the darkening night. There was a small pavilion here also, a meeting place for the amirs, and water in the main long pool, its fountains silent in the cold. To his right, along the path, there were oil diyas in terracotta shades, lighting the way upward to the final terrace, where no man not connected to the imperial family had ever been allowed—for this last and highest piece of land in the Shalimar Bagh was the zenana garden.

The steps were steep here, almost at thigh level, but Najabat ran up them quickly and stood panting at the very top, unable to believe what he saw. The cold of the night was dispelled by a hundred coal braziers in the open air, smoking gently with the warm perfume of aloewood. There was light everywhere, along every pathway, set atop the broad and unusual eaves of the pavilion at the far end, scattered along the polished marble floor inside the pavilion like the night sky come to rest upon the earth in all of its brilliance. Here, the water flowed in a cold rush over the walls, and inset in the walls behind the water were niches filled with the glimmer of more diyas—turning the whole cascade of water into a sheet of gold. The woman stood in one of the central arches of the baradari, her back to him. Najabat waited until the pounding of his heart from running up the stairs had subsided, laid a hand on his chest, and ran lightly up the pathways, skipping over the diyas strewn in his way until he reached the bottom of the three small steps leading up. He stood there waiting for her to turn and acknowledge him, for she must have heard the sound of his footsteps. A moment passed, and then another, and the fine sheen of sweat on his brow cooled and froze on his skin.

'Your Highness,' he said.

'So you have come.'

At the sound of her voice, he felt a flutter of discomfort. It had been many months since he had heard her speak, but the music of her laughter and her words had been seared into his brain. This was not the same woman, he thought, then dismissed that notion as soon as it came, for who else could she be?

'Will you turn to look at me?' he said, greatly daring, 'or have I offended you? I flatter myself that you would not have honoured me with this summons if I had. It was an error on my part, one I am greatly ashamed of, one I should not have given credulity to.'

'What have you heard, Mirza Najabat Khan?'

This time he had to lean forward to hear her. 'Nothing I can talk about, Your Highness. It was women's talk.' He laughed. 'I mean that it came to me from my zenana, and stupid as it was, I believed it. But I know you . . . in that short space of time we spent together I came to know you better than I know my wives. If I say that they mean nothing to me, and you . . . everything, would you believe it? That which we set in motion on the night we played chaugan together will not be stopped again, by any person's doing.'

She took a deep breath, and he watched her shoulders straighten and collapse under the quivering furs on her back. 'And what of my Bapa?' she asked.

'I respect His Majesty,' he said, 'but I do not agree with his injunctions that you must not marry. If it is to be so, and we are bound to obey his wishes, *this* must suffice for us, Your Highness.'

The woman swung around then, the furs of her cloak whispering on the floor. Najabat moved towards her, up one step, his right arm out to clasp her hand. His fingers fell upon her sleeve, and he felt the softness of the velvet band around it just as he looked into her face. The light of the baradari glowed upon her skin and the dark frame of hair shimmering with pearls. Something, even in her moving to meet him, had struck him as unusual, but when he saw her he found himself looking at a strange woman, not the one who had dwelt in his thoughts for all these days. He stepped back, almost slipping and falling in his attempt to get away from her.

'Did you expect my sister?' she said. 'Why, though, Mirza Najabat? You were amenable enough when we met in your tent on the way to Agra.'

'Your Highness,' he said, bowing in the taslim, his hand falling to the ground and up again four times almost automatically. 'I was mistaken, forgive me.' Thoughts jostled in his mind, her words finally coming to rest in clarity. *She* was the first woman he had seen, Princess Roshanara Begam; the second one, who had splendidly trounced him in chaugan, was Jahanara. The rumours were about Jahanara, and when he glanced up again at the spite drawing up her eyebrows and at the sneer around her lush mouth, he recognized clearly that Roshanara had created the gossip about Princess Jahanara. He felt helpless standing there, his arms hanging loosely by his sides, thinking only of her deceit in calling him to Shalimar Bagh on the pretext of being her sister. He could barely remember what he had said to her, how he had begged to be forgiven, how he had shown his love for Jahanara to this woman. He felt a little cold touch on his cheek and looked up to see a few snowflakes mist gently into the gardens.

'This is not a game, Your Highness,' he said, intensely furious. 'You have deliberately lied to me. The letter came in Jahanara Begam's name, and—'

'Not in her name, Mirza Najabat Khan.' Her voice was sharp. 'If you had only stopped to read it carefully, you would have seen that it was not signed.'

'But it was her seal.'

'Would you have come if I had written?'

'No,' he said quietly. 'For you I would not have come. You committed a folly in visiting me in my tent, put my reputation in jeopardy, knowing that, if we were caught, it would be my head loosened from my neck and not yours.'

'And what did the Begam Sahib do later?'

'That was different, Your Highness. I could not dare to think of you in such . . . terms; my affections lie with your sister.'

She waved a hand in his direction, a slew of gold bangles tinkling with the movement. 'Go, Mirza Najabat Khan. I have heard enough of your insults. But remember,' she said as he turned and began walking down the pathway, 'that I will recall your words for the rest of my life.'

'If I have insulted you, Your Highness,' he said, stopping once to look back, 'then you have deserved every word.'

'I will tell Bapa,' Roshanara said in an undertone, and so he did not hear her. Even if he had, he would not have cared; he just wanted to get away.

Najabat fled down the terrace and the stairs to the middle level and the bottom one, where his shikara waited for him. He was deeply distressed and did not notice that the first few flurries of snow had thickened as they talked, and the flakes were now pouring down upon him, coating his bare head and his shoulders even as he ran. He came to rest at the pier, winded, shaking with rage. His shikara was nowhere to be seen, and the copious falling snow had killed all noise; even the sound of his harsh breathing seemed to be somewhere in the distance. The light of the night sky had almost turned into day with the snow a sheer blue, and he could see down the canal, the trees on its banks canting over in black streaks. And then he noticed the shikara pulled up along the edge of the pier, its trappings of gold and gilt dusted with snow. A woman sat under the shelter of the gold-tasselled awning, clad in white, a hand on the boat's rim, snow laid over her exposed skin. She had long fingers, fine and shapely, and Najabat saw the glint of diamonds on her rings.

Her unremitting gaze was upon him, her eyes dark, lips purple in the cold. She was shivering. He crossed his arms and watched her—snow piling upon his eyebrows and his eyelashes, whitening his beard—waiting for the smallest movement from Princess Jahanara Begam that he could take as an invitation to leap to her side.

seventeen

The princess should be married to the chief general at the court, whose name was Nezabet Can (Najabat Khan), a man descended from the royal family of Balq (Balkh). He was brave and well-proportioned; but Shaista Khan, brother-in-law of Shahjahan . . . said to him (Shahjahan) that it was not advisable to make such a marriage, because when married to the said princess the husband would necessarily have to be placed in the same rank as any other prince.

—WILLIAM IRVINE (trans.)
Storiado Mogor, or Mogul India, 1653–1708
by Niccolao Manucci

Kashmir
Thursday, 13 April 1634
15 Shawwal A.H. 1043

Until the end of his life, Najabat Khan would never recall how he had boarded the shikara on the pier outside Shalimar Bagh—whether the princess had beckoned to him in the still blue luminescence created by the softly falling snow, or if he had made the first move. He did remember that a eunuch had steadied the boat as he climbed in and handed him a pair of oars. The eunuch had actually let the oars clatter to the floor of the shikara, but neither Najabat nor Jahanara paid heed to his temper. It must have been Ishaq Beg, Najabat thought later; no other man who considered his neck precious would dare to display his displeasure in front of an amir of the court and a royal princess.

Najabat thrust the shikara from the dock and turned the craft around, his back to the lake as they went down the canal. He sensed, rather than saw, four other boats detach themselves from the bank around the Bagh and follow them, and as he rowed, four more materialized in front. Eunuchs filled the guard boats, seated with their backs to Jahanara and Najabat, spears held aloft, daggers folded into their cummerbunds.

They went thus in a scattered procession and swung out into the wide expanse of the lake at the end of the canal. The snowstorm, if it could be called that, had subsided as inaudibly as it had come into a flutter of white in the sky. Even in that short time, the half hour it had taken for Najabat to row them to the lake, snow had piled on the mountains, whitening their peaks; the houses on the edge of the lake had mantles of white on their wood roofs; the branches of the trees were carved out against the darkness. Only the lake glimmered indigo and black, seemingly untouched by the late-season snow. And around them, lights glowed gold from the houses, boats and piers.

All the way down, they had been subdued themselves, as though not trusting their voices, with only the mellifluous and rhythmic dip of the oars to keep them company. At first, Jahanara had searched Najabat's face with her intense gaze, and then, perhaps a blush had come over her skin—he could not tell—and she had turned to the banks of the canal to present him with her profile. Najabat had not taken his eyes off her, except to rest them upon the slender line of her neck, the unseen hands folded now in a fox fur muff in her lap, the sway of her shoulders as the shikara rocked. When they broke into the lake, the skies opened up above them, still grey with snow-bearing clouds. Their escort spread out into the waters, at enough of a distance now that the boats were mere specks.

'Are we not to speak, Your Highness?' Najabat said finally, resting his aching arms and allowing the shikara to drift.

'I wonder,' she said, with a deep breath, 'if I did right in coming here tonight.'

'If you had not,' he said simply, 'I would have had no way of contacting you again.'

'And yet, it was for you to do so.'

'I spoke at great length about my folly to your sister,' he said. 'I listened too much, paid too little heed to my own feelings . . . I was wrong.' He said more, all that he had told Roshanara, even his last words to her and how he had been mistaken in thinking her to have been Jahanara at the encampment.

'So what now?' Princess Jahanara said. She removed her hands from the muff and laid them on the sides of the boat. 'What are we to do?'

He wiped his face and chin of the wet, melting snow. 'I, a commander of five thousand horses in His Majesty's service, have been a coward, Your Highness. I have been afraid, uncertain of the emperor's temper if he were to find out . . . But I was curious, I admit it readily.' He chuckled. 'It is not every day that a royal princess commands an amir to her side, and when I began to think of the consequences of being discovered, it weakened my resolve. Now, if you will have me, I will not betray you again.'

Najabat reached forward and took her warm hands into his own. She slipped her hands out of his clasp and held his instead, rubbing her fingers over his frigid skin.

'This is not a game to me, Mirza Najabat Khan,' she said. 'I have . . . given my heart to you. Perhaps it sounds foolish, perhaps I ought not to be talking like this either—'

'I know,' he said. 'I also know that my heart is yours until I die. If we were other people—more common, less important—we would have had the succour of the rituals of everyday life, a marriage and children. But as it stands, the emperor will not allow you to be taken from his zenana to grace mine, and I understand his sentiments readily; they are no less than I feel myself. But if you will permit me to be your husband, and will let it be our secret . . .' He shook his head in disgust. 'I am a soldier, Your Highness, with no words within me for courting or poetry. I fear that I do not say what I want to well enough.'

'So we are to live our separate lives,' she said carefully, and Najabat felt an ache in his chest at her words. 'And meet every now and then.'

He shrugged. 'So it would seem Allah has ordained for us. Little snatches of happiness.'

He picked up the oars again and began to row.

'What will happen after my Bapa dies, Mirza Najabat?' she asked.

'I do not know, Your Highness,' he said frankly, glancing over his shoulder as the shikara glided through the water. 'It depends on who will wear the crown.'

'Dara,' she said decisively. 'Why would you doubt that?'

He looked at her in surprise. 'I beg your pardon, Highness, but there is no such certainty. Prince Dara Shikoh has His Majesty's favour, but the nobles at court . . . we all think of Prince Aurangzeb as being more qualified. He has courage, that young man, and an unwavering resolve. And he is polite, well mannered—all that a royal prince should be.' He stopped abruptly, sensing he had said too much. It was not the first time he had heard of Jahanara's love for Dara, and he had hoped it was just a rumor, because Dara was impudent, irreverent, too flighty for them to consider as an emperor. He was like a well-groomed horse, petted and cared for, and not put through its paces daily. Even Prince Shuja had gone to the Deccan to aid Mahabat Khan in the fight there—a battle they had lost, true, but his mettle had been tested at war. Princes who lived in the soft lap of the imperial court could not rule over an unruly empire, with its fluid boundaries and its insurgencies within. And yet, though Aurangzeb was also still at court and untried as a soldier, he was vocal and he had tact. After the news of Dara's insult of Sadullah Khan had spread through the court, Prince Aurangzeb had sent him a magnificently caparisoned elephant and four horses as a gift, supposedly for no reason, in actuality as an apology for his wayward older brother. The amirs had spoken of the gift also, though Sadullah Khan had merely acknowledged it and said nothing; it created an aura of goodwill around the young Aurangzeb. That, Najabat thought, and his brashness at the elephant fight nearly a year ago, when Dara had fled and Aurangzeb had faced the raging Sukhdar. The nobles had long memories, and, in the end, the empire would come to rest only in the safekeeping of the man who had their support—it was a simple and inviolable rule for governing over such a large and unwieldy empire.

'I cannot agree with you,' Jahanara said finally. 'Dara will be emperor after Bapa. His Majesty himself thinks so.'

'Why, Your Highness?' Najabat asked gently.

'It will go against all laws of nature to put a younger son on the throne while the eldest is willing and able to rule,' she said stubbornly, and then she had the grace to redden, for she never forgot that Shah Jahan was the third son, that he had caused Prince Khusrau's death, that on the way to the throne that was now his, other brothers and cousins, older or not, had died.

Najabat released the oars and clasped her hands to kiss them. 'Then we will have to disagree with each other on this, Jahanara. It matters little to me. I would have insisted, I freely admit, that my wives have the same opinions as mine, but you are to do as you will. I only beg that you be careful, that if I give you information that comes from court, you will listen and use it to your advantage. In your well-being lies mine, my love.'

It was the first time he had used her name and called out to her with words of love.

But she only replied, 'I am not used to being told what to do, Mirza Najabat.'

'Then I will not speak further.'

They had docked now at another pier, on the eastern bank of Dal Lake. A long row of lanterns, dusted with snow, their light muted, framed the outer edges of the dock and led the way up a path to a haveli, its windows picked out by the glow of diyas inside.

'Where are we?'

'At my house,' he said. 'I have been bold, as you see, bringing you here without your permission.'

She was silent for a long while, her eyes shining with laughter when she looked up at him. 'Not today,' she said.

He felt a pang of frustration. She was lovely and, to him, unreachable. Whatever she wanted, however, he would give her.

'When then?' he asked.

'Tomorrow.' She signalled into the dark night, and a shikara came up to dock by their side. Ishaq Beg helped her in.

'You must learn to wait, Mirza Najabat Khan,' she said as the boat moved away towards the western bank of the lake above which the Hari Parbat fort was illumined in streaks of light. 'We have, after all, the rest of our lives.'

They met the next day as the sun pulled into the horizon, leaving skies wrought in russet red, ochre gold, and tangerine orange. It had been a long day for Jahanara, heavy with anticipation, her skin tingling, her every nerve on edge. She had thought of nothing, and no one, but Najabat. In the early morning a missive had come to her from her Bapa, a gilded farman rolled and reposing on a bed of green silk.

'Take it away,' she had said to Ishaq. 'There is no time today for matters of state. Take it away and tell Bapa I said so.' This last imperiously.

'You should look at it, Highness,' Ishaq had said, eyes aglitter.

'No. Order my bath, bring out my clothes and my jewels and my perfumes. Not today, Ishaq.'

'Perhaps you would consider bathing in the garden, Your Highness,' Ishaq said slyly. 'The view is quite magnificent from there.'

Princess Jahanara Begam reached then for the farman and opened it. Her first surprise was to see the letter in Bapa's hand;

he usually let the court scribes earn their keep. Her second was that it was addressed to her.

> My darling Jahanara, forgive me if I intrude upon your time when we are here on a holiday, but the business of the empire must be conducted as usual—there is no rest for kings, or indeed their offspring. Perhaps this is not *truly* the empire's business, but when a king writes to his daughter—a royal princess whose every word must be of as much importance as his own—it is no less than that. I have seen you admire the Nur Afza garden that my father commissioned, and so . . . it is yours now, my child. Change the name if you wish, do anything that takes your fancy, but if I may suggest—call it still Nur Afza, 'Light Increasing', for your presence there, my dearest daughter, can mean only an increase in the garden's brilliance. The royal seal reposes with you; use it at the bottom of the letter so this might become an official order.

'Why now, Ishaq?' Jahanara had asked, bemused, even as her eunuch brought her the inkwell, the block of ink, a gold cup of water and the *Uzuk* in its velvet sack.

'The princess went to your father last night, your Highness, upon her return from Shalimar,' he had murmured, watching as she laid the seal upon the paper and then taking the Uzuk from her and wiping it carefully.

'And he gives me a gift the next day,' Jahanara had said.

When the morning had slipped into the afternoon, Ishaq had an enormous copper bathtub brought into the blue-floored pavilion of the Nur Afza and set in the centre. This early in the year, even at midday, there was yet a biting chill in the air; after all, it had snowed on the previous night. So Ishaq had placed coal braziers worked in silver and gold filigree around the edges, their gentle smoke perfumed with tiny sandalwood chips. Jahanara had undressed in this warm fug and stood patiently as slave girls massaged her body with oils flavoured with frankincense and camphor. Then she had slipped into the steaming bathwater and lain there, the tiredness of her muscles creeping away, her limbs loose and rested by the end. She had not lifted even a finger in her bath—the servants had soaped her arms and legs with the froth of soap nuts, washed her hair in chamomile and kesu flowers, dried it over a brazier with the scent of the sandalwood threading its way through the strands. They had smoothed her hair, braided it, and pinned it to her head with pink and white pearls. More eunuchs had brought in outfits, holding each reverently—ghagaras dripping with diamonds and pearls, rubies and emeralds, cholis so thickly embroidered in zari that they were more gold than cloth, veils so delicate and gossamer that each could be pulled through a finger ring. They had laid out her jewels in velvet cases on the floor of the baradari, and Jahanara had chosen the set she wanted to wear by pointing at it—pearls and rubies, sprinkled with tiny diamonds, for her ears, her neck, in a long chain at the parting of her hair, bangles that rode up to her elbows. When the veil had cascaded over all this finery, she had turned to Ishaq Beg, suddenly anxious. 'Will he like me?'

The eunuch had bowed, words caught in his throat. He was but half a man, and yet he could barely talk when he looked at his mistress; her beauty, at this moment when she was on her way to meet her lover, was such as he had never seen before. 'Mirza Najabat Khan would be a fool not to, Your Highness,' he had said. 'May I accompany you?'

'No.' She was already moving away, the fabric of her skirts swishing over the floor, her mind, her heart, her every sense already given to Najabat.

Now this, Jahanara thought, as they stood in Najabat Khan's house on the edge of the lake, watching the sun set. His hand, warm and sturdy, was at her waist. He was standing close to her, and she could almost hear the rapid beating of his heart. All of her confidence and bravado had melted into nothing by the time she had reached the pier and found him waiting there, and she had barely been able to look at him. Now she did, meeting his gaze, feeling the skin of her face heat as his eyes dropped to her mouth. She bit her lip. The past few times she had been with him, it was in the blue-black light of the night, his eyebrows shadowing his cheeks, his presence more felt than seen.

'Come,' he said softly. 'I do not wish to hurry you, my love, but we have so little time. When do you have to be back at the fort?'

'By morning,' she said.

He placed a finger on her mouth and tugged the lower lip free from her teeth. When she began to smile, he dipped his head and kissed her. The hand on her waist was joined by the other, and he turned her fully into his arms. She raised her hands to clasp around his neck, breathing in his scent, feeling loved and wanted. When he led her to the divan in the room, she did not resist, following where he went hungrily. The back of her choli was threaded through cherry-size pearls, and she waited, her eyes sparkling with laughter, as he undid them one by one, kneeling at the back. Doing them up had taken her slave girls close to an hour; under Najabat's impatient hands, the choli slipped off her shoulders in ten excruciatingly long minutes.

'Are you afraid?' he asked, his face pressed against her body.

'Not any more. This I have wanted for a very long time,' she said simply, bending to kiss his forehead. When he gathered hold of her again, she saw that he was trembling, and soon she forgot everything around her—the deepening gold from the diyas' light, the shimmer of silk under them, the warm room, the skies turning blue and then indigo. This was indeed love, she thought, this bliss in a lover's arms, the taste of his skin, the touch of his lips upon her, the oblivion of lust.

~

The imperial party returned to the Indo-Gangetic plains in September, even as the air in the valley of Srinagar cooled in anticipation of the coming winter and the green of the trees turned to the yellows, ambers, browns and reds of autumn. The scenery, the stay itself had been restful for all of them, and the normal business of the court was conducted even so far a distance from

Lahore and Agra. The passes were open, and every day, runners sprinted through in both directions, into the mountains and down to the plains, bringing news from every corner—minor rebellions quashed, sons and daughters born to vassal kings and governors, and Mahabat Khan's death far south in the Deccan.

This last was the one piece of news that had jolted the amirs and the emperor alike—they had not even known that the Khan-i-khanan was ailing, and now there was the information of his death. The law of escheat required all of the Mughal general's vast property to revert to his emperor—and it did, nominally, before Shah Jahan graciously bequeathed the whole upon Mahabat Khan's heirs. He kept, however, Mahabat Khan's stable of elephants, fine, rigorous animals so cherished that they had been brought up on a diet of lotus leaves and pods and Persian melons. More troublesome was to find an adequate Commander-in-Chief for the Mughal imperial forces, a man who could be respected, followed, supported by the nobles, and Shah Jahan gave the post to Abul Hasan, his father-in-law and grandfather to his children. Abul had little experience in war, more in the field of cunning, for it was he who had captured the throne for Shah Jahan, and this was payback. Abul's rank was elevated to seven thousand horses, his personal income raised, and his wealth now made him richer than any other man in the empire except for the emperor himself and the royal princes. And, of course, Jahanara.

A month after they had settled back in Agra, Prince Aurangzeb celebrated his sixteenth birthday. There was no weighing this time, but Emperor Shah Jahan gave him his first rank at court and made him a commander of ten thousand horses. A few months later, he was sent to conquer the rebellious Bundela king in the south. Just as he had predicted, Aurangzeb was banished from court, never to return again as a cherished son (which he had never been), unless . . . he came to don the crown to the empire. But, as matters stood with Dara—treasured and valued Dara—the only way Aurangzeb could rule the empire would be to wrench the crown from his father's head and murder his brother. That, he thought gloomily as he rode away, he could not even dream of doing.

When he departed, there was only one other brother besides Dara still at court—Murad, who was ten years old, still a child, very much, actually, a child, who had none of Aurangzeb's fiery and impossible ambitions. So Aurangzeb left behind two brothers and two sisters—one who had promised to be his ally in all things political for purely personal reasons; one who was staunchly Dara's ally in all things political and personal for no reason at all, or so it seemed to Aurangzeb. But Jahanara did not care what Aurangzeb thought; she had other things on her mind.

She was pregnant.

eighteen

To prevent dissensions among the three generals, who were practically of equal rank, Shahjahan appointed Prince Aurangzib to the supreme command . . . but Aurangzib's post . . . was more nominal than real . . . and if he gained any experience it was that of an onlooker. He had nothing to do with the practical side of it.

—BANARSI PRASAD SAKSENA,
History of Shahjahan of Dilhi

The Deccan
Sunday, 28 January 1635
9 Sha'baan A.H. 1044

Some thirty years before, the kingdom of Orchha, if it could even be called by such a cohesive name, had been a tract of scrub, desert, and heat-stunted forests. A Rajput chieftain, Bir Singh Bundela, ruled here—his lands were flung out as far as his eye could see, his men gave him allegiance on the sword, his bed was a sun-warmed rock, his sleep was shattered nightly by the howls of jackals. Bundela was one of numerous warring chieftains in Mughal India who held on to their little pockets of lawlessness by marauding hapless passers-by, feasted on their belongings, knew little of the man who, so distant in Agra, called himself their emperor. One day, a furtive message came to him from Prince Salim, Emperor Akbar's son. For the sum of five thousand rupees, Salim needed the head of a courtier, Abul Fazl. The Bundela chief did not question why Salim wanted Fazl's life, only set out on his murderous mission. Five thousand rupees was a vast—immensely vast—reward, and so Bir Singh sought out and chased Fazl and cornered him, wounded and resting under the shade of a tree. He did not demur as he chopped off Fazl's head, wrapped it in straw, and sent it to Prince Salim. He then took his money and disappeared to wait out the end of Akbar's reign, for by now he knew Fazl to have been a valued courtier and friend of the emperor, and he knew that, if he were sighted *anywhere* in the empire, the emperor would just as quickly slice off his head.

A few years later, Salim became Emperor Jahangir, and at the coronation Bir Singh came out of hiding to be granted the lands of Orchha as his kingdom and the title of Raja. These were good times for the Bundela king—he was finally a king of something, land and brick and mortar; his coffers increased daily with raids into neighbouring fiefdoms, and his emperor was benevolent enough to ignore his infractions. By the time Bir Singh died, he was a rich and content man, who had passed on some of his belligerence and self-entitlement to his son Jhujhar Singh.

The crown changed hands in 1627, and the new emperor, Shah Jahan, not quite as understanding as his father had been, demanded a meeting to discuss all this unaccounted-for acquisition of wealth. Jhujhar, who was in Agra for the coronation festivities, fled to his estates in Orchha. The imperial army followed, vanquished him, and compelled him to join the army in the Deccan wars. By 1635, Jhujhar had returned again to Orchha, leaving a son as surety in the Deccan. But fighting was in his blood, so he began forays into other kingdoms again, much as his father had done—and hunted down Raja Prem Narayan, captured his fort at Chauragadh, forced the Raja to send his wives and the women of his zenana to a funeral pyre and to get himself killed on the battlefield.

Emperor Shah Jahan roared at Jhujhar from Kashmir—surrender the Chauragadh fort to the imperial generals, or pay retribution for the spoils and present yourself at court *immediately*. Jhujhar ignored his emperor and sent word to his son to escape from the imperial army in the Deccan and find his way home so that they could fight out this battle together from their stronghold at Orchha.

This, then, was Shah Jahan's response to the errant Bundela king. He sent three generals at the head of a twenty-thousand-strong army to Orchha, with Aurangzeb to command the men, accompanied by the emperor's brother-in-law Shaista Khan to advise and counsel the sixteen-year-old prince.

The fort and the palaces at Orchha fell on the fourth day after Aurangzeb arrived in the area, fervent, his nose scenting battle. On that morning, soldiers set off mines on the fort's ramparts, blew a massive hole in the ten-foot-thick walls, and stormed their way inside. The imperial army spread quickly through the palaces, crashing through studded doors, dragging out the servants and soldiers and beheading them on the spot, spilling the stored grains and shattering water vessels.

With the stench of gunpowder still washing his nostrils, Prince Aurangzeb clanked his way in, tripping on the heavy armour and mail he wore, barely able to see through the eye guard of his helmet. A tight complement of guards hedged him in as he swept through the courtyards, his sword drawn and dragging his wrist down with its unused weight. Someone smashed a terracotta pot, and a shard cut into his upper arm. Even before he began to bleed, a couple of soldiers came bearing bandages, which they slapped on to stanch the trickle of blood.

'Don't,' Prince Aurangzeb muttered, sweating in embarrassment. 'I'm fine.'

'Your Highness,' a soldier said kindly, 'you must be safe; Mirza Shaista Khan has entrusted your well-being to us.'

'I'm at *war,* you dolt,' Aurangzeb shouted, pushing his hand away. He wiped his forehead unthinkingly, and the armour scratched against his fine skin, drawing blood again. At war, he thought, was that what this was? He waved off the soldiers and sat down on a stone bench in the centre of the courtyard.

Aurangzeb lifted his head, weary already, when the men brought out a woman and began to tear off her clothes.

'Stop!' he yelled. 'Raja Jhujhar has left the palaces; there is no need to search here any more.'

At the sound of his voice, the soldiers halted, and one of them yanked the woman by the hair and led her out of the yard, her screams melting into the dust.

'Bring her back!' Aurangzeb roared. But no one paid heed to him. He turned in rage to Khan Duran, one of the generals his father had sent along with him, and said, 'Why do they not listen to me?'

'As His Highness wishes,' Khan Duran said. He had barely raised his voice, and yet, amid all the shouting and the noise, the men seemed to have heard him. The girl was brought in; someone had thrown a thin cotton sheet over her shoulders. She stood in front of Aurangzeb, shivering, her face mutinous.

'Where is the Raja?' Aurangzeb asked her.

She stared at him, uncomprehending, and then shook her head.

'Your Highness,' Khan Duran said, 'she is nothing. If they have left her here, she must be little more than a servant. It will not do to question her. I have news that Raja Jhujhar and his son have fled to their palace in Datiya. We will follow them there.'

'Tonight?' Aurangzeb asked, already counting the hours until departure.

'No,' Khan Duran said, his hands spread out, his shoulders rising in an exquisitely dismissive gesture. 'There is no need for haste—wherever the Raja goes now, we will find him. With Orchha ours, and Datiya soon to be ours, the Raja is as good as dead. The rebellion is over, Your Highness. We have won.'

Aurangzeb nodded bitterly. Over, and so soon. What had they really done? Nothing. What sort of a command had this been? He had arrived at Orchha a little less than a week ago, but his uncle had cautioned him against storming the fort until Khan Duran had come in with his own army. So Aurangzeb had spent the next three days in waiting, his army encamped outside the fort, winnowed out over the plains in a massive show of force, their tents baking in the heat, the flags on the posts wilting. A smear of ochre in the eastern horizon had heralded Khan Duran, and then the three generals had closeted themselves in a tent in conference—which Aurangzeb had insisted upon attending. There had been less talk of war and more revelry, as though victory was already theirs. Wine had flowed, women had danced, and the soldiers had sung bawdy songs around campfires until they all straggled to bed in the brief moment of cool before the break of dawn. The next morning, almost desultorily, the generals had sent sorties towards the fort to assess the battlements and scout locations for mines. One hole in the wall and they were in. An hour later it was obvious that they had been guarding an empty fort.

The prince returned to his tent and allowed his slaves to divest him of the armour. The pieces fell to the floor and lay there glittering, their shine barely dulled in all the fighting. A smudge of black—dirt, Aurangzeb thought with disgust, not the blood of an enemy—streaked one of his cheeks, and when he wiped it off, it disappeared. His horse still pranced around outside, neighing at the inactivity. He had ridden him harder in play at chaugan than here in battle. Why had his father sent him here? The generals treated him like a child; one of them had actually applauded when he suggested setting a mine under cover of night—they had long decided it to be the course of action, of course, but this Aurangzeb realized only when the army set it off within ten minutes of his suggestion. His father had fought against the Rana of Mewar and vanquished him when he was not much older than Aurangzeb, and no one would have dared to suggest that it had been one of his generals who had led that assault. But it was only too obvious that he was a puppet here, merely a token commander. The three generals, older men, long in the service of the empire and well acquainted with one another, had trounced the Raja of Orchha without any effort at all. Now they would not even allow him to go after the fleeing Jhujhar. He would be caught, they said, in good time, for he had nowhere to go other than south to the Deccani kingdoms, where he was sure to be killed first and questioned later about his defection.

He sighed and sat down in the warm bath that the eunuchs brought in for him. Keeping his hands carefully out of the water, Aurangzeb began two letters—one to his father, telling him of their victory, and another to Jahanara—and wrote a paragraph in each in turn.

All is well by the grace of Allah, he began in both, but the letter to his father had this salutation: *Your imperial Majesty, your third son begs your attention,* and to his sister, he said, *My dearest Jahan, I pray that this finds you well, as I am indeed, to be able to write to a sister so beloved.*

When he had written that first line, he laid down his quill on the little teak table beside his bath and put his head in his hands, remembering their last meeting, a few months ago, before he had departed Agra for this . . . war.

He had taken leave of Dara and Nadira, but only because he had had to, standing at the door of their apartments to say goodbye. Dara had nodded and waved a languid hand at him, and Nadira, the cousin they had grown up with, as much their sister then as she was now, had said, 'Go with Allah, Aurangzeb. May He grant you success in your mission.'

'A very important mission,' Dara had said, lifting his head from the divan's cushions, laughter bubbling out of him.

'What do you mean?' Aurangzeb had asked, flushing, erect with his soldier's bearing at the door. How could Dara bear to lounge in such a slothful manner? Was this the behaviour of kings?

'I hear Mirza Shaista Khan is being sent along to be your nursemaid.'

'Our uncle,' Aurangzeb had said stiffly, 'wishes to be in the south with me. I am a commander of ten thousand horses, Dara; I do not need anyone to look after me.'

'Go without him then,' Dara had said slyly. 'Why not suggest this to Bapa and see what he says?'

'I have to leave now,' Aurangzeb had replied, and marched away.

When he had gone into Jahanara's apartments, he had stepped in farther, all the way up to her as she leaned forward against the small writing desk set on the rugs, her head laid on her arms. She had not realized he was there until he sat down and touched her on the shoulder. And then, she had started and laughed. 'I did not expect you.'

'I sent word that I would be coming.'

'I had forgotten.' She had turned away again, her gaze moving beyond the windows to the brightness outside. Overhead, a punkah had flapped forward and back on its wooden pole, creaking every now and then. It had a rope tied to one end of the pole, which was then strung out along the ceiling to the verandah through a hole in the wall. On his way here, Aurangzeb had passed the punkah girl, tugging at the rope tirelessly so that cool air would eddy around the princess's apartments. He had sat awkwardly by his sister's side, on his knees, wishing that she would look at him and talk to him. He had barely seen her in Srinagar; each time he had visited her rooms it was only to be told that she had gone to the gardens at Shalimar or Nishat, or that she was with their Bapa or in a shikara on the lake. Almost as if she were a man and could leave the zenana when she pleased, without questions.

'I depart tomorrow,' he had said.

'Bapa has given you a great honour, Aurangzeb,' she had said. 'Even Shuja did not have such a high rank when he was sent to the Deccan.'

'I deserve it,' he had said. 'I am a royal prince.'

She had sat up, frowning. 'We are all royal, none different than another.'

He had looked at her anxiously, noting the shadows beneath her eyes, the whiteness around her mouth. 'You are tired.'

'I have been listless ever since we returned from Srinagar. Perhaps it is the heat here, even so late in the year. In the valley, there would be a chill in the air during the nights and the early mornings, the trees would begin to shed their leaves, painting carpets of red and gold at their feet . . .' She had rubbed her neck and lifted the heavy hair from her nape. 'Why did we have to come back, Aurangzeb?'

'The empire is here, Jahan. This is where we rule, where we are kings. Srinagar is a pleasant interlude, but life is not all pleasure,' he had said, and she had glanced at him thoughtfully. He had hesitated. 'Will you miss me?'

She had been silent for so long that he had begun to doubt she would ever speak, then she had said gently, 'I will always miss you, Aurangzeb. But I wish sometimes that you were not so insistent on having your way.'

Happiness had filled him at those first words, such as he had never heard from her, and then he had glowered. 'I am not that one.'

'No, not Dara,' Jahanara had said. 'He will only get, in the end, what he deserves as the heir to the empire.' She paused. 'You must go now; I have to lie down for a while.'

Aurangzeb had risen to his feet and stood looking down at his sister's bowed head. He had wished for something more coming here, some token of her affection, a little gift perhaps from her to him—a handkerchief, a sandalwood box in which she kept her jewellery, a ring from her finger—something for him to remember and hold close to his heart when he was on the battlefield. There were times when he could not explain even to himself why he had so much love for her, why he admired her so much. When he was emperor . . . she would always have a place in his zenana, one more exalted than his wives or his concubines. If Jahan was supreme here, in Bapa's harem, she would be more powerful in his. He had shifted his weight on his feet, wanting to tell her this and knowing how ridiculous it would sound. He was a young prince on the way to his first command, his father had lost none of his potency and was hardly likely to step aside for him, and besides, there was Dara. There was always Dara, whom Jahanara loved as unreasonably as he, Aurangzeb, esteemed her.

'Bapa asked Mirza Najabat Khan to stay back in Srinagar and lead the campaign there,' he had said, unable to stop himself even as the words came from his mouth.

When Jahanara had stood up—almost like an old woman, putting her hands on the floor to raise herself—a flush had stained her face and neck. Her eyebrows had been drawn together over eyes that were very, very angry. 'What are you saying, Aurangzeb?'

He had felt himself vacillate, half-fearful of her reaction. She must know that there was only one reason he had brought up Najabat Khan's name in her presence. There had been talk, all summer long, souring the crisp air of the mountains and rendering his stay so unpleasant that he had been forced to speak. How could he make her understand this? 'It is good for Mirza Najabat Khan to be away from court, Jahan,' he had said quietly. 'We all, and I mean all of us, the men and women of our family, have to present ourselves pure and unblemished to the people of the empire. How will they look upon us to lead if we are ourselves tarnished? Take care, Jahan.'

'Go!' She had swept to the windows and would not turn to look at him again. Silently, he had kissed his hand and sent the kiss flying towards her rigid back. 'Aurangzeb'—her voice had been acid—'you take too much upon yourself. It's not for you to tell me what I must do and what I must not. Come back when you've had some experience of the world yourself, and talk with me then.'

He had not replied because he had felt that there was no response he could make that would satisfy her. She would realize one day that he had been right; Aurangzeb was content to wait until then, knowing that he had done his duty in attempting to protect Jahanara, who was misguided in her actions and needed his succour. One day, she would even accept it.

The water of his bath cooled as Aurangzeb sat in thought in his tent at Orchha. He could hear the soldiers shouting and singing outside, their voices slurred by alcohol and opium, its sweet, sickly smell permeating even the canvas walls of his tent. It was still an hour to sunset, and they were already drunk, he thought, nauseated. If he had been the true commander here, he would have put a stop to all of these unseemly festivities, ordered a halt for prayer five times a day, had the camp swept free of the women of ill repute and the nautch girls.

He dried his hands on a towel and picked up his quill again, blocking out the sounds of carousing with an ease that came only from practice. When Aurangzeb wanted, he could concentrate in a matter of minutes on something to the exclusion of all else. He wrote, steadily, almost identical letters to his father and his sister.

> Here in Orchha, the erstwhile Raja Jhujhar and his father, Raja Bir Singh, have chosen their seat with the eye of an architect and a landscaper, without, I understand, having the benefit of either of these. How could these people from the plains have the kind of insight we have into such matters? But the countryside is fine in parts, and the palaces stand in a place of eminence. The river Betwa flows through this dry, baked, brown dirt, creating broad bands of opulent forests and farmlands along its banks, as though it carries the green within its clear blue heart. During the day, partridges, wild fowl and bustards scurry across our path—they are plentiful, and I have already shot a fair number. The trees hide other animals—the *nilgau,* deer, tigers, and leopards. Wild elephants trumpet all night long, especially when a female is due to give birth, which the soldiers tell me should be anytime now, and we are all fearful of entering the forest for the next few days. The Betwa's waters are sweet and cool to a parched throat, the palaces are of a fashion I have not seen anywhere else in Hindustan, with their flat roofs, their *chattris* in our style, some domes here and there, all standing in a ring in the river.

> The Betwa is unusual in this, it splits into two at a point and curves east and west, meeting to form one stream again farther south, and the Rajas have built their palaces in the centre of this loop of the river, so that from the rooftops one sees the calm of azure water all around, creating an island.

He read over what he had written and copied it onto Jahanara's letter. This would be the first time he had communicated with her since he left her apartments at the fort at Agra without saying goodbye. Though he had muttered the word at the doorway, he did not think she had heard. But she would be interested in reading what he had to say here, this much he assured himself, because he had tried to copy Emperor Babur's writing style from the *Baburnama,* a book precious to both his father and Jahan. He could not keep from adding these words at the end of Jahanara's letter, because he really did not know how to be humble—*I will touch only briefly upon the matter we talked of last . . . Whatever happens, I will look after you, Jahan.*

rauza-i-munavvara
The Luminous Tomb

I always thought one of the chief faults of Hindustan was that there was no running water . . . A few days after coming to Agra, I crossed the Jumna with this plan in mind and scouted around for places to build gardens, but everywhere I looked was so unpleasant and desolate that I crossed back in great disgust.

—WHEELER M. THACKSTON (trans. and ed.),
The Baburnama: Memoirs of Babur, Prince and Emperor

Agra
Thursday, 1 February 1635
13 Sha'baan A.H. 1044

With the riverfront terrace completed, the tomb itself rose rapidly into the sky. When workers raised wooden walkways on stilts to build the dome of the central, marble monument, two other walkways zigzagged up to the top of the Miham Khana and the mosque on either side. All three buildings were constructed from brick and mortar, layer upon layer, with thick walls, domes and arches, so that they would endure in their unsullied, new-built splendour five hundred years from now. But the facing of the main tomb was attired in the speckled white marble that Ustad Ahmad Lahori had convinced Emperor Shah Jahan to use, and the mosque on the left and the Miham Khana on the right, absolutely identical to each other in look if not in function, were clad in red sandstone. These two latter buildings, guardians of the Luminous Tomb through time, were to provide sanctuaries for the meetings of the nobles and commoners and hallowed places for prayer.

With all the aspects of the riverfront terrace finished, Ahmad Lahori stepped again onto the platform of the Great Gate and viewed his creation. The earth gaped to the tomb itself from where he stood, and the sun had carved out a space for itself in the roasted dirt and turned all of their skins a corroded brown, broiled their brows, desiccated their insides. It was finally time to begin planting in the gardens. For almost four years, they had all laboured in the hundred-degree heat of the summers without even the meagre shade of a sapling to cover them, and now that the main part of the tomb's complex was done, they could breathe and rest as they performed the pleasurable task of raising greenery.

The first thing to do in the tomb's gardens was to build the four immense sandstone pathways that would meet at right angles in the very centre. Here would float a pool in white marble with severe square rims on the outside and voluted edges on the inside. There would be five fountains in this pool to mist water into the scorching air of the summer, and the waters would be clean and cool, for pilgrims to stop at, wash their faces, drink from the cupped palms of their hands. The main pathway that led from the Great Gate on the south to the tomb itself in the north would be similarly interspersed with fountains; the pathway crossing it, from east to west—thus dividing the gardens into the traditional charbagh—would be a blank walking path.

With the pool in place, Ahmad Lahori began drawing up plans to bring in the water. He experimented with various engineering styles, visited the gardens around Agra, especially the first imperial garden, built by Emperor Babur some one hundred years ago, and mulled over an ingenious technique by which to lift water from the Yamuna and into the gardens of the Taj Mahal. While

Lahori was pondering how to conceal the workings of the system, so that it would seem as though the gardens produced water out of the heat and dust and the emerald trees, he met a Venetian, a traveller who was writing a history of India, or so he said to the great architect. Only mildly curious about this foreigner (for there were so many in Agra), Lahori invited him home for a meal so that the women of his zenana could have a look at him through the latticework net that divided the public and private spaces of his house. Amid the tittering and laughter from behind the screen, as the women examined the man's red hair and his sweaty red beard and colourless eyes, Lahori let slip his dilemma about the gardens of the Taj, and the Venetian, in turn, boasted of some ancient waterworks in a country called Rome. Lahori clapped his hands, gestured to shoo the women away, and sent his guest on his way to write his history as he would, laden with gifts of silk cloth, a mule to carry his belongings in all of his wanderings, and a manservant. Lahori spent the night sketching, for the Venetian had given him an idea he wanted to explore, and he had not had the heart to tell the man that, though the waterworks he spoke of had been in Rome for some one thousand years, in Hindustan they had existed for much longer.

An inlet was dug out from the river on the western side of the complex—the side which housed the mosque on the riverfront terrace—and here batches of sixty-two oxen went around in endless circles so that a waterwheel with buffalo-hide buckets could scoop water in turn and tilt it into an elevated aqueduct with channels open to the sky. The aqueduct ended in three large cisterns raised to the level of the western compound wall, and the entire system lay outside the western wall of the Luminous Tomb's gardens. From the cisterns, a lone pipe snaked its way into the wall and then downward, and the elevation was just enough so that when the pipes were connected with the fountain spouts of the central pool and the long pool of the north–south pathway, water gushed and played as it was intended to do.

In the gardens themselves, all the pipes, made of copper or kiln-fired or sunbaked terracotta, were buried inside the stone pathways—if a leak developed, or the system failed to work, the stone would have to be broken and lifted from the ground for the fixing. But Ahmad Lahori had just finished constructing a tomb formed of luminescence—a little seeping of water did not worry him, and, confident of his design, he boldly interred all the pipes in stone so that water would be seen, heard, touched and felt in abundance in the gardens but its source would be concealed from view.

With the water in place, they began to lay out the trees in the sixteen quadrants of land in the gardens—each of the four quadrants formed by the main pathways had then been split into another four. Tall cypresses, chenars, evergreens, cotton trees and medlars all struck root along the pathways in groups of two and three, and under their welcome, opaque shade, Lahori put stone benches to rest aching legs. The remainder of the gardens was left all light, brilliant and searing during the day, blue and silver in the moonlight. And here, in consultation with the empire's most expert landscapers and with agreement from his emperor (by correspondence), Ustad Lahori laid out a series of parterres of finely wrought, slender sandstone pieces in the shapes of stars, rectangles, squares and octagons, and crammed these with flowers. The land around the parterres was the green of a painstakingly cultivated lawn. And in this lush jade were jewel points of colour according to the season—heavy pink and purple roses from Kabul, burnt orange marigolds, white carnations, sweating poppies, tulips and daffodils from the gardens of Kashmir.

And that was how the living frame for the building was formed, the sumptuous cool greens of the trees, the scent of flowers, and, floating above it all, the shimmering white of the Luminous Tomb.

nineteen

The underside of the canopy is covered with diamonds and pearls, with a fringe of pearls all round, and above the canopy . . . there is a peacock with an elevated tail made of blue sapphires . . . the body of gold inlaid with precious stones, having a large ruby in front of the breast, whence hangs a pear-shaped pearl of 50 carats or thereabouts.

—WILLIAM CROOKE (ed.) AND V. BALL (trans.),
Travels in India
by Jean-Baptiste Tavernier

Agra
Saturday, 10 February 1635
22 Sha'baan A.H. 1044

Seven years in the making, Emperor Shah Jahan thought as he ascended the three steps to the Peacock Throne and sank down on the main gaddi—a mattress thickly stuffed with cotton and upholstered in red velvet embroidered in gold zari and minute pearls. He was alone in the Diwan-i-khas at the fort at Agra, having sent all the guards and eunuchs outside, and this was the first time he was seeing the throne which he had commissioned soon after his coronation. Bibadal Khan, the superintendent of the imperial karkhanas, had begged to be allowed at this viewing, wishing to see his emperor's reaction for himself, to note His

Majesty's pleasure when his eye lit upon the glitter of gold and precious stones, to see whether he had executed this task to his ruler's satisfaction. But Shah Jahan had banished him also, wishing for some quiet from the bustle of life that surrounded him daily. He had carved out this time from his sleep, rising before the sun as usual for the early-morning jharoka, and then, instead of returning to the zenana for a few hours of sleep, he had turned to the Diwan-i-khas, where the Peacock Throne would be unveiled to the amirs in the evening.

It was the month of February, and an impenetrable mist eddied into the courtyard from the Yamuna below, turning the battlements of the fort waxen, hiding from view the waters themselves. The white marble of the Diwan-i-khas's pillars was dim and cold to the touch, and with the throne positioned in the centre of the balcony, even the inlay work in blues and reds seemed to have lost its lustre. For the Peacock Throne was brilliant. It was in the shape of a platform, six feet by four feet, atop four thick stumps clad in beaten gold sheets. On the main platform, on three sides of the throne, were arranged twelve pillars, which held up the canopy—the front, where the emperor would sit and face the court, was open. Inside the pillars was a raised back for the throne, constructed of solid gold and inlaid with a thousand shimmering gems.

Shah Jahan had picked out the stones himself over the years, as merchants and governors of provinces far and near brought him these jewels from their lands. He had paid for the stones according to the value assessed on them by the court jewellers and rewarded the men who brought them with increased mansabs and grants of estates, so that it would never be said that the emperor took and did not give back in return. And this, he thought in wonder, looking up at the inside of the canopy—a sky filled with an impossible sparkle—was the final result. The canopy was studded with thickly set emeralds, diamonds and rubies, with a fringe of perfectly matched teardrop-shaped pearls. Each of the pillars was also made of gold, and emblazoned on each of them were two peacocks, their tails set with sapphires and rubies, their eyes of emeralds. Bouquets of flowers sprang to life on either side of the peacocks, their details picked out in rubies, diamonds and topazes. The sides of the steps leading up—for these too were part of the throne and would not be used anywhere else in his palaces—were also inlaid in patterns of flowers and geometric designs. In the centre of the backing for the throne was a diamond the size of his fist, some one hundred carats in weight. When he sat on his throne, this diamond would shimmer over his turban, meant to inspire awe in his audience as it shed its dazzling shine over him.

He felt the light from the throne glow over him, encompass him, lend him its glory even on this hazy morning. With the sun caressing the stones, as it would when it leaned over west later this evening, he would seem on fire. This, he thought, was not only the privilege of kingship but the duty of a king—to present his person as omnipotent, all-knowing, commanding, ablaze in the radiance of jewels and precious stones, which represented wealth and power. The Peacock Throne had cost the imperial treasury, in its making, a little over ten million rupees, twice the expense of the Luminous Tomb. And that was just the price for the exquisite workmanship—the jewels had cost another hundred and ten million rupees.

Emperor Shah Jahan rose and walked from the throne until he was a few feet away, then turned to look again at the marvel he had created out of gold and stone. As valuable as the gemstones of the throne were on the open market, there was one ruby—a Balas ruby from the mines at Badakhshan, embedded into the tail feathers of the central peacock—which had a history dear to him. Many years ago, Shah Abbas of Persia had sent this Timur ruby to Shah Jahan's father, Emperor Jahangir, and on it were engraved the names of the descendants of Timur the Lame. First, Timur himself, then Mir Shah Rukh, Ulug Beg, Shah Abbas, Akbar and Jahangir. The ruby had come as a gift from his father in happier times, just after his victories in the Deccan, because Jahangir had recognized his son's fondness—nay, fascination—for jewels of the first water and was aware that no other present would be as welcome. Shah Jahan had had his own name inscribed below, knowing with a certainty even then—when his hold on the crown was so shaky—that only kings had their names engraved on the ruby and that he intended to be emperor or die in the attempt.

Now, he thought, no other king whose name was on that jewel would leave a legacy such as his for posterity. The *rauza-i-munavvara,* the gorgeous apartments at the fort at Agra, the entire new city of Shahjahanabad, the gardens in Kashmir, his own father's tomb at Lahore . . . and this glorious throne.

As the mists around the fort and in the courtyard of the Diwan-i-khas loosened in the heat of the wakening sun, the emperor saw a lone figure striding up and down the terrace on the riverfront. Jahanara moved awkwardly, with none of her usual grace and elegance, hampered by the skirts of her ghagara and the long, full cloak she wore over it. Her arms were crossed over her chest and rested on the small bulge of her belly.

He leaned against one of the pillars and watched her stumble, trip, right herself. She cast a quick glance at him, but at that moment the sun broke over the roof of the courtyard and blinded her. She was waiting, he thought, to see if he was ready to retire to his apartments for a nap before his breakfast and the first of his duties at the Hall of Public Audience. He had known she would be there, even though he had ordered the Diwan-i-khas emptied before he stepped in, wanting to savour the beauty of the Peacock Throne for himself. And so she was. How far along was she? To his experienced eye—and he had sired sixteen children, including those from his other wives—it seemed like five months, perhaps six. Yet she barely showed. In a month she would be ungainly and big, and there would be no hiding her fatigue and her still-present nausea from him or anyone else. The women of the zenana knew, of course, as they were wont to, yet not a word had been breathed in his presence or in the corridors or at court.

His heart ached as he watched his beloved daughter negotiate this hurdle all by herself. He could not talk to her about it; she would not want it, for it would mean admitting the presence of Najabat Khan, and admitting also that his strict injunction against her ever marrying had led her to this. She had asked him to let her go on a pilgrimage to Ajmer and Delhi and had said that it would take a few months, four, maybe five or more. Could he spare her for that time?

Two days ago, they had both received Aurangzeb's letters, filled with his exhausting praise of Orchha and the victory there. Earlier intelligence had informed the emperor that Raja Jhujhar and his son had escaped into the Deccani kingdoms and been killed there—all of the Raja's possessions were now in imperial hands. Jahanara's eyebrows had knotted in anger as she read her letter, but she did not offer to show it to her father.

Emperor Shah Jahan sighed, the Peacock Throne forgotten, the troubles of his children overwhelming him. Dara was his firstborn son, the one to whom he intended to leave this empire, yet he was unsatisfactory, too flighty in matters of politics, too interested in books and learning. Never a good combination for a sovereign—for the hand on the sword must always be mightier than the one holding the quill. Shuja and Murad were disappointing in their own ways, fire and frost, not enough of one, sometimes too much of the other. Aurangzeb was strong, levelheaded, cut from the cloth of kings, but far too intolerant to be a good one. And—Shah Jahan rubbed the back of his neck slowly—there was that one incident from the past . . .

When Arjumand had been pregnant with Shuja at Ajmer, in the last days before giving birth, she had craved apples. Servants had been sent into the June heat to look for them; there were none to be found in that season, but Arjumand had been so insistent and unreasonable that they had all doubted her ability to survive the confinement. Shah Jahan had gone out himself, scouring the bazaars in the hope of an early apple from Kashmir or Persia or Qandahar, his pockets laden with gold mohurs. And then a passing fakir, unshaved and unwashed for many days, had reached into his filthy robes and brought out two perfectly formed golden red apples, their skins smooth, fragrant in the sun-fired air. Shah Jahan had given him a bag of gold, which the fakir had waved away, accepting only one gold mohur instead and leaving him with this prophecy—that a son would be born to him who would be, in the end, the death of him. And that son would be marked with a scar at birth.

Of his four sons, only Aurangzeb had a birthmark, on the middle of his back in the indentation of his spine, shaped like a scorpion's claw. Over the years it had faded, but Shah Jahan had seen it and had never been able to find much empathy with his third son because of it, much as Arjumand herself had tried to dispel his fears.

The fakir had also curiously said that when Shah Jahan was going to die, his hands would smell of apples—it was a fruit he never ate after that day, even though his wife did not lose her love or fascination for it.

When it came to his daughters, Shah Jahan thought only of one; the others hardly mattered to him. And in Jahanara, Shah Jahan saw all the qualities her brothers lacked . . . but she was a mere woman.

He stepped onto the terrace and joined her along the balustrade, where they stood in silence, their fingers linked, looking out at the Luminous Tomb's white marble dome.

'When do you leave, my dear?' he asked.

'You give me permission then, Bapa?'

He put his arm around her and kissed her forehead. 'I have decided to take the court with me to the south to sample some of the fine hunting Aurangzeb boasts about.' Her eyes widened in relief—she had been dreading that he would want to join her, he knew—and he continued, 'It will also give me a chance to oversee the campaign there. You will go safely?'

She nodded, watching her hands.

'And return to me safely?'

She held his gaze. 'I have nowhere else to go, Bapa. My place is with you.'

'Go then, prepare for your travels. I will miss you, my love.'

They parted as he gently nudged her towards her apartments in the zenana, leaving him to go to his alone. Her steps were hurried. Emperor Shah Jahan knew that he sent his heart with his oldest child, and if she were to die, as his wife had, in childbirth, he would no longer have the capacity to rule, and the empire would fall into Dara's hands even if he had not yet proved himself capable.

The next three months passed in a daze for Jahanara, alone at the Taragarh fort at Ajmer with her ladies-in-waiting and Ishaq Beg. Her stop at Delhi on the way here had been brief—she had visited her great-great-grandfather Emperor Humayun's tomb and meditated at the dargah of Shaikh Nizamuddin Auliya, a Sufi saint of the Chisti order who had died in the early part of the fourteenth century. She had not known what she was praying for as she knelt by the saint's grave, then rose to her feet clumsily, for even that little effort had caused a shortness of breath. She had thought that she would stay here for a while, but Ishaq had insisted that they continue their journey, fearful that the child would come too soon if she exerted herself.

And so they had found their way to Ajmer and the hill fort of Taragarh, a meagre five hundred feet above sea level, meagre only compared to the mighty Himalayas she had left behind some six months ago. Ajmer was on the southern tip of the great Thar Desert, which laid itself out in bands of brown sand over the northwestern edge of the empire. Here, there was the hint of desolation in the orange and red hills of the Aravalli Range, which curved and humpbacked like mystical animals in repose, their sides dotted with faded green shrubs and the occasional tree that defied the sun, the heat, the aridity to provide a scant shade under its desiccated branches. The fort itself had been built in the fourteenth century, the stronghold and residence of the Chauhan kings, who had bowed to Emperor Akbar's suzerainty. The building inside climbed up the hillside, sharply vertical, the heavy stone bleached to a whiteness, perforated with arches, topped with ornate chattris, with curved eaves over the windows that mimicked the arcs of the verandah arches. The stone, quarried from the womb of the Aravalli, was unyielding to the chisel and the hammer, and, consequently, the walls of the palaces, both inside and out, were uncarved. Instead, on her first visit to the fort, Jahanara found painted walls in her apartments and in all the public spaces—lushly brushed with indigos, greens, reds, oranges, yellows, turquoise, each painting a story from Hindu mythology, panel after panel lit by the western sun as it flooded the plains on its way to rest.

Here, in these decorated halls of the zenana, Jahanara spent many an hour, tracing her hand over the warm stone, marvelling at the forever unknown artists—merely men for hire—who had left their marks in colour and fable. The city of Ajmer, mostly composed of the mansions of the nobles who had accompanied the Mughal emperors here on their own pilgrimages to the dargah of Khwaja Muinuddin Chisti, another Sufi saint, spread out below the crenellated walls of the fort near and around the saint's tomb. And this was why Jahanara had made the journey to Ajmer also. Her interest in Sufism had been fuelled by Dara, who had given her books to read, allowed her to sit behind a curtain when the holy men came to visit him and discuss their philosophies, read poetry with her. In the early days after discovering herself to be with child, Jahanara had felt bereft, not knowing to whom to turn for help, if indeed help was available to her. She had been deeply fearful of Bapa's reaction to the news, not that she intended to talk with him about it, but . . . he would be disappointed. Najabat Khan had stayed back in Srinagar, and she had written to him, knowing he would be happy, as she was, happy and afraid. His response had been for her to fly to him, find sanctuary in his haveli in Srinagar, and give birth to their child under his protection—as things ought to be. For a while, a few weeks, Jahanara too had cherished this thought, until her Bapa had fallen ill with a fever that left him shivering in the torrid heat of Agra, and though exhausted herself, she had nursed him back to health.

That dream had shrivelled. She had taken the bold step of accepting Najabat Khan as her husband without the sanction of a marriage; now she would have to carry and have their child by herself—this was the path she had chosen. Over the next five months, she had continued her duties in the zenana and at court as always, thinking and planning for the future, and, most surprisingly, the suggestion to visit the dargahs of the Sufi saints had come from Dara by way of Nadira. They knew, they all knew, Jahanara thought, and accepted their discreetness gratefully, for she could not have borne a public proclamation of her plight. The only person who had genuinely been unaware had been Aurangzeb, his ears buzzing with rumours of a possible alliance with Najabat Khan; he had not grasped how far matters had come. But Aurangzeb had always been this self-centred, stifling her with his supposed love but unwilling to think of her—what she wanted and needed.

One evening, as the sun waned in the skies over Ajmer, Jahanara ordered her palanquin to be made ready for another visit to Khwaja Muinuddin Chisti's grave at the foothill of Taragarh. It was the month of May, and the heat of the desert had built up to sweltering proportions; even as the sun yanked its last golden rays beyond the horizon, the air broiled. Ishaq Beg accompanied her, and she heard him pant as he ran down the steep ramp that led from the fort to its principal entrance, the Hathian Pol, with its two carved elephants adorning the front. The streets were quiet at this time of day, and, through the sheer curtains of the palanquin, Jahanara saw the quick flames of cooking fires inside the houses, women bent over smoking chulhas, bareheaded, their brows beaded with sweat. She had grown big now, her belly ballooning in front of her, her toes no longer visible unless she put them up on a cushion, and this she did very little, not wanting to see the swollen skin around her ankles and the sharp green of the veins in her feet. Every movement was an agony, although the four men who carried her palanquin jogged on soft feet, the poles of her conveyance resting on wads of cloth upon their shoulders.

A mile from the dargah's entrance, she stopped the palanquin and got out arduously, using her hands to hoist herself to a standing position, her legs trembling as they bore her weight.

'I will walk,' she said firmly to Ishaq Beg, who opened his mouth to protest and then shut it, recognizing from the rigid way she held herself that she was not going to argue about this. She slipped her chappals from her feet, and this time he did demur, but she would not listen. Her grandfather, her great-grandfather, her father—they had all approached Muinuddin Chisti's tomb on foot, barefoot in homage to the saint, to whom they had gone to pray in times of need and, when their prayers were answered, in times of rejoicing.

Descended from the Prophet Muhammad, Muinuddin Chisti was born in Persia in the twelfth century and spent part of his life in Samarkand and Bukhara in search of spiritual instruction. Although he had not left a book of his teachings, his disciples talked of his having had a vision from the Prophet himself telling him to go to Hindustan, and so he did. Here he found an acceptance of his beliefs, a range of followers from both the Hindu and Muslim faiths, but he refused the patronage of the kings, preferring to remain apolitical. He had finally come to stay at Ajmer, in the very heart of a kingdom whose ruler was Hindu, and here he had remained, buried under a simple slab of local stone. His disciples had spread his teachings, and Nizamuddin Auliya, the saint whose grave Jahanara had visited in Delhi, was also a disciple of his, three generations removed.

When Jahanara began to walk down the bazaar street that led to the first of the gateways to the dargah, she noticed that the imperial guards had already warned the people of her presence. The long street was empty, the shops had drapes over their fronts, and behind them, lit by oil diyas, she saw the shadowed figures of the shopkeepers and their assistants, motionless and listening to her footsteps as she passed by. She had time to think during that walk, the stones on the path biting into her feet, her heaviness dragging upon her, her breath coming in gasps, the heat closing in.

The Mughal kings had a long history with the Chisti Sufi saints; Emperor Akbar had always revered Muinuddin Chisti, but it was another Sufi saint of the same order—Shaikh Salim Chisti—whom he had considered to have blessed his empire. For it was to Salim Chisti that Akbar—twenty-six years old and married for more than ten years—had gone in prayer and pilgrimage, begging for an heir to his empire. Salim Chisti had lived in a cave near the village of Sikri, a few miles from Agra, and he had promised the emperor three fine sons. When they were born, the first of them had been named after the Sufi saint. That Prince Salim became Jahanara's grandfather Emperor Jahangir.

The man who had brought Chisti Sufism into Hindustan, however, the man from whom all these disciples were descended and who had rendered help and succour to the Mughal kings when they faced hardships, was Khwaja Muinuddin Chisti at Ajmer. Emperor Humayun had built a dome over his grave; Emperor Akbar had erected a massive gateway to the tomb and a mosque inside its main courtyard. At some point, a Hindu Raja had paved that courtyard with slabs of white marble, chill to the touch even in the peak of summer, shimmering in the light of the sun. Jahanara's father had built another mosque in the compound, and yet another gateway leading in, and it was this gate that Jahanara now entered, pausing to rest below the portal.

The dargah had been cleared of loiterers and worshippers so that she could come here. In front of her were two stone platforms, each with carved steps leading to the top, where mammoth cauldrons had been sunk into the mortar. They were both of brass, aged to blackness, widemouthed and shallow, and used for cooking a sweet concoction of rice, milk, sugarcane juice, raisins, almonds and pistachios to feed the poor and the pilgrims. The bigger one had been given to the dargah by her great-grandfather, the smaller one by Emperor Jahangir—he had knelt at one of the four openings in the steps and lit the first fire that burned under this cauldron himself, and when the fire had begun to take life and the khichri had begun to bubble, he had stirred it with his own hands.

She skirted around the cauldrons and went up the steps to the Khwaja's tomb, halting at the doorway to pray. The Khadims, the caretakers of the tomb, lurked somewhere in the shadows, their faces angled away from her. They did not know who she was, or why she occupied the fortress of Taragarh, but they doubtless guessed that she had some imperial connections, for she had been coming to the grave three times a week in the past few months, and every time they were asked either to leave or to glue their eyes to the ground for fear of looking at her. They were getting tired of her, she thought as she heard their quiet mutterings echoing in the hush of the tomb. In the bazaar, even with everyone kept indoors so that she could walk unmolested by the gazes of the common men, there had been the noise of horses neighing, cows lowing, women chattering, the tinkle of the coppersmiths' hammers, the rustle of hay, the barks of dogs. Here, there was a complete absence of sound. Even in death, the Muinuddin Chisti brought tranquillity around himself. There was an indefinable aroma in the air, a combination of the attar of roses, the incense of myrrh, of jasmine, of the cool of the marble, of the heat of a desert baked over many centuries.

Jahanara leaned against one of the walls in silence until her feet ached, and then she left the tomb and walked around it. A yellow moon floated in the sky, its light so thin that she had to watch the diyas flickering around the tomb to find her way. The marble was smooth under her feet, its mortar lines barely felt. She joyfully placed a hand over her belly as the child kicked hard against her pelvis. It had been quiet all day, and Jahanara had remembered the women of the zenana saying that a child's moving inside meant good health, so she had come here, forcing her tired limbs to take her down the bazaar streets and into the saint's tomb to pray for her child.

And now her son was telling her that he was all right, that he had been, perhaps, asleep, lazy, slothful, unmindful of his mother's concern. She patted her belly again, and he knocked against that spot. She stopped, paling in the feeble light of the newly risen moon. For a gush of something warm had flooded between her legs.

rauza-i-munavvara
The Luminous Tomb

Of all the tombs at Agra, that of the wife of Shahjahan is the most splendid. He purposely made it near the Tasimacan . . . The Tasimacan is a large bazaar, consisting of six large courts all surrounded with porticoes, under which are chambers for the use of merchants, and an enormous quantity of cottons is sold there. The tomb of this Begam, or sultan queen, is at the east end of the town by the side of the river.

—WILLIAM CROOKE (ed.) AND V. BALL (trans.),
Travels in India
by Jean-Baptiste Tavernier

Agra
Wednesday, 2 May 1635
14 Zi'l-Qa'da A.H. 1044

'And this will be the Taj Ganj?' At the sound of a large crash, Roshanara ducked involuntarily, and the eunuchs guarding her gathered in a tight circle, their arms stretched out. The man standing behind her ran towards the wooden pathway, held up on stilts, which had just collapsed, raising a thin fog of dust. Men shouted; hands disappeared into the rubble as workers were raised out of it, dusted off. The man scuttled around the periphery of the accident and then came running back to stand behind the princess again.

'I beg pardon, Your Highness,' Ustad Ahmad Lahori said. 'A minor incident; no one is hurt. The men will have the planks up again in no time at all.' When he realized that she was not listening, he went on, 'His Majesty had decided that this will be called the Taj Ganj or the Taj Makan. The bazaar streets will be here, along with the four caravanserais. This part of the *rauza*'s complex will be as large as the gardens of the tomb.' He stopped and waited for her response. It was a long time in coming, and Lahori dared a quick look at her back. Why was she here? Why the interest now, so many years into the tomb's making? Other royals, even the Begam Sahib, had come by often, wandering through the dirt, picking their way between the workers and the foremen, curious about this monument their father was constructing for their mother. It was Lahori's job, as architect, to accompany them when they came, and he resented even that little time taken away from his true work. But it had been pleasant, and at times beneficial, for, a few days after Princess Jahanara's visit, his wives had been invited to spend a week within the walls of the imperial zenana, and they had returned happy, flushed by the honour shown to them. But this princess, the emperor's second daughter, had never yet shown any curiosity about the Luminous Tomb and had come here before only for the 'urs ceremonies.

'Splendid,' Roshanara said eventually. 'You have done well, Ustad Lahori.' She waved in a vague dismissal.

Lahori bowed and backed away slowly. Of course it was splendid, he thought, and he didn't need this girl, this woman, to tell him so. Why *was* she here? Simply bored? The emperor was himself in the Deccan, the Begam Sahib in Ajmer, it was said, and Princess Roshanara had chosen to remain here at Agra.

Roshanara took a deep breath and coughed, the red sandstone dust clogging her nostrils. Her eyes watered, her skin was coated with the dust, and she was hot even under the shade of the white umbrellas held up by her attendants. Around her there was the sound of metal on stone, the thick mixing of mortar, the subdued murmurs of the men and women working on the site. When she left, they would talk and shout, she knew—all this quiet was in deference to her being here.

The Taj Ganj, she thought, looking at the walls being erected. In most tombs, the Jilaukhana also contained the sarai area—a place of rest for the pilgrims, the travellers, the curious and the tourists. But Bapa had specified that there would be a third area altogether for this purpose, and the Jilaukhana, the forecourt, would house only another bazaar and quarters for the Khadims, the tomb attendants. This, the Ganj, was south of the Jilaukhana, accessed through the southern gateway of the forecourt.

It was a simple square, a compound wall enclosing its four sides. Within, there were two streets, one north–south, the other east–west, and these two streets, which sliced the Taj Ganj into its own charbagh shape with four quadrants, were the main access roads within the walls. Every quadrant was then further closed off with high walls, and the square courtyards formed inside had verandahs on all four sides and rooms beyond—a hundred and thirty-six rooms per quadrant. The sarais were self-contained units, each with its outhouses, kitchens, hammams, storerooms and guards.

At the point where the two streets met in the centre of the Taj Ganj, the corners of the four sarai walls would have chamfered edges, cut out enough to accommodate a gateway in each corner that would lead into the sarai and be shut at night to keep out thieves and bandits. Along the entire outer walls of the sarais, fronting the streets, were a series of verandahs with little rooms beyond, and here was the marketplace of the Taj Ganj. The bazaars, when they came into being, would be lushly stocked with every item of trade available in the empire, no matter how distant its origin or how dear its price.

Standing at the centre of the Taj Ganj, Roshanara imagined what the bazaars would be like in a few years—a sight she would never see, for if she visited the bazaar, it would be under guard, the shops closed, the streets emptied.

There would be jewellers who worked in delicate pearls and gold, their wares lustrous in the morning sun, their shops surrounded by veiled women who would watch them with eyes filled with lust and envy. Copper and brass workers hammering away on cups, water vessels, spoons and plates. Grocers laying out their produce in rows, fresh from the earth, harvested as the sun lifted its sizzling head over the horizon. Betel nut sellers hanging the heart-shaped leaves from jute strings around their stalls, enveloped in a jungle of shiny green. Cloth merchants swinging their fabrics from one end to another—shimmering silks the colour of sunsets, chiffons flimsier than summer clouds, gleaming cottons in blues and grays. Flower merchants in corners, surrounded by freshly picked peonies, roses, marigolds, lilies, jasmine and jacaranda, still heavy with dew, saturating the air with their fragrance.

Everywhere in the Taj Ganj, this new city for repose and trade, would be the sounds of bustle and life. Jugglers and buffoons cavorting in the streets, a throng of women—some veiled, some not—their eyes brilliant with kohl, their skin browned by heat and grime, their arms strong from working in their houses. And behind them, down the southern gateway into the Jilaukhana, through the Great Gate, would lie the hushed tomb, with its luxuriant gardens, its fountains, its pearl dome, and the smooth-flowing Yamuna beyond.

Roshanara sighed. The Luminous Tomb was a massive undertaking, most of it already in place. The riverfront terrace and its buildings were completed, the Jilaukhana constructed, the work begun here in the Taj Ganj. In a few years, all the details—the dado panels in the tomb, the inlay work, the writing of the suras around the edges of the portals—would also be finished. And all this, she thought, for Mama. Had she been so precious to Bapa then? Yes . . . perhaps, but in the building of the tomb, Bapa had forgotten, overlooked, its initial purpose, thinking more of himself and his fame as the patron than of Mama, who lay here. Roshanara had suggested as much during the second 'urs, and her father and Jahan had both been outraged. She rubbed her forehead. They had not appreciated her honesty then, or later, when she had informed Bapa of Jahan's furtive alliance with Najabat Khan. She could not remember that abortive meeting at the Shalimar gardens without being outraged. How had he dared to speak to her thus? And the very next day, Jahan had visited him in his house . . . and spent the night.

Now she was in Ajmer, ostensibly on a pilgrimage.

'Shall we leave, Your Highness?'

'Not yet,' Roshanara snapped. Why did it surprise them all so much that she would want to oversee the building of Mama's tomb? What else did she have to do here, with Bapa away, the court with him, half the zenana in the Deccan, the other half in Agra? It was laughable, the manner in which everyone had accepted Jahanara's excuse of visiting the Shaikh's tomb. What would she do with the child when she returned? Bring him into the zenana as a waif she had picked up, or send him away?

'Your Highness.' The eunuch was insistent, his hand now on her elbow, nudging her out of the Taj Ganj. 'We must leave.'

This time Roshanara let him guide her steps. She took one last look around and felt a small bite of envy. This mausoleum, in all of its magnificent parts, would pin Bapa into history more firmly than the numerous official biographies he had commissioned, the children he would leave behind, the farmans he dictated to rule the empire. And because of its beauty, posterity would think of Mama also as this most loved woman. What of her, Roshanara? Would anyone remember her? Jahan would have her child, one she could not acknowledge in public, true, but she would leave a little of herself in the world. Roshanara had nothing. No powerful lover at court, no opportunity to become a mother . . . perhaps even no tomb to tell future generations that she had once lived.

Fretful and furious, she went back to her apartments to write again to Aurangzeb in the Deccan. He responded rarely, and then only in brief. She told him this time the actual reason Jahanara had gone to Ajmer and why she had not accompanied their father. *A fact, Aurangzeb,* she wrote. *I would not speak of this if it were not true. You see how she has fallen low in my estimate and must now do so in yours also?*

When the letter was signed and sealed and on its way, Roshanara called for the musician's son—the same man who had gone to pleasure her sister—for the night. She felt as though she was taking something away from Jahanara, since she couldn't, after all, shake the love that her father, Najabat Khan, Dara and even Aurangzeb had for her older sister.

When Mehrunnisa had built the little white, lavishly inlaid tomb for her father, she had packed the gardens with fruit trees—guavas, mangoes, pomegranates—to supply a continuous and perpetual income for the tomb. That money would go towards salaries for the tomb's attendants and repairs on the structure itself when necessary. Emperor Shah Jahan had levelled the earth, rerouted the river, and raised a magnificent monument over his wife's remains that cost him five million rupees when it was completed. A handful of fruit trees in the gardens would not provide enough of an income for the upkeep of the tomb. So he had built the Taj Ganj. From the rental of the rooms of its caravanserais—whose fame would spread all over the empire and so would rarely lack occupants—and the taxes and rents on the shops in the bazaar streets came two-thirds of the funds required to maintain the tomb, provide alms to the poor on Mumtaz Mahal's death anniversaries, and pay the imams who recited verses from the Quran on-site, as well as the caretakers. For the remaining third, Shah Jahan created an endowment of the annual revenues from thirty villages around Agra, and the total paid to the administrators of the tomb was three hundred thousand rupees a year.

By the time Amanat Khan—the only man responsible for the construction of the Taj who, as calligrapher, was given this privilege—appended his last signature on the tomb's complex, in 1647, on the north-facing portal of the Great Gate, Emperor Shah Jahan had turned his attention to the extensive capital he was building in the old city of Delhi. And by 1647, the tomb was complete in all of its parts—the white marble mausoleum; the Miham Khana and the mosque on the riverfront terrace; the mature trees and shrubs and the incandescent pools of the garden; the forecourt, with its dazzling Great Gate; the humming and thriving Taj Ganj with its merchants, its travellers and its customers.

A common visitor, or even an esteemed amir at court, entered and viewed the Taj Mahal thus, from the Taj Ganj, with its cacophony of sounds; to the Jilaukhana, snug with the heated reds of the sandstone in its smaller bazaar streets and its verandahs; up the stairs to the Great Gate, on which the inscriptions in Arabic called all believers to step into Paradise; immediately beyond into the tranquil shade and fragrance of the garden; and finally to the astounding white marble vision of that most Luminous Tomb.

twenty

Another no less saintly but more tender comforter he had in his daughter Jahanara, whose loving care atoned for the cruelty of all his other offspring. This princess . . . practically led the life of a nun in the harem of Agra fort.

—JADUNATH SARKAR,
A Short History of Aurangzib, 1618–1707

Ajmer
Tuesday, 15 May 1635
27 Zi'l-Qa'da A.H. 1044

Flamingos called out to one another across the breadth of Ana Sagar Lake. As Jahanara watched, they took flight and skimmed over the water, their bodies pewter grey, the darker tips of their wings and their beaks disappearing into the gloom beyond. She clasped her arms around a pillar in the baradari and rested her head against the soothing marble as a pain began again. The first one had come within ten minutes of her waters breaking, even as she stood in the courtyard of the tomb, wondering stupidly what was happening, though she knew every moment in a woman's labour in intimate detail, having been present at many birthings—those of her mother and other women of the zenana, the numerous cousins and aunts.

Now she felt the tightening grip of an invisible hand around her tailbone, and at the same time, another seemed to constrict around her heart and lungs—it was not so much a *pain* as a discomfort, extreme and unflinching. The flight of the flamingos had stirred a breeze over the shimmering water, and it came spiralling around the baradari, laying its fingers along her flushed skin. She counted the seconds under her breath. Then the pain died, leaving her body beaten, her hands quivering. In the few moments of quiet, she lifted her gaze to the lake, thankful that she had ordered her slaves to bring her here to the pavilions her father had built along the Ana Sagar and not back to the fort, where the walls still retained the heat of the day and the air broiled inside her apartments.

'Will you walk, Your Highness?' Ishaq Beg asked, offering her his arm.

She nodded and leaned gratefully against him as they took slow steps along the waterfront. Somewhere behind them in the baradari, her servants and ladies-in-waiting had set up a bed with silken coverings, stools for the midwives, who were gathered just beyond in the gardens, carpets on the ground for them to sit on. When Jahanara had arrived at the lake's pavilions, thick curtains streamed from every archway, blocking the slight wind, enclosing all the air inside. She had ordered the curtains to be torn down to open the baradari to a view of the waters, as was intended under any other circumstance. The women had balked. A royal princess laid out in childbirth for the whole world to see? Who would see her? Jahanara had demanded. A tight cordon of soldiers guarded all the entrances to the lake; the baradari sat atop an eminence, its occupants hardly visible to anyone on the banks, and if the lanterns were extinguished, they would all be one with the light of the moon—or shadows in the shade of the arches. If any man dared to raise his eyes to the baradari and was discovered, he would not see the sun rise the next morning; if he dared to and was not caught, he could still not say that he had seen anything at all.

'Does he know, Ishaq?' she asked softly, feeling her legs ease with the exercise.

'A message is on its way, Your Highness.' He paused and looked down at her. 'I have written to Mirza Najabat Khan every day since our arrival here; he insisted upon news.'

'More often than I have,' she said. 'I could not bring myself to write, even'—she laid her other hand on the rise of her belly—'to the father of this child.'

'I have seen many women, Your Highness, in such a state as yours, and they have all been obsessed with the life within them, living as though in a dream, unwilling to heed everyday matters. Perhaps especially with the first one.'

'I do not know that I will experience this again,' she said simply, even as her eyebrows drew together in the first spasms of another labour pain. She laid her head on his shoulder as a whiteness bore down upon her eyes, as her breath caught in her throat. She was determined not to cry out, and so shut her teeth on her lip until a little streak of blood dribbled down her chin. When she looked up at the end, it was to present a pale face with a ribbon of red from her lip to her neck.

'I am tired,' she said. 'How much longer, Ishaq?'

'I do not know, Your Highness. Perhaps one of the women would . . . if only you will let them attend to you.'

She laughed, a thin and faint laugh belying her fatigue. There had been a time, early in the pregnancy, when she could not have borne to be touched, her skin throbbing with sensitivity at every place, the baths with the slave girls a torture until she had commanded them away, the gentle hand of her father on her shoulder a torment. It had been during this time that Aurangzeb had come to bid her farewell. She knew that he wanted to embrace her, to lay a kiss upon her cheek, but she had turned away, loath almost to share of herself any more with anyone. The child inside was everything; he had consumed her, drawn upon all of her vast energy, eaten up her tolerance. All that had remained unchanged until today, when the labour began. Even in the warm air of Ajmer, Ishaq's grasp had been comforting, his shoulder a blessing . . . but the women who waited, midwives and servants, they were strangers, and yet when the time came for the child to be born, it would be their fingers that would caress her womb, their hands that would pull him out, clean him up, prepare and apply the poultices that would heal her.

Another pain came, taking her so much by surprise that she doubled up and fell to her knees. This time it blinded her, drew every thought out of her head, and she did not protest when the women came to lift her and carry her to the bed. They were the ones who smoothed the sweat-matted hair on her brow, who wiped her face with cool towels dipped in rosewater, who massaged her distended belly with their capable and soft hands. At some point during the next few hours—she could no longer tell how time had passed—she heard a midwife say, 'Bear down, Your Highness; the child's head has crowned.'

Ishaq was by her side, on his knees, one of his hands clutching hers, her fingernails leaving slashes of red upon his palm. She had never listened to an order from a menial, rarely even from her father or her brothers. But she did now, with an enormous effort, forcing the child from her body and out into the world.

Silence followed. Jahanara's heart contracted with fear. 'Is he all right? Say something.'

She heard the midwife slap the child across his buttocks, and he opened his mouth in a huge, reedy wail that echoed off the pillars of the baradari and swept into the brilliance of the lake beyond. Jahanara, who had not cried when she discovered that she was pregnant, never shed a tear when her fatigue, both emotional and physical, was great, found tears welling in her eyes and flowing down her cheeks. Ishaq cried also, quietly, his tears dampening his mistress's hand.

'Give him to me,' she commanded. 'Now.'

A midwife brought the child. He was so slight, hardly even a weight in her arms. They were still in the shadows, silver moonlight beyond the arches of the baradari, and they carried her bed to the edge so that she could look upon his face.

'Hush,' she said, her voice breaking, when his cries broke out again. 'Hush, my little king, now you are safe with your mother.' She talked on, words of nonsense, of endearment, not even knowing where they came from. He quieted again, his eyes riveted on her face. She touched the black eyebrows that winged thickly above his eyes, already meeting in the middle, the lush head of still damp hair, the perfectly curved ears, the rosebud of a mouth. He turned his face and nuzzled against her breast, and an ache began to build inside her.

'Your Highness,' Ishaq said at her shoulder. 'It is better not to . . . it will form too much of an attachment. The wet nurse waits; hand the baby to her.'

If it had been any other royal princess, or a noblewoman, in the normal course of events the baby's mouth would have sought the wet nurse's breast so that the new mother did not have to spoil her figure—a woman's perfect body, immaculate even after childbirth, was much prized. But whom did she have to please? Jahanara thought, overwhelmed by an unexpected desire. The baby began to cry again, his face turning crimson, his fists balled as though ready for a fight.

'Just one time, Ishaq,' she said, pleading, her fingers struggling with the ties of her choli.

'I do not understand—' he said, but he helped her loosen the strings that held her bodice together at the back and watched as she offered her breast to the child.

The baby rooted around until he found the nipple and began to suckle. Jahanara leaned back against the pillow, her body melting, her limbs liquefied. This was love, she thought, such love as she had never had before, as she would never again experience. For the rest of the night, she lay with her son in her arms, thinking of the name she had chosen for him, as the moon waned in the sky, to be replaced by the glow on the eastern horizon that heralded dawn. She was invigorated, alive, not any more in need of sleep. When the child woke, she kissed him on his lips, gave him her breast at regular intervals, forgetting the promise she had made to her eunuch. The slaves came to take him from her briefly, to change his wet clothing and dry him. She sat up and watched until they brought him back to her.

She would have to give him up, but with force of will she forbade her mind to think of the parting, focusing only on the present.

As the morning flung its skeins of red and gold on the still-dark sky, she propped herself up on an elbow, the child snuggled against her, and wrote to Najabat Khan. At the very top of the page, she wrote *All is well by the grace of Allah,* so that he knew this letter brought him nothing but good news.

> You have a son at last, my lord, and it is I who have given him to you. He sleeps by my side, his fist curled against his exquisite face, my milk still fragrant upon his lips. You see, I could not resist, though I know that from now on he will belong only to you . . . never, you must promise me this, to the women of your zenana. There must be only one woman in his life, the mother he will never know, but you must talk to him of me, tell him that his coming has shown me why I live. Keep him with you, on your travels and on your campaigns; I know you will cherish him because he is mine also.
>
> I want to call him Antarah, after the Arab poet, for it is his work I have been reading, his poetry that has lulled me to sleep on many a difficult night. I must go, my son stirs, and soon he will open his mouth in hunger.

She laid down the quill and sprinkled sand on the writing to blot the ink before she folded and sealed it with her own seal—a single rose with six unfurled petals, a multifaceted diamond in the centre that left its perfect imprint upon the wax, and tiny script upon one of the petals—reversed in the seal, righted upon the stamp—which read *By the order of her imperial Highness, the Begam Sahib Jahanara.*

Later in the afternoon, when she had woken from a deep sleep, which had wrung all the fatigue from her limbs and left her clear eyed and bright, Ishaq Beg handed her a letter from Emperor Shah Jahan. It was written upon paper woven with gold and sealed with the imperial seal, which he had taken with him but which normally reposed with her in the zenana. In it were only two lines. *I hear you are well again, beta, and have completed your pilgrimage. When will you be returning home?*

She held the child to her, laid her lips upon his soft skin, drank in his fragrance, and when he began to wail because she would not bare her breast, she handed him to the waiting wet nurse. He howled for a while, already sensing different milk upon his tongue, and resisted as long as his little strength held out, but in the end, he grasped at that strange breast and drank the woman's milk as he had his mother's. Princess Jahanara spent the day with her face in her hands, dry of tears, her heart hardening within her. Antarah had never been hers; it was madness for her to have allowed him to suckle at her breast. For the next two days, her breasts swelled with milk and rubbed painfully against the silk of her cholis, and she had to undo the ties at her back to ease the ache. Her nipples leaked when she heard her son's cries—real and imagined—but Jahanara doggedly stayed in her bed, not once asking for the child to be brought to her.

On the fourth day after his birth, they all returned to the zenana apartments at Taragarh fort, and, at twilight, Ishaq ushered in a veiled woman, who bowed to her princess and waited by the doorway for a summons to enter.

'Why do you cover your face?' Jahanara asked sharply. 'How am I to know that you are his wife?'

The woman proffered a letter, which she laid on the carpets in front of Jahanara, and receded a few steps. In it was the hand of the man she loved, the man who had fathered her child, and he told her that this woman was one of his wives, childless herself, to whom he had given the responsibility of bringing up

Jahanara's child. She would look after him well and treasure him as she would her own.

'Take off your veil.'

'Your Highness,' the woman mumbled, 'it is better this way. I will never harm your child . . . and never consider him mine; you must rest assured of that. But he is my husband's son, and my lord has commanded me to be his nurse and his caretaker; I would do nothing to disobey his orders.'

Ishaq brought the baby, swaddled in silk, one chubby hand over the top of the swaddling, his face blissful in repose. The woman craned her neck to look at the child, took one step forward, and then fell back. Her arms, which had risen involuntarily upon seeing Antarah, returned to her sides. Jahanara touched the baby on his forehead, on his nose and cheeks, and on his lips, she then brought that hand to her own mouth and motioned to Ishaq to lay the child in the woman's arms. The baby settled deeply into the cradle she had made and turned his face to her with a small sigh.

'Go,' Jahanara said, her voice threaded with ache. 'An imperial guard will escort you back to Agra. Thank you.'

The woman bowed again, silently, and let herself out.

Some three weeks later, Jahanara set out for Agra herself. She had memorized her son's face, thinking that she would never see him again, but already, she had forgotten the perfume of his little body, the rounded curves of his cheeks, the fans of eyelashes against his skin as he slept. She was on her way to resume her duties as the Begam Sahib of her father's harem, for he had written to say that both Aurangzeb and Murad were to be married, to two of the daughters of Shahnawaz Khan Safavi, a powerful amir at court, who could trace his lineage so closely to the Persian Empire that he still carried the name Safavi.

Jahanara had to prepare the gifts, schedule the various events, play hostess to the two weddings. Murad was only fifteen years old, she thought, and he would already have a wife. She, who was the best loved of all of her father's children, had just given up her only child because she would never marry. She worked all day long, every day, giving orders, overseeing arrangements, greeting visitors, reading to her father, who did not seem to want to let her out of his sight. It was when she collapsed in her bed that the tears came, filling her with an immeasurable ache, choking her throat. When she did sleep, it was to awaken still fatigued, her dreams crammed with thoughts of Antarah, of Najabat, of her brothers' wives, who could openly carry children in their wombs, bear them in comfort, never send them away.

When Emperor Jahangir had lost Qandahar in 1622 to the Persian Shah, Emperor Shah Jahan—then Prince Khurram—had refused to come north from the safety of the Deccan to help. Instead, taking advantage of his father's attention being focused elsewhere, he had thundered into Agra in the hope of capturing the treasury. Emperor Jahangir had left Lahore with a large army to meet the forces of his errant son, had vanquished him and sent him into exile. But Qandahar had fallen to Shah Abbas of Persia.

Even some fifteen years after the event, Emperor Shah Jahan could not shake off the impression that he had been solely responsible for the loss of Qandahar. From the very first year of his reign, he had given orders to Said Khan, the governor of Kabul, to send out diplomatic missions to the Persian governor of Qandahar, Ali Mardan Khan, in the hope that he could be convinced to betray his Shah. And so it had happened. Without a single shot fired, or a single life lost, Qandahar became Mughal territory again. When Princess Jahanara heard the news, she suggested to her father that Ali Mardan Khan should offer his allegiance in person. That way, the governorship of the newly acquired Qandahar could be given to Said Khan himself. It was a brilliant diplomatic move—for Said Khan was firmly on the

Mughal side and could not be swayed into releasing Qandahar again to the Persians without a fight.

When he came to Agra, Ali Mardan Khan was feted and given a large mansab at court, while Jahanara watched him carefully from behind the zenana screen in the imperial durbar.

A month later, she said that he was an able general and a warrior, court life would not befit him, but the governorship of Kashmir would. So Ali Mardan Khan, who had just begun to chafe at the rituals and duties at court, went gladly to the Himalayan kingdom of Kashmir—what had started for him as a wise manoeuvre to enter the service of Emperor Shah Jahan by giving up Qandahar had culminated in his becoming one of the most trusted generals at court. Before the year ended, his emperor had rewarded his loyalty by making him the Amir-ul-umra.

With the majority of the work completed on the Luminous Tomb, Ustad Ahmad Lahori and his emperor shifted their attention to Delhi and the new city of Shahjahanabad. An auspicious date was determined by the court astrologers, and on Friday, the twenty-ninth of April, 1639, workers began levelling ground on the banks of the Yamuna. Stonecutters, ornamental sculptors, masons and carpenters left Agra for Delhi, and, just as they had near the Taj Mahal, they set up their shacks and shanties to settle in for a few years of toil.

And so Jahanara returned to her place in the imperial zenana and her tasks as though nothing much had happened in the months she had been gone. But she had left a part of herself in the child she had borne, and she came back carrying a huge, painful void within her. Bapa had not noticed anything amiss, she had thought when she watched him at Aurangzeb's and Murad's weddings—the laughing and joyful father of the grooms, a patronizing hand on their father-in-law's shoulder, which the man accepted gratefully as a token of his emperor's esteem. There was colour and light around her from the celebrations and a small pinpoint of darkness where Antarah lay in her memories. Roshanara commented once upon how emaciated she had become during her pilgrimage, how the flesh had wasted from her bones. 'Quite swiftly, is it not, Jahan?' she had asked in front of Aurangzeb and his wife Dilras Begam.

The prince, intent on his meal, had lifted his head at the statement and gazed long and thoughtfully upon Jahanara, and she had met his eyes unflinchingly. A shadow crossed his face, something akin to disgust, and Jahanara felt a wave of hatred wash over her. For she had heard another story about this brother of hers, whom she was being forced to fete on the occasion of his marriage—that he had dissuaded their father from thinking of a marriage between Jahanara and Najabat Khan. She knew, in her heart she knew that Bapa had come to that decision himself . . . and her father she could not fault, but Aurangzeb had no business interfering in anything to do with her. The story also went that Aurangzeb had been clever enough not to talk with Shah Jahan himself but had persuaded their uncle Shaista Khan—a man to whom the emperor was more likely to pay heed—to do so. Now, when she ached for her child every day, when she turned her face away from the children in the zenana because none of them was hers, she fantasized about a marriage to Najabat, Antarah with them always . . . It was because of Aurangzeb, she thought bitterly, that Antarah lived in Najabat Khan's haveli on the other bank of the Yamuna. Perhaps not more than a mile away, but she could not see her child, touch him, breathe his essence, and he could just as well have been on the far corner of the world.

She bade farewell to Aurangzeb and Dilras when they went back to the Deccan, where he was governor, and turned away almost at once, so she did not see him look back time and again and did not see jealousy map his wife's young and pretty face. When he wrote, Jahanara did not reply. Antarah was brought up as Najabat Khan's son; who his mother was, no one cared about or asked, since every amir in the empire assumed that he was born of some woman—wife or concubine—in Najabat's zenana. It was his father's name that was important. And that was why

Princess Jahanara stayed away from Antarah, and her siblings followed her lead. Dara, at court by her side, never mentioned her absence or the fine lines of pain drawn upon her forehead. Shuja and Murad were away ruling their own provinces. Roshanara smiled and raged alternately, unable to do anything to her quietly powerful sister.

In the end, it was Aurangzeb, with his rigid views on propriety and decency, who reached out a hand to his sister's son, a boy she would never acknowledge in public.

twenty-one

Begam-Saheb formed [an] attachment . . . for . . . a young nobleman remarkable for grace and mental accomplishments, full of spirit and ambition . . . [but her father] had indeed already entertained some suspicion of an improper intercourse between the favoured Nobelman and the Princess.

—ARCHIBALD CONSTABLE (ed.) AND IRVING BROCK (trans.),
Travels in the Mogul Empire, A.D. 1656–1668
by François Bernier

Agra
Saturday, 25 July 1643
27 Jumada al-awwal A.H. 1053

For months, they had all watched the heavens with anxious eyes, the fields lying fallow, the rice crop shrivelling under the sun's blazing gaze, the skies a pale blue without even the glimmer of a cloud. The rains had come in June, and again a few weeks later, but splattering so weakly onto the parched earth as to barely settle the dust. Winds raged and howled around Agra, white-hot, blowing dirt, searing skins, and clogging noses.

The boys, ranging in age from six to eight, gathered together in the archery maidan outside the fort's walls—in an open field of beaten mud ringed by a grove of tamarind trees. In the very centre was the target in the shape of a man, ten feet tall, clad in the armour and mail of the Mughal armies. The target was made of stuffed cotton and wood chips, its arms akimbo, a helmet of steel thrust on its head. Ten boys were mounted on stocky Turki horses in a silent circle around the target. It was high noon, the end of the second pahr of the day, and the sun rode overhead, leaching their shadows tightly into the ground. Each boy held his head cocked, listening for the archery master's signal, his concentration absolute even as the heated wind curved around the maidan raising a vortex of dust.

'Which one is yours, Mirza Najabat Khan?'

Najabat turned swiftly at the sound of that voice and bent in the taslim when he saw Prince Aurangzeb. When he had completed his salutation, he moved two steps back so that he was behind his prince and said, 'The fourth from our right, Your Highness. The boy in white.'

Aurangzeb gazed at Antarah, stroking his beard thoughtfully. He saw a lean boy who seemed more mature than eight years old, his expression intent and serious. Antarah glanced at them and raised his hand to his father with a quick smile that lit up his face. 'Muhammad Sultan is here also.'

'Your son, Your Highness?' Najabat asked in surprise. 'Forgive me; I did not know the royal princes were at this lesson. Antarah . . . did not tell me.'

'So she named him Antarah, after the poet,' Aurangzeb murmured, more to himself than to his companion. Najabat bowed his head and did not respond. The two men stood under one of the tamarind trees, in the deep gloom of its shade, and beyond them the maidan glowed in the stark light of the sun. 'A good name,' Aurangzeb said. 'And he is a fine-looking boy. You must be pleased with him, Najabat.' Then, turning towards him, 'Are you?'

The amir met his prince's gaze evenly. 'He is my only son, Your Highness, and he makes me proud . . . always.'

Aurangzeb nodded. 'And his mother?' he asked carelessly. 'Is she equally so?'

A silence followed while Najabat pondered upon this question. Men of royalty, of nobility, were not given to talking of the women of their harems—if a woman was mentioned at all, her name was bandied about with ease. But Najabat knew that Aurangzeb was asking him about Princess Jahanara, and this was not a casual encounter, for the prince had found his way to his side, approached him, and inquired directly about his son . . . and the prince's sister's son. What was he to say, though?

Jahanara disliked this brother of hers, for reasons Najabat could not well fathom, and so they were sure not to have talked about Najabat or Antarah. If she had confided in anyone at all, Najabat thought. It was only with him that she was open and enchanting, words spilling out of her mouth; in the zenana she always had a burdensome role to play—a daughter, the Begam Sahib, a sister—and the weight of all her responsibilities kept her mute about her personal life. This immeasurable strength of character was what had attracted him to her and was the aspect of her personality he least understood.

'His mother,' Najabat said, choosing his words carefully, 'has blessed my life in more ways than one, Your Highness. We are both proud and happy that Antarah is our son—there is no reason to be otherwise.'

Again that shrewd look from under lowered brows. 'You think so? There is a correct way of living . . . and a wrong one. I wish sometimes that I could convince my sisters of it.' Aurangzeb lifted his shoulders in an eloquent gesture of defeat. 'But they are not members of my zenana; if they were, things would be different. However, we are here to talk of your son.'

'And yours, Your Highness,' Najabat said, determined not to answer all the veiled inferences. He too had heard of Aurangzeb's interference in the supposed matter of an alliance between Jahanara and him, but, unlike the princess, he held no grudges. Because the emperor would never have agreed himself, and Prince Dara would not have either, although he had told Jahanara that he would allow her to marry when he wore the crown—that was nonsense, Najabat thought; there were far too many obstacles in their way, and if they had waited, Antarah would not be here. The past eight years had gladdened Najabat's heart beyond measure, and though he cherished the stolen moments with Jahanara when he came down to Agra, the boy was always in his home to remind him of his mother in his actions and his mannerisms. When Jahanara and he met, as they had the previous night, they passed half their time in talking of Antarah, some in their love for each other, and the rest as Najabat watched her sleep in his arms, at peace as she never was in the imperial zenana.

A shot reverberated over the dusty maidan as the archery master lifted his musket and fired into the air. The horses whinnied and skittered about on their hooves, and then, one by one, in a well-orchestrated dance, the ten boys nudged the animals' flanks with their stirrups and began to ride around the target. None of the boys was holding his reins; instead these were tucked into the saddles of their horses, so they gripped their mounts only with their legs and feet. The boys held composite bows—short, curved, and immensely strong bows made of mango wood, deer horn and buffalo sinew, covered with lacquered enamel and leather. The strings of the bows were made of a thin and tough animal hide, and they had quivers filled with sixty arrows each slung over their backs. Every boy had a different coloured arrow—red, blue, green, purple, yellow, black, or gold, as Najabat saw in the prince's quiver. The fletchings of the arrows were made of crane feathers, and, in Prince Muhammad Sultan's quiver, the fletchings were of eagle feathers, as befitted a royal prince.

'Who do you think will win, Mirza Najabat Khan?' Prince Aurangzeb asked, covering his mouth and nose as the dust from the riding churned its way towards them.

Najabat only had eyes for his son, steadily upright in the saddle, his bow held aloft in his left hand, his right trembling in the vicinity of his quiver. 'Antarah, Your Highness,' he said softly. 'I beg pardon for saying this, but the prince is two years younger than my son, who has more experience and is the master's favourite in this sport.'

To his surprise, Aurangzeb laughed aloud. It was a sound so rarely heard at court—where the prince had a reputation for being a morose and sullen man, unlike his brilliant brother Dara—that Najabat tore his gaze away from his son and glanced at him.

'Well said, Mirza Najabat Khan,' Aurangzeb said. 'I do not wager; I dislike such diversions excessively, but if your son wins, you must come and serve under my command in the Deccan. That will be your reward.'

The riders had been steadily gaining speed around the target, their horses moving smoothly in a rhythm, each horse's nose a few feet away from the preceding one's tail. The master fired another shot. The boys dipped into their quivers in a fluid motion, fit their arrows into their bows, and let loose the arrows across the maidan. A mélange of colours flashed under the bright sun, and all the arrows found their marks in the target from all sides as the boys rode around. But Najabat watched only Antarah's slight figure as he thundered past his father again and again, his heart in his mouth, praying that every arrow would find its way to the target and not beyond, to hit his son. All the young boys were experts at their craft, and they had been specially chosen for this most dangerous of all archery sports because they were superb riders, able to guide their horses with little prods from their knees, capable of keeping their seats, and adept at hitting the target every time they took aim. The question was which one would empty his quiver before the ending shot rang out.

Four minutes later, the master called for the end of the game, and the boys gracefully pulled up their horses and waited again, panting, their gazes fixed upon the half-broken target, which was littered with arrows. To Najabat, leaning out from the shade of the tamarind, it seemed that one colour predominated—purple, that of the arrows Antarah had carried in his quiver. Najabat could not see his son, for he had stopped on the other side of the target. The two fathers watched in silence as the archery master ran swiftly around his charges, emptying their quivers and counting the arrows left in them. When he reached Antarah, he held his quiver aloft; not one arrow remained.

'Four minutes,' Prince Aurangzeb said. 'So he shot an arrow an average of every four seconds, Mirza Najabat Khan. I did well in not making a wager with you. He has his father's skill on the battlefield and will be formidable when he comes of age.'

Shaking with relief and joy, Najabat bowed to Aurangzeb. 'Thank you, Your Highness . . . for everything. I am honoured that you choose to ask me to serve under you, and if I am ever given that opportunity, I shall take it.' He knew, and his prince knew, that this was more than a mere promise to serve—Najabat Khan had declared his fealty to Aurangzeb because he admired him. If there was ever a question as to which prince he thought should wear the crown, it had been amply answered today.

When Aurangzeb left and Najabat lifted himself from his bow, he found Antarah loping madly through the dust towards him. The boy flung himself upon his father and grasped him about the waist, hiding his face briefly in Najabat's qaba. Najabat held him away so he could see that he was not injured in any way, and then he kissed him lightly on his sweaty forehead.

'Oh, Papa,' Antarah said. 'Did you see what I just did?'

'Yes,' Najabat replied, and then, turning him towards another corner of the maidan, he pointed with a finger. 'Look.'

A woman stood under the trees holding her veil in place. They could barely see her through the thick dust that still floated above the maidan, but they did see her touch her heart and then her mouth, as though she had sent a kiss towards them across the length of the field.

'Is she my mother?' Antarah asked, his young face serious, squinting to look better.

'She could be anyone.'

'Tell me,' Antarah said, facing his father.

Najabat put an arm around his son's shoulders and pulled him close. He put his lips on his head and said quietly, 'Yes, she is. Beta, matters between your mother and me are . . . complicated, so difficult to explain, but I wanted you to know that she was here, that she wanted to be here because she loves you very much. Do you understand?'

Antarah shook his head. 'No.'

His father sighed. 'Perhaps when you are older, you will. Come, we must go home now.'

Princess Jahanara Begam stayed on at the edge of the field long after Najabat and Antarah had gone, long after the maidan had emptied and the horses had been led away. Her heart had finally stopped its crazy pounding, and she leaned against a tree trunk, exhausted, as though she had taken part in the competition herself. Pride washed over her at Antarah's antics, at the elegant way he had ridden his horse, at the speed with which he had shot the arrows, at the impatience in his manner while he had waited for the master to take down the quiver from his back. She had seen the empty quiver long before he had and known that he had won. And when he realized this, he had leapt down from his horse and thundered across the ground to his father. At that moment, she had nearly called out to him. But then, almost as soon as he had reached Najabat, there had been that gift from him to her as he turned Antarah towards her. Perhaps he had told him who she was, and so the boy had looked long and hard at her. She put her face against the rough bark of the tree and closed her eyes. As the years passed, she had come closer and closer to Antarah—in the beginning she had kept the width of the Yamuna between them, but she had started stepping nearer as time passed. Although he had whirled past her as he rode around the target, she had been but ten feet from him and had seen him clearly—that thin face, those determined eyes, that open mouth through which he had breathed, his intense concentration.

'Your Highness,' Ishaq said by her side.

She raised herself and dusted off her hands. 'Yes, I know, we must go too now. How long before I can see him again, Ishaq?'

'Who can say, Your Highness? But I would advise not too soon, and not too often. People will talk, and it will affect the boy.'

She let her eunuch lead her from the maidan and allowed him to help her onto her horse. The waiting eunuchs formed a tight guard around her as they picked their way through the scrub to the palaces at the fort. When they reached her apartments, she lay down on a divan, the soft swish of the punkahs feeding cool air into the rooms, and relived every moment of the game. Tomorrow night, she would see Najabat again, and they would talk of their son. In a few months, perhaps more, there would be another snatched opportunity to see Antarah. In the meantime, she had her duties as the Begam Sahib—and this was more than most women were given. Perhaps one day she would be close enough to her son to reach out and touch his hand and hold it within hers. She was his mother, and though she did not think he would ever address her with that title, it was enough for her that she had given birth to him, given him life, and still watched over him. And this she would do for as long as she was alive.

And so she dreamt of the future. Not knowing that, very soon, death would come pounding at her door.

twenty-two

It happened one night while engaged in such-like dances that the thin rainment steeped in perfumed oils of the princess's favourite dancing-woman caught fire, and from the great love she bore to her, the princess came to her aid, and thus was burnt herself on the chest . . . I was admitted on familiar terms to this house, and I was in the deep confidence of the principal ladies and eunuchs in her service.

—WILLIAM IRVINE (trans.)
Storiado Mogor, or Mogul India, 1653–1708
by Niccolao Manucci

Agra
Sunday, 26 March 1644
17 Muharram A.H. 1054

'How many years have I been Emperor, Jahan?'

Princess Jahanara looked up from the book and closed it over her finger to mark her place. 'Sixteen, Bapa,' she said. 'You know this number well.'

'Yes,' Emperor Shah Jahan said drowsily, adjusting the pillows behind his back so that he could be more comfortable.

It was the middle of the second pahr of the night, around eleven o'clock, and they heard the night watchman's footsteps echo over the stone platform below the emperor's apartments. The windows had been thrown open to capture what little coolness the night afforded, for even this early in the year, after a relatively cool winter, Agra steamed, presaging a torrid summer. Parrots cawed outside, disturbed from their sleep by the watchman; a dog barked somewhere in the distance; the city of Agra slowly ground to a halt as the nobles returned to their homes on the banks of the Yamuna. It had been a busy day for both of them; the emperor had been engrossed in his state duties and Jahanara in listening to and sifting through the various petitions that had come to the zenana—dowries for the marriages of orphan girls, a destitute woman divorced by her husband because he had taken a younger wife, another sold into slavery by her parents. Towards all of them she had opened her hand and her purse and written out nishans—royal edicts—that would be implicitly obeyed, perhaps more than the show of money. She heard these stories every day, more than once a day, and each time she gave thanks to Allah that she had been born a princess, that her father was the sovereign of the richest empire in the world.

'You have a birthday coming up soon. I will have a surprise for you, my dear,' Emperor Shah Jahan said.

Jahanara was sitting on the plush red Persian carpets on the floor beside her father's low bed, leaning her back near where his pillows rested. From here, she could see him only if she turned her head fully. It was how he liked her to read to him, so that he could look over her shoulder at the pages, read along if he wanted, although his eyes had weakened so much in the past few years that he almost never attempted to study a page any more but had the Mir Tozak at court, or the eunuchs in the zenana, read out every piece of paper that came to his attention.

'What is it, Bapa?' she asked, smiling, tilting her head back so that her bright eyes looked up at him.

'It will not be much of a surprise if I tell you, beta,' he said firmly. 'You will just have to wait and see.'

She nodded, removed her finger from the pages of the book, and shut it. Bapa was in a talkative mood tonight, as he often was these days, reminiscing about her mother at times, about matters of state at times. They had read all the books in the imperial libraries, poetry and prose, more than once. He had even read the biography she had written on Khwaja Muinuddin Chisti, in which she had spoken of the months she had spent at Ajmer waiting for the birth of her child (though not mentioning it specifically), and the tranquillity the saint's dargah had brought to her in those turbulent times, when, although alone, she was never far from the thoughts of her father and her brother. And so Emperor Shah Jahan had learned of what his daughter had done not from her but from her words on paper. She knew that on festival days, when they celebrated the Nauroz in February, or Diwali, or Id, he sent caravans of gifts to Mirza Najabat Khan in the name of his son, Antarah. On one occasion, when Jahanara had not been at the Diwan-i-am, the boy had been presented to his emperor by his father. It had all been very correct and official—just as Shah Jahan noticed and granted royal favour to the progeny of his other amirs, so too he had done for Najabat Khan. But her heart had gladdened when she heard of it, and she thought that, as close as they were, as close as a father and a daughter could be, this one secret they would never talk about. It was enough for Jahanara that it was acknowledged.

Upon their return from Kashmir last year, Najabat Khan had also been recalled to the plains and sent to serve under Prince Aurangzeb in the Deccan. He had been asked where he would like to be—at court with Dara, in Multan with Murad, in Bengal with Shuja, or in the Deccan with Aurangzeb. Married and settled into family life, each of the three younger sons had a command and a governorship so that they would not be idle and foster thoughts of rebellion. Dara alone stayed at the imperial court, and so high was the esteem in which he was held that a gold gaddi had been set in the durbar hall just below the emperor's throne. It was the first time a royal prince, indeed anyone, had sat in a Mughal emperor's presence through the long hours at the Diwan-i-am. Emperor Jahangir had set such a place for Shah Jahan once, while he was still in favour with his father, but it had been a token gesture—Shah Jahan had remained standing, albeit near the chair that proclaimed him the heir apparent.

But despite Jahanara's pleas that he should stay on in Agra, Najabat had left for the Deccan.

'I am a soldier, Jahan,' he had said, 'and the ceremonies at court can satisfy me for only so long. I must be in the midst of a battle.'

'Why not go to Bengal or Multan then?' she had asked.

'Because Prince Aurangzeb is the most able of all the emperor's sons. I know'—he held up his hand—'you disagree, but I must choose what is best for me.'

And so he had gone and taken Antarah with him. Her son was nearly nine years old and had long ago graduated from his father's zenana apartments to the mardana—the male quarters of the household—and Najabat told her that he was bold, fearless, with a quick tongue, almost like a girl in that last part.

She held these little pieces of information close to her heart, the only luxury she allowed herself; she had not asked to see him when he went to the Deccan. Her place was here, by her father's side.

'What is this you are wearing?' Emperor Shah Jahan asked, lifting the thin chiffon of her clothing. She wore seven layers of the fabric, in muted browns and greens, so that, together, they covered her shoulders and flowed down to her knees like the waters of the Yamuna outside. Underneath she wore a choli, more a wisp of gold cloth than anything, tied around her back with strings, and there was very little covering her legs.

'I devised this myself, Bapa,' she said. 'Do you like it? It keeps me cool in the day's heat.'

'You are too exposed, Jahan,' he grumbled. 'But I am an old man, what do I know of women's wear? Your Mama would never have shown herself to me in this way.'

'And I am not Mama.' She rose to put the book away on a little sandalwood table and smoothed the silk sheet over her father, tucking it in under his arms. When she bent down to kiss him on his forehead, he said, 'You are a good child.'

'I know,' she said. 'Sleep well, Bapa.'

Emperor Shah Jahan watched as she blew out the lamps in his apartments, turned to glance at him in the sudden darkness, and then let herself out the door, shutting it gently behind her. The aroma of jacaranda lingered in her wake. He twisted to his side and tucked a hand under his cheek. Tomorrow, he would give orders for the diamond and emerald necklace he was planning on giving her for her birthday, and when it came, he would put it around her neck himself. The surprise was to be a drama set to music of Amir Khusrau's poems that he had ordered the court musicians to write and perform. Khusrau, a thirteenth-century poet, had been an ardent devotee of the Sufi saint Nizamuddin Auliya, and his grave lay within the same courtyard as the saint's—it was said that he had wasted away at Nizamuddin's burial site and had died soon after. During her pilgrimage to the saint's tomb, Jahanara had always stopped to offer prayers to Khusrau also, and they both knew his poems verse by verse, line by line. He had been blessed by Allah, Emperor Shah Jahan thought, in a wife whom he had loved, in a child who was now his entire life. He slept. Five minutes later, his world exploded.

As Jahanara returned to her apartments, shadows detached themselves from the walls outside her father's rooms and followed her. Two slave girls and two eunuchs. She did not need protection inside the fort at Agra, but these servants were ever present to tend to her every need, listen for and obey her every command, pick up anything she dropped, carry her if she was tired. They were, in that, very much like her own shadow, trailing at a discreet distance so that she barely saw them or heard them, and she had stopped paying heed to their presence many years ago.

A row of oil diyas lit the way down the long corridor she was passing through—they were set in the centre like a chain of gold, their light pooling in bright circles, the rest of the corridor in semi-darkness. It was a warm, still night, and the flames stood vertical and unwavering.

She could hear the sound of her bare feet on the cool marble, the tinkle of her anklets muffled in the chiffon that her father had derided as too transparent. She looked down upon herself and smiled. It was true, she thought, for her skin glimmered even through the cloth, her legs sleek and muscular, her arms long and smooth, her stomach flat, and her waist slender. She would be thirty years old in six days, but she did not look it—sixteen, perhaps twenty, but she felt more comfortable in her body and herself than she had at those ages. In Mughal India, she was considered past the age of desirability—there were creatures in the zenana who had been banished to its farthest quarters because of this, no longer presented to her Bapa as choices for a night.

But they were poor individuals, much like the women who came to appeal to her; they had no names or titles to speak of, no wealth to rely upon. There were only a few women in the empire to whom age would be of little matter, and Princess Jahanara Begam was the first of those.

She had found a single grey hair at her temple the day before and had hurriedly brushed it into the darker, denser hair around her face. A few more strands and she would have to dye the whole to retain her youthful appearance. She had wondered then if Najabat would still find her pleasing when she grew old, and now, as she went down the corridor, the palace sleeping around her, she laughed out loud. It was a rich sound that echoed off the walls and made the slaves pause in their stride. Jahanara had not stopped, though; she went on, and in doing so put a much greater distance between her and them—those few steps would be her undoing.

A breeze came in through the arches that faced the river, opulent and sweet, filled with the essence of the blooming raat-ki-rani flowers in the gardens. Jahanara turned her head and involuntarily moved to the middle of the corridor. The soft wind swept over the diyas' flames, and they reached out greedily to lick at the first layer of chiffon she was wearing.

For a few seconds no one noticed that her clothes were ablaze. Jahanara sensed rapid warmth at her legs, gazed disbelievingly at the flames sucking their way upward, and raised her hands to fend them off. Her sleeves caught fire; an immense heat seared through the skin on her back when her long, thick plait of hair was set ablaze.

The two slave girls came pounding down the length of the corridor, threw themselves upon their mistress, and flapped wildly at the flames. Their clothing began to burn. Still, they persisted. By the time the eunuchs reached them, the two girls were human infernos, more likely to harm Jahanara than to save her. The men flung the girls away and dragged drapes down to smother the fire on their princess.

'Bapa!' she screamed. Just once, before she felt the flames singe through her choli and blister the skin under her breasts. She felt the weight of one of the eunuchs as he pitched himself onto her, shouting for help all the while. Her skin came away in patches upon his clothing, and smoke smouldered from her hair and her hands. Her eyes grew heavy; the intense pain from the burning came to smother her chest and cease the beating of her heart. She found it difficult to breathe and closed her eyes as darkness fell upon her.

The corridor was now crowded with eunuchs and maids, holding the cloths of their turbans or their veils to their noses to keep from smelling the awful stench of burning flesh. The fire had spread through the curtains on the verandah arches—but the brick and sandstone walls of the fort quenched its ravage. Ishaq Beg came tearing from his bed, knelt heavily by his unconscious princess, then lifted her in his arms to carry her away, his face streaming with tears.

The two slaves lay where they had fallen—in a heap, charred to ashes on the stone floor.

The news spread swiftly on the heels of the imperial runners, and the empire held its breath, waiting to hear more about the fate of the Begam Sahib. Every day, crowds of veiled women gathered in masses around the zenana's main gates, begging for any bit of information about the woman who had been so generous to them in their times of need. They brought gifts for her—a gold medallion which was a treasured family heirloom, rough-hewn toy carts and soldiers that their sons had made, baskets of vegetables scrabbled out of the hard, unforgiving dirt of their gardens, water lilies from ponds, pink-fleshed guavas they had stolen from an amir's estate.

In Burhanpur, Prince Aurangzeb stared in disbelief at his father's broken and unwieldy handwriting sprawled across the page; when he put the paper to his face, it seemed to reek of burning hair. *I pray daily to Allah,* his father had written, *but she seems not to be any better for all of my prayers. Oh, Aurangzeb, what have we done to deserve this tragedy? Where have I gone wrong? Is it, as the Hindus say, a sin of my past life come to revisit me now? She lies before me even as I write, still and unmoving, her breath so shallow that I have to lay my ear upon her chest to assure myself that she is still alive. Dara and I take turns at her bedside, watching her through the nights. If I could give up my life for your sister, I would—the empire is nothing compared to this sorrow.*

Aurangzeb covered his face with his hands and wept, and the sound of his harsh sobs was the first indication to the ladies of his zenana that something was amiss. His first wife, Dilras Begam, made a movement with her hand, and the music in the gallery above stilled abruptly.

'What is it, my lord?'

'Jahanara is unwell,' he said slowly, lifting a tear-streaked face to her.

'A fever?' she asked, her features toughening from their normal prettiness. She was aware of her husband's near obsession with his older sister, whom she considered cold and distant towards them all. Why, the gifts at the wedding had been paltry, and she, Dilras, was a descendant of the Shah of Persia—surely more was due to her position and status. Dilras overlooked, while in these unpleasant ruminations—made more so by a raging envy that Aurangzeb's attention seemed not to be all her own—the fact that the Shah of Persia had conveniently forgotten the connection, and that the Mughal emperors were the highest royalty in the land and she had been fortunate to be connected to the imperial family.

He handed her his father's letter. 'I have to find Mirza Najabat Khan.'

He instructed his men and his household to prepare for the journey to Agra that very night, and they set out at the first glimmer of dawn, riding hard through the heated days, barely resting when darkness came. Aurangzeb had spent his last night at Burhanpur arguing with Dilras about the necessity of going to Agra and giving orders to his generals on the management of the armies and the need to be alert at all times against the threat from the Deccani kingdoms—this last he did perfunctorily, since he knew the men to be as able commanders as he was; most of them had spent their lives here in this very quest. But the Deccan was his responsibility; after sending him here eight years ago to overthrow Raja Jhujhar, Emperor Shah Jahan had officially given him the viceroyalty of the Deccan, and Aurangzeb had made Burhanpur his headquarters.

During the trip back to Agra, he had time to think. In recent months, there had been an upsurge of rebellion among his many generals, and he suspected that reports besmirching his character had found their way to his father. He had noticed that Shah Jahan had not asked him to come to Agra to see his sister, but he did not mind that so much, grateful that his father had at least seen fit to write to him and not have the report brought through the impersonal means of the runners who crisscrossed the empire.

It was a self-serving letter, he thought at times, as the sun beat down upon his bare head and the earth stretched brown and parched around him, unrelieved by greenery or shade. Bapa always seemed to think of himself first and others later—even in this period of grief, he was more concerned about how he might have brought this to happen and not about what Jahan was suffering.

Aurangzeb's entourage entered Agra at the end of April 1644, and he camped on the outskirts with his men and his zenana, knowing that a grown son, with his own household and servants, would not be received within the fort. Or perhaps he knew that *he* would not be welcome—no matter, Aurangzeb was here for Jahan. He sent word to his father of his arrival and settled down to wait for an appointment.

In Bengal, Prince Shah Shuja moved more leisurely. He had been away from the imperial court for so many years that he felt the bonds with his father and his siblings fraying; his life was different now, and they were no longer children. He mourned the possible loss of beauty that Jahanara—a woman had so little else to offer—would suffer; it was a shame that this misfortune had occurred, but she did not need her looks any more; she was old. He thought of all this in a very kind manner, for he was genuinely fond of Jahan . . . or, rather, had been very fond of Jahan. So he waited awhile for more news, and then he heard that both Aurangzeb and Murad were on their way, and he knew that politically it would be prudent for him to be at court also. Thinking thus now, he set out for Agra.

Four hundred and fifty miles northwest from Agra, in the province of Multan, Prince Murad had also received the report of his sister's scrape with death. He too was married, a father twice over, more master of his harem than his brother Aurangzeb, who was known to be dominated by his wife. Murad, married to Dilras's younger sister, was continually appreciative that his father had chosen the more agreeable sister for his wife. So Murad gave his commands, saw that they were obeyed, amassed his men, and set out for Agra. He arrived around the same time Aurangzeb did but was granted his audience with Jahanara before his older brother. Perhaps it was simply luck that it happened so, or perhaps Aurangzeb's missive had lost its way before being delivered, or perhaps both letters from the two sons had arrived at the same time, but the emperor's hand had more naturally stretched to Murad's first and then, after a week, to Aurangzeb's.

Princess Jahanara knew little about her brothers' movements and would not have cared if she had. Every day that she could open her eyes was a gift from Allah, and her every night was threaded with dreams of pain and terror, some real, some imagined. It would take her a long time to recover—two other women, slaves, had died; she herself could have died if the eunuchs had not risked their lives to save hers. So, she would not know until very late that her Bapa, acting upon pressure from Dara, would offend Aurangzeb. If she had been well, she would have advised caution . . . and Emperor Shah Jahan would have listened to her, as he always did.

By the time she realized anything, it was too late. And this one little insult would sow the seeds for a turning point in the empire's history.

twenty-three

Jahanara . . . was on the verge of death for four months, during which Shah Jahan made only the briefest of appearances at his daily durbar in the diwan-i-am and spent much of his time praying at her bedside. Her brothers returned from their various posts to be with her, and it was in this charged atmosphere that Aurangzeb was dismissed and humiliated.

—BAMBER GASCOIGNE, *The Great Moguls*

Agra
Saturday, 21 May 1644
14 Rabi' al-awwal A.H. 1054

For the first time in many days, Jahanara felt rested when she awoke. It was early yet, not quite day—the sky outside her window was clotted with twinkling stars, their light fading as she watched. For the first time also, she had not cried out for the relief of opium when her eyes opened or felt the scorch of the burn on her back. For many days after the fire, she could smell her own flesh, putrid and puckered, and, to her mind, still smouldering as the pain blazed through her. She had no recollection any more of the event itself; she remembered bidding her father goodnight, remembered exulting in the fineness of her figure, the smoothness of her skin. When she came to this thought, tears inevitably filled her eyes and blurred her vision.

And she cried again this morning because she had the blessing of a lessening of the pain, and because she knew that the fire had disfigured her. With a shaking hand, she drew the sheet away. Her fingers encountered ridges along the fronts and backs of her thighs, creases against her spine, a raised fold of flesh along the right side of her waist. She turned her face into her pillow and cried with great, heaving moans. The blemishes would never go, even years from now, if she lived that long; patches of discolour on her body would show the mark of the fire as surely as if it still burned her. She had been proud of herself, thinking as she walked that being thirty years of age was no great difficulty for a royal princess who had her beauty, her immense wealth, the love of her father and her brothers—would it be enough to have just the latter two now? Would she still be revered and respected as she had been? Though who at court would ever see her in this state? She had never presented herself before the amirs and would never do so in the future; any flaws she suffered would be just a myth to the men and to the rest of the empire. But she had lost something here, something that crushed her vanity, the only weapon a woman had, and had most certainly lost Najabat Khan's love. He would not find it difficult to replace her, she thought miserably; even if the women of his zenana were not to his liking, there were others, always others, concubines and slaves. And he was a virile, demanding man who would give her his love in words and tokens of affection but would be too disgusted to caress her again.

'Jahan, are you awake?'

She turned her face to the door and hurriedly wiped away the tears. Aurangzeb came running into the room on his bare feet and knelt by her side. The imperial hakims had warned them to keep her room as hygienic as possible to avoid infection, and his face and hands dripped with water from a recent washing.

'You are crying,' he said accusatorily, touching her damp pillow with the back of his hand. 'Why? I'm here now and will look after you for as long as you want me.'

'Aurangzeb,' she said in exasperation. 'You appear like an apparition. I thought you hundreds of miles away in the Deccan, and you open the door and bound in without notice. Where is Bapa? Does he know you are here? Does he even know you are in Agra?'

Aurangzeb grimaced, an ugliness twisting his mouth. He had been a fine figure at sixteen, stocky (he seemed to have stopped growing at fourteen), with a hooked and curved nose, a wide forehead, high cheekbones. All that was unfinished about him at that age had come to completion now, at twenty-six. He had always been restless, she thought, as he moved around on his knees, shifting his weight from one thigh to the other, his hands smoothing her sheet. His knuckles brushed against her hip, and she cried out.

'Don't touch me.'

'Sorry.' He bent to kiss the edge of the mattress, afraid to touch her again, then he raised himself on his elbows and searched her face. 'There are no signs of the fire on your neck and above,' he said.

'I did not know,' she replied. 'They have not allowed me a mirror.'

'I will be your mirror then, Jahan,' he said eagerly, moving as though to divest her of the sheet. 'Would you like me to see?'

'No!' she shouted. 'No one must see. No one can see me like this.'

Behind them, Ishaq opened the door and slipped just inside, his face grim. 'Do you wish for the prince to leave, Your Highness?'

Aurangzeb turned in surprise. He rose and stood before Jahanara's bed, his arms dangling loosely by his sides, his attitude utterly imperial. For a long while the two men—one a mere eunuch, really half a man, the other who had thoughts of being his sovereign—stared at each other.

'Can you make me leave, Ishaq?' Prince Aurangzeb's voice was quiet.

'If necessary, Your Highness,' Ishaq said bleakly. 'It has been a scant two months since the burning, and Her Highness is still grievously unwell. Your presence causes her discomfort, as perhaps it always has—and I beg pardon for pointing out what is, after all, the truth. You should have gained the emperor's full permission before coming here today and waited until the princess was ready to receive you. The servants told me of your presence, and I have come in haste only to find you upsetting my mistress.'

Much of this conversation passed in a blur for Jahanara, for her legs and back had begun pulsating again with little stabs of pain, and she felt the oozing of pus from the burns as the sheet below her became damp, as her breathing seemed to constrict. She shifted in her bed and said, 'Go, Aurangzeb. Thank you for coming, but go now.'

He bent his head and touched her elbow softly, hoping she could feel that little dab. Her features were filled with pain; her gaze had wandered again to the windows and the lightening sky beyond, and her limbs had started to tremble. That was the last lucid sentence he heard from her.

'I do not approve,' he said finally, assuming the pompous tone he employed when talking of such matters, 'of your . . . connection with an amir at court. I had thought it unbecoming then, and I still do now. You are a woman, Jahanara, and should have behaved with more modesty, for in your discretion lies the reputation of the male members of the imperial family.' Ishaq grasped his prince's hand hard and began to drag him backward. His grip was secure, and Aurangzeb wondered about the courage of this man—did he not feel his head parting from his neck by daring to lay a hand on an imperial prince? Jahanara started to moan, so Aurangzeb cut short his diatribe and ended with 'Remember, Jahan, I do this against my best instincts.'

She had already slipped into oblivion by the time Ishaq Beg pulled Aurangzeb out of her apartments and marched him, not too gently, to the outer doors of the zenana. When he came back, he found another man waiting in the antechamber to his princess's rooms, seated cross-legged on the floor, his back against the wall, his face tranquil.

'Come,' Ishaq said, not marvelling at Najabat Khan's presence. 'She is asleep and will be for a while now. In her being able to sleep lies her cure, for then she is unconscious of the pain, both physical and emotional. Her brother distressed her, but *you* I know she wants to see. I am only surprised that Prince Aurangzeb brought you to Agra with him and smuggled you into the zenana. But then, I am surprised by everything he does.'

Najabat Khan shrugged. 'He truly cares for his sister, Ishaq, as much as you and I do—and though he does not approve of'—he hesitated for a moment—'us, and as much as he would like to be as beloved by her as I am, he is an honest man, at least with himself.'

Ishaq raised his eyebrows, his incredulity clearly evident. 'You view the prince differently then,' he said at last. 'Everyone must have his opinion, however wrong he may be.'

They entered the room together to find Jahanara deeply asleep, the sheet twisted around her legs and arms. Ishaq freed the fabric, bathed her bare limbs with cool water, and changed the thin muslin dressings. Before the dressings went on, he lathered her burns with an ointment of calendula and aloe. Another eunuch came to help him lift Jahanara from the bed to a divan while they stripped her sheets and laid out fresh ones. She slept all through, breathing a small sigh of comfort when her body felt the coolness of the new sheets. And all the while, Najabat Khan leaned against the doorjamb, watching the woman he loved.

'When will she eat?' he asked.

Ishaq shook his head, washing his hands in a basin of warm water. 'I do not know, Mirza Najabat Khan. If we are lucky, she will take a little of a watered-down *khichri* or a tablespoon of stew. It is hard to say.'

'Thank you for allowing me to stay. I had no idea that she was so unwell and would never have known if I had not seen this for myself. Can I . . . be here longer?'

The eunuch turned his sharp gaze upon him. 'Until mid-afternoon. Both the emperor and Prince Dara spent the night in Princess Jahanara's apartments—it will be at least that time before they return to her side. I, however, am always here.'

So when she awoke again, in a few hours, it was to see Najabat Khan at her bedside, seated on a little stool, his hands resting on his knees.

'The day is full of surprises though it has just begun,' she whispered. 'I don't wish to be vain, but I have never wanted to appear before you like this. If you had stayed away, you would have remembered me as when we first met.'

He tilted his head, pretending to think. He had taken off his turban and pushed back the hair from his forehead. In all these past years of seeing and more often not seeing him, usually in some shade of semi-darkness (for they still had to be cautious), she had not noticed the deep grooves of a more or less permanent frown above his eyebrows. His skin was a blistered brown, as though he had just arrived from a battlefield and a war fought in the arms of the afternoon sun. His silk qaba was white, the loose pajamas he wore below also white—both shot with thin lines of silver. He had been here for a while, she thought, noting the creases on his clothing. How long had she slept?

'Do you mean when Dara first brought us together all those years ago?' There was a teasing smile in his voice. 'I did not see you then, Jahan, merely heard your voice. Little enough for a man to base all his love upon. I will remember holding your body in my arms under a waning moon, the scent of your mouth upon mine, the caress of your fingers.' He watched her struggle with shyness, a blush flooding her face and neck as she turned from him.

'Hush,' she said.

He took her hands in his large ones and kissed them. 'You cannot be bashful with me; I will not allow it. Where is the woman who mocked me in the chaugan grounds and defeated me so soundly? Where is that bold woman who came in her shikara to take me with her down the canal and into the waters of the

Dal, and insisted that I row? You did all of this when you barely knew me; now, when you are familiar with every thought in my head and know me to love you beyond every other being on this earth, you cannot turn your face away.'

She glanced upon their linked hands and stole her fingers around his, feeling his warmth and his vitality come into her. 'It all seems so long ago. I wonder . . . if I will have any courage again. My body has been beaten, Najabat. It feels as though my soul has . . . died.'

He leaned over her and laid his face against the curve of her neck, an ache in his heart when he realized that she had grown emaciated in these past months, her collarbone jutting sharply against his cheek. He did not dare to gather her tightly into his arms as he wanted to but had to content himself with laying his hands around her slight figure so that she sensed his embrace even if she could not feel it. When he spoke, his voice was muffled. 'You must get well, Jahan; you *will* get well. If I were allowed to be by your side always, then I would be here. The duty your father and Dara do for you—it is mine under the gaze of Allah, for I am your husband.'

She felt his warm tears against her skin and was glad for that sensation, glad to feel anything at all. 'You cry for me?'

'Only because you are in pain and I can do so little about it.'

'The hakims have prepared some miraculous ointments, and the pain is so faint now I hardly feel it.'

'You lie,' he said. 'Remember that I will always know if you lie.'

She laughed at that, a shrill, unused laugh that cracked its way from her throat. She did not need to ask any more, of herself or of Najabat, if he would find her desirable and attractive. She knew he would because he had defied all the rules of the zenana to find his way here.

'Are we to thank Aurangzeb for this bounty?' she asked.

'He brought me along,' Najabat said simply. 'I was the prince's to command; if he had chosen, I could have been left behind in the Deccan. I would still have fled to you, and perhaps Ishaq would have taken pity on me and allowed me to creep into your apartments for a brief look before the imperial army captured me.' He shrugged. 'This is much better.'

'Aurangzeb is a pretentious snob,' she said. 'His ideas have not changed since he was twelve years old, and I sometimes think that he still speaks like a child—the same passion for his causes, the complete lack of forbearance for any other opinion.' She shook her head with a smile. 'I must be better if I can muster the energy to be angry at him.'

'He came all the way from the Deccan to see you, Jahan. I saw his suffering on the journey,' Najabat said.

'So did Shuja and Murad.' She took a deep breath. 'I am being intolerant myself, and I do not even know why.'

Ishaq Beg brought in a bowl of steaming stew—flour dumplings cooked in chicken broth, flavoured with cumin, chilli powder and salt, sprinkled with a few leaves of coriander. He left it by her side and went out, winking at his mistress and keeping his gaze stoically away from the amir.

'He has always disapproved, you know,' Jahanara said. 'But I understand that he writes to you.'

Najabat smiled. 'His letters about you are almost as welcome as yours are. They tell me more, certainly, more than you care to reveal. I have taken some trouble to cultivate Ishaq, as you see, or he would not leave to me this most precious task of feeding you.'

'I am not hungry.' Her eyebrows met in stubbornness in the centre of her forehead.

'Of course you are.' He lifted her head and fed her the stew, spoonful by spoonful, until she had finished almost the whole thing and the spoon clattered into the emptiness of the bowl. He wiped her mouth with the sleeve of his qaba and then bent his head to kiss her.

'I brought someone along,' he said.

Her voice was faint. 'I have wished to see him for so many years . . .'

Najabat went to the door, and Antarah stepped into the room. Jahanara felt her heart flood with love. She was already very tired from this meeting with Najabat, first apprehensive, then so immensely joyful that her heart had swelled to bursting within her. This, the extravagance of seeing her son up close for the first time, under such circumstances, was almost too much. But she welcomed it. He was a solemn little creature, she thought, already so much like the man he would become. The sturdiness she had seen from across the Yamuna and the lean lines of his body at the archery grounds were apparent now in his nicely muscled arms and legs, slim waist, robust shoulders, clear skin and bright eyes. He had gleaming black hair, smooth and long beyond his ears—the curls of childhood had vanished. He came forward fearlessly, though he must have been afraid, Jahanara thought, for it was the first time he was being introduced to her, and this very first time he had to see her thus—ravaged by a fire.

Antarah bowed in the chahar taslim, rising from it with his right hand on his forehead. 'Your Highness, this is a pleasure indeed.'

'How correctly he speaks, Najabat,' Jahanara said. 'Did you teach him?'

Najabat nodded, watching their son with a smile.

'Do you know who I am?' she asked.

The boy bit his lower lip and rushed to kneel by her side. He cried manfully, trying to hide his tears on the sheet covering her, ending by wiping his eyes and laying a small kiss on the edge of the sheet. 'Will you become well again, Your Highness?'

She caressed his head, exhausted by the day's events. 'I will now, Antarah,' she said. 'Being able to see you . . . is one of many blessings in my life from Allah. Go, my love, I tire now. Go, and remember me with affection if you can.'

Najabat and Antarah rose to leave, but from the door Najabat returned for a brief moment. He set his lips against her forehead and watched her slip into sleep again. Before she did so fully, he said, 'Call for me again, Jahan, when you are well. I will wait, no matter how long it takes.'

A few days later, Jahanara suffered a relapse—her burns became infected, her breathing slowed almost to nothing, and when she opened her eyes she did not recognize anyone in the room. Prince Aurangzeb sent his father a purse of five hundred gold rupees every day, begging him to slip it under his sister's pillow for the night and to distribute it among the poor in the morning. Emperor Shah Jahan did so himself, adding to the purse to bring the amount to a thousand rupees. Hakims travelled long distances to reach Agra with their potions and prophecies, each hoping to be the one who would effect a cure and gain renown as the saviour of the princess. The emperor listened tirelessly to each of them, afraid that if he dismissed anyone too summarily he might indeed be taking away his beloved child's right to live. The days passed thus until a fakir in the streets spoke softly through song of being the one who would bring about a treatment, and word of him filtered into the imperial palaces. Remembering the first fakir, who had so fortuitously given him two apples for his wife in the midst of a broiling summer, Shah Jahan summoned this man into the zenana and ordered him to make good on his promises.

The man brought a variety of herbs from the filthy sack he carried on his back—the thick, broad leaves of aloe vera, the stems and bark of witch hazel, the skin of a young plantain. He fanned these out on the marble floor of a courtyard in the Anguri Bagh in front of his emperor, who sat on the steps leading to the pavilions that looked over the Yamuna and watched him. He asked for milk, honey and an egg, and servants scurried to do his bidding. Buffaloes attached to the imperial kitchens were freshly milked, and the milk, still frothing and warm, was poured into a gold jar, its neck tied with a clean piece of muslin. Eunuchs rooted for the newest egg they could find, one that had just dropped from the hen, and cradled it in silk cloth as they brought it to the courtyard. The honey came from the imperial apiaries, golden, liquid, and fragrant with the jasmines that had created the nectar. With a lot of grunting and some chanting, the fakir broke the egg, carefully decanted the yellow from the white, and used the latter in his concoction along with the rest of the ingredients.

When he was done, he held up a small bowl of cool, whitish paste in both his hands as an offering to his sovereign. 'It will not work unless I make it myself, Your Majesty.'

Shah Jahan rose to grab the vessel from his begrimed hands. 'If it works, you will make it yourself every day, and when the princess recovers, you will own a mansion on the banks of the Yamuna, any one you choose, even one currently occupied.'

He ran to his daughter's apartments and smeared the salve on her himself, praying all the while. Her burns seemed to wane upon first contact, but he continued praying, hoping that he was seeing not what he wanted to see but what actually was. But no, an hour later, she fell into a profound sleep and stopped moving restlessly on the bed. Two days later, the wounds dried up. A month later, they had almost completely healed, and she slept more soundly and woke refreshed and laughing.

This second fakir was heaped with riches, and Emperor Shah Jahan could not help but think that perhaps the first one had also spoken the truth all those years ago.

Remembering that first fakir, Shah Jahan studied the letters he had received from disgruntled commanders of the imperial army in the Deccan—all condemning in a veiled manner Aurangzeb's conduct in the various sorties the army had led into the Deccani kingdoms. Elephants captured from one foray had not been sent to the imperial stables, or the jewellery from one stormed fort now adorned the ladies of the prince's zenana, or something even as simple as the prince not allowing the foraging parties to stray too far, afraid of their being ambushed, and so the campaign had to be abandoned in a few short weeks because of a lack of fuel and water. Taken by itself, each accusation was spiteful, and Shah Jahan would not have paid heed to them. But he was troubled about Jahanara, how slowly she was recovering, and felt how weak his heart had become from this constant battering of uncertainty—and he took it out on the son he did not like. Prince Dara Shikoh, reading the missives over his father's shoulder, added his protests also.

At the end of May 1644, Shah Jahan wrote a curt letter to Aurangzeb, still encamped outside Agra waiting out his sister's illness, and told him that, because of the reports that had reached him about Aurangzeb's misconduct, he was now dismissed from the viceroyalty of the Deccan and could not return to Burhanpur.

As a final insult to his son, the emperor sent Saif Khan, one of his brothers-in-law, to take over the now-vacant governorship. Aurangzeb had assiduously cultivated all of his powerful relations, but he had neglected Saif Khan, who was married to his mother's sister Mallika Banu. Now he smouldered with envy that Saif would go to Burhanpur, live in the palaces he had remodelled himself, take over an easily managed army that Aurangzeb had trained.

The prince had lost yet another supporter recently, his grandfather Abul Hasan—Mumtaz Mahal's father, who was buried at Lahore in 1641 in a fine tomb with blue tile work across from the crypt of Emperor Jahangir. Both men had been fathers of royalty—Abul's daughter was Empress Mumtaz Mahal, and Jahangir's son was Emperor Shah Jahan. The difference was, of course, that Jahangir himself had been emperor, so his mausoleum was grander. And though Abul's sister Mehrunnisa had been empress and wife of Jahangir, space for her final resting place was allotted farther away.

It was—Aurangzeb thought disconsolately when he received his father's missive—a lesson in kingship. Better to die a monarch than a deposed one or an unwanted one—his status at death would determine the shape, size and structure of the tomb that would house his remains. And the grander it was—Aurangzeb had just visited the Luminous Tomb and marvelled, unwillingly, at the elegance of his father's inspired design—the more likely posterity would be to remember him.

He wondered what he would do now and waited daily for some news from his father. What came was a condescending invitation from Dara to visit the splendid mansion he had lately built on the banks of the Yamuna near the fort, with all the copious monies their father had bestowed upon him.

twenty-four

As it was the summer season, an underground room had been constructed close to the river, and mirrors from Aleppo . . . had been hung . . . Dara conducted Shah Jahan and his brothers to see how the room looked. Muhammad Aurangzib sat down close to the door leading in and out of the room. Dara . . . winked at the Emperor, as if to say, 'See where he is sitting.'

—JADUNATH SARKAR, *Anecdotes of Aurangzib*

Agra
Thursday, 2 June 1644
26 Rabi' al-awwal A.H. 1054

The mansion—really more of a palace to rival the ones inside the fort at Agra—was massive, stretching its length along the Yamuna and its breadth landward into a grove of mango and guava trees that cast their dense shade on the beaten earth and were filled with the bright green of a thousand parrots. The birds dropped half-eaten fruit on the ground, greedily consuming all they could find, unmindful of the waste. Mammoth pink and blue snakes, fashioned out of fragrant sandalwood, nestled in the branches of the trees, realistic even to their forked tongues raised into the air, but the parrots were undeterred. They cried out to one another in their raucous language, swarmed in and out of the leaves, flying so low that the imperial malis, who took care of the garden, had to duck at times. They squabbled over pieces of guava, scolded the humans from their perches, serene in the knowledge that they could not be caught.

Dara came running to the colossal wood-and-metal-studded doors of his palace, pushing the slaves aside, laughing as he ushered his father and his brothers in. 'The birds are unmanageable.'

'Why don't you take a musket and shoot them?' Aurangzeb asked coolly.

Dara shuddered. 'Kill them, you mean? You were always violent, Aurangzeb. There is little harm in the parrots; they create an inconvenience, that is all. But come in and see my marvellous house. What do you think of it, Bapa?'

They wandered through all the rooms as the breeze from the Yamuna dried the sweat on their brows and cooled their heated skin. It was a strange procession, Prince Aurangzeb thought as he lingered behind his father and his brothers. They had always been feted and entertained on Bapa's bounty, or Jahan had played hostess to them in the zenana, offering dinners and nautch girls, but here was Dara assuming the role of patron. He could not bring himself to consider this invitation as a mere pleasure for them all—they were grown men, scattered around the empire; opportunities, such as this one, to gather in one place, to break bread together, to mull over the problems of their inheritance were rare. He saw it instead as a show of might by Dara. A magnificent mansion with no expense spared—gold-and-enamel-inlaid censers in every room, silk curtains from Bengal, marble floors from the Rajput kingdoms, ivory figurines from Africa, the best sandstone from Fatehpur-Sikri. Everywhere the eye went, it met with plenty, an open hand for purchases, with, it seemed to say, the vast coffers of the imperial treasury behind it. Aurangzeb had seen Dara's chair in the Diwan-i-am, one he had refused to occupy for the month that Aurangzeb had been in Agra, saying that he would consider himself blessed to sit in his father's presence when Jahanara was finally recovered. It was she who had exhorted the four brothers to meet—this luncheon was her idea.

Overwhelmed by the quiet opulence of Dara's house, Aurangzeb followed the party to an underground room whittled into the banks of the river. It was long, with a high ceiling carved out in red sandstone, lit brilliantly by hundreds of oil diyas in niches along the walls. The wisping smoke from the diyas flung a glaze over Aurangzeb's eyes and made them water. Dara had commissioned a new carpet for the room, thirty feet long, twenty feet wide, in blue with a white border. It had taken the weavers two years to make. The pile was thick and lush, and their bare feet sank into its embrace. Luxurious as Aurangzeb's camp in Agra was, there was a real gratification in being able to stand upon a finished floor, feel the solidity of walls enclosing him and a ceiling over his head. He had come to loathe the encampment, for it meant he was in temporary circumstances here—no longer the head of a state, with no place to call his own, no people to govern. In the same breath that Shah Jahan had dismissed Aurangzeb from the Deccan governorship he had lauded Murad for . . . something; Aurangzeb could no longer remember what it had been. But it had warranted a public audience at court, a khilat and a gold dagger, a nod of approval in front of the nobles in the Diwan-i-am.

They sat down to eat. Eunuchs filed in with a large red tablecloth, which they laid on the carpet in front of the divans. And then they brought in the food from the kitchens of the mansion. Aurangzeb noted that the dishes, in gold and silver, were each tied with white and red muslin, with a paper tag attached to the top knot on which the Khansamah, the superintendent of the kitchens, had written the name of the dish and its ingredients and placed his seal upon the knot but a few minutes ago. The dishes were untied, and a royal taster, his face covered with a cotton mask, his hands gloved in white cotton, dipped a spoon into each preparation and took the spoon to his mouth, lifting the cloth over his face. His nose and mouth were normally covered when not engaged in the actual operation of tasting so that his breath or saliva would not defile the food. Then every dish was laid out, and Aurangzeb took a deep breath, his mouth watering.

There were smoky brown curries of lamb and goat, still bubbling in their rich gravies, and piles of warm naans, creamy and perfectly baked, peeled from the walls of the underground ovens, their undersides crisp. A whole roasted chicken, warm and moist, steamed on a silver platter, cooked with a spice rub of garlic and coriander seeds, marinated overnight in yogurt. The rice came from the foothills of the Himalayas, aromatic on its own but seasoned further with strands of golden saffron and garnished with cashews, raisins and anise fried in ghee. There were fifteen plates of cooked vegetables, potatoes, new peas, spinach swirled with cream, plump beans, stuffed brinjals—each spiced differently, subtly, so that Aurangzeb had to taste every morsel on his plate and ponder upon the recipe. The cucumbers and the carrots in the salad had been picked from the imperial vegetable gardens that morning, still scattered with dew, and they were crunchy and melted in the mouth with their spare dressing of lime juice, salt, pepper and sesame oil.

Aurangzeb ate with relish, though he had decided that there were other matters more engaging to his mind and his body than food. He felt a comfort he had not sensed in a long while, ever since he had decided to be on a simple diet, but the food was delicious, and he promised himself that this would be the last time he would indulge himself so.

At the end of the meal, Dara rose and said, 'I must go see about the entertainment, if you will excuse me.'

They all murmured assent, replete, content, lying back on their divans. When Dara departed, he shut the door, and Aurangzeb's head jerked up. He realized that they were alone except for a handful of aged retainers, too old to do anything if there was danger. Here, in Dara's cool underground room, the door had closed upon all the rivals his brother had for the throne. He jumped up and rushed to the door. It did not give immediately to his shoulder, and he heaved against it until it swung open, mocking him—it had not been locked after all. He sat panting on the doorstep, enraged at having allowed himself to be placed in such a vulnerable position.

'What are you doing, Aurangzeb?' Emperor Shah Jahan asked, a slice of irritation in his voice.

Aurangzeb bowed from the door. 'Bapa, I prefer to sit here.'

Dara returned and found him blocking the way. 'Will you move? How will the musicians enter if you are here?'

'Why was it necessary for you to go personally to see about the arrangements, Dara? Could you not have sent a slave?'

Dara shrugged, gazing down at his brother. 'You are a fool, Aurangzeb. This is my house, you are my guest, and you dare question my movements?'

In the end, the entertainers had to manoeuvre around the seated prince to find their way inside. Aurangzeb refused to budge, listening to the music with half an ear, wishing himself anywhere but there. His father and his brothers drank steadily, wine brought in from the Abdar Khana in gold flasks set with emeralds and rubies. He had put a hand over his goblet when the wine was first served and tried to exhort the others to follow his example, but they had laughed.

'Drink, Aurangzeb,' Murad said, smiling, 'and perhaps it will loosen the stiffness of your countenance. How does your wife bear your glum face every day?'

The melodic sound of the sitar grated on his ears—in his encampment he had put a halt to all such amusement; the food was the plainest, music had no place, and the camp was dry. If his amirs wished to indulge in liquor, they had to do it elsewhere. He leaned against the doorjamb and watched them get drunk, laugh, and make jokes he did not find in the least humorous, and his head began to ache. Down the stairs leading to this room came the faint song of the muezzin calling the faithful to prayer: *Allah u Allah u Akbar*.

He stood, tried to capture his father's attention, failed to do so, and turned and ran up the stairs so that he could find an open space on the terrace to lay out his prayer rug, kneel towards Mecca, and pray. When he came back, he found the door shut and locked from the inside, two dour guards stationed outside. 'You must return to your camp, Your Highness,' one said diffidently. 'His Majesty has so ordered.'

That evening, Emperor Shah Jahan sent Aurangzeb a long and bitter letter about his lack of courtesy to his older brother and his inattentiveness as a guest, and said, *Do not show your face to me again, Aurangzeb, until you have accounted for your strange behaviour to my satisfaction.*

Four months later, Jahanara recovered fully and went back to Ajmer and Khwaja Muinuddin Chisti's tomb to give thanks for her health. She remembered that Aurangzeb had come all the way from the Deccan to see her, and, given when he had arrived at Agra, he must have left Burhanpur very soon after receiving news of the fire. So she wrote to her estranged brother, telling him to stop sulking in his camp and come to court and beg their father's pardon. He wrote back telling her that he did not trust Dara and mentioned finally his fear that they would all have been murdered that day in a room that could have been their tomb forever. This news gave Emperor Shah Jahan and Jahanara some pause, for though they did not believe it to be true, Aurangzeb had acted, in being distrustful of his brothers, as a royal prince should.

Two months later, Shah Jahan gave Aurangzeb the governorship of Gujarat and told him to stop his aimless wanderings around the empire and settle down to his duty.

The rift thus begun between Aurangzeb and his father never really healed. Here, then, was the beginning of the end.

A year later, when the imperial party was again on a summer visit to Kashmir, Nazar Muhammad Khan, the governor of Balkh, attempted to capture the city of Kabul. He did not succeed. Shah Jahan was enraged at the presumption of this petty governor in making an assault on the mighty Mughal Empire and sent the imperial forces out to capture Balkh in retaliation. The emperor used this excuse—and it would have done as well as any other—for he had long wanted to annex Balkh and Badakhshan. He sent Prince Murad at the head of the army under the guardianship of Ali Mardan Khan, the Amir-ul-umra, and equipped him with a mighty force—fifty thousand cavalry, ten thousand infantry all loaded with guns, muskets and cannons. Balkh crumbled even before the imperials came within sight, and Murad was ordered to stay on and solidify his hold. But then, winter set in, the land was harsh, the cold severe, the air dry, the mountains forbidding, and dissent set into the imperial camp. Murad was a weak leader, unable to control his men, and they looted the countryside, wreaked havoc in the villages, laid desolation wherever they went, and he begged his father to allow him to return to Hindustan.

While this was happening, another branch of the army conquered Badakhshan, routed out the ruler, killed him and took possession of the land and its famed ruby mines. Eventually, disgusted with Murad's lack of spine, Emperor Shah Jahan divested Aurangzeb of the Gujarat governorship and gave him Balkh and Badakhshan instead.

The whole operation was a mistake from the beginning, for Aurangzeb was outfitted with an army only twenty-five thousand strong, cavalry and infantry, and, even before he arrived to take possession, his force was whittled down severely, raided in surprise attacks by the Uzbegs. In the meantime, the dispossessed governor of Balkh, Nazar Muhammad Khan, the man who had dared to attack Kabul, had been secretly amassing forces of his own to take back his lands. When Aurangzeb arrived in Balkh, he barely had the time to gather the wealth of the treasury, load it on horseback, elephants and camels, and flee back to Hindustan via the Arbang pass in the Hindukush mountains. They came home in deep winter again through a pass heavily laden with snow, pursued by enemy forces who decimated large chunks of their rearguard. Five thousand men died, along with thousands of pack animals, some slipping and falling in the ice, buried under the snow before the break of dawn.

Immensely weary, with a racking cough in his chest, Aurangzeb wandered back to Lahore with his attenuated army, half the treasure he had started with interred in the layers of ice in the mountains, to rest there for all eternity. While Murad had merited a mere slap on his wrist for his abortive attempt at holding Balkh, Shah Jahan complained indignantly about Aurangzeb for his part in losing it and the paucity of the booty he had dragged back with him. He sent Aurangzeb to Multan as governor, telling him that this was his last chance to prove his loyalty to his father.

A month later, Shah Abbas II of Persia sacked Qandahar, overthrew the imperial forces, and established his own mighty army to wait for Mughal retaliation. And so, as it had in most of the history of the Mughal kings in India, Qandahar passed from the hands of the Mughals to the Persians.

It was an insult, and one Emperor Shah Jahan was quick to respond to, for he was aware that he had been lax in the security of Qandahar, having pulled out all but the minimum of forces for the futile conquest of Balkh. He sent a stern letter to Prince Aurangzeb—recognizing that, of all his sons, the one he disliked most was the most likely to be a strong commander—and sent along with him this time an impressive host of grandees of the empire, the Grand Vizier Sadullah Khan, Raja Jai Singh, Ali Mardan Khan, Rustum Khan and Raja Bithaldas, and a massive army.

'Is this wise, Bapa?' Jahanara asked as she glanced at the imperial farman her father had brought to her for affixing the royal seal.

'Qandahar must be part of the empire again, beta,' Shah Jahan replied. 'It is rightfully ours.'

'True,' Jahanara said. Though the Persians did not think so; that much was evident. They had a history with Qandahar and dated their aggression to a promise, now long forgotten, by Emperor Humayun to the Shah of Persia. The Shah had provided Humayun with forces to retake India with an understanding that, since Qandahar had to be conquered first (on the way into Hindustan), Humayun would relinquish it to the Persians after his mission had been completed. The Mughal kings, of course, did not give Qandahar to the Persians . . . so they took it, and lost it, and now had taken it again.

'Why the worry?' Shah Jahan asked, noting the lines on her forehead.

She shook her head. 'It's nothing. Just that so many of the big amirs are to be on this campaign, under Aurangzeb's command. And, Bapa, he has a fluent tongue.'

'But they are *my* generals, beta.'

'Even so.' She pressed the *Uzuk* on the farman and waited for the imprint to dry. Perhaps Bapa was right and she fretted too much over too little. But she had heard whispers about her brother's influence over the nobles, his unexpected friendships with them, even of their . . . support—no, that was not the right word, but their liking for him. Najabat Khan was with him, as was Antarah. They had both journeyed with Aurangzeb to Balkh, and during all the months of waiting—when the only news that filtered through the dense winter passes was upsetting at best—Jahanara had prayed for the safety of the man she loved and the son she had borne. When they met at Lahore, Najabat had said that Prince Aurangzeb had insisted upon Antarah riding beside him.

'He looked after our boy, Jahan,' Najabat Khan had told her.

Jahanara had not responded. So perhaps Aurangzeb had; what of it? It was his duty as a commander to bring his men back safely. On the one hand, he still berated her in letters for the sin she had committed; on the other, he kept watch over Najabat and Antarah. Now they were all to travel to Qandahar, and it would be a short campaign, sweet and swift. Surely.

In the end, the sixteen-year-old boy king Shah Abbas II of Persia was more canny and powerful than the Mughal armies expected. They laid siege to Qandahar for three months, surrounding the fort and keeping water, grains and fodder from going in, but the fort held out. Aurangzeb was recalled, and Dara was sent in his place, because Jahanara insisted that he ought also to have a command. Dara went better equipped than Aurangzeb in men, horses, cannons, muskets, battering rams and guns, and spent five fruitless months trying to pummel his way into the fort. He did not succeed either.

A dispirited, weary Aurangzeb fled to the Deccan and to Burhanpur after his father stripped him of his provinces—Kabul and Multan—and gave them to the favoured Dara instead. And there, in the place where his mother had died, he gave Jahanara more cause for fury.

At the age of thirty-five, Prince Aurangzeb fell in love for the first time in his life.

twenty-five

When the throne of kingship of this country became adorned with the accession of the king of heavenly dignity, Muhammad Aurangzeb Bahadur 'Alamgir Padshah Ghazi, His Majesty [Shah Jahan], in accordance with the expediency of Fate, was forced into involuntary seclusion inside the fort of Akbarabad.

—From the *Amal-i-Salih* of Muhammad Salih Kambo, in
W.E. BEGLEY AND Z.A. DESAI,
Taj Mahal: The Illumined Tomb

Delhi
Thursday, 13 September 1657
5 Zi'l-Hijja A.H. 1067

'Bapa!'

Jahanara woke to the sound of her own voice. But no one stirred around her; the slave girls in her apartments still slept, and outside in the verandah she could hear Ishaq Beg's soft snores.

She rose noiselessly, pushed aside the sheet that covered her, and put her feet on the cloth carpet, waiting for the flaming pain along her right side to subside. This was the legacy of her burning all those years ago; sometimes, mostly in the middle of the night, she would wake to a searing burn, relive those bewildering moments when she saw her legs on fire, her chiffon skirts wisp into nothing, feel the agony again in excruciating detail. Now it seemed to her that the unpleasant stink of her burning flesh hung about the rooms, stifling her breath. And then she remembered hearing her father call out to her.

Jahanara gathered her ghagara around her knees and went to the door leading into the gardens. Once in the verandah, she descended the marble steps of the Rang Mahal and fled down the pathway leading to the Khas Mahal at Delhi fort—the private apartments of her father.

A full moon glowed in the sky above, painting the gardens she passed with bright silver and deep shadows. The evergreens lining the path seemed to take on the guise of men, and she heard the eunuchs stiffen when they heard her footsteps and then bow when they recognized their Begam Sahib. At the *baithak* of the Khas Mahal, the sitting room with its cusped arches, a shaft of moonlight came to strike the floor and lend radiance to the ceiling of white marble inlaid with precious stones that were blue, green and red in the day, now a dark indigo—like a painting captured in black and white. The stocky Kashmiri ladies who guarded the emperor's inner sanctum stepped forward and then back again in one motion, bending their heads in salute, and Jahanara went into the central chamber, where her father lay on his bed.

A lone diya cast its thin light around the room made fully of marble—the walls, the ceiling, the floor, all embellished in the same pietra dura inlay that the outside baithak boasted. But here, the sound of her feet was softened in the deep nap of Persian carpets, and, despite the blistering September night, coal braziers burned faintly, heating the air. Jahanara stood looking down at her father, the skin on her back breaking out into a sweat.

'What is it, Jahan?'

She sat down next to him. 'I thought I heard you call out to me.'

He turned bleary eyes towards her. 'I did. I did not expect you to have heard me. It was nothing . . . a dream . . . a nightmare.'

She caught one of his hands and held it to her cheek, thinking that it was very warm. He had a fever again, and his forehead was sketched with lines of pain. Emperor Shah Jahan had fallen ill some ten days ago of strangury. His stomach was distended, his legs had swollen to twice their size, and he could no longer hold himself upright, let alone take any steps. The court physicians had come with their plethora of cures—poultices to reduce the swelling, potions to restore the health of his urinary tract. It was an old complaint that came and went as it wished, and he was an aged man, as he often said, sixty-five years old this year. But with each coming, the illness stayed longer, affected him more, left him further weakened, and it took him more time to recover.

Jahanara clapped her hands lightly, and, when a eunuch bowed his way in, she said, 'A basin of cool water and a towel. Immediately.'

'Yes, Your Highness.' He retreated, returned in a few minutes as bidden, and set the basin at her side, the clean, white towel draped over the bowl.

Shah Jahan shivered. 'Make sure the water is not too cold, beta. I could not bear the cold—this heat from the braziers, it keeps my blood running and calms the trembles in my limbs, even gives me some relief from the ache.' His words were slurred and slow but lucid enough.

'You have a fever, Bapa,' she said firmly, dipping the towel into the water and wringing it to damp, not dry. Then she folded it lengthwise and placed it on his heated forehead. The cloth warmed alarmingly soon, and Jahanara realized, after a moment of panic, that the temperature in the room was as much to blame as the fever ravaging her father's body. Twenty minutes later, the emperor's breathing slowed and he fell asleep, his hand on his daughter's shoulder so that she could not move without waking him again.

She leaned back against his bed, as she had done for so many nights, whether he was well or not, and closed her eyes also, her heart heavy with foreboding. When Shah Jahan had fallen ill—almost from the next day, when he had been forced to cancel all of his public appearances—the empire had begun to hum with dissatisfaction. Though she was confined to the sickroom, nursing her father, these comments had reached even her ears, fractured, splintered bits of words and phrases of information. *The emperor was dying. The throne would be vacant. Who would be the next king?* In the twenty-nine years that Emperor Shah Jahan had ruled, he had only once missed jharoka appearances or not presented himself at court—and that had been because of a death, his wife's. Even during the previous attacks of strangury, with an uncertain carriage, pain that bent him double, a whitening around the corners of his mouth and at his temples, Bapa had stood before the people in the morning jharoka, dragging himself to bed afterward and sleeping the day away. But this time he had refused, and it had been a long ten days that there had been no sign of Emperor Shah Jahan at the Shah Burj of the Delhi fort.

Jahanara watched the Kashmiri guards change shifts sometime during the third pahr of the night, exchanging muted talk, that did not reach her ears, and their weapons—spears, daggers, shields.

Word had also come to her that Aurangzeb had gathered his army in the Deccan and was making his way north in response to his father's poor health. What did he mean by this? And Aurangzeb had been made powerful by *them*—all of them—recently. Inadvertently perhaps, but still . . .

A few months ago, Mir Jumla, prime minister in a Deccani kingdom, had proposed to defect to the empire if Shah Jahan would provide him with protection. In return, he had offered a bag of diamonds that he claimed were mined in Golkonda. Aurangzeb had assumed the governorship of the Deccan again, and Shah Jahan had sent him orders to allow Mir Jumla safe passage into Mughal land, and then to provide him with an escort to court so that the emperor could see these brilliant stones for himself and judge their worth. If there was an abiding fault in her father, Jahanara thought, it was his intense love for these inanimate things—to her the diamonds were simply stones, doubtless of immense value, and their cool lustre had lit her arms and neck many times, made her feel beautiful, wanted, desired. But she had felt so even clad in only a string of flowers, freshly picked, dewy from the night. When the stones had come, she almost changed her mind. For Mir Jumla had held out the best stone in his palm in an open *durbar*—as massive as his large fist, ablaze like the sun at high noon, seeming to draw all the light of the Diwan-i-am into its brilliant heart. It had appeared alive and throbbed in the hand of the man who had brought it.

The next day, despite Dara's and her repeated cautions, Emperor Shah Jahan had sent a fifty-thousand-strong army to the Deccan to be under Aurangzeb's command and given him orders to invade Golkonda. If there were more diamonds to be found in the Golkonda mines, they had to belong to him, first and last. What of strengthening Aurangzeb in the Deccan? they had asked their father, and he had laughed, saying only that his third son was a fool and would not know how to rebel against his father even if he tried. The fever of greed had caught Emperor Shah Jahan firmly, and he thought of all the monuments and forts he had built so far, the immensely rich Peacock Throne (though it was only one of seven upon which he gave audience), and decided that possession of the world's most magnificent diamonds—which were to be found in Golkonda if that one diamond was any indication—would make him the world's most potent monarch.

Dara and Jahanara had talked for long hours, knowing that their father was aging, that, in some senses, he was losing control of his mental faculties. When Jahanara thought of these discussions, she cringed. If she had not agreed with Dara all those months ago, perhaps he would have behaved better when their father had fallen ill this time. In the ten days that had passed, Dara had closed down all the roads leading into Shahjahanabad, not allowed any news to seep out, and taken over the role of sovereign. He gave all the orders at court, and, because of his lack of tact, he had offended too many of the old and powerful nobles at court. When they had come hesitantly to beg information about their king, Dara had had his eunuchs drive them away from the Lahore Gate that led into the fort. Before he had shut the doors,

Roshanara Begam had slipped away, and Jahanara heard later that she had gone down the Yamuna to Agra and established herself in Aurangzeb's house there.

All these years Roshanara had been sending secret missives to Aurangzeb; this Jahanara knew well, since she had intercepted and read some, but they seemed harmless—spiteful, vituperative letters insulting her father and her sister, sometimes Dara, always ending with a profession of deep love for Aurangzeb. Jahanara had been too disgusted to read more than a few, and if Aurangzeb replied to Roshan, she did not know about it, and so she suspected that he did not. He, on the other hand, had been deeply involved until now in a . . . *love* affair.

The girl, for she was barely seventeen years old, was a concubine in her uncle Saif Khan's harem, called Hira Bai. Aurangzeb had seen her in Zainabad Bagh, when he had gone there to pray at the baradari where their mother had initially been buried, and a variety of tales had reached Jahanara's ears about the beginnings of this silly affair. Hira Bai had been holding down a branch of a flowering mango tree, the blooms framing her pretty face, and Aurangzeb had fallen into a faint upon first seeing her. There were reports also that Saif Khan had declined to let her go, but it was not so, Jahanara knew, for the two men had exchanged women from their respective harems—Aurangzeb giving up some concubine for Hira Bai, whom he titled Zainabadi Begam after the place where he had first seen and so precipitately fallen in love with her. He had spent hours at her feet, singing songs to her, reading poetry, or watching her sleep—neglecting all of his other duties. Already in trouble with Bapa about his handling of the Balkh and Qandahar affairs, Aurangzeb had further ignored his father's commands and laid himself out in the service of an insipid, though supposedly beautiful, concubine. Jahanara had written to him then, for the first time voluntarily. *You have had the temerity to stand in judgement on my love for Mirza Najabat Khan, and what do you do now—moon about a child young enough to be* your *child? Younger, in fact, than your own children? Does she even have the capacity for conversation, Aurangzeb?*

He had not replied for a long while, and when he did, it was to say simply that she had hurt him profoundly, and if she could only know Zainabadi as he knew her, she would come to love her also. Besides, he was a man, with a man's needs, and she was a woman in purdah who should have had the prudence to remain behind the veil and not attempt to besmirch all of their reputations.

It was this affair Bapa had referred to when he called Aurangzeb a fool, but Jahanara was afraid that her brother was a fool no longer. The woman, that girl child, had died recently of consumption, and Aurangzeb had no further distractions to take his mind away from his early ambition. With Dara being so stubborn, perhaps Aurangzeb had no other alternative than to be aggressive. But they were both behaving as though Bapa was on his deathbed.

When Shah Jahan woke to his daughter's touch the next morning, she said to him, 'Bapa, you must show yourself at the jharoka this morning.' She would not listen to any more protests from him or, surprisingly enough, from Dara, who ought to have known better—for if his father was shown to be alive he still had some standing at court, even as the heir apparent. If the amirs at court thought Shah Jahan dead, Dara would not find many of them supportive of him.

They carried Emperor Shah Jahan to the jharoka balcony, and two eunuchs propped him up below the balustrade. Hidden behind his back, Jahanara lifted one of his arms so that he could wave to the crowds below. The men roared out their greeting, 'Padshah Salamat!' But they fell quiet too soon after, and a forest of murmurs rose and buzzed along the banks of the Yamuna as Shah Jahan stepped back and disappeared through the silk curtain because he could not stand any more. By that night, rumours droned from one mouth to another that the emperor was dead and that a substitute had been found for the jharoka, but that no one who had seen the man had been deceived for an instant.

In the Deccan, the news of Shah Jahan's illness came to Prince Aurangzeb one morning after he had finished his first prayer of the day. He stayed kneeling on his prayer rug, facing west, towards Mecca, the tight roll of the letter in front of him. Over the past few years, he had taken to writing to everyone he knew, and then some others he did not—letters of mere salutation, of respect when the amir at court was barely known to him and greater in years, of humour to his peers (in age, for in status there were none). And finally, he had been writing to his brothers, Shuja in Bengal and Murad, who had been sent back to govern Multan. So their missives had crisscrossed the empire for a while, frequent enough to set up special runners for this imperial purpose and to construct sarais for these runners, who were kept on a permanent salary, which Aurangzeb willingly paid.

Murad was six years younger than he, Shuja two years older, and though they had come together originally because of their intense, and so naturally unspoken, dislike of Dara, Aurangzeb did not think either of them was capable of ruling the empire. But then he had never thought so. He had made sure that each wrote to the other *through* him—he told Murad that he wanted to read all of his letters to Shuja, just for the news, and so that Murad would not have to repeat the same in another letter to him, and that he wanted to add postscripts to Murad's letters so that Shuja would receive news from both Multan and the Deccan at one time. His two brothers had believed him, so they had but little contact with each other directly.

To the nobles at court, whether they openly supported him or not, Aurangzeb penned noncommittal notes, merely to keep in touch, he said, and every bit of information in the empire was valuable to him, so if they chose to share it with him he would be honoured. He sent presents of silks and jewels when their children were married and when their grandchildren were born, or ivory and silver figurines when they built new homes and sent him invitations to their housewarmings. To most of these matters, he attended himself, asking the advice of none of his ministers or nobles, keeping his own counsel.

Now this. Prince Aurangzeb had been visited by a vision this morning while he prayed—a flash of radiance had filled the darkness under his eyelids and set his limbs quivering. The letter, he thought, had something to do with it. He willed himself into serenity, wiped his face with his hands, rolled the prayer rug and handed it to an attendant eunuch, then sat cross-legged on the floor to open and read the news of his father's illness. He set the paper down with shaking hands. How old was he this year? Thirty-nine. If he became emperor, he would have at least thirty years to rule.

For the next week, Aurangzeb moved patiently through his duties in the Deccan, never seeming flurried or flustered. Because his fingertips were constantly stained with the ink from his quill, and because he wore white—a non-colour more in keeping with his asceticism—he held his hands away from his qaba and his person awkwardly, as though he was reaching out to something. He wrote letters late into the night, every night, and woke in the mornings with dark circles around his eyes. But his energy did not flag; it was quiet and burned with a relentless flame. In carrying the letters, the imperial runners zigzagged over almost every established route, and some new ones, patterning the map of Hindustan with sets of lines, but they did not touch the heart, the city of Delhi. For Dara had closed down all the arteries into Shahjahanabad, and for what Aurangzeb wanted to achieve, he did not need to reach out to Delhi.

To each of his other two brothers, he offered his backing, indeed, his ardent wish for *them* to be emperor, and he told both of them to wait for a short period to assure themselves that their Bapa was dying, or dead, and read the khutba in their names in their provinces.

There were three bastions of sovereignty in Mughal India—the khutba, the ability to issue imperial farmans, and the minting of coins in the name of the emperor. In the vast and far-flung empire, where communications between provinces and states took days if not weeks, the muezzins in the mosques sang out the official proclamation of sovereignty, the khutba—'All hail the mighty Emperor, Lord of our lands.' This they did every Friday before the noon prayers, so that the populace would know on a weekly basis towards whom they should be bowing their heads.

Murad and Shuja proclaimed themselves kings in Multan and Bengal, and at the same time, Prince Aurangzeb brought together his men, including the mammoth army his father had so providentially sent him to conquer Golkonda, and spoke to them of his designs. They were to leave for Agra the next day. He did tell his commanders and generals that his father was dead—nothing else, certainly not the idea of a coup, would have persuaded them to move—and that there was a danger that Dara would become king.

You see, my dearest Jahan, Najabat Khan wrote from the Deccan,

> how perfidious the two princes are to announce themselves sovereign even before the emperor is dead? My prince, Aurangzeb, is more discreet. We have started for Agra with an army, for he believes Prince Dara wishes him ill, and perhaps it is just a show of might on his part . . . how can I fault this? I am a soldier myself and recognize the value of the sword. Against my advice, Prince Aurangzeb has halted our march five days out of Burhanpur; he says that we left in a hurry and these past few days would have afforded all the amirs a chance to decide whether they want to offer their allegiance to him . . . or slip out of camp in the dark of the night to Prince Dara, whose army is said to be on its way to meet us.
>
> Aurangzeb is assured that we will thrash Prince Dara's army, the part that he sends here, and then we will move ahead to meet the rest near Agra so that we can release the emperor and you from your captivity.

As they waited out the next two days, Prince Aurangzeb wrote again to every amir who had been sent in command of forces against him, asked for their loyalty, and promised them riches when he became emperor. There was no hiding any more the fact that he was on his way to depose his father, who had committed a grievous wrong in allowing Dara control of the empire even before he was dead. Dara hated him, did Bapa not know that? Aurangzeb had always been a good and respectful son, but Bapa had always favoured the weakling Dara—how could Shah Jahan even bear to think of handing his precious empire to someone so incompetent?

And so he revealed his intentions fully and directly. Prince Aurangzeb was in rebellion, much as his father had been thirty years ago against *his* father, and there was only one way this would end—someone would die.

Dara's armies were routed over the next few days, and by the time Prince Aurangzeb arrived at Agra, only a skeleton of forces, mostly from the imperial bodyguards, the Ahadis, surrounded the fort.

Princess Jahanara received Najabat Khan's letter around this time, and when he begged for an audience, she refused him one, furious that his faith in her brother was unshakable. Her own, in Dara, was wavering.

For it was true what Najabat had said—Bapa and she had been held prisoner in the fort at Delhi, their movements restricted, Dara himself not available to respond to any questions. She had been fearful for the first time in her life and it was a real, palpable anxiety, because she did not know what was happening outside the zenana's walls or how this was all going to end. She did write to Najabat Khan in Aurangzeb's encampment outside the fort. *Leave him, my lord,* she said.

> You did not listen to me all those years ago when I cautioned you against putting too much trust in my third brother, and now you and he are camped outside my father's palaces awaiting

> his surrender. His surrender? From what? He is Emperor Shah Jahan—your king, your monarch, your master. Bapa has sent Aurangzeb a splendid sword, which he has called the 'Alamgir', the Conqueror of the Universe, as a token of his friendship. Why then does this worthless son of my father's wait for the emperor's submission? A son cannot wear the crown upon his head while his father is still alive; every regulation, legal and moral, rebels against this, and yet it would seem this is what Aurangzeb wants. Does he? And where is Murad? Why is there no news of him?

Najabat Khan did not respond for a long while to this missive, knowing that he and his beloved princess were on two sides of an ever-widening void. Everything she wrote in the letter was accurate—Aurangzeb's intentions and their consequences. But he had sworn fidelity to the prince; he had vanquished Prince Dara's army and sent him fleeing north, and . . . Najabat had taken Prince Murad prisoner and escorted him to the fort at Gwalior, which was the imperial penitentiary. He did not think Murad would leave there alive.

At Agra, on the thirty-first of July, 1658, some ten months after his father had fallen ill, Aurangzeb conducted a small ceremony in Princess Jahanara's garden on the eastern bank of the Yamuna and announced that he was now emperor. For his title, he chose Alamgir—the same name as that of the sword his Bapa had presented him. Shah Jahan had been King of the World; Aurangzeb was now Emperor Alamgir—Conqueror of the Universe. Then, with Najabat Khan and a large army, he set off to pursue his oldest brother.

Over the next few months, Dara was constantly on the move—Lahore, Multan, Sindh, Cutch, back to Gujarat, Ajmer, Ahmadabad, back again to Sindh, hoping to get some refuge, finally, from the Shah of Persia. Aurangzeb's men hounded him through the empire, a step or just a few behind him at all times—so assiduously had Aurangzeb cultivated the friendships and the loyalties of the grandees of the empire, so detested was Dara himself. Finally, in 1659, a year after Aurangzeb had proclaimed himself emperor of Hindustan, Dara was betrayed to the imperial forces by a tribal chieftain who had ostensibly been helping him escape.

He was brought to Delhi, paraded through the streets seated backward on a donkey, and his head was sliced off the next morning . . . and sent in a silver box to Emperor Shah Jahan and Jahanara at the Agra fort.

Shuja was killed a year later, and in 1662, Aurangzeb put the imprisoned Murad out of his misery by hanging him. Now only his sisters were left. Roshanara had come to live in his harem, but Jahanara had refused even to speak to him these past three years. He went to see her at Agra, bareheaded, holding his imperial turban in his hands.

~

'What is it, Aurangzeb?' Jahanara asked dully. 'What murder have you come to boast of now?'

It was a few days after Murad's death, and when Jahanara had received the news, she had stared dumbly at the messenger, Ishaq Beg, unable to comprehend for a moment who he was talking about. Then she remembered that little boy who had wrapped his arms around her waist and muffled his sobs in the silk of her ghagara on the day they had buried their mother in Burhanpur. She thought of the innocent trust he had always had in all of them, that Aurangzeb had used to his advantage. She was fatigued now, almost every day, her heart toughened against hurt, and it had been almost torn asunder on the day she opened the box from Aurangzeb and saw Dara's bloody head inside. She had not been able to hide the bloodstains on her hands from her father, and so Bapa had known also. Aurangzeb had left them at the fort at Agra, confined within its walls. The first month after he had had the khutba read in his name, he had written to her and begged her to come and be with him.

Jahanara leaned against the warm teak of the door to her apartments and set her ear to the wood, listening for a sound from the other side.

But Aurangzeb was silent. She had not responded to his many pleadings—what did they mean, anyway? How could she leave Bapa and go out? Who would look after him? And if he were to be allowed out with her, what amir at court would profess loyalty to his vicious son? She realized that Aurangzeb never meant to see his father again or consent to his showing himself in public—it would be fatal for the sovereignty Aurangzeb had just set up for himself.

'Jahan,' Emperor Aurangzeb said in an injured voice, beating his fist lightly against the door. 'You hurt me with such words. Do you think if Dara or Shuja or Murad were alive, they would allow me to be king? My head would have rolled in the courtyard—I have done nothing but protect my interests.'

'You were always selfish,' Jahanara said bitterly, 'always thinking about yourself.'

'This empire,' Aurangzeb said, 'is rightfully mine. Bapa had allowed it to become rife with a rot, the singing, the dancing girls, the rivers of wine. People do not even heed the call for prayer, do you know? I stop whatever imperial activity I am engrossed in and kneel to pray; I intend to set an example for the citizens of the empire by my actions. Allah has ordained that my head feel the weight of the crown, Jahan. If I were not convinced of this, I would have given up this battle a long time ago and retired from court life to meditate and pray.'

Jahanara slid down the length of the door and sat on the floor, her hands clasped in front of her. It was the first time since that war of succession that she had deigned to talk with her brother—the only brother she had now, she thought sadly. Once they had been a splendid family. Dara, with his height and striking handsomeness; Shuja, with his habit of looking towards her for approval; Murad, with his serious intent—they had all been good men. Jahanara did not think she could say that of Aurangzeb.

She was inside her apartments, ten inches of wood between her and Aurangzeb. He might be emperor, she thought with tired irony, but he still could not command a meeting with her, even though she was his prisoner and had defied his orders and his demands by remaining by the side of their father, whom he seemed to detest. Where did that hatred come from? And then, because she was a reasonable woman, Jahanara remembered all of their persecutions of Aurangzeb. The major ones—his being stripped of his governorships more than once, and the petty ones, when she had refused to meet him, or not responded to his letters, or made fun of him.

Ishaq Beg strode up and down the corridor, his gaze purposeful, his hand on a dagger tucked into his cummerbund, as if he expected his emperor to come rushing through the door at any moment to take his mistress's life. She shook her head and smiled at him. Then, since Aurangzeb doubtless listened still beyond the door, she said, 'What are you going to do, Ishaq? He probably has the entire army waiting behind him. Well, he would not bring an army to subdue a mere woman, but a few guards at least. Aurangzeb has become fastidious; he was not that in his youth, but now he will not soil his hands by killing me himself. Someone will be delegated to do it.'

'He will have to kill me first, Your Highness,' Ishaq said, and Jahanara was touched by his devotion.

'Come back to court life, Jahan. I beg this of you,' Aurangzeb said softly. 'Let me at least see you and take you with me. Is it right that my sister must live thus?'

'Your father does,' she replied in a harsh voice. 'Have you no feelings for him?'

Emperor Shah Jahan coughed from the Shah Burj of the Agra fort, where his bed had been laid out for him, and the sound of that cough travelled through the corridor to Jahanara's ears. She rose from the door.

'I have to go now, Aurangzeb, Bapa needs me.'

His voice was muffled. 'I need you too, Jahan.'

'I think,' she said deliberately, 'that you have never wanted or believed in anyone but yourself. I sometimes wonder how you could have turned out so differently from us. We had the same upbringing, and while I once could have said that there was something of the familiar in you . . . I can no longer. Go, Aurangzeb, I will not leave Bapa's side for the rest of his life.'

'Then,' he said, knocking against the wood one last time, 'you must stay there until he dies.'

twenty-six

Though Jahanara grieved overmuch inwardly at the gloom that enveloped the citadel, yet she did not permit the windy tempests of the heart to blow her about and uproot the moorings of her personality . . . She had a woman's body but a man's mind. Though defeated, never did she own that the reverses had galled her.

—MUNI LAL, *Shah Jahan*

Agra
Tuesday, 20 March 1663
10 Sha'baan A.H. 1073

An errant thunderstorm at twilight left smoky clouds and tangerine skies over Agra. Then darkness came to cover it all, and already-muted sounds dulled into silence. Lamps flickered here and there, uncertain and subdued, remnants of a capital city left to die. A few people walked the streets, aimless, wandering. For the last six years, Agra had been quiet, ever since Emperor Aurangzeb had moved his court to Delhi and the city of Shahjahanabad, which his father had built. The bazaars were empty, custom slow and hesitant. Even the Taj Ganj, with its magnificent sarais, which Shah Jahan had envisioned as a thrumming, thriving place, filled with people eager to see his wife's tomb, was hushed.

In the fort, the corridors were deserted, dust lying over the many windows, the gardens untended, flowers wilting for lack of water. Princess Jahanara stood in her apartments, looking out at the languid Yamuna below. These were the rooms her Bapa had constructed for her in the Anguri Bagh, with their smoothly curved Bangala roofs, their vast verandahs filled with marble latticework screens that filtered coolness from the waters of the river and swept it into every corner.

March already, she thought, of another year . . . how many since they came to Agra after Bapa's illness? Some five and a half. If she had been told that her life would have been thus, shut away in the palaces, a handful of attendants to minister to them and guard them, she would not have believed it. Even now, it was difficult to comprehend. That Aurangzeb had indeed been emperor for so long, that Bapa had struggled to live . . . and had lived for so long, cursing the son who had brought this about. Tomorrow, they would celebrate Nauroz, the New Year, at the beginning of spring.

She pressed her forehead against the screen and closed her eyes. Remembering. All she had now were her thoughts that stretched into long days and desolate nights. The Nauroz festival was a time of rebirth, of happiness, music in the hallways and at court, amirs with cheerful faces, the giving of gifts, the receiving of them. Food in plenty. Wine in the fountains. Jahanara had heard that Aurangzeb's court was more austere. In Delhi, the Nauroz would be celebrated with a mere gesture—no elaborate meals, no laughter, certainly no alcohol. If the amirs wished to drink, they did so in their homes, in the safety of their *zenanas*—even the public houses had been shut. The emperor's bounty in these stark times was measured by cloth caps that he stitched himself. Even with the pall over her, Jahanara could not help grinning. Bapa had given his nobles grants of land, jagirs and estates, higher ranks, more money, jewels from the treasury, positions of repute. Aurangzeb, the fool, gave them *caps*. He had said that he had too much time on his hands after matters of state had been attended to, so he kept busy with his scissors, his length of dreary cloth, his needle and his cotton thread.

She wondered what the amirs thought of this, what they dared to think of the man they had put on the throne of the empire. The man who had imprisoned his father and his sister and had killed all of his brothers. Remorse? Had they finally realized their stupidity? She was to find out from one of them at least.

'Jahan.'

Jahanara's heart began a mad thumping, and she forgot everything she wanted to ask; every bit of bitterness fled. She turned, saw Najabat, and put her hands over her face, overcome with love.

He came to her side with quick steps and enfolded her in his arms. He was trembling, much as she was. It had been some six years since he had held her thus, and yet, there was nothing unfamiliar. The scent of his skin, the strength of his grasp, the rub of his beard on the top of her head. He pulled away to look at her. He had aged, she thought, his eyebrows fully white, his hair thinning on the top. But his fingers were warm on her skin, his mouth . . . She leaned into him and laid her lips on his. She did not speak when he lifted her effortlessly and carried her to the divan, undoing her choli and her ghagara, laying her out in front of his gaze. His hands went across her body, flitting gently over the scars from the burning on her stomach, back and thighs, rising to cup her breasts. She began to cry, and he wiped her tears away, kissing the sounds from her mouth. A lone jackal howled below at the waterfront, but Jahanara and Najabat did not hear it as they hungrily reached for each other, as they kissed and loved in the heated night.

When they were done, she lay on the divan on her side, Najabat's head buried in the curve of her shoulder, their breaths easing.

'I have missed you.'

'I thought,' he said, 'that I would never see you again, my love. Thank you for summoning me to your side.'

A long pause. 'What do you think we will do now, my lord?'

He turned her over and put his palms on her face. 'Come to my house, Jahan, leave this fort. Live in my zenana; let me look after you as I ought to.'

She pulled his hands away, all the anger she had felt rising in her again. 'And what of my Bapa? Who will take care of him? You don't think—Aurangzeb and you don't stop to consider that he is a broken, beaten man. What will he do if I am not here?'

He rested his head on the pillow, pain drawing lines on his brow. 'I'm sorry. Things . . . could have gone differently. If Prince Dara, indeed the other princes also, had only paid heed to His Majesty's claim on the throne, they would still be alive. My hands'—he lifted them up and they shook—'are stained with their blood. I have no right to ask anything of you, Jahan. I am not your husband, merely the father of your child.'

Jahanara rose to draw a *peshwaz* over herself and sat down again, cross-legged. 'If Antarah deserted you when you most needed him, Najabat. If—'

When he said nothing, she continued, 'It was not necessary to have killed the princes.' But she knew, all too well, that it had been. That Najabat had been following Aurangzeb's orders when he hounded Dara over the empire, when he sent Murad to the prison at Gwalior, when he stood by as Shuja was killed. But she recalled that moment when Dara's head had come to them in a silver box, his eyes closed, an almost foolish expression on his face. She had known then just how powerless they had all become, how difficult it would have been to stop Aurangzeb once he had begun this war of succession. And he had succeeded, much as Bapa had all those years ago when the throne became his.

In the gardens beyond, the cicadas had begun their incessant chirping. A woman's voice, lustrous in song, floated in the warm night air from the banks of the river. Najabat put a hand on Jahanara's thigh, daringly, and she let it lie, thinking of another night so many years ago—thirty or so—when she had listened to a woman singing while waiting for a lover. Since Najabat and she had come together in Kashmir, there had been no necessity for any other man. He had been everything to her. She bent to kiss his hand, held it in hers, sketched lines over the back and in his warm palm.

'Why did you call for me, Jahan?'

'I missed you,' she said again, looking at him, her eyes fixed on his face. She had missed him. So much. Perhaps—and she was being honest with herself—more than she had before, when she had been busy in the zenana, at court, by her Bapa's side. But as much as she loved her father, he was an inadequate companion—ill most of the time, querulous and demanding at others—and she was tired of being in pain all the time. So . . . this little interlude.

'And nothing else?' he asked.

She looked away. 'There can be nothing else. I do not stay with Bapa because it is my duty . . . though it *is*. I adore my father, and when he dies, Najabat, it will be my hand that will close his eyes, my image he will take with him on his final journey.'

'So he told me also,' Najabat said in a low voice.

'Who?'

'Your son. He said that I must not come between you, that this must be your decision, that you must do as you please, because you are no mere woman.'

Antarah had said that to Najabat. Princess Jahanara Begam leaned over and kissed her lover again, buried her mouth in his neck and cried. She had not seen her son in many years either, and there was no easy way to beckon him to her side, not as she had done his father. He was more or less a stranger to her, a gift from Allah to be cherished in brief moments, and each time she saw him, she marvelled at how he had grown, what a fine young man he had become, how endearing, how beloved. Antarah was twenty-eight years old, a father himself, with his own zenana, and the title of Shah Alam from his emperor—Aurangzeb's sly way of acknowledging her lover and her son. As if she cared, Jahanara thought. But she did care, in some part of her heart, that her child should be so lauded at court, that his achievements should be recognized, that his father should be proud of him. Only the fact that Aurangzeb's hand had signed the imperial farman granting Antarah his new title was troubling.

'Is he a good emperor?' she asked, her voice muffled.

Najabat did not reply for a while, his breathing even. 'Perhaps,' he said finally. 'It's too early to tell yet.'

So Najabat was disappointed too. In the past few years, Jahanara had been thinking about kingship and empires also. Dara would have been little better, this she saw now, because the empire needed a king with a warrior's heart and his had been that of a poet. Shuja and Murad would have been too precipitous in their decisions, too raw. Aurangzeb she had always considered would have been a bad sovereign, and he was proving himself thus. An ache came over her. Was this then the end of the Mughals? Who would rule after Aurangzeb? Did he think all of his numerous sons would forget the lessons he had demonstrated for them in grabbing the throne? Just as he doubtless was waiting for his father's death, so were his sons awaiting their grandfather's death, because he had taught them this. With no respect, no consideration, no pity, no sympathy . . . no real feeling, how could the empire survive?

'You should go now, my lord,' she said.

Najabat dressed slowly, deliberately stretching out the minutes in Jahanara's apartments. He did not take his gaze from her face. 'Will I see you again, Jahan?'

She shook her head.

'We don't have much time left. I am fifty-six years old this year, my love. What if I were to die?' He said this with a little smile on his face.

'And I will be fifty next year, Najabat,' she said, coming into his arms one last time. 'But my place is here with Bapa. If Allah wills it, when Bapa dies, I will come out of the fort. Aurangzeb still wants me in his zenana.' She grimaced. 'He has promised me the title of Padshah Begam. Roshan, I hear, is merely Shah Begam; he still waits for me, you see.'

'You see how much you are loved on the outside?'

'And on the inside, here, by my father.' She stepped back and raised her hand in farewell.

~

'How long, beta?' Emperor Shah Jahan asked. His hair had whitened after his wife's death, thirty-two years ago, but now it had taken on the sickly, yellowed sheen of a beaten man who had been lying in his bed for a long while.

'Nine years,' Jahanara said slowly, leaning over her father. She could hear the harsh rasp in his breathing, the rumble in his voice as he spoke, and knew him to be frail and failing. If he would last the night, she thought, perhaps he would last another few years, but she saw nothing but defeat in his rheumy eyes, smelled the sourness in his breath, felt the too tight clutch of his hands around hers . . . as though he knew too. 'We have been here for nine years, Bapa.'

They were in the Shah Burj at Agra fort—the octagonal balcony jutting out from the battlements of the fort, clad in white marble, inlaid with semi-precious stones—where Shah Jahan had commanded elephant fights in the pounded earth maidan below, where the crowds had thronged in the early mornings, hoping for a glimpse to reassure themselves that he was alive and well.

'I wonder,' Emperor Shah Jahan said now, turning his face to the view beyond the arches of the Shah Burj and the glow of the white marble dome in the distance, 'if anyone even believes that I still live. Is Aurangzeb a good sovereign, beta?'

'There is talk in the streets that he intends to reissue the jizya.'

Emperor Shah Jahan smiled, though it was a weak smile and cost him an effort, at the end of which he began to cough from deep within his chest. When the coughing had finally stopped, he laid his aged face in the curve of his daughter's shoulder and said, 'Aurangzeb was always a fool; he must know that he cannot rule a largely Hindu empire by offending almost all of its inhabitants. There will be rebellions. He is a fool.'

Jahanara stroked her father's hair. Emperor Akbar had abolished the jizya when he began to build his empire in Hindustan—it was a tax on non-Muslims, a head tax, paid for the mere fact that a person was a Hindu. There were other rules surrounding the jizya that created fear and loathing and, in doing so, an atmosphere of unrest. One of them was that no more than three Hindus could talk on the streets together or congregate in one another's houses, for they would be automatically considered to have been in collusion against the emperor and so fined or jailed. But Aurangzeb was always too rigid in his beliefs. Since the meeting with Najabat three years ago, reluctantly on her part, Jahanara had begun to correspond with Aurangzeb. She still refused to see him or to enter his zenana, but she did write to him, and when she had heard this news, her letter had been fiery. She had called him stupid also, and much more, but he had not listened.

She laid her father back on the pillows, and he picked up her hand and kissed it. 'I am not very accomplished at farewells, Jahan. You saw how difficult it was for me to let go your Mama.'

Jahanara stilled his words. 'Not yet, Bapa. You must not talk thus.'

He grasped at her wrist to pull away her hands and say, 'I smell apples on my skin; it means death, my dear.'

So he still remembered that prophecy from fifty years ago, when the fakir had warned him that one of his sons would cause him grief and that, when the time came for him to go, his hands would be scented with the aroma of apples. She leaned over and put her nose in the cup of his hand, and there she smelled it too, the scent of the fruit.

She sobbed then, bending her head to let the tears pour over the wrinkled skin of his knuckles, beset by an abrupt fear of the emptiness his dying would leave. They had been so isolated for the past nine years, left here with a sprinkling of retainers—eunuchs and slaves. It was said that there was still a heavy guard outside the fort's walls, but she had never seen the soldiers herself. Aurangzeb had sealed all the entrances to the fort except for one, and left only a man-size opening in that one. All of their food—grains, vegetables, meat, water—was brought through that doorway and inspected carefully before it was allowed in. And so they had lived, Bapa and she, alone and for the most part even happy. He had talked for long hours about his childhood and his youth, about growing up in the care of his grandfather Emperor Akbar and his favourite wife, Ruqayya Sultan Begam, who had adopted him—no, forcibly removed him from his mother's quarters into hers. Jahanara had not met her great-grandfather, and even her grandfather Emperor Jahangir was but a faint memory to her. But her Bapa's stories had told her so much about them—more than the official histories could ever record, more than posterity would ever know. An old man's ramblings, Shah Jahan had said, now when he had nothing else to do.

'There is your Mama,' Shah Jahan said softly, and they both turned to gaze out at the Luminous Tomb. Oil diyas burned around the perimeter of the dome, and they could see it sparkle along the curve of the river, the light from the lamps reaching up to cast the freestanding minarets as marble swords spearing the skies. Mists had begun to roll outward from the river's cool winter waters, and the tomb seemed to float above, untethered from the ground.

'Bapa,' she said. 'Now you must sleep.'

'You have been good to me, Jahan.' He tried to speak again, but the words choked his throat and he cried soundlessly. Jahanara put her arms around him and laid her head lightly on his thin chest. They stayed like that for a long time, until she heard her father's breathing calm into a rhythm as he slept. She closed her eyes, willing him to live, knowing that he probably would not.

When she woke suddenly, cold and shivering, she could no longer hear the sound of his heart under her ear. It was the thirty-first of January, 1666—nine years after his son Aurangzeb had incarcerated him in Agra.

rauza-i-munavvara
The Luminous Tomb

Upon my grave when I shall die,
No lamps shall burn nor jasmine lie,
No candle, with unsteady flame,
Serve as a reminder of my fame,
No bulbul chanting overhead,
Shall tell the world that I am dead.

—SYLVIA CROWE AND SHEILA HAYWOOD,
The Gardens of Mughal India

Agra
Monday, 1 February 1666
26 Rajab A.H. 1076

There were spies in the fort in Emperor Aurangzeb's service, and even as Princess Jahanara's wails brought the servants to her father's bedside, the news flew to the emperor in Delhi. He was wakened in the middle of the night, a word whispered in his ear. Aurangzeb knelt by his bed in prayer with an immense sense of relief. He was, finally, the sole and undisputed king of the empire.

As the mists spun around Agra an hour before dawn, there was the muffled sound of hammers on brick as the barricaded doorway at the foot of the battlements was smashed open.

Jahanara watched dry-eyed as her father's body was cleaned and washed by two of his favourite ministers—Sadullah Khan and Ali Mardan Khan—and wrapped in three shrouds of white cloth. The old amirs then lifted their emperor's body upon their shoulders and bore it down the stairs, moving as carefully as their aged limbs would allow them, to carry him across the maidan and onto the simple barge waiting on the river's bank. They hesitated when the veiled princess followed them, and one of the men began to protest, but her stride was firm, her attitude inflexible—Jahanara meant to bury her father herself; she had earned the right to do so.

Another doorway had been opened in the Luminous Tomb, leading from the riverfront terrace to the subterranean rooms below, and here the two men deposited their burden upon the cool marble floor. In the few hours since his death, a grave had already been cleaved into the ground beside the sarcophagus of Mumtaz Mahal.

At the end of the second pahr of the day, the noon hour, the men lowered Emperor Shah Jahan's body into the ground and recited the Fatiha. Jahanara stood at one corner, still veiled, but she stepped forward now to lift a handful of earth and throw it upon her father's body.

'You are with Mama now, Bapa,' she whispered, then moved back to her place as the gravediggers piled mud over the grave and laid a white marble slab on top of it.

In time, another sarcophagus would be raised over the emperor's remains, and Emperor Aurangzeb would order a similar one in the upper chamber of the tomb, by the side of his mother's. Unlike his mother's cenotaph, this one would not be inscribed and inlaid with verses from the Quran—Amanat Khan had died a few years earlier, and no other calligrapher could be trusted with the task—but instead would be decorated with a forest of flowers in blues, greens and reds. Only the most careful of observers would notice the difference—what they would see instead was that the emperor's cenotaph was bigger than his wife's, that it sat off centre within the marble railing surrounding the cenotaphs, as though he had never meant to rest by his wife's side for all eternity.

When Jahanara stepped out onto the riverfront terrace, she took a deep breath of the cool, moist air. It had begun to rain, just as it had on the day that her mother had been buried. This was a winter rain, chilly, blowing about with gusts of wind. She knew that Aurangzeb, who had not attended the burial, was waiting for her in her apartments as he had promised that he would, to renew his exhortations that she come to his zenana, return to court life, come under his protection, as a sister should. She *would* talk to him now, she thought; before it would have been a betrayal of her father . . . now it did not matter.

The imperial barge was already docked at the pier below the Taj Mahal, the boatmen clad in white, its awnings of a rich and russet red. Jahanara went down the stairs of the Tahkhana, which consisted of the rooms fronting the Yamuna carved into the sandstone base of the tomb, and paused when she saw the man standing at the foot of the pier. Najabat Khan put out a hand, and she went forward to meet him.

Emperor Shah Jahan, who had ruled over the richest and most glorious empire in the world, had died a pauper's death. There had been no state funeral, no alms given to the poor, no recitals of the Quran over his grave in the ponderous voices of the imams—just a hurried flight from the fort to the tomb, a lone daughter to watch him go to his final rest, a couple of old ministers who had defied their emperor to perform this final duty for the man they had loved.

But she did not know that, despite all of her Bapa's achievements in stone and marble—the apartments in Agra fort, the glorious city of Shahjahanabad, the gardens of Kashmir—this tomb would eventually cast all of their lives in its elegant shadow. She did not know, as she boarded the barge and sat next to Najabat, her heart exploding with pain and joy, that, though her father had died a broken, unhappy man, his name would come to typify the grandeur and majesty of the Mughal Empire in Hindustan. That posterity would remember *him,* not his ancestors or his son or the useless sons of his son, with awe—and if he had known this, at least he might have died in some peace.

Because he would always be revered and respected as the man who had built that most Luminous Tomb.

Afterword

Why Jahanara? Readers of *The Twentieth Wife* and *The Feast of Roses* will notice that I've skipped a generation in Mughal history for this one, *Shadow Princess.* Mumtaz Mahal (Arjumand Banu Begam) appears in the aforementioned novels—as a child, as a young woman whose hopes of marriage have been blighted by circumstances beyond her control, and as a new wife, incredibly fecund, absurdly in love with her husband. When she dies, four years into his reign as Emperor Shah Jahan, he builds the Taj Mahal in her memory.

By then Jahanara is seventeen years old, forced to carry the weight of an imperial zenana, in the nebulous position of being a beloved daughter and yet the most important woman in the harem and at court for the rest of her father's life.

Mughal women, especially of the imperial family, lived behind a veil both literally and figuratively. They were rarely seen at public occasions, and then only in the fluttering of their fingers or a bold and curious eye through a latticework screen, or a *hukm* or *nishan* (imperial command) sent to a noble with a specific order.

When I began reading and researching facts about the life of Mehrunnisa, Empress Nur Jahan, for my first two novels, I found only brief mentions of her in seventeenth-century Mughal sources. Even Emperor Jahangir remarks on her fewer than a handful of times in his memoirs; a couple of references are telling, true, but for the history of her life, before she married Jahangir and after, I had to rely upon the small allusions in the accounts of the merchants from the British and Dutch East India companies and other travellers' tales. In some, Mehrunnisa is the ideal wife and companion; in others (court documents from Shah Jahan's reign), she is the epitome of evil—cunning, sly, dominating and overly ambitious. Yet, despite this paucity of material, there emerged a more or less complete picture of the woman.

It was during these readings that I stumbled upon Niccolao Manucci's portraits of the two princesses—Jahanara and Roshanara—and knew, even that early on, that they would find a place in a future novel. They were both said to have been powerful women in their own right: Jahanara almost from the moment of her mother's death, Roshanara from behind the walls of Aurangzeb's zenana. There were other stories—of men smuggled into the harem for their pleasure, of an injunction against their ever being married, of rumours about the love Shah Jahan had for Jahanara, and, finally, the fact that each of these women championed a different brother as the next Emperor. And only one of them was, naturally, successful in the end. Yet, it was the other, Jahanara, who became the Padshah Begam of Aurangzeb's harem once her father died and she could leave the confines of the fort at Agra.

The facts of Jahanara's life—when and where she was born; the income her father gave her; her hold over him and the love he had for her (which led to speculations about their true relationship, based upon, as far as I can see, some loose bazaar gossip, which probably had its origins in the harem itself)—are readily documented in official court papers and the travelogues of foreign visitors to India. I chose not to believe in the incest for two primary reasons: one, the rumours began as early as six months after Mumtaz Mahal's death, even before her body was disinterred from Burhanpur and brought to Agra; and two, Emperor Shah Jahan did not live out the rest of his life as a saint—he had a vigorous sex life, with reports of more than one dalliance with the wives of his nobles.

There are two broadly defined sources for Mughal history during Shah Jahan's rule. The first set consists of the official biographies the emperor commissioned; at least eight men lent their names to various prose and verse histories. The second set is easier to read, not as bombastic in language, gossipy in style, and of somewhat suspect authenticity—these are the tales of travellers, foreigners who found themselves in India by chance or intent. They either settled in and stayed or spent a few years or months in desultory wanderings, noting aspects of Mughal culture, cuisine, manners and customs, picking up bazaar chatter and recording it in their journals.

In most accounts, Jahanara comes across as a woman of stupendous power, imagination, strength and piety; there is very little of the human left in her. Only this interesting tidbit—a stray mention by Manucci of a possible alliance with a noble at court, Najabat Khan. This alliance leads to nothing, for she is known not to have married. Yet, from that one aside, I built up the entire love story in *Shadow Princess.* Najabat Khan did have a son, named Shah Alam, in Aurangzeb's court, and his background and history are as recounted. There is no mention, though, in any official documentation, of Shah Alam's mother.

All the royal historians cite the emperor's immense grief at Mumtaz Mahal's death and the fact that he considered giving up his empire—relegated to a minor footnote, since Shah Jahan continued to rule for over a quarter of a century. Lahori is most eloquent in his *Padshah Nama*: 'It was repeatedly uttered by his divine revelation-interpreting tongue that, if the heavy burden of the divine deputyship . . . had not been imposed on this seeker of the will of God . . . he would have certainly abandoned the high-ranked vast empire of Hindustan and divided among the princes of noble birth this extensive kingdom.' To me, these casual lines were important. Shah Jahan would not have considered Murad (seven years old) or Aurangzeb (thirteen) or perhaps even Shah Shuja (fifteen) as fit for the throne—he was undoubtedly thinking of his eldest son, Dara Shikoh, who, at sixteen years of age, was the crown prince. All of a sudden, this historical postscript was significant, because I believe that the lines of loyalty began to be drawn from this moment, a few days after Mumtaz Mahal died. The Mughal princes all had rights to the throne by law. It was enough to have been born male—whether to a wife or to a concubine—and to have a steady hand on the sword, a heart unmoved by excessive sympathy, and a voice fluent enough in diplomacy to court the backing of the powerful amirs. In the end, it was Dara who lacked judgement, Aurangzeb who had it, despite, or perhaps because of, his stubborn will and his inflexibility in matters relating to religion. Everything that happened over the next twenty-seven years of their father's reign came back to this time, when Jahanara supported Dara, and Roshanara supported Aurangzeb. This prince, on more shaky ground than the favoured Dara, worked assiduously to woo his other brothers and the nobles at court.

A note on the Islamic dates used at the beginnings of the chapters. The dates are applied based on the Hijri calendar of twelve lunar months (instead of the Gregorian solar months) and begin on the Gregorian calendar in AD 622, the year the Prophet Muhammad emigrated from Mecca to Medina (known as the Hijra). The Hijri years are abbreviated AH, from the Latin *anno Hegirae*—the year of the Hijra. The official biographers of Emperor Shah Jahan's court use the Hijri calendar to date events and occasions; in some instances I've used their actual dates, in others I converted Gregorian dates into Hijri using an online source: http://www.islamicfinder.org/Hcal/index. php.

Today, a visitor to the Taj Mahal enters through the western gateway of the Jilaukhana—the forecourt to the tomb. The Taj Ganj, south of the forecourt, is no longer a part of the complex; it has been built over extensively over the years with bazaars and houses, some of which still bear parts of the original stonework. But the Great Gate remains. As does the view Jahanara must have seen when she stepped onto the platform of the gate and looked down the length of the garden at the riverfront terrace, with its mausoleum in the centre, the mosque on the left, the Miham Khana on the right.

Shadow Princess ends nine years into Aurangzeb's reign and fifteen years before Jahanara dies. She settles, finally, into her once-loathed brother's harem and again supersedes her sister Roshanara by acquiring the title Padshah Begam—the chief lady of the zenana. Surely the rivalry that drove their lives would have reared its head once more, even though they were older and perhaps wiser. Official sources, and those unofficial, don't mention why Jahanara loved Dara so passionately or why she supported him, or why indeed she disliked Aurangzeb so much.

But even though the sources don't give reasons for the adoration Aurangzeb, in his turn, had for the sister who refused to espouse his ambitions, in giving her a home and the premier position in his harem, he amply demonstrated that devotion.

Indu Sundaresan
March 2009

Acknowledgements

Thanks go: first, to the early readers of *Shadow Princess*, my friends Janet Lee Carey and Phillip Winberry, for being willing to plow through an unrevised manuscript and comment upon it.

To my agent Sandy Dijkstra and everyone at the Sandra Dijkstra Literary Agency, for everything—how hard they work, how carefully they read my work, how well they champion it, and how nice they all are; this last is a true and unexpected blessing.

To other nice people: my publisher, Judith Curr, and my editor, Malaika Adero, for their support, encouragement and counsel on my work.

To the very first reader of any manuscript-in-progress, my husband, Uday. And to Uday and Sitara for making me happy enough to write.

And finally, to the two library systems near home—the King County Library System, and the University of Washington's Suzzallo and Allen libraries—for their superb (and expanding) collection of work on India, which has provided me with invaluable research material for *Shadow Princess*.

Bibliography of Select Works

Ball, V., trans., and William Crooke, ed. *Travels in India by Jean-Baptiste Tavernier, Baron of Aubonne.* London: Oxford University Press, 1925.

Begam, Qamar Jahan, and Begam Jahanara. *Princess Jahān Arā Begam: Her Life and Works.* Karachi: S.M. Hamid Ali, 1991.

Begley, W.E., ed., and Ziyaud-Din A. Desai, comp. *The Shah Jahan Nama of Inayat Khan: An Abridged History of the Mughal Emperor Shah Jahan, Compiled by His Royal Librarian: The Nineteenth-Century Manuscript Translation of A.R. Fuller* (British Library, add. 30,777). Delhi: Oxford University Press, 1990.

Begley, W.E., and Ziyaud-Din A. Desai. *Taj Mahal: The Illumined Tomb: An Anthology of Seventeenth-Century Mughal and European Documentary Sources.* Cambridge, Mass.: Aga Khan Program for Islamic Architecture, 1989.

Blochmann, H., trans., and S.L. Goomer. *The Ain-i-Akbari by Abul-Fazl Allami.* Delhi: Aadiesh Book Depot, 1965.

Constable, Archibald, ed., and Irving Brock, trans. *Travels in the Mogul Empire,* AD 1656–1668, by François Bernier. Delhi: S. Chand, 1968.

Elliot, H. M. *Shah Jahan.* Lahore: Sh Mubarak Ali, 1875. Reprint 1975.

Eraly, Abraham. *The Mughal Throne: The Saga of India's Great Emperors.* London: Phoenix, 2004.

———. *The Mughal World: Life in India's Golden Age.* New Delhi: Penguin Books India, 2007.

Gascoigne, Bamber, and Christina Gascoigne. *A Brief History of the Great Moguls.* New York: Carroll & Graf, 2002.

Hansen, Waldemar. *The Peacock Throne: The Drama of Mogul India.* New York: Holt, Rinehart and Winston, 1972.

Hoyland, J.S., trans., and S.N. Banerjee, annot. *The Empire of the Great Mogul: A Translation of De Laet's 'Description of India and Fragment of Indian History'.* Delhi: Idarah-I Adabiyat-I Delli, 1975.

Irvine, William, trans. *Storia do Mogor, or Mogul India, 1653–1708, by Niccolao Manucci.* Calcutta: Editions Indian, 1965.

Khan, Mubarak Ali. *The Court of the Great Mughuls (Based on Persian Sources).* Lahore: Book Traders, 1986.

Koch, Ebba, and Richard André Barraud. *The Complete Taj Mahal: And the Riverfront Gardens of Agra.* London: Thames & Hudson, 2006.

Lal, Muni. *Shah Jahan.* New Delhi: Vikas Publishing House, 1986.

Misra, Neeru. *Succession and Imperial Leadership Among the Mughals, 1526–1707.* Delhi: Konark Publishers, 1993.

Misra, Rekha. *Women in Mughal India (AD 1526–1748).* Delhi: Munshiram Manoharlal, 1967.

Qanungo, Kalika Ranjan. *Dara Shukoh.* Calcutta: S.C. Sarkar, 1935.

Saksena, Banarsi Prasad. *History of Shahjahan of Dihli.* Allahabad: Indian Press, 1932.

Schimmel, Annemarie, Corinne Attwood, and Burzine K. Waghmar. *The Empire of the Great Mughals: History, Art, and Culture.* New Delhi: Oxford University Press, 2005.

Thackston, Wheeler M., ed. and trans. *The Baburnama: Memoirs of Babur, Prince and Emperor.* New York: Modern Library, 2002.

Tillotson, G.H.R. *Mughal India.* London: Penguin Books, 1991.

Glossary

Amir	nobleman
Bagh	garden
Baithak	seating area
Baradari	pavilion
Chahar Taslim	form of salutation in which the hand is raised to the head four times, as opposed to the traditional three of the *taslim*
Chajja	eave
Charbagh	garden divided into four quadrants by two intersecting walkways; Persian in origin
Chattri	literally 'umbrella' or 'canopy'; here a dome-shaped pavilion built over a funerary site
Chaugan	polo
Choli	bodice, blouse
Chukkar	period of play in polo, usually seven minutes long
Chulha	fireplace with walls for cooking
Chunam	a type of plaster made with quicklime and sand
Dargah	tomb of a Sufi saint
Dholak	double-headed hand drum
Diya	lamp
Durbar	court proceeding
Farman	imperial edict; almost exclusively the privilege of the Emperor
Firangi	foreigner
Gaddi	seat
Ghagara	pleated, full-length skirt

Ghari	measure of time; approximately twenty-four minutes; the day and night were divided into twenty-four gharis
Ghariyali	timekeeper
Hakim	physician
Halva	sweet confection
Hammam	bathhouse
Havaldar	policeman
Haveli	house, mansion
Hinabandi	ceremony, part of the wedding celebrations, during which henna is applied to the bride's hands and feet
Howdah	canopied seat, usually on an elephant or a camel
Huzoor	sire
Imam	Muslim spiritual leader
Jagir	estate, parcel of land
Jali	screen
Jharoka	overhanging balcony used by the Emperor for audiences
Karkhana	workshop, atelier
Khazana	treasure
Khilat	Arabic for 'dress'; here a specific coat given by the Emperor to a subject
Khus	aromatic grass
Khutba	proclamation of sovereignty; usually before the noon prayers at mosques around the empire
Khichri	mixture of rice, lentils, and ghee; usually poor people's food
Konish	form of salutation
Maidan	open field
Mali	gardener
Mansab	military rank denoted by the number of cavalry and infantry a noble had under his command
Mardana	men's quarters in the house
Mast	intoxicated; when referring to elephants, 'energetic'
Matka	earthenware pot
Mehr	gift from the groom to the bride during the wedding ceremony

Mirza	title for a nobleman
Mohur	gold coin
Mulla	man trained in Islamic law and tradition
Nadiri	sleeveless, thigh-length coat
Nautch	dance
Nilgau	a bluish-gray wild ox
Nishan	imperial edict; usually the privilege of queens, princesses,and princes
Pahr	measure of time, the length of a watch; the day and night were divided into four pahrs each
Pargana	land holding
Peshwaz	long-sleeved, high-waisted garment that flowed to the knees
Pishtaq	portal, entry
Punkah	fan
Purdah	literally 'curtain'; here to mean the veil
Qaba	overcoat with long sleeves
Qazi	judge who rules in accordance with Islamic law
Rauza	tomb
Sachaq	customary wedding gift to the bride
Salah	ritual prayer
Sarai	rest house for travellers
Sehra	headdress worn by the groom during a wedding ceremony
Shamiana	canopy, tent
Shikara	slim wooden boat used in Kashmir
Sura	Arabic for 'chapter' of the Quran
Taslim	form of salutation
'Urs	death anniversary
Uzuk	royal seal
Zari	gold or silver wire thread used in embroidery
Zenana	harem quarters or the women within; consisted of wives, concubines, mothers, sisters, cousins—any women who required shelter and were related to the imperial family